Surrender Becomes Her

Also by Shirlee Busbee

Seduction Becomes Her

Scandal Becomes Her

Surrender Becomes Her

SHIRLEE BUSBEE

ZEBRA BOOKS
KENSINGTON PUBLISHING CORP.

ZEBRA BOOKS are published by

Kensington Publishing Corp.
119 West 40th Street
New York, NY 10018

Copyright © 2009 by Shirlee Busbee

ISBN 978-1-61523-299-4

Printed in the United States of America

To some dear, <u>dear</u> American Shetland Pony friends:
PAT MICHIELSSEN for all the laughter and pony tales
we've shared over the years and JIM CURRY
for all the same, as well as advice and the WINS
we've shared. <u>American</u> Shetlands Rule!

And

To HOWARD, oh, just for everything!

Prologue

Devon, England
Spring, 1795

"Why won't you give it to me?" Isabel demanded, hands fisted on her small hips in a most ungenteel manner. "It's not as if the money doesn't belong to me. It's mine! You have no right to hoard it."

A shaft of late afternoon sun shone in through the long windows of the library, transforming her red hair into a halo of fire and Marcus was struck again at how often his seventeen-year-old ward reminded him of fire. Sometimes she resembled nothing more than an appealing, cheerful little fire and other times, as now, despite her diminutive stature, a dangerous tower of flames ready to burst into a conflagration that could leave him seared to the bone. Already feeling as if his skin was singed, he very much feared that today was going to end with a conflagration.

The discussion, if one dared to call it such, was taking place in the comfortable library at Sherbrook Hall, Marcus's country estate in Devon, and had begun some ten minutes earlier when Isabel had burst into the house demanding to see her guardian. At once! Since Miss Isabel had run tame through the Hall all her life, the butler, Thompson, with unruffled aplomb, had promptly shown the young lady into the library and gone in search of the master of the house. The instant Marcus had stepped into the room, Isabel had launched her attack and he had been attempting, not very successfully, to defuse another explosive situation with his tempestuous ward.

"I have every right," he said patiently. "I am your guardian and as such it is my duty to see that you do not squander your fortune before you come of age or marry."

Isabel stamped her foot. "You know very well," she said hotly, "that my father never intended for *you* to be my guardian! Uncle James should be my guardian—not you."

Which was true, Marcus admitted to himself. Isabel's father, Sir George, had been nearly seventy when he had stunned the neighborhood by marrying a woman young enough to be his granddaughter and had promptly fathered a child. To Sir George's joy, Isabel had been born a scant ten months later. His death at eighty, when Isabel had been ten years old, had come as no great surprise to anyone. It was the death of Marcus's own father some four years ago that had come as a shock to everyone. At the age of fifty-nine, the elder Mr. Sherbrook had gone to bed one night full of rude health, never to awaken the next morning. Numb with grief and disbelief, he had been informed by his solicitor several weeks later that in addition to inheriting his father's wealth and estates, he had also inherited the guardianship of Sir George's only child, thirteen-year-old Isabel. Marcus had been aghast, assuming like everyone else that Sir George's younger brother, James, would become Isabel's guardian. But such was not the case. At the time the agreement had been drawn up, Sir George had not felt that James, a committed bachelor living in London, would make a good guardian for his daughter. A much better choice, he had decided, would be his dear friend and neighbor, Mr. Sherbrook. Unfortunately, Sir George had not distinguished between the elder Mr. Sherbrook and the younger Mr. Sherbrook and had made no provision for the death of Mr. Sherbrook senior. Consequently, though everyone knew Sir George had never envisioned the son of his best friend being his daughter's guardian, that is exactly what happened. Even now Marcus felt a wave of incredulity flood through him. He had been only twenty-three years old at the time. What had he known about being the guardian of a young woman? *Not much more,* he thought wryly, *than I know at this very moment.*

"Don't pretend you don't know what I'm talking about," Isabel said, when he remained silent. "You were not meant to be my guardian."

"I'll grant you that," Marcus replied, "but since your father made no other provisions for your welfare before he died and no one expected my father to die so unexpectedly, I'm afraid that we are, er, stuck with each other."

Isabel shrugged. "I know all that and, generally," she admitted grudgingly, her quick temper subsiding a trifle, "you're not so very bad. I just don't understand why you have to be so, so *stubborn* about this one thing. It is not as if I am even asking for such a huge sum. Your new curricle and that lovely pair of blacks you bought cost more than I am asking you to give me." Her eyes narrowed. "And it *is* my money. Not yours." When Marcus said nothing, she muttered, "And it would not be squandered."

"That is a matter of opinion," he said. She scowled at him and he grinned. "Come now," he coaxed, his cool gray eyes full of amusement, "you know that as your guardian there is little that I deny you, but it would be remiss of me in this instance to allow you to spend a small fortune on a horse." He shook his head. "Especially *that* horse."

Her temper flared and her topaz-colored eyes narrowed. "And what, pray tell, is wrong with Tempest?"

"There is nothing wrong with him. The price Leggett is asking for him, while high, is not exorbitant. And I'll agree that the stallion is beautiful. His bloodline is impeccable and anyone with an eye for good horseflesh would be proud to own him."

Her black expression cleared instantly and a blinding smile

crossed her small, vivid features. "Oh, Marcus, he *is* a wonderful stallion, is he not?"

Marcus nodded, bemused, in spite of himself, by that smile. "Yes, he is." Recalling himself, he added, "But he is not for you."

The smile vanished like the sun behind a thundercloud. "And why not?"

"Because," he said bluntly, "you don't have the strength or the experience to handle an animal of that size and spirit right now." He smiled faintly. "You're both young and untrained and you'd probably kill each other within a week." At her gasp of outrage, he held up a hand. "But there's another reason I won't fund this latest fidget of yours. How many times have you concocted one outrageous scheme after another, only to lose interest within a fortnight? Remember when you were going to breed goats? Or you were certain that you wanted to raise chickens? If memory serves, the goats nearly ate your aunt Agatha's rose garden to the ground before they could be sent to market and as for the chickens. . . . Wasn't there something about a rooster and the rosewood newel post of the main staircase in Denham Manor?" Ignoring the storm gathering in her eyes, he continued, "Now you say you want to breed horses, but what about next month or next year? Something else to consider: what will happen to your horses, all your plans, when you go to London next year for the Season?" He shook his head, smiling at her. "I know you. By summer your head will be full of nothing more than ball gowns and all manner of fripperies, the parties and the balls that you will be attending next spring, and the gentlemen you will have falling at your feet. And when you marry, as you surely will, brat, you will have no time or thought of horse breeding. The expenditure for Tempest will have been wasted."

Her ready temper returned in an instant and her small hands clenched into fists. "Unfair!" she protested furiously. "I was eleven years old when I wanted the chickens and it wasn't my fault the rooster flew into the house; Papa's old dog, Lucy, chased him there," she said defensively. "It's true the goats ate Aunt Agatha's roses last fall, but it was good for them. This year you can't even tell that the goats had ravaged them and the bloom has been spectacular. Even Aunt Agatha said so." She shot him a look of dislike. "And it wasn't all of the roses, just some of them."

Ignoring her outburst, Marcus said, "My point is that you haven't a very good history of following through with these fancies that take you. How do I know that Tempest and your scheme to raise horses isn't just another case of goats in the roses and roosters in the house?"

She glared at him, rage and hurt mingling in her breast. Why couldn't he understand that Tempest and the grand stud farm she imagined had *nothing* to do with goats and roosters! Her wretched guardian knew very well that she loved horses, had loved them all her life and, she thought resentfully, was very good with them; everyone said so. Even Marcus admitted—when he wasn't being so aggravatingly mule-headed!—that she had an uncanny ability with horses. It was unfair and unkind of him to throw her disasters with the goats and chickens in her face. Those were childish pastimes. She was an adult now, making adult decisions. Why, oh why, couldn't he see that? Why did he persist in seeing her as a child? Still think of her as a child to be petted and indulged and sent away when convenient?

Isabel had only to take a glance in the cheval glass in her room to know the answer to that question, she thought miserably. She still *looked* a child. Barely five feet tall and fashioned upon a slim, fairylike frame, and to her great disappointment, with no bosom to speak of, it was likely that decades would pass before her family and friends stopped thinking of her as a child. It didn't help that fate had given her a mop of unruly red hair and—gasp!—a sprinkling of freckles across her nose that no amount of buttermilk or cucumbers could erase. She found no fault with her nose itself; it was, she had decided a few months ago, a rather nice nose, finely formed with a saucy tilt to the tip. No one denied that her eyes, large, lustrous, and framed by dark lashes of marvelous length and thickness, were her best feature. But fine eyes or not, nothing, not even the fact that she had left behind the schoolroom weeks ago, was going to make anyone view her any differently as long as she remained the size and shape of a ten-year-old boy! Especially not Marcus Sherbrook. With a painful twist in her heart she realized that she wanted him to see her as a young woman. He never would, though—not as long as she was trapped in this childish, boyish body, she thought bitterly. Misery welled up inside her. She was never going to be a tall, stately beauty; she was condemned to spend her life short, flat chested, and freckled! It was so unfair!

Fighting back the urge to burst into tears, she lifted her chin and said with commendable calm, "You have every right to believe that Tempest is merely a whim of mine, but if, as you said, he is an animal that anyone would be proud to own, then there is no reason for me not to buy him. If, as you think will happen, I grow tired of him in a few months, he should be able to be sold for the same price I paid for him. I would lose no money on the transaction."

Marcus regarded her steadily for several moments. Isabel had always been hard for him to resist, and as the years had passed and she had blossomed into an appealing young woman, he'd found it more and more difficult not to indulge her every wish. And he cursed this blasted guardianship that frequently put them at daggers drawing. It hadn't always been so. There'd been a time that, like a precocious kitten, she'd scampered at his heels and he'd been happy for her to do so. He couldn't explain it, but from the moment he'd seen her, a babe in arms, with that red hair so bright and vivid that he'd been astonished his fingertips hadn't been burned when he'd touched the silky nap, she'd held a special place in his affections.

Though Isabel had been born to wealth and position, Marcus was very conscious that her life had not been without problems. Her mother had died tragically before Isabel's second birthday and, despite a doting father, it couldn't have been easy for her to grow up without a mother. She had adored her father; oddly enough the two of them rattled around happily in Denham Manor, completely satisfied with each other's company. His death had hit her hard. Sir James, her uncle, wasn't unkind, but he couldn't replace Sir George in her affections, and his wife, Agatha . . . Marcus's jaw clenched. Talk about history repeating itself! Sir James had followed in his brother's footsteps in more ways than one. Stunning the neighborhood once again, two years ago he had tossed aside his bachelorhood and married a woman half his age: Agatha Paley, Isabel's governess!

Marcus had never liked Miss Paley, not even when his mother insisted that she was an exceptional governess and precisely what Isabel needed. At the time she'd been hired, he'd thought her too strict, too cold and unfeeling for someone like Isabel, but to his regret, he'd allowed his mother to override his objections. It had not been a good match: Isabel, impetuous and spirited, and Miss Paley, cold and rigid. He'd known that Isabel had been dreadfully unhappy, but before he could change the situation, Miss Paley had stolen the march on him and married Sir James. He still wondered how she had brought that about, but it didn't matter; what mattered was that the former Miss Paley was now Lady Agatha, Isabel's aunt, and the former governess made certain that everyone knew *she* ruled Denham Manor. His expression softened as he stared down into Isabel's face. Poor little mite. Living under Agatha's icy fist couldn't be pleasant.

He grimaced. Who was he to deny Isabel something that made her happy? As she'd said, if she lost interest, the stallion could always be sold. He worried, though, about the danger. Tempest was aptly named; he was a big, powerful two-year-old stallion. Marcus knew. He'd seen the horse. The moment he'd gotten wind of Isabel's interest, he'd made it his business to look into it. Despite himself, he'd been impressed when Leggett, a man known for his excellent horses, had led out the magnificent chestnut stallion with the nearly white mane and tail and four white stockings. If Isabel had not already spotted the horse, he'd have purchased him on the spot. He couldn't argue with the animal's quality, pedigree, or price, and Isabel was right; the horse could always be sold if her interest waned. He took a deep breath, hoping he wasn't making a mistake.

Her eyes fixed anxiously on Marcus's dark face, Isabel felt despair roil through her. He was going to say no. She just knew it. Neither defeat nor patience were her best-known virtues and she took refuge in that volatile temper of hers. "If I want to throw it away on a bloody horse it is my right," she declared furiously. "Furthermore, you're a mean-spirited beast and I hate you! Do you hear? I hate you! Oh! I cannot wait until I am no longer your ward and no longer have to deal with a clutch-fisted miser like you."

The words he had been about to speak died in his throat and, his own temper spiking, Marcus snapped, "Believe me, you little devil, I live for the time that you are no longer an albatross forever hanging around my neck! No more than you do I live for the day I am relieved of this abominable guardianship." Grimly, he added, "But until you come of age or marry, I *am* your guardian and control your fortune."

"Well, we'll just see about that, won't we?" she taunted, temper riding her hard. "It'd serve you right if I married the first man I saw just to spite you."

"If you could find a man mad enough to take on a viper-tongued little shrew like you, I'd shake his hand and congratulate him!" he snarled before he thought about it. Even as the words left his mouth, he wanted to snatch them back, but the damage was done.

"Viper tongued? How dare you!" She dashed away tears of hurt and fury. "You'll be sorry," she promised fiercely, rushing toward the door that led from the library. "You'll see. You'll be sorry."

Flinging open the door, she rushed from the room.

Stillness descended upon the room with the power of a thunderclap and Marcus stared dazed at the open doorway through which Isabel had disappeared. Torn between the urge to go after her and tell her she could have the bloody horse and the determination not to let her see how easily she could manipulate him, he stood rooted to the spot.

He took a deep breath and shook his head. Isabel could be explosive, but sometimes, as now, dealing with her was like grappling with a tornado. She swept in without warning, blasted everything in her path, and then—poof!—stormed away to wreak havoc somewhere else.

As Marcus stood there, staring blankly at nothing at all, a tall, striking woman, wearing a narrow-skirted gown of dove-gray muslin trimmed with black corded silk, walked through the door and into the room. Her silver-dusted black hair was caught up in a chignon at the back of her head and she wore a necklace of jet beads around her throat.

Seeing the baffled, angry bewilderment on her son's handsome face, she smiled. Amused understanding in her brilliant green eyes, she asked, "Isabel?"

Marcus flashed her a quick smile. "Who else? She has her heart set on buying that horse. I cannot feel that it is wise." He shook his head. "But I was about to tell her she could, when she gave me a tongue lashing I am not likely to forget and charged from the room." He sent his mother a helpless look. "What am I to do with her? I know nothing of being a guardian to someone like Isabel."

Seating herself on the sofa before a black marble fireplace and arranging her muslin skirts to suit her, Mrs. Sherbrook said, "Give her a little while to vent her temper and then I am sure if you talk to her, you will be able to make your peace with her. You know that Isabel's temper tantrums never last long and that she is always contrite afterward."

Marcus looked uneasy. "I don't know. She was very angry."

"She may have been, but since she is a sweet child—" At her son's snort, she amended, "Usually a sweet child, the next time you see her, you will discover it was nothing more than a tempest in a teapot and you will be able to put this incident behind you."

If Mrs. Sherbrook had known just how hurt and furious Isabel was she might not have been so sanguine. Wiping angry tears from her eyes, Isabel raced down the broad steps of Sherbrook Hall and snatched the reins from the Sherbrook groom holding her horse. In one swift movement, she mounted the horse and kicked the startled gelding into a wild gallop. Heedless of anyone that might have been unfortunate enough to meet her, she careened down the long driveway that led from Sherbrook Hall and onto the main road. Reaching the wider thoroughfare, common sense asserted itself and she pulled the bay into a more sober pace and in the waning April sunlight rode toward Denham Manor.

So I'm a viper-tongued shrew, am I, she thought wrathfully. *And no man would want to marry me, would he?* Her lips thinned. *We shall see about* that!

Her head full of schemes to show Mr. Marcus Sherbrook just how badly he had misjudged her, she finished the journey. Tossing the reins to the groom who met her at the stables, she slid from her horse. Nursing her wounds and not wishing to face Aunt Agatha or her uncle, Sir James, she set off toward the lake that divided the Denham property from their neighbor, Lord Manning.

She often walked to the lake when she was angry or troubled; something about the placid blue waters and the green forest with its sprinkling of artfully planted flowers and

shrubs that meandered along its curving length gave her solace and soothed her raging emotions.

Stepping from the woods, she noticed a small boat on the
lake and, too unhappy to make pleasant company, she was
about to disappear back into the trees when a hearty male
voice called out her name.

Recognizing Hugh Manning, Lord Manning's youngest son,
at the oars, she waved half-heartedly and watched as he began
to row toward the Denham side of the lake. Until the previous
winter she had hardly known Hugh; he had left the neighborhood prior to her father's death and sailed to India to begin
his career with the East India Trading Company. His return
in September for a long sojourn at home before returning to
his post in Bombay had put the entire area in a dither. For
weeks following his return there were parties and dinners in
his honor, everyone agog to hear tales of that far-off mystical
place, India. Isabel found his company enjoyable and, coupled
with the friendship between her uncle and Lord Manning, an
easy intimacy had sprung up between them. Even if Hugh
was nearly thirty, the fact that he was a personable, charming
young man had not escaped her notice and she understood
completely why the squire's daughter thought him very handsome with his darkly tanned skin, fair hair, and deep blue eyes.

Since January, Hugh had been traveling about England
and had only returned a week ago and within days was
preparing to sail back to his post in Bombay. Isabel knew
that Lord Manning was dreading his departure; Hugh was
not likely to return from India again for years and Lord
Manning feared he might never see his youngest son again.
He'd said as much one evening last week when he'd come to
dine at Denham Manor.

Reaching shore, Hugh leaped nimbly onto the muddy
ground. After pulling the boat aground enough so that it
would not float away, he turned and smiled at Isabel.

"It's been a lovely day, hasn't it?" he said. He glanced up

at the blue sky and added wistfully, "There is nothing like an April sky in England. I think what I miss most in India is a sky just that particular shade of blue." He took in a deep breath. "And the scents of an English spring—daffodils, roses, and lilacs in bloom."

Bruised and wounded from her exchange with Marcus, she didn't want any company, but when Hugh suggested that they sit on one of the stone benches nearby, she agreed.

It didn't take Isabel long to realize from his long face and comments that Hugh Manning was nearly as unhappy as she was. A frown between her brows, she asked, "Don't you want to return to India? I thought you were looking forward to going back."

His gaze on the lake, he said, "I'd rather join a regiment and fight against the French," he said. "With the war on the continent going so badly, England needs all the fighting men she can gather."

Isabel stared at him. "I didn't know that you wanted to be in the Army."

"Army, Navy, it wouldn't make any difference," he said carelessly. Glumly, he admitted, "I'll be honest, Izzy, I'm finding the prospect of returning to Bombay unappealing. At least the military would provide an opportunity for adventure. What I wouldn't give to be with Hood's fleet in the Mediterranean!" He cast her a miserable glance. "Once the exoticness dissipates, you do not know how boring life in India can be. Everything is the same day after day. I'd like a bit of excitement."

"I would think living in a land where one can ride elephants and see monkeys and tigers roaming about would be exciting enough!"

He shrugged. "Oh, there are moments to be sure and generally I am happy with my lot, but I had hoped to . . ." He took a deep breath. "I had hoped to take a wife with me when I returned. I have done well in Bombay and I now have the assets to support a wife and family in style and comfort." Hugh laughed bitterly. "I had it all planned: I'd come home, find a bride, and return to Bombay with my wife by my side, ready to start my family. Instead, in less than three days I sail alone back to India."

Isabel nearly jumped out of her skin at his words, staring at Hugh with large, wondering eyes. Had fate sent her an opportunity? An opportunity not only to show Marcus how very wrong he was, but an opportunity to escape once and for all from a home she no longer thought of as hers, from a woman whose sole purpose seemed to be to make her miserable. "D-d-did no one suit your fancy?" she forced herself to ask.

His eyes on the shore of the lake, he muttered, "There was a young lady. . . . She's the reason I have been away for so long. I offered for her, but her father turned me down."

"But why?" Isabel cried, upset for him. "Surely you explained your situation to him? And told him that you are Baron Manning's son?"

"Oh, I did all that," he said, "but Mr. Halford didn't want his daughter buried alive in India. He has a nice *local* gentleman all picked out for her, one who will inherit a title."

"And she? What did she want?"

"What difference does it make," he snapped. "Her father said no and Roseanne wouldn't stand up to him."

Her tender heart aching for him, feeling his pain, she slipped her little hand into his. "I'm very sorry, Hugh," she said softly.

His fingers tightened on hers and he looked down at her. "Thank you, Izzy. You're the only one I've told about Roseanne." He brushed back a lock of her unruly hair. "Did you know that she has red hair, too? Not as dark as yours and her eyes are blue . . . blue as the English sky."

He frowned, noticing for the first time the signs of tears on her cheeks. "What is this?" he asked. "Have you been crying? Who has been making you unhappy? I'll run him through for you, if you like."

She shook her head. "It doesn't matter."

"But it does," Hugh argued gently. "I don't like seeing my little friend upset. What can I do to make you happy again?"

The words popped out before she had time to consider them. "You could marry me and take me to India with you."

Goggle-eyed, Hugh stared at her. "Marry you! What put that bee in your bonnet?"

Averting her face, she said stiffly, "Never mind. I shouldn't have said anything."

"But you did. Why?" he persisted, looking at her as if he'd never seen her before.

"Because you want a wife and I-I-I can't bear to be treated like a child anymore by Aunt Agatha. And Marcus—!" Anguish and temper coiled in her breast and she exclaimed, "Oh, how I wish I was a thousand miles away from here!" Her eyes locked on his, she said desperately, "If we were to be married, we'd both get what we want."

They stared at each other for a long time, Hugh thinking of the lonely years in India without the benefit of a wife at his side; Isabel ignoring that little voice that shrieked in her ear that she was being reckless and foolish—just as Marcus always scolded. What did she care? she thought painfully. There was nothing in England for her.

"Are you certain?" Hugh asked, knowing he shouldn't carry this conversation further, yet unable to help himself. This was madness. There were many reasons why he should get up and walk away but he remained firmly where he was. Isabel wouldn't be the wife of his heart, but he'd be good to her and who knew? In time they might love one another, but if they did not, surely liking and respect would carry them through? And he wouldn't face years, decades, alone in India.

His expression troubled, Hugh asked, "What of your aunt and uncle? What will they say of this?"

Her eyes met his steadily. "They will say that I am too young. That I don't know my own mind."

"Oh, well, then," he said dispiritedly, "it wouldn't work."

"But it *will*," cried Isabel. "It doesn't matter what they will think. Once we are married there is nothing Marc—they can do." Her eyes fixed beseechingly on his, she said, "Oh, please, Hugh. I promise you I shall be a good wife. *Please!*"

Lost in her great golden eyes, Hugh's good sense wavered. She was a fetching little thing. . . . He liked her. . . . He pictured his empty bungalow in India and saw the years stretch out emptily before him with only hard work and plenty of it to give him satisfaction; Isabel could change all that. . . . There would be children. . . .

His decision made, Hugh stood up and paced in front of her. "If your aunt and uncle disapprove, it will have to be a runaway match. We can be married in London by special license before my ship sails." He looked uneasily at her. "I don't know if I can arrange passage for you, and I *must* be on that ship, the company is expecting me back by a certain date—I cannot delay. You might," he warned, "have to remain in London with your maid for several weeks before another ship will be sailing for India. You could stay at m'father's townhouse; he keeps a small staff in residence, so they would see to your needs." He paused. "That might not be a bad idea. I can sign the necessary papers and leave instructions with my solicitor to get your affairs in order. And you will have time to shop for necessities. I'll prepare a list for you." He looked down at her, doubt still lurking in his blue eyes. "I plan to leave tomorrow, just after daybreak. If this is really what you want, you must gather your things and slip out of the house; I will meet you at the gates of Denham Manor. By the time anyone knows you're gone, we'll be well on our way to London."

Captured by the knowledge that in one fell swoop she'd be escaping from everything that made her unhappy, Isabel nodded. The sudden prospect of traveling to way-off India, of seeing live tigers, elephants, and who knew what other magical creatures dancing in her brain, took her breath away.

She leaped to her feet and flung her arms around Hugh's neck. "I promise I will be a good wife and never make you regret this moment," she vowed passionately. Ignoring the tiny pang in the region of her heart when Marcus's handsome face flashed before her gaze, she hugged Hugh even tighter, pushing the image away. "I promise."

Hugh took a deep breath. "Well, then, my dear, it appears before we are much older, we shall be man and wife—and on our way to India!"

Chapter 1

"That woman!" Marcus Sherbrook snarled in tones of ill-concealed temper as he paced the library of Sherbrook Hall.

His mother looked up from her embroidery, a faint smile on her lips. "I presume you are speaking of Isabel Manning?" At his curt nod, she asked, "And what has poor Isabel done now to put you in such a taking?"

Stopping his perambulations before one of the long windows of the library, he stared out at the impeccable expanse of grounds, garden, and wooded area. April was a lovely month in England and this April was proving to be no different. The roses were budded, some blooming; pansies in a bright array of purple, yellow, blue, and white turned their sweet faces up to the sun; and in the distance he could see the white and pink clouds of blossoms that ringed the apple trees in the orchard.

It was a tranquil view, a view worthy of a wealthy gentleman's estate, the carefully planned garden and woodland rolling out serenely to meet the undulating Devon hills green with spring grass. Normally he took pride and satisfaction in the view but not today. Today, Isabel had managed to once again disrupt his orderly life and he wished, not for the first time, that having made a runaway match with Hugh Manning thirteen years ago and blithely sailing away to India that she'd had the good sense to stay there.

Marcus's fists clenched at his sides, a faint memory of searing anguish sliding through him. He never again wanted to feel the ripping pain he experienced when he realized that it was true: Isabel had run away and married Hugh Manning. He'd been dazed, full of disbelief when he'd first learned the news from her agitated uncle, Sir James, but as the truth had become known, something deep within him, some fragile emotion he hadn't been aware of, shriveled and died. Fury had come later, and he had spent several months after Isabel's marriage hating her and damning her to hell. Eventually, his own good common sense had asserted itself. In command of himself once more, he reminded himself calmly how much he had loathed the guardianship and in time convinced himself that he was quite satisfied with the way the affair had turned out. His tiresome ward was safely married to an honorable man; her fortune was in Hugh's capable hands and they were half a world away from him. Where she should have damn well *stayed*, he thought bitterly.

Marcus winced. He wasn't being fair and he knew it. One would think, he admitted, in the decade since Hugh had died and Isabel had returned to England, her two-year-old son toddling at her side, that he would have become accustomed to Isabel living right under his nose. He hadn't, and he'd discovered almost immediately that the easiest way for him to deal with Isabel's disruptive presence in the neighborhood was simply to ignore her. It wasn't hard for him to do. At any social affair that they both attended, after doing the polite thing—and Marcus was always polite—he promptly disappeared into the card room set aside for the gentlemen. He did not reappear until time to bid his host good night, and if his mother had accompanied him, and she often did, escort her home. He had also become adept at avoiding any small gathering in which he would come face-to-face with Hugh's widow. He couldn't explain his tactics, but he wasn't unaware that it had something to do with the gaping wound her marriage had caused him. Stunned by the depth of pain he'd felt at that time, he was determined to never feel that way again, which meant he kept Isabel as far away from his well-ordered life as possible.

Avoiding Isabel Manning had become habitual for him and it helped that he was frequently out of the area, sometimes gone from home for weeks or months at a time. Unlike Isabel, whose movements were hampered not only by the simple fact that she was female, but by her son's need of her as well, Marcus could and did come and go as he pleased. He was most comfortable in his own home but he often traveled to visit friends and relatives and even undertook the occasional brief trip to London when it suited him.

One of his favorite places to visit was the home of his cousin, Julian, the Earl of Wyndham and his charming countess, Nell, and their growing brood of children. Another of his cousins, Charles Weston, lived near Julian and, while there had been some constraint between Charles and Marcus in the past, these days he found Charles's company very agreeable. In fact, he had returned not long ago from attending Charles's wedding to a charming young lady in Cornwall. Everyone who knew him agreed that Charles's marriage to Daphne Beaumont would be the making of him. After the wedding, while most of the guests had departed, Marcus, Julian, and Nell had remained at Beaumont Place for an extended visit with the newlyweds. Thinking of that visit and what they had uncovered in the bowels of the ancient house, once a Norman keep, caused a ripple of unease to pass through him. There had been some ugly events that he would not ever forget, and as for the ghosts . . . He shook himself. Here at home, surrounded by the calm and familiar, the *normal*, Marcus wondered if his memory of what had transpired during those last days of his visit wasn't a bit faulty. Living at

Beaumont Place, with Charles and Daphne insisting it was true, it had not been difficult to believe the place was haunted by a pair of ghosts, but staring out at the sunny expanse before him that belief was shaken. Did he really believe in such things? Spirits of the dead capering about? Ghosts floating mistily in the air? Before his visit to Beaumont Place he would have sworn not, but . . .

A sudden vision of Isabel's vivid face flashed across his mind. She wouldn't have hesitated a moment in believing that Beaumont Place was haunted. She would have enjoyed immensely grappling with ghosts and such. He almost smiled as he pictured the excitement that would have glittered in her eyes but then he remembered that he had a grievance with Mrs. Hugh Manning and scowled. Why the devil couldn't she stay out of his life?

She'd hated being his ward and he'd not found the experience an unalloyed pleasure either. At least when she'd returned to England and stepped off the ship from India a decade ago, he reminded himself, she hadn't been *his* responsibility any longer. In those days old Lord Manning had had the joyless task of dealing with her fits and starts and thank God for that, he thought with suspect piety.

Of course, Manning didn't consider having Isabel and her son underfoot a burden. Their arrival, Marcus admitted, had probably saved the baron from simply wasting away with grief. Through a series of dreadful events, Lord Manning lost his eldest son, Robert, and his son's pregnant wife in a boating accident and then, not four months later, news of Hugh's death in India reached him. The letters, each with their terrible news, had likely crossed each other on the ocean. The old man had been shattered and Marcus feared his will to live had died with his two sons.

Isabel and Edmund's return to England had brought about a remarkable change in Lord Manning. Though grieving over Robert's death and Hugh's demise from a cobra bite while in the back country of India inspecting goods destined for the

East India Trading Company warehouses in Bombay, Lord Manning had been beside himself with joy to welcome Hugh's widow and only child into his home. Isabel's fortune would have allowed her to live where she pleased, but there had never been any question of her living anywhere but at Manning Court with her late husband's father. She'd wanted to return to the neighborhood of her youth, and her son, Edmund, was the elderly baron's heir and sole link with his dead son; he adored the boy. And there was no denying that Edmund was the very picture of his father at the same age. Marcus's expression softened and his mouth twitched. And as charming a blond-haired, blue-eyed scamp as he'd ever seen, he thought affectionately.

When she wasn't disrupting his well-ordered life, and putting aside the tragic loss of her husband, Marcus considered Isabel's return to the neighborhood ten years ago a happy occurrence for his neighbor. Like a welcome spring breeze, she and Edmund had swept into Manning Court and pushed out the crushing sadness and heavy shadows that would have, no doubt, sent Lord Manning to the grave. Within weeks of her arrival, there was a spring in milord's step once again and a twinkle in his faded blue eyes and Marcus was grateful for that. He scowled. But he bloody well wasn't grateful for Isabel's unwarranted intrusion into his carefully arranged life!

"Are you going to tell me what Isabel has done?" asked his mother, interrupting his thoughts, "or are you simply going to stand there glaring out the window?"

"I was not glaring," Marcus said austerely. "I was merely admiring the view."

"Of course you were," his mother agreed, smiling. "But tell me: what has Isabel done now to put you in such a taking?"

He sighed, his anger dissipating "It's that horse of hers—Tempest. He jumped the fences, the same fences I have warned her needed to be raised if she was going to keep a stallion in that paddock, and I found the beast this morning sporting with a half dozen of our mares. Worse, Jasmine, the chestnut with the wide blaze that I intended to have bred this afternoon to Nonesuch, had already fallen to his charms. It's possible Tempest may have covered another mare or two, there's no telling at this point."

His mother kept her eyes on her needle. "I seem to remember, oh, years ago, you mentioning that you wished you'd bred him a few more times before you sold him to Isabel when she returned from India."

He shrugged. "I would have, but once she returned to England, I didn't have much choice but to turn him over to her— immediately!"

"Well, it was the only fair thing to do; after all, she *did* discover him first."

"I know that, Mother," he said dryly. "I would have suggested she buy him from me myself once she settled into Manning Court, if she'd given me a chance to do so."

Something suspiciously like a giggle escaped Mrs. Sherbrook. "If you could have seen your face when she found out you owned him and stormed in here accusing you of stealing him while her back was turned."

Marcus grinned. "She was in rare form, wasn't she? I had to feel the top of my head afterward to make certain I still had hair and that I hadn't been scorched bald."

Selecting a pale green thread, his mother rethreaded her needle. "What did she say when you told her about Tempest, ah, sporting with your mares?"

His lips thinned. "She was not a bit sorry or contrite! Looking down her nose at me, she very graciously told me that if any of the mares turned up in foal that she'd be happy to either buy any mare that became pregnant from Tempest's, ah, visit or the foal when it was weaned—whichever I preferred."

"And you told her?"

He sent his mother a look and this time she did giggle.

"Oh, Marcus! If you only knew how happy I am to know that something can shake the stuffiness from you."

"Stuffy!" he exclaimed, ruffled. "Why is it that just because I don't flaunt a different opera dancer on my arm every week, habitually drink myself under the table, gamble my fortune away, or spur my horse up the steps of the chapel, that everyone thinks that I am a dull fellow? Is there something wrong with preferring a calm, well-ordered life? Or something deviant to liking peace and tranquillity and seeking not to have one's life constantly in an uproar?"

He looked so mystified that Mrs. Sherbrook shook her head in despair. Her tall, handsome son was nearly forty years old, and even she thought it unnatural that he had never caused her a moment's despair. There had been no wild scrapes or daring romps even when he had been a young man. He had been ever affectionate, courteous, and dutiful and could be depended upon to do the right thing and keep a calm head in the midst of crisis, for which she was devotedly thankful . . . most of the time. He was a son to be proud of, and she was. Very. The problem was that she rather thought that he should have, at least once in his life, thrown caution to the wind and plunged into some sort of scandalous escapade. Not so *very* scandalous, she reminded herself cautiously, just enough to add a little excitement to his life and shake him from the staid, stolid path he seemed destined to follow. When he continued to stare at her with that same mystified expression, she admitted, "No, there is nothing wrong with wanting the familiar. And I am truly blessed that you have never caused me to hide my face in shame. Quite the contrary, I have always been very proud of you, but Marcus, you are not in your dotage. Yet you have always behaved and acted like someone twice your age." Almost wistfully she asked, "Have you never wanted to escape from the humdrum of country life? Ever longed for adventure or felt a need to kick over the traces and leave behind the common, the routine?"

"Are you saying you *want* me to be a libertine?" he demanded incredulously. "Shall I set the neighborhood gossiping by risking life and limb by racing my curricle against the mail coach and fill the house with rakes and gamesters and squealing bits of muslin while you hide yourself away upstairs to avoid being accosted in your own home? A fine fellow I should look!"

"No! Oh, no," cried Mrs. Sherbrook, horrified by the image he conjured up. "Of course not," she said more calmly a second longer. "It is merely that you have always been such a *good* son—I could not ask for one better—but your father's death when you were so young and the responsibilities it placed on you . . ."

"I was twenty-three, Mother, not a schoolboy." He smiled at her. "Old enough to know my own mind. If I had yearned for the delights of London there was nothing stopping me from enjoying them." He grinned at her. "And I have from time to time. Enjoyed them immensely." He sat down on the sofa beside her. Taking one of her hands in his, he kissed it. "Mother, why is it that you, everyone—Julian and Charles included—find it so hard to believe that I am quite content with my life?" he asked, puzzled. "Understand me: if I were not, I would change it. You must believe me when I swear to you that I enjoy living in the country. I even enjoy escorting you on your yearly trek to London for the Season and—"

"And you hotfoot it back to Sherbrook Hall just as soon as you decently can," his mother murmured.

"Guilty! But the whirlwind of parties and balls that so appeal to you bore me to death. And as for chasing after opera dancers or playing deep in some hell on Pall Mall or drinking myself under the table . . ." He snorted. "Those rakish pastimes have never held any allure for me." He smiled whimsically at her. "Don't you see—I'm content with my life."

Her gaze rested thoughtfully on him. "I don't know that I'd want to settle for 'content,' if I were you."

"What? You would have me miserable?" he teased. "Dissatisfied? Unhappy?"

She sighed inwardly. Marcus was everything a mother could hope for: affectionate, generous, honorable, a most worthy man, but . . . One could be *too* worthy. Staring at him, her heart couldn't help but swell with love and pride. He was tall and broad-shouldered, yet leanly built, and she knew he commanded attention whenever he entered a room. Women admired him; she'd seen the speculative glances sent his way, glances he wasn't even aware of, she thought dispiritedly. But for all the attention he attracted, he was not traditionally handsome. His features were too bold, his jaw and chin remarkably determined, but the frankly carnal curve of his full bottom lip made the female of the sex forget about those imperfections and dwell on the implicit promise of that tempting mouth. His mother often thought it a shame he hadn't inherited the color of her own emerald eyes, but looking into those intelligent gray eyes his father had passed on to him, she was not displeased; they were striking in his dark face. But for all the intelligence in those gray eyes, he couldn't see that there was something very wrong about a handsome, virile man being "content" to live the life of a monk, buried in the country! Her gaze narrowed. Of course, she could be wrong about the monkish part; her son, for all his virtues, was hardly likely to tell her if he kept a mistress in town.

"Oh, this is a silly conversation," she said abruptly, putting aside her embroidery.

"And who, may I ask, started it?" Marcus asked, a twinkle in those gray eyes, as he stood up.

She smiled. "My turn to cry guilty." Getting to her feet and shaking out the skirts of her gown, she asked, "Is it all arranged for us to leave next week for London? I received a letter from Lady Bullard yesterday. She writes that Parliament is in session and that the Season has already begun. I do not wish to delay our departure too long."

"I have everything well in hand," Marcus replied as he accompanied her from the room. "Provided you have all your gowns packed and the weather holds we should leave on Tuesday."

Events went as Marcus had planned. The following Tuesday, he escorted his mother, her companion, Mrs. Shelby, and several of the estate servants to London and saw them comfortably settled in the Sherbrook townhouse. The annual trip by his mother to town gave him an opportunity to visit his tailor and his boot-maker, resupply himself with those articles that could only be obtained in London, and show his face at White's and a few other gentlemen's clubs that he belonged to. He hadn't lied when he said he enjoyed escorting his mother to London. He did, just as he enjoyed the clamor of the city, the color and the bustle; enjoyed greeting old friends and hearing the latest on-dits and even casting a considering eye on the latest crop of well-born females to flood the Marriage Mart. But a fortnight in the city was about all he could endure and late April found him once more at Sherbrook Hall.

Jasmine, the blaze-faced chestnut mare, and a sleek black mare that traced her ancestry directly to the Darnley Arabian, had not come back into season and Marcus accepted the fact that next March a pair of Tempest foals would be born on his estate. Despite his plans to breed the mares to his own stallion, Nonesuch, he was not displeased, but he was uneasy. There was no telling the outcome when dealing with Isabel.

Walking back from the stables to the main house that warm April morning, he considered his options. He could leave her in ignorance until after the foals were born or he could write her a note telling her that, if all went well, there would be two extra Tempest foals on the ground next year. Or, he could simply ride over to Manning Court and tell her in person. The note, he thought cravenly. The note would be easiest.

Yet when he found himself seated in his office, the blank

page of paper before him, the quill in hand, he discovered a disinclination to hide behind a mere note. Placing the quill in its stand, he pushed back from the cherrywood desk and stood up.

The day was pleasant, perfect for a ride, he told himself. There was no reason why he couldn't ride over to Manning Court and tell Isabel the news. A faint smile lurked at the corners of his mouth. And watch her antics as she tries to bamboozle me out of the two mares.

Whistling cheerfully, he left the office and headed to the stables. Shortly, astride a handsome black gelding, he rode through the rolling countryside, enjoying the sound of the song-birds and the dappled shade afforded by the ancient oaks.

The Manning and Denham estates both adjoined the Sherbrook lands and the three families had always been good friends as well as neighbors. Lord Manning was Marcus's neighbor on the north and Sir James, Isabel's uncle, on the east, and beside the public road there were several private pathways crossing from one property to the other. Taking a shortcut through the forest, Marcus was soon riding on Manning land.

He was still some distance from the main house when he heard the sound of raised voices. He recognized Isabel's voice instantly, even if the words were not clear. By the sound of it, she was angry and ringing a peal over some poor unfortunate, but there was something in her voice, some note that made Marcus kick the gelding into a trot.

As he rode nearer he heard Isabel say clearly, "And that's the end of it! Do not approach me again. Next time, I'll set the hounds on you and the devil be damned!"

There was the low growl of a man's voice and then Isabel cried, "How *dare* you! Unhand me, you blackguard!"

Marcus rounded the bend in the narrow, leafy lane and came upon Isabel and a burly fellow he did not recognize standing in a small clearing off to one side. He recognized the type, though: former military, if the cut of his hair and jacket and the arrangement of his cravat was anything to go by. A pair of horses was tied to a nearby tree.

It was immediately apparent to Marcus that this was no mere chance meeting. The two combatants were concentrating on each other and for a second neither was aware of Marcus's approach. The man had one hand wrapped tightly around Isabel's upper arm and she was struggling to escape. From the glimpse Marcus had of her face, she was more furious than afraid and yet there was something in her features that made Marcus's gut tighten and aroused all his protective instincts.

His calm demeanor at odds with the spurt of hot rage that raced through him at the sight of the stranger's grip on Isabel's upper arm, Marcus said brusquely, "I believe that the lady made a request. I would suggest that you follow it. *Now.*"

Isabel's gaze jerked in his direction and her eyes widened when she saw him just a few yards away sitting astride the big black horse. Embarrassment mingled with fear flitted across her features before she mastered herself and schooled her face into a polite mask. The embarrassment Marcus understood. But fear? Good God! She had no reason to fear *him*.

The stranger took Marcus's measure, and whatever he saw in Marcus's face made him drop his hand from Isabel's arm and take a step away from her. Smiling, the stranger said, "There is no reason for you to be staring daggers at me. This is merely a misunderstanding between old friends." He looked at Isabel and prompted in a silky undertone that raised Marcus's hackles even more, "Isn't that right, my dear Mrs. Manning?"

Isabel nodded, her eyes not meeting Marcus's. "Y-y-yes. Major Whitley w-w-was Hugh's friend in India. He was stationed near us in Bombay for a number of years." A flush on her cheeks, she added hurriedly, "He recently retired from the Army and was visiting friends in the neighborhood. When he learned that I lived nearby he came to call."

Isabel had never been a very good liar, but Marcus gave

her full marks for trying. He didn't doubt that some of what she said was true, perhaps all of it, but she was leaving a great deal unsaid and that aroused his curiosity—that and Major Whitley's threatening manner. *He* might bully Isabel all he pleased, Marcus decided instantly, but he damn well wasn't going to allow anyone else that liberty. Swinging down from his horse and holding the reins lightly in one gloved hand, he walked up to where they stood.

Stopping a few feet from Whitley, Marcus drawled, "Ah, so you knew Mr. and Mrs. Manning in India, did you?"

Whitley inclined his head, his dark eyes watchful. "Yes. Hugh and I met while I was stationed in India." He sent Marcus a man-to-man smile. "We were merry bachelors together in those days and I considered Hugh one of my boon companions. His marriage did not change our friendship and once Mrs. Manning joined him in Bombay, she frequently invited me to dine at their home." He flashed a glance at Isabel. "For which I am forever grateful. Mrs. Manning was a most gracious hostess to a poor bachelor officer. She and Manning often entertained several of us stationed there."

Whitley was a big and burly man and his dark hair was lightly peppered with silver. His black eyes were set under well-marked brows and at one time he might have been considered quite handsome, but lines of dissipation blurred and distorted his once chiseled features. Marcus disliked him on sight.

"An Army officer," Marcus remarked politely. "Retired. Recently." He looked perplexed. "How very odd. With Castlereagh at the War Department again and the gossip buzzing 'round the country about a possible invasion of the continent by Sir Wellesley this summer, I would have thought that the military would have use of an experienced officer like yourself. I vaguely remember a friend in the Army saying not long ago that the war with France was making advancement up the ranks easier and that for a career man it was a capital time to be in the service."

Whitley ignored the implication that there was something unseemly about the timing of his retirement and shrugged. "I regret I won't be part of the force that finally beats Napoleon, but after over twenty years in the military, I felt the need for a change."

"Ah. And this, er, need for change brought you to Devon?" At Whitley's nod, Marcus asked, "Do you intend to visit long in the neighborhood?"

Whitley's eyes slid to Isabel. His gaze returning to Marcus, he smiled and said, "My plans are not firm yet. I find that there are, ah, certain attractions in the area not to be found elsewhere."

"Really?" Marcus murmured, his skepticism insultingly overt. "Now, that I do find most odd, indeed! We have no particular geographical sites of interest nearby and while the Devon coast is spectacular in places, we are situated some miles inland from its charms." The expression in his gray eyes unreadable, he said in a voice just shy of sarcastic, "Do you know, I have lived here all my life and I cannot at the moment call to mind those, er, 'certain attractions' that would hold the attention of a seasoned traveler like yourself. Perhaps you would care to share specifics with me? Especially since I seem to have overlooked them."

Whitley did not like either Marcus's tone or the persistent questioning, but he wasn't going to let the other man rattle him. Seeking guidance in dealing with this tall, formidable gentleman, he cast Isabel a glance. But there was no guidance to be found from that quarter; her pretty mouth half open, her eyes wide and startled, Isabel was staring at Marcus as if she had never seen him before.

If she didn't know better, Isabel thought incredulously, she'd swear that Marcus—staid, sober, excruciatingly polite *Marcus*—was determined to provoke a fight with an utter stranger! Uneasily, she stared at that rigid jaw and those cool gray eyes, wondering where the cordial, amiable, oh, and sometimes infuriating, gentleman she had known most of her life had gone.

Since Isabel was no help, Whitley said lightly, "I find that strangers to an area are more likely to see gems all around ... gems that are overlooked by those who pass them by every day."

"That may be true," Marcus agreed. "But I'd still like to know of which gems you speak."

Whitley's lips tightened. Was the man obtuse? In no mood to continue to exchange veiled remarks with an irritating stranger, Whitley considered his next move. Ordinarily, in the face of the blunt hostility radiating from the stranger, he might have retreated and returned at a better time, but Isabel's show of spirit needed to be dealt with immediately. If she thought she could fob him off so easily, she would soon learn to her cost that such was not the case! He slanted another assessing look at the newcomer and stifled an oath. Unless he missed his guess the fellow wasn't going to give ground anytime soon. So who the devil was this country bumpkin? Realizing that the stranger had never introduced himself, Whitley said, "I'm sorry, but I don't believe you gave me your name."

"I am Marcus Sherbrook," Marcus answered, no sign of his normal friendliness in his voice.

"Not the 'clutch-fisted, monster guardian' who drove our dear Mrs. Manning from England?" exclaimed Whitley, an expression of astonishment crossing his face.

Unsmiling, Marcus glanced at Isabel, who dropped her eyes and had the grace to blush. Looking back at Whitley, he bowed and said coolly, "The same. Although, I believe that 'former clutch-fisted, monster guardian' would be the correct title these days."

"I must say," Whitley remarked, "that I am most happy to make your acquaintance. Since my dear Mrs. Manning spoke of you so often, why, I feel that I know you already."

A derisive gleam in his eyes, Marcus murmured, "How fortunate for me that my reputation goes before me." *And if this black-eyed knave,* Marcus thought grimly, *calls Isabel "my dear Mrs. Manning" in that smarmy tone of voice one more time* . . . His hand formed into a formidable fist and the satisfying image of that same fist smashing into Whitley's face whipped through his mind.

Unaware of how close he was to having his claret drawn, Whitley laughed. "Having met you I see now that the picture Mrs. Manning painted of you as an absolute ogre was misleading."

An edge to her voice, Isabel joined the conversation. "If you will remember I was very young at the time I made those remarks."

"Very true," said Whitley, "but you were quite adamant about it. I remember listening to numerous complaints about your wretched guardian's unreasonable behavior and his selfish habit of forever thwarting your plans."

Isabel risked a contrite glance at Marcus's face. "It was a long time ago and has no place in this conversation," she said tightly.

"But it is so delicious, my dear," Whitley said, staring at Isabel with a small, spiteful smile. "From your comments I was expecting to meet a veritable monster and instead I see before me a sensible gentleman."

"As Mrs. Manning stated, it was a long time ago," Marcus said flatly, not liking Whitley's malicious enjoyment of Isabel's embarrassment and disliking even more the furtive apprehensive looks Isabel flashed Whitley whenever she thought herself unobserved. She was afraid of the man, Marcus concluded ominously. But why? He realized that the why didn't matter: what mattered was that Isabel was frightened of this "friend" from her past and that it was in his power to shelter her from whatever threat Whitley represented. Abruptly, Marcus said, "It has been, ah, an enlightening meeting but if you will excuse us now, Mrs. Manning and I have business to discuss."

Whitley stiffened. "I do not wish to be rude, sir, but I believe that you were the one who interrupted my business with Mrs. Manning."

A glint leaped to the gray eyes. "Perhaps you misunderstood me," said Marcus icily. "I have asked you politely to leave. I suggest you do so before I forget my manners."

Major Whitley had not survived twenty years in the military without recognizing the need for a strategic retreat. He had no idea how much of a threat Sherbrook represented, but it occurred to him that a wise man would abandon the field at this point. He looked at Isabel. There would be other meetings. Meetings that did not include the overbearing Mr. Sherbrook.

It went against the grain, but Whitley smiled and murmured, "Ah, it appears I did misunderstand. Forgive me." Meeting Marcus's cool gaze, he added, "Until we meet again, Mr. Sherbrook."

Turning to Isabel, Whitley took her hand in his and bowed. His bow completed, he stood before Isabel and smiled. Not a nice smile. "It has been a pleasure renewing our acquaintance," he said. "I look forward to seeing you again. We have much to discuss about the old days in Bombay, don't we, my dear."

Marcus watched the exchange closely, frowning. Surely the damn fellow wasn't *threatening* Isabel? But even more telling was the slight shrinking away of Isabel's body from Whitley's and the swiftly concealed flicker of fear he glimpsed in her eyes. His own eyes narrowed. It appeared he was going to have to take decisive action and he could think of only one way that would rout the fellow and ensure Isabel's protection from further advances.

Marcus strolled over and, taking Isabel's hand from Whitley's, he held her cold little fingers in his, and said, "Mrs. Manning and I will let you know when it will be convenient for you to call."

"I think that Mrs. Manning can issue her own invitations," Whitley snapped. "She doesn't need your permission."

"Ah, you're wrong there," Marcus said. Smiling warmly down at Isabel, he lifted her hand to his lips and pressed a kiss on her knuckles. Looking back at Whitley, he added, "You see, Mrs. Manning has recently done me the honor of accepting my proposal. As her future husband, Mrs. Manning will be asking my permission for a great many things."

Chapter 2

"Pray tell me," Isabel demanded sarcastically, "what maggot has gotten into your brain? How dare you tell Whitley that we are engaged! Of all the nonsensical notions!" Her entire body vibrating with suppressed emotion, she glared at him and Marcus correctly deduced that it was not delight that caused her reaction.

Once Whitley had taken his abrupt leave from the newly betrothed pair, in an uncomfortable silence they had ridden to Manning Court. They were presently standing in the handsome office in the main wing of Squire Manning's impressive stables, the heavy mahogany door firmly shut behind them. Yellow sunlight poured into the room from the bank of narrow windows that overlooked several paddocks in which long-legged Thoroughbred mares and foals gamboled on the lush green grass.

Arms crossed over his chest, his admirable shoulders resting comfortably against the doorframe, Marcus regarded her thoughtfully. Now why, he wondered, did I even entertain for a second the idea that she might be grateful for my intervention? He grimaced. How could he have ever forgotten that stubborn streak of independence? It had led to many a wrangle between them in the past and it appeared that nothing had changed. In his own mind, he had acted in a responsible manner, honorable even, and Isabel was furious with him. Why wasn't he surprised?

His appreciative gaze followed her trim little form as she stalked around the office. In an amber-colored riding habit trimmed in bronze braided silk, her red hair caught back by a green and brown plaid bow at the nape of her neck, a few bright tendrils brushing her cheeks, she made a fetching sight. Or would have, he admitted, if she hadn't been scowling so dreadfully.

Isabel flounced down in the padded leather chair behind a massive oak desk and, leaning her elbows on the top of the desk, buried her head in her hands. In muffled tones, she asked, "How could you have done something so reckless and irresponsible? Good God! What *were* you thinking?"

That was a very good question, Marcus admitted. He had no idea what he had been thinking when he'd made his bold announcement. *Not true*, whispered a part of his brain; he knew very well what he had been thinking. It had been apparent to him from the first that Isabel was frightened of Whitley and had needed protection from whatever danger the fellow represented; the announcement of her betrothal to himself had provided it. Certainly, it had rocked the major onto his heels and cut the ground beneath him, Marcus thought contentedly, recalling the look on the major's face. Marcus didn't usually take pleasure in another person's discomfort, but he was forced to admit that Whitley's stunned expression and rapid retreat had given him a great deal of pleasure. The only thing that would have given him greater pleasure, he decided, would have been to draw the major's cork and he was hopeful that the major would give him another opportunity to do just that.

Whitley may have retreated but Marcus did not delude himself that he had heard the last of the man. Whitley had some hold over Isabel; that had been obvious to him, not so much from what Marcus had overheard, although that was damning in itself, but from Isabel's reactions. He had not mistaken the fear in her eyes or her uncharacteristic reaction to his sudden announcement of their betrothal.

She had not said a word, merely flashed him a complicated look of mingled astonishment, relief, dismay, and consternation before dropping her gaze. Isabel knew as well as he that he had been lying through his teeth, but she had not denied to Whitley that such a betrothal existed and that was curious. Isabel was perfectly capable of tearing a strip off him, several strips if she was angry enough, Marcus admitted, wincing, certain memories of past conflicts when they were much younger rising up in his mind, but she had stoically allowed his words to stand. There had been no outcry, no outrage, and no explosive denial—and he'd been halfway prepared to have his words hurled back in his face. But she had said nothing, even her expression giving nothing away, yet he remembered distinctly her fingers tightening on his and the nearly imperceptible movement of her body nearer to his. Whatever she might be saying now, she *had* been grateful for his intervention. And was probably furious with herself, he thought wryly, for feeling so.

Pushing himself away from the doorjamb, Marcus wandered around the office. "I wouldn't worry overmuch about it," he said finally. "It's not as if I'd sent a notice to the *Times*."

Her head snapped up, her angry gaze boring into his. "Since it was to Whitley that you made your outrageous announcement, you won't need to send a notice to the *Times*; he is the biggest gossip alive. Have no fear, half of Devon will know before nightfall." Her gaze fell and she said bitterly, "One of the reasons for his popularity in Bombay with all the hostesses was that one could be assured of learning the latest rumors and tittle-tattle. He had the knack of knowing everything the moment it occurred."

"And does he know something about you?" Marcus asked quietly.

"Of course not!"

She said the words with enough vehemence to almost convince Marcus. Almost. He frowned. Not only was she frightened of Whitley but she wasn't willing to talk about it. And how could he help her, Marcus wondered acidly, if she wouldn't share with him whatever it was Whitley held over her head?

He studied the elegant little profile presented to him as she stared out of the windows. Thirteen years had passed since they had confronted each other that fateful morning at Sherbrook Hall, but Isabel's face showed few signs of the passing years. It was true she no longer looked the child she had been then; she was a woman now; she had been a wife, a mother, and a widow. Those events had not left her untouched, but the passing milestones in her life had only refined and honed the character and steel beneath the soft youthfulness. There was a mature beauty to her face that had not been there thirteen years ago and, though her gaze was averted from him, Marcus was conscious that her eyes, once so innocent, these days held worldly knowledge, adult awareness . . . and tightly held secrets.

They knew each other so well, yet not at all, he admitted. Though she had lived all of her thirty years, except for the time in India, within just a few miles of him, in recent memory they had had little contact, beyond the few social affairs that they had both attended. He knew her son better than he did Isabel, having traveled with the old baron and Edmund to Scotland for an annual fishing trip the past five years. Those weeks in Scotland with Edmund traipsing at his heels had been most enjoyable and he had developed a strong fondness for the boy. Though his contact was mostly with her son and father-in-law, Marcus could not help but hear of Isabel's doings from time to time from his mother and other friends in the neighborhood, and Lord Manning frequently mentioned events in the Manning household, which naturally included information about Isabel. But for all Marcus knew of Isabel's life at Manning Court, he did not know her,

not as he had known the much younger Isabel, and he suddenly regretted that fact.

This was a woman before him now, with a woman's cares
and concerns, and he had not the first clue as to what went
on in that lovely head of hers. Marcus sighed. Nothing
would convince him that she didn't have a serious problem in
the burly form of Major Whitley but it was apparent she was
not going to share whatever that problem was with him. At
least not yet. . . .

Wandering over to the windows, Marcus stared out at the
mares and foals in the paddocks in front of him. "Whitley is
a stranger to the area," he said, "and though he intimated he
might visit longer, I suspect that my announcement today will
send him about his business." He sent her a long look over
his shoulder. "I don't think that Major Whitley will be a
problem for you any longer."

"I didn't have a problem with Whitley," she said evenly,
"but your actions today have certainly created one for us."

Turning away from the window, Marcus walked over to
stop in front of the desk. Looking down at her, he said, "I
doubt it. Only the three of us know what I said."

"And you think Whitley will keep his mouth shut?" Isabel
asked incredulously. She snorted. "I told you he is the biggest
gossip alive. Even if he thought your statement untrue, he
will pass it along the first chance he gets—if for no other reason than to cause trouble. You must believe me: he delights in
throwing the cat amongst the pigeons."

Marcus shrugged. "I wouldn't worry overmuch about
what a stranger just passing through the neighborhood has
to say. We can deny his words and let it be known amongst
our friends and family that the major misunderstood. As long
as we give it no credence, others will follow suit."

For a minute Isabel looked hopeful, then her face fell. "It
won't do. Think of the gossip."

"Gossip will pass. We can stand the nonsense." Growing
irritated by her manner—after all, he'd only been trying to

help—he said, "I don't know why you must turn this into a Siddons' tragedy."

"Perhaps because I don't relish being the subject of gossip and speculation?"

She had a point and he was beginning to wish he'd simply written her a damn note about Tempest and the foals. If he'd done that, at this moment he'd be comfortably at home and would never have come across the ugly little scene between Whitley and Isabel and felt compelled to interfere. So why *had* he interfered . . . and in such a dramatic manner? He knew better than to tangle in Isabel's affairs. Yet with no thought of the consequences, he had leaped willy-nilly into the fray and, even more astonishing, he was not sorry. The reason for his unprecedented behavior remained: Isabel had needed his protection and he had provided it.

He didn't see that there was such a problem. Even if Whitley did blab, everyone who knew them would think the idea of a betrothal between them a huge jest. Why couldn't she see that no one in their right mind would think that they would make a match of it? Good Lord! They'd barely spoken to each other in years. The whole idea was ludicrous!

Testily, he said, "If you don't like denying it, we shall claim that it is true and in a few weeks you can cry off. Say we don't suit or something."

"What? You would have me be the jilt?" she demanded indignantly.

"Well, I can't be the one to cry off," he argued. "Bad *ton*! Everyone would think me a scoundrel."

"At the moment," she snapped, "I think you *are* a scoundrel!"

"Thank you very much for that," he said bitterly. "I do you a favor and this is the thanks I get for my efforts."

"If you will remember," she said from between gritted teeth, "I didn't ask you to grant me any favors."

With an effort Marcus held onto his temper. In hindsight, he agreed that his way of protecting her from Whitley had been poorly conceived, outrageous certainly, and he marveled that he acted so precipitously. Though he showed no signs of it, he was a trifle stunned by his wildly uncharacteristic behavior. Marriage had never crossed his thoughts until he had uttered those fateful words, and the mind fairly boggled at the notion of his being married to Isabel. Bloody hell! To any woman, for that matter, he thought candidly, but especially to *Isabel*! Most unsettling, however, was the knowledge that he had not spared one thought to the consequences of what he was doing. He had simply reacted to the situation. And just look where it had gotten him.

Reviewing the situation, Marcus saw that there were . . . difficulties, problems even, arising from his hasty and ill-thought-out actions, but he was confident that they could brush through the affair fairly easily. If they kept their heads about them and didn't do anything foolish, all would soon be right and tight.

A huge chasm suddenly yawned before Marcus as it occurred to him that if the major was friends with one of his mother's boon companions such as Lady Carver, the formidable wife of Viscount Carver, or Squire Bassett and his wife, that they might not escape unscathed. Another equally uncomfortable thought occurred to him. What if Whitley was an intimate of Garrett Manning, Lord Manning's nephew? If Garrett learned of the engagement, it would only be a short time before Lord Manning did. The horrifying possibility of marriage to Isabel loomed large in his mind and a hunted expression crossed his handsome face as the enormity of what he had done hit him like a cannon ball.

In a feeble voice, Marcus asked, "Er, who are the friends that Whitley is visiting?" He swallowed and said more firmly, "The outcome will depend upon who they are and their consequence in the area—and how likely they are to be believed."

Isabel hesitated, then muttered, "He is staying at the Stag Horn Inn."

Marcus frowned. "I thought you said he was visiting with friends?"

She sent him a look. "It seemed the simplest explanation at the time. I didn't realize then that you were going to end up announcing that we were betrothed."

Marcus ignored the last part of her statement. Hopefully, he asked, "So he doesn't actually know anyone in the neighborhood?"

"No. But before you think we've gotten off scot-free I would remind you that Keating's youngest boy, Sam, is Edmund's boon companion and that the eldest son, Will, is one of my uncle's footman at Denham Manor. Don't forget: Keating's wife is a bosom friend of Lord Carver's Cook. If any one of the Keating family hear of the engagement . . ."

Her words dashed the faint flicker of hope the information that Whitley was a stranger in the area had aroused. Marcus was well acquainted with Keating, the voluble innkeeper of the Stag Horn, and his gossipy wife. If they learned of the betrothal from Whitley . . . He closed his eyes as if in pain.

Isabel watched him closely and smiled maliciously. "Exactly. All Whitley has to do is breathe one word to Keating and the cat will be out of the bag."

Opening his eyes, Marcus shuddered and nodded. "And of course, Whitley, being a nosy sort, will no doubt make inquiries, or at the very least make mention of the engagement. Even as we speak, the news is probably already spreading through the servant grapevine."

"And from there it is only a matter of hours before it travels from the servants' hall up to the master and mistress of the household," Isabel said wearily.

Bleakly they regarded each other. Isabel's eyes were the first to drop. She was furious with him, yet she could not prevent the skip of her pulse or the sudden leap of her heart whenever their eyes met. Even as angry as she was with him, she could not deny that he was still the handsomest man she had ever met. Nor could she pretend that, at least initially, she had not been grateful for his intervention. For that first split second after he had made his astonishing announcement, she had allowed herself to feel safe and protected— emotions she had not felt for a very long time.

From beneath lowered lashes she considered that dark, dearly familiar face, her heart aching as she wondered why she had found his guardianship so onerous. She could admit now that Marcus had never been anything but fair and kind to her, and she had been too full of herself, too stubborn, too *young* to see it. In those long-ago days, he had only to suggest one thing for her to immediately want the opposite. At every turn, and with great relish, she had defied him and fought him, heaping scorn and insult upon him in the process. It wasn't surprising that in the decade since her return to England he had avoided her like the pox. She'd certainly given him no reason not to, she thought mournfully. And now . . .

Marcus's words broke into her thoughts. "I *am* sorry," he offered gently. "I only meant to help you, not create this sort of complication."

"Complication?" Isabel asked, torn between temper and tears. Didn't the man understand? Whatever his motives, he had completely overset her life. "A complication," she explained tartly, "is having accepted two different invitations for dinner! Not embarking upon marriage with a woman you loathe!"

"I don't loathe you," Marcus said sharply. "You can be an infuriating little devil at times, but I have always had a fondness for you."

"Not a very good basis for marriage," she said miserably, staring blankly at her hands where they rested on the desk.

Marcus moved to her side, his big hand warmly covering hers. "But not such a bad one either, poppet." She glanced up at him, her golden-brown eyes swimming in tears. His breath caught, pain knifing through him at the sight of those tears. He could never bear to see Isabel unhappy, even when she had made him furious. Brushing aside one of those bright tendrils of hair near her cheek, he said bracingly, "Come now! Cheer up! I have it on good authority that marriage, even between strangers, is not the end of the world. We are not strangers." He smiled at her. "We have known each other all our lives, surely that gives us an advantage? And our marriage is not a sure thing; Whitley may hold his tongue."

Isabel shook her head. "Not he. Believe me, he *will* snoop about and not rest until he finds out what he wants to know." Her voice thickened. "It is what he does best."

Frowning, Marcus said, "Isabel, don't you think it's time for you to tell me what is really going on here?"

She tried to jerk her hand away but he held on tight. "No," he said, "you are not running away and you are not throwing a tantrum. What does Whitley hold over you?"

"N-n-nothing! You have mistaken the situation."

"I did not mistake your fear of him, nor did I mistake your dislike of him. If there is no reason for you to be beholden to him, why did you meet him this morning? Why didn't you send him away with a flea in his ear?" His voice sharpened. "And don't try to lie to me."

"You are mistaken," she repeated stubbornly.

"I didn't see him holding you against your will?" he asked dryly. "Nor, I suppose you'll tell me, I didn't hear you threatening to set the dogs on him if he didn't leave you alone?"

Finally freeing her hand from him, Isabel jumped to her feet. Putting half the room between them, she said, "Major Whitley was presumptuous. He thought to make more of our friendship in India than there actually was. When he overstepped the bounds, I gave him a well-deserved set down. There was nothing more to it."

She was lying through her pretty little lips, but Marcus knew from past confrontations that pushing her would gain him nothing. If she didn't want to tell him the truth, she damn well wouldn't, and the more he pushed, the more she'd dig in her heels. Sighing, he said, "Very well, have it your way." He leaned a hip onto the corner of the desk and, staring at his booted foot, he said, "It would seem that my intervention was unneeded and I apologize for that, but it doesn't solve our problem."

"And we wouldn't have a problem," she reminded him sweetly, "if you hadn't interfered in matters that are none of your business!"

"True, but I did interfere and, unfortunately, we must deal with the results." Still staring at his gleaming boot, he said, "We have a few options though none are foolproof. We can hope that Whitley says nothing and the problem simply vanishes; or the moment we are faced with it, we can ridicule any notion that we are actually engaged and hope we convince our family and friends, or . . ."

"Or we can make the announcement ourselves and marry each other," Isabel said flatly.

"Unless, of course, you wish to follow my earlier suggestion and cry off in a few weeks?"

She sent him a burning look. "I told you I do not wish to be labeled a jilt."

"Then what do you want to do?" he asked patiently. "Since this is my doing, I am willing to follow your lead."

"You are being far too amiable about this whole affair," she said suspiciously. "Don't you realize that we may very well find ourselves married to each other?"

Marcus was trying very hard not to think of that option, but as the minutes ticked by, he suspected that before much longer he would find himself truly engaged to Isabel . . . and at some point in the future, married to her. He closed his eyes and shuddered, the earthshaking upheaval marriage would cause in his life looming before him. Good God! What had he done? If the marriage came to pass, Isabel and her son would live at Sherbrook Hall and his well-ordered, comfortable existence would be a thing of the past. In a matter of months, he would no longer be the carefree bachelor able to arrange his life as he saw fit; he would be a married man with a stepson! Married, he thought, horrified. To Isabel.

Marcus couldn't explain it, but he was aware that underneath his horror and undeniable panic there lurked a curious sensation of excitement and anticipation. Given the choice, he might have wished there was some other way out of the dilemma his hasty words had created, but he wasn't even certain of that. His gaze traveled down her slim form and for the first time he saw her, *really* saw her. She was, he realized astounded, a fascinating female . . . a female he would enjoy taking to bed. In that instant memories of his once irritating ward or the to-be-avoided-at-all-costs widow of Hugh Manning vanished. Feeling as if he'd been struck by a bolt of lightning, he stared awestruck at her, aware that she was an immensely attractive woman, a very attractive woman whose sweetly rounded body held all sorts of secrets he wanted— no, *needed*—to learn. His eyes on her small, high bosom, he imagined their softness and weight in his hands, their taste upon his tongue; desire flared. In that second, he wanted nothing more than to close the short distance between them, take her into his arms, kiss that saucy mouth, and caress those tempting breasts. His breathing thickened and, suddenly conscious of the indecent bulge in his breeches, Marcus stood up and retreated to the window.

Keeping his back to her, he fought to control his unruly body, but his awareness of Isabel as a *woman* would not go away. His body one long ache of desire, he stared doggedly out at the foals and mares and concentrated on not giving in to the urge to discover the silky flesh he knew lay under that fashionable riding habit.

His voice harsher than he intended, he said, "If we have to marry, we have to marry."

Marcus heard her quick steps as she came up beside him. "Don't you understand, you big dolt?" she said furiously. "I do not wish to be married! Not to you or anyone!"

Frowning, he half-turned to look at her. "Did you love him so much?"

Isabel made a vexed sound. "What was between Hugh and me is none of your business. I simply do not wish to be married again."

"Well, then," Marcus said slowly, "you have to choose which of our not-very-attractive options will suit you best."

Isabel glared at him. "And I wouldn't have to if you'd minded your own business."

"I've apologized already," he reminded her. "I can do no more than that."

Spinning on her heels, Isabel walked over to the desk and once more sank down into the chair behind it. Elbows on the desk, she buried her head in her hands again and muttered, "It isn't just a matter of which option would suit me best, but which option will cause the least amount of trouble and gossip. I have my son to think of—and my father-in-law, both of whom would be delighted if I did marry you."

"Really?" Marcus asked, smiling foolishly and inexplicably pleased.

She raised her head enough to send him a speaking look before dropping it into her hands again. "Yes, Edmund thinks you are top-of-the-trees and my father-in-law has hinted recently how fortuitous it would be if I were to marry again . . . to, say, a neighbor or someone who didn't live very far away so that he could see his grandson whenever he wanted."

He almost said "really" again, but caught himself in time; instead, he said, "I had no idea that Manning wished for you to marry again." Frowning, he added, "I would have thought marriage would be the last thing he'd want for you."

"It may have escaped your notice, but this past year or so," she began tartly, "my father-in-law and Mrs. Appleton have been coyly circling each other. You'd have noticed if you didn't always disappear into the card room."

Marcus was acquainted with Clara Appleton. A plump,

easy-going matron his mother's age, she was also one of his mother's circle of friends and a frequent guest at Sherbrook Hall. Mrs. Appleton's husband, a retired admiral, had died five years ago and had left her comfortably situated and Marcus hadn't been aware that the lady had been looking to marry again. Certainly his mother had never mentioned it, or that the baron was thinking of marriage. But it wasn't his business, so he shrugged and said, "If he wants to marry her, why doesn't he? What does your marriage have to do with it?"

"He hasn't discussed it with me," Isabel explained, "but I think he's hesitant to ask her to marry him while Edmund and I are living at Manning Court. He doesn't want me to feel pushed aside, nor does he want his new wife to have to deal with another woman in the house. If I were to marry you, it would solve all his problems. He could marry Mrs. Appleton and yet Edmund and I would be living right next door."

Something occurred to Marcus. "Does my mother know all this?"

"I assume so. She and Mrs. Appleton are great friends and your mother and my father-in-law have always been neighbors as well as friends. I'd be surprised if she didn't know."

"Er, do you think your father-in-law has mentioned to her his hopes for you and me?"

"Probably," she admitted with a faint smile. "I often find them with their heads together and yet the moment I come up to them, the conversation stops." She eyed him curiously. "Why do you ask?"

Marcus rubbed his jaw. "Before my mother left for London she seemed mightily concerned about the state of my life. Now I know why."

"She *said* something about it to you?" Isabel asked, astonished.

Marcus shook his head. "No." Grinning, he added, "She just seemed fixated on the idea that I couldn't possibly be happy doing just as I pleased. Thought I needed a little excitement or some such."

"So *that's* why you acted so outrageously!" exclaimed Isabel, her eyes darkening with temper. "You thought you'd liven up your existence by destroying mine."

"No, it ain't!" protested Marcus, although now that he thought of it, he did wonder if that hadn't been part of the reason. Had his mother's words been at the back of his mind? He considered it, then dismissed it. No, his announcement had had nothing to do with his mother's concerns and everything to do with the need to spike Whitley's guns and provide cover for Isabel.

For a moment they regarded each other, and then Isabel asked miserably, "What are we going to do?"

Marcus shrugged. "I've given you our options, unpleasant though they may be."

She leaned forward intently and said, "You do understand that marriage between us is out of the question?" Her gaze dropped and she said thickly, "After Hugh died..." She swallowed. "After Hugh died I swore that I would never marry again. It has nothing to do with you. It is just that there are ... reasons why marriage to you or anyone is impossible. I will not marry again."

Studying the top of her down-bent head, Marcus scowled. Upon Hugh's death, Isabel had taken a vow of chastity? Now that was just plain silly. She was a lovely young woman. She had much to offer a man and there was no earthly reason for her to lock herself away like a novice in a nunnery. The more he thought about it, the more annoyed Marcus became. Hugh Manning had been a fine young man, but he couldn't bring himself to believe that Isabel had loved her husband so much that she could not even bear the thought of marriage to another man. It was, he decided, downright insulting. Why, he had as much to offer a wife as Hugh! How the devil did she know that he wouldn't prove to be an even better husband than Hugh had been?

Hastily reminding himself that a comparison between his husbandly virtues and a dead man's wasn't the point, Marcus cleared his throat and said, "Since you are determined not to marry me, we have only two choices." He ticked them off on his fingers. "One, if word of a betrothal between us becomes public, we deny it and paint Whitley as a malicious spreader of gossip, or, two, we confirm it and at some later date, you will have to cry off." Dryly, he added, "Since you refuse to marry me, I'm afraid you may have to face being labeled a jilt after all . . . and please remember that it is your choice. I *did* offer to marry you."

Softly she said, "Yes, I'm aware of that and I appreciate it. And if the worst happens and I am labeled a jilt . . ." Her jaw clenched. "It will be unpleasant for a few weeks or months and I can only hope that my father-in-law and Edmund do not suffer from the gossip and speculation."

"So what do you propose we do?" Marcus asked. "Deny or confirm, if the question arises?"

They discussed the matter for several minutes longer, before Isabel said, "We can do nothing until we learn what Whitley will do with the information." She bit her lower lip. "He might, though I doubt it, say nothing, but that would be totally out of character for him. I think we have to simply wait to see if he does spread the word. . . ." She made a face. "And if he does, then we shall confirm our engagement and a few weeks later, I shall cry off."

Reluctantly, Marcus agreed and shortly he took his leave of her and rode toward Sherbrook Hall. His thoughts heavy, Marcus had much to consider. Whitley had some power over Isabel. Whatever it was, and Marcus didn't doubt that it was serious indeed, she was unwilling to tell him what it was or let him help her. He supposed he should be offended that she was willing to face social disgrace and rampant gossip rather than marry him. He half smiled. How could he have expected any other reaction from Isabel? She'd been confounding him since birth.

But the situation with Whitley was no smiling matter and, thinking of the major, his expression darkened. He would have to deal with Whitley. Isabel might refuse to marry him, but she could not prevent him from doing just as he pleased in the matter of Major Whitley. Whatever power or secret Whitley held over Isabel had to be discovered and destroyed and he was just the man to do it. A lethal, dangerous glitter lit his eyes. Julian or Charles would have instantly recognized that glitter and applauded its appearance with relief and enthusiasm. The tiger that both cousins knew had to live within the cautious and amiable Marcus Sherbrook had finally awakened.

Chapter 3

Isabel misjudged Whitley. Even with Sherbrook's stunning announcement echoing in his ears, he did not immediately head back to the Stag Horn Inn and start ferreting around for information. Instead, he kicked his horse into a gallop and rode toward the coast. His schemes involving Isabel may not have played out as he had hoped, but he would consider his next move at a more convenient time. He could brood and plot later; right now, he was focused on another little plan dear to his heart—one that he was confident would pay a much bigger dividend.

Several miles later, the terrain changed dramatically and, the closer he came to the coast, the neat farms and forested areas of the gentle hills gave way to bare, windswept, wildly undulating ground. Coming to a divide in the road, he dug in his vest pocket and pulled out a scrap of paper. After a glance at the directions he'd scrawled down, he turned his horse off the main road and onto a path that appeared little more than an animal track. After several turns, the restless English Channel came into view and the scent of the sea was strong in the air, a crisp wind blowing across the increasingly barren ground. Spying the small dwelling and the ramshackle outbuildings behind it in a narrow, desolate gully below him, he carefully guided his horse down the thin, twisting path.

Arriving at his destination, he pulled his horse to a stop

and dismounted. His boots had hardly hit the ground when an ugly black and tan mongrel of mainly mastiff heritage came charging and snarling from around the side of the house.

"Badger! Down!" yelled the roughly garbed, stocky man who ran close on the heels of the dog. "Down, you blasted cur, *down*! Down, I say!"

The dog, still grumbling fiercely, dropped to the ground but never took his yellow eyes off Whitley.

Seeing the pistol that had magically appeared in Whitley's hand, the other man said, "Put that away! Badger won't attack you . . . this time."

Slowly putting away the pistol, Whitley said, "Such a welcome. I am quite overcome."

The other man smiled grimly. "We don't like strangers around here. Be glad I knew you was coming and saw you on the trail; I was tying up the other dogs."

Nodding to a sea-wind-blasted tree nearby, the man said, "Tie your horse there. We can talk inside."

Glad to be out of the buffeting winds, Whitley tied his horse and followed the other man inside the house. A small fire burned in the fireplace. The air inside the house was thick and close, the smell of animals, unwashed bodies, and countless meals cooked over the fire stung Whitley's nostrils.

Gingerly he seated himself in the rough wooden chair indicated by his host and accepted, with some reluctance, the pewter mug of amber liquid pushed into his hand.

Taking a sip, Whitley discovered the liquor was some of the finest French brandy he'd ever tasted. "Very nice," he said, as he swirled the liquid around and delicately sniffed. "Not what I expected."

The other man laughed. "You'll find that here in the West Country we've grown to appreciate the bounty from across the Channel." His jovial manner disappearing, he asked bluntly, "And now what need, major, do you have of someone like my poor self?"

Whitley was aware that the whole south and east coast of

England was rife with smugglers, and during his stay in the Devonshire area he had been surprised at how open the common folk were about the smugglers in their midst. But then it hadn't taken him long to realize that in this neighborhood nearly everyone was in one way or another touched by the smugglers. From the farmer who turned a blind eye when oxen and horses vanished from the barn overnight, or the laborers who pocketed a bit of the ready for a night's work, or the landowners who discovered a half anker of brandy or a few yards of lace or silk left discreetly behind, all benefited from the smuggler. Most inhabitants near the coast had friends or relatives who either plied the trade themselves or helped the smugglers. All were united against the Revenuers.

Whitley's initial, discreet interest in the smuggling community had been met with blank-faced silence, but once suspicion had been erased that he might be a preventive man in disguise, it hadn't taken him very long to learn what he wanted. Peter Collard, a local fisherman, *might* be helpful if one wanted to do a spot of private business. Whitley and Collard had met for the first time last night at the Stag Horn and, after sizing him up, Collard had agreed to a second meeting.

"Someone mentioned that you're a very able sea captain and that your ship, the *Sea Tiger*, is bigger and better armed than any cutter in the Revenue Service." Whitley took another swallow of his brandy and said carefully, "I heard a, er, rumor that if someone was wishful of escaping the eyes of the authorities and sailing for a French port that you're the man to see about passage."

Collard looked down into his mug. "People talk. Don't mean 'tis true."

Whitley bit back an oath, impatient with the fencing. "Let's pretend it is true," he said sharply. "And if it is true, what would one be expected to pay for a message to be delivered to a certain individual in Cherbourg . . . and waiting a few days for a reply?"

Collard left off contemplating the contents of his mug and his brandy and stared hard at Whitley. "And would you be the one wishful of having such a note delivered?"

"I would."

Collard studied him a few minutes longer, then named a price. It was higher than Whitley had expected, but since Collard was considered the best, he decided it was worth it. The last thing he wanted was for his message to Charbonneau to end up in the hands of the Revenue Service, or at the bottom of the English Channel.

Not wanting to appear too eager, Whitley haggled on the price, and eventually a deal was struck. They discussed the details over a second mug of brandy, and when Whitley rode away, he was satisfied that at least one of his schemes was unfolding as planned.

Having settled with Collard, Whitley turned his thoughts to this morning's disastrous meeting with Isabel. Nothing had gone as he had assumed it would, and all during the long ride back to the inn, anger and resentment festered inside of him.

By the time he returned to the Stag Horn he was in a thoroughly foul mood and his thoughts about Isabel Manning and Mr. Sherbrook were *not* kind. Spying the innkeeper, Keating, behind the lovingly polished oak counter in the main room, his gaze narrowed and he considered how he might discover more about the irritating Mr. Sherbrook . . . and more important, the engagement between Mrs. Hugh Manning and Sherbrook.

The news that Isabel was engaged had been a facer, Whitley admitted sourly, even as he smiled and watched Keating pour him a foaming mug of dark ale. Taking his ale with him, Whitley retreated to a small table in the corner to nurse his drink as well as his wounds. Isabel was proving more difficult to handle than he had first thought and, since his hold on her was tenuous at best, he had to pick his way with care. He had been positive that she would panic and agree to anything he wanted, to keep him from even hinting about his suspicions. It had been a decided setback when she had proved to be so obstinate. She'd eagerly paid him when he first confronted her and he had assumed that she would continue to pay to keep his mouth shut about what may or may not have happened in India. With his pockets newly plump, he would have happily ridden away . . . for a while.

Whitley viewed blackmail as an investment, one that if he were careful and didn't get greedy, would keep paying for years and years and years. His problem, in Isabel's case, was that he had no tangible proof and could only bluff—which he was rather adept at doing. His lips thinned. Unfortunately, it appeared that Mrs. Manning was equally skillful; damn her!

Until this morning he had been confident that he could frighten Isabel into parting with a great deal more money for the promise of his silence, but the prospect of a fiancé changed the entire situation. Biting back a curse, he swallowed a deep draught of ale. That bloody Sherbrook!

Arriving in the area three days ago, Whitley had established himself at the inn and made friends with Keating and his wife and a few of the regulars. Having elicited Collard's name, he then concentrated on pumping everyone for more information, ostensibly about the neighborhood, giving out that, though a stranger, he thought to settle nearby. His goal, however, had been to learn what Mrs. Hugh Manning had been doing in the ten years since she left India. Having no access to Isabel's circle of friends or relatives, he'd been forced to use Keating and the like for information. It was surprising, he thought, what the common folk knew about the doings of the likes of Mrs. Hugh Manning. He'd been gratified to learn that she had been living quietly with her son at Manning Court in the home of her father-in-law, Lord Manning, and was well thought of and liked in the neighborhood. There had been no mention of any engagement or courting gentlemen.

It was pure mischance that had brought Whitley to Devonshire and Isabel's doorstep. Newly retired, and with little but his government pension to sustain him, Whitley had immediately set into motion several long-held plans to arrange a very, *very* comfortable retirement for himself. While in London, he'd dropped in to visit several old friends now stationed at the Horse Guards. He smiled. Renewing former associations had proved useful. Having accomplished what he wanted to in London, it was then time to turn his attention to those individuals he'd known in the past and that he thought might be vulnerable to blackmail. Since he had need of someone like Collard and wanted to put some distance between himself and London and any repercussions that might arise, he had chosen Devonshire as a likely locale for the furtherance of his schemes. That Isabel happened to live in the district was pure chance, but it made her the first of several old acquaintances in England that he planned to visit.

Having discovered her still-unmarried state, he had an idea that marriage to a woman of fortune might not be so very disagreeable. Her son was the heir to a barony and the current holder of the title was elderly, Manning Court was a handsome house; he was confident that he could live quite comfortably there. Marriage to Isabel would have banished the disagreeable necessity of buying and setting up his own place, and it was unlikely, even with his various schemes to increase his ready cash, that he could afford a country estate like Manning Court. And even if he could afford to purchase such a grand place, the upkeep would have proven ruinous. Besides, why spend his own money when he could spend someone else's?

Sherbrook's advent on the scene certainly put paid to any notion of marrying Isabel and helping himself to her fortune. Sipping his ale, he brooded on the unfairness of fate. Isabel was not to his taste, a little skinny, hot-at-hand, and far too outspoken, but in order to get his hands on her fortune, he could have swallowed his distaste. Marriage to Isabel had never been a sure thing, and the way she was refusing to pay him to keep his mouth shut and go away had made the prospect of his being able to bring her to the altar even more unlikely. Still, it rankled to discover that someone was there before him.

Reviewing the meeting with Sherbrook this morning, he frowned. With his nose for scandal and gossip, he'd wager a purse full of yellow boys that there was something havy cavy about that engagement. There'd been nothing of May or orange blossoms about the pair of them and the more he thought of it, the more convinced he became that if Isabel and Sherbrook were engaged there was something unusual about it. Something he could use to his advantage?

After mulling the situation over for several moments Whitley finally gave up. He couldn't see any way, at this time, that he could turn the engagement to his benefit, but he did intend to snoop about and see what he could find out.

Returning to the counter with his empty mug, he allowed Keating to pour him another. Leaning against the bar, he sipped his second mug of ale slowly and made light conversation with Keating, angling for an opening to drop in mention of Sherbrook.

An interruption occurred a few minutes later with the arrival of two youths. Jostling with each other, as boys will do, they approached the bar. Cheeky grins on each grimy face, they demanded lemonade.

Smiling, Keating served the two boys. Whitley recognized the one boy with the dark, lank hair and round, friendly features as a member of Keating's numerous brood. The other boy was blond-haired, taller, and slimmer, and though his clothes were in as deplorable a state as the other boy's, the material and workmanship bespoke wealth. Whitley's gaze sharpened as he studied the newcomer. The resemblance to Hugh Manning was striking. So this was Hugh's son. How very, very providential.

Having served his newest patrons, wiping a glass with a small white towel as he stood next to the bar, Keating asked,

"And what have you two young hellions been up to today? If I had to hazard a guess, I'd say it appears you've been wrestling in the mud." He bent a teasing look on the taller boy. "I'll wager that when Lord Manning and your mother agreed to let you miss term at Eton after you broke your leg at Christmas, they didn't expect you to spend the time cavorting with this scamp. What *have* you been doing to end up in such a state?"

Both boys burst out laughing and the brown-haired one said, "Farmer Foster's sow farrowed last night, Pa, and half the piglets ended up in the pen next door. He promised us a penny each if we'd catch them and throw them back where they belong. Coo! It was a dirty job. Squealing piglets everywhere and slippery as the devil in the mud and that old sow . . . We were half afraid she break through the walls of her pen and eat us up."

Keating's nose twitched. "It smells as if you have brought home half of Foster's farm with you." Glancing at the taller boy, he said, "And you, Master Edmund, while I expect Sam to come home looking like a ruffian, I'll wager your mother will not be pleased when she catches sight of you."

Edmund grinned, his blue eyes sparkling. "Mother says that boys are meant to be dirty and that when I grow up I will have a long time in which to be a proper gentleman. All she asks is that I don't come to the table covered in muck or keep lizards in my room."

Whitley cleared his throat and asked, "Did I hear the name Manning? Would that be any relation to Mrs. Hugh Manning?"

Edmund looked at him and said politely, "Yes, sir. Mrs. Manning is my mother."

Whitley smiled charmingly. "What a coincidence! I visited with your mother only this morning. We are old friends; we knew each other in India."

Edmund's very blue eyes lit up. "You knew Mother in India?" Eagerly, he added, "Did you know my father?"

"Why, yes, I did," Whitley replied easily. "Your father and

I were great friends. I knew him even before he married your mother."

"By Jove!" Edmund exclaimed, his face flushed with excitement. "That's wonderful! Has Mother invited you to stay at Manning Court? I know that Grandfather will be most pleased to meet a friend of my father's from India." Shyly, he added, "I hope you do not think me too forward, but my father died so long ago and I know very little of him. Mother and Grandfather have told me all they can about him, but Mother doesn't like to talk about India, I think it is too painful for her and reminds her of his death. I would be most gratified to learn more about my father from someone who knew him then."

Whitley was conscious that Keating was watching him with a considering eye. Previously Whitley had given no hint that he had known Isabel—had stated, in fact, that he was a stranger to the area—and he was now worried that his claiming of a prior relationship with Mrs. Manning might arouse suspicion. Behind his jovial manner, Keating was a knowing one and Whitley doubted that much went on in the neighborhood that the innkeeper, or his wife, wasn't privy to.

"Quite a coincidence," Keating said slowly, his mild blue eyes fixed on Whitley's face, "you being friends with Mrs. Manning."

Whitley looked innocent. "You could have knocked me over with a feather when I met her by accident this morning. I pulled my horse aside to allow a lady to pass on the pathway I was riding and realized I knew her. We recognized each other in an instant. It is hard to say which of us was the most astonished."

"I'll wager Mother was elated to see you," said Edmund, "and that she can't wait to tell my grandfather the good news. Did she invite you to come to dine tonight?"

Taking spiteful pleasure in the problems he could see arising for Isabel once her son returned home, Whitley smiled. "No, she didn't," he replied, "but I think that was because she was distracted by the gentleman who joined us within a few minutes of our meeting. A Mr. Sherbrook? Tall, imposing fellow? A neighbor, I believe?"

Edmund grinned. "Mr. Sherbrook is a great friend of mine, but he and Mother usually avoid each other. I imagine Mother was too busy thinking of a way to escape from him and forgot to invite you."

"Ah, now, Master Edmund, I think you've bothered Major Whitley enough," Keating interposed.

Whitley hid his annoyance, knowing very well what Keating was about. The innkeeper obviously thought that Edmund had said enough and was trying to divert him and, while it irritated him, Whitley was quite satisfied with the results of this little conversation. It was going to be even more satisfying when he dropped his last bit of news.

Astonishment crossing his face, Whitley said, "I'm sure that I don't quite understand. There was no sign of your mother wishing to avoid Mr. Sherbrook's company this morning. Quite the contrary: Mr. Sherbrook announced that they were betrothed."

A stunned silence descended. Enjoying himself immensely, Whitley stared from one shocked face to the other.

"You must have misunderstood him," said Keating, frowning. "There's been no hint of an engagement between them."

"Mother and Mr. Sherbrook? Oh, that can't be right," blurted out Edmund, his eyes nearly starting from his face.

"Mr. Sherbrook was bamming you," Sam Keating said bluntly. "Everyone knows that they can't abide each other."

Whitley shrugged. "I'm sorry, gentlemen, but Mr. Sherbrook plainly stated that he and Mrs. Manning were engaged."

"And Mother didn't toss the words back in his teeth?" demanded Edmund.

"No. In fact, as I recall, she most becomingly allowed him to kiss her hand and looked at him as if he had hung the moon." Whitley cleared his throat. "It was quite touching really."

The other three looked at each other, then back at Whitley.

"Gammon!" said Keating forcefully. "I've never heard such nonsense!"

"What nonsense?" asked his wife as she bustled into the room, carrying a tray of clean glasses and mugs.

Keating, Edmund, and Sam all began to speak at once and, after a moment of listening to their babble, Mrs. Keating put down the tray on the counter and, raising a hand, said, "One at a time, if you please."

Sending Whitley a dour look, Keating said, "Let him tell you. He's the one who said it."

Fixing a friendly gaze on the major, Mrs. Keating said, "Well, major? What is it that has these three loobys in a fret?"

"Why, only the news that Mrs. Manning and Mr. Sherbrook are engaged to be married," he murmured. "Mr. Sherbrook told me so himself just this morning. Mrs. Manning was right by his side when he told me of their betrothal."

Mrs. Keating looked startled. Her round, plump face perplexed, she muttered, "Never say so! There's been never a hint of such a thing." Thoughtfully, she added, "Although Mr. Sherbrook would play his cards close to his vest and Mrs. Manning ain't one to wash her linen in public. . . ." A smile curved her lips. "I always did think that the pair of them went to an awful lot of trouble to avoid each other. Mayhap, they only wanted to do their courting in private."

She glanced at Edmund, who was standing and staring at her open-mouthed. "Well, my young man, what do you think about having Sherbrook for a stepfather?"

Edmund's mouth shut with a snap. He swallowed. Took a deep breath. An expression of awed delight on his young face, he breathed, "I would like it above anything! And Grandfather will be over the moon. He has said to me time and again that Sherbrook would make Mother an excellent husband—if she wasn't too stubborn to see it."

Keating laughed. "Yes, I can hear the old baron saying just such a thing."

Immensely pleased with the results of his meddling, Whitley said, "I suspect that your mother will tell you all about it when you arrive home."

"Indeed, she will!" Edmund said with a laugh. Putting his empty glass on the counter, Edmund bid the others good-bye and flew from the room.

Isabel was enjoying a cup of tea with her father-in-law in the small green salon that the family used when not entertaining. It was a pleasant room: gold-patterned pale green silk covered the walls; cream-colored drapes adorned the long windows; and a thick, wool rug in shades of green, cream, and rose hid most of the gleaming walnut parquet floor. Comfortable sofas and chairs done in the same three shades as the rug were scattered about; elegant satinwood tables flanked several pieces of the furniture.

Despite the fine spring weather, as the day waned there was a trifle chill in the air and a small blaze burned in the dark green marble fireplace. Taking advantage of the warmth of the fire, Isabel and Lord Manning were seated nearby.

Isabel had just lifted her cup of tea to her mouth, when the double doors to the room swung open and Edmund catapulted into the salon. As always, her heart swelled with joy when she saw her son. He was, she thought with justified maternal pride, a fine boy.

There was little of Isabel to be seen in Edmund's young face. He was clearly his father's son, having inherited Hugh's wheat-fair hair, bright blue eyes, winning smile, and rugged build. The old baron often said that Edmund could have been Hugh's twin at the same age.

Those same bright blue eyes full of feverish excitement, Edmund rushed up to stand in front of his mother. "Is it true?" he demanded eagerly. "Are you going to marry Mr. Sherbrook? Your friend, Major Whitley, said that Mr. Sherbrook told him so this morning and that you did not deny it. Oh, Mother, it is wonderful!" Turning to glance at his grandfather, Edmund said, "It is just what you wanted. Mother is to marry Mr. Sherbrook!"

Recovering quickly from his astonishment, his lined features reflecting the same excited delight as Edmund's, Lord Manning leaned forward in his chair and exclaimed, "Oh, my dear! This is the best news an old man could hear. You, married to Sherbrook! I could not have asked for anything more wonderful." Springing to his feet with a youthful vigor that belied his age, he crossed the room and pulled on the bell rope. "We must have champagne to celebrate this marvelous news!"

As if turned to stone, her welcoming smile frozen on her lips, Isabel still held her cup of tea halfway up to her mouth. Blindsided, she barely managed to keep the panic that threatened to choke her from showing. Plain, brutal desperation broke her free from the icy paralysis Edmund's announcement had caused and with shaking fingers she carefully set down her cup, grateful she didn't spill a drop. *Whitley!* May his black soul rot in hell! Sick fury burned through her and she cursed Major Whitley with a fluency and an inventiveness that would have scorched polite society's raised eyebrows.

She'd known the risk of Marcus's reckless announcement becoming public had been great; she just hadn't been prepared for it to happen so soon, or to come home to roost in her lap so swiftly. Staring at the ecstatic faces of her son and father-in-law, like a rat escaping a sinking ship she scrambled for a way out of her predicament.

Seeing their open pleasure, their sheer joy, she realized immediately that denying the engagement was out of the question. She could no more have destroyed those delighted expressions than she could have danced on a knife blade. For the time being, the engagement would stand.

In that instant, she felt a prison door snap shut. Looking from one happy face to the other, she doubted even an emphatic denial would bring them to their senses. *They* wanted this marriage and she had not, until this moment, understood how very much. Fighting back panic, she searched for another way out of this predicament, but no matter how frantically she searched, thanks to Whitley, there was no escape. She would have to marry Sherbrook. Not to escape being labeled a jilt, she thought sickly; that name she would have gladly borne. No, she would have to marry Sherbrook because of all the innocent people she loved and that were now part of this damnable situation, and who would be devastated if she cried off.

Looking into her son's excited face, with a hollow feeling in her chest, she knew that she would never allow him to believe in a fantasy world in which she was going to marry Marcus and then shatter it in a few weeks by ending the engagement. Her gaze slid to her father-in-law, finding an identical expression of joy on his face. Her stalwart, kind, generous father-in-law. How could she lead him in such a cruel dance? To let him think his dearest wish was to come true and then rip it away from him? And what of Mrs. Appleton? Before the day ended, she didn't doubt that Lord Manning would have sent the widow news of the engagement, and that in a few days, weeks at the most, another engagement would be announced. How could she let them believe she would marry Marcus, allow them to build hopes and dreams, make plans of their own, and then with a few careless words lay waste to everything? She could not.

Wanting to bury her head in her hands and howl, Isabel flashed a blinding smile to the men of her family. "La! You have found us out," she said with hardly a tremor in her voice. "Marcus and I had thought to keep it to ourselves for a few weeks, but he was so gratified by my acceptance that he blurted out the news to the first person he met."

The butler's entrance into the room saved her from further speech.

"Champagne!" ordered Lord Manning joyfully. "The best

in the cellar. And tell Cook to prepare a feast for dinner tonight: Mrs. Manning is to marry Mr. Sherbrook."

His face wreathed in smiles, the butler, Deering, bowed low and murmured, "Allow me to congratulate you, Madame, and to say that the staff will be very happy at the news."

"Enough of that," interrupted Lord Manning. "I want that champagne. Oh, and bring me some writing materials. I must invite Sherbrook to dinner tonight." His smile widened. "And Mrs. Appleton."

"I'll do that," Isabel said hastily. Rising to her feet, she said, "Let me but dash off a note to M-M-Marcus and Mrs. Appleton and I shall return and enjoy a glass of champagne with you."

Shortly, Marcus was reading his betrothed's scribbled note. There was nothing loverlike about it.

> *Marcus,* she wrote, *Edmund brought home the news of our engagement this afternoon. His path crossed Whitley's and Whitley wasted no time in telling him. My father-in-law is beside himself with joy. He would like you to come to dine this evening.*
>
> *I would appreciate a word with you first. I will be waiting for you in the east garden.*
> *Isabel*

Chapter 4

Assuming Isabel didn't want anyone to know of their meeting, Marcus did not, as was his wont, ride up to the massive front entrance of Manning Court that evening. Nearly as familiar with the layout of the grounds of Lord Manning's estate as he was with his own, he approached the house from the rear and discreetly tied his horse to a large lime tree that grew near the edge of the extensive gardens that surrounded the house.

Entering through a delicate iron-worked gate set in the stone walls that surrounded the gardens, Marcus leisurely walked down one of the crushed rock pathways that meandered through the meticulously maintained shrubs and perennials. The scent of roses and lilacs hung heavy in the air and, following a bend in the path, he came upon a charming bower covered with pink roses, flanked by several purple lilac bushes. A stone bench was in the middle of the bower and, at his approach, the small figure seated there leaped upright.

"Oh, thank goodness, you are here!" cried Isabel, looking charming in a high waisted confection of white India muslin embroidered with gold thread. Her vivid red hair was caught up in a pair of braids arranged in bandeaux across the top of her head and several curls had been coaxed to frame her face. A pair of beige cameo earrings graced her ears and a small matching cameo locket hanging from a gold chain around her neck was her only jewelry.

Marcus's breath caught at the sight of her, and his heart, usually a most reliable organ, leaped like a gigged frog in his chest. He'd been hoping that his unexpected awareness of Isabel as a desirable female earlier in the day had been a not-ever-to-be-repeated aberration. He'd convinced himself that when next he faced her he would be able to view her only as his former troublesome ward and Hugh Manning's widow and nothing more. Certainly he did *not* want to see her as a woman he'd enjoy in his bed. Unfortunately, before him stood a woman who made his pulse pound and caused the most indecent thoughts to dance in his head.

A certain part of his anatomy swelled in readiness and, cursing it and himself, he desperately sought to regain his composure. But composure seemed to have entirely deserted him and he couldn't tear his eyes away from her dainty form and face. Rocked back on his heels by his reaction to her, he wondered bewilderedly why he had never before noticed the sweet curve of her bottom lip or the gentle swell of her breasts revealed by the low neckline of her gown. His fingers twitched and it was all he could do to stop them from cupping her head and bringing that impossibly tempting mouth next to his. It would be so easy. . . .

His hand actually lifted, his body already anticipating the taste and texture of her mouth when Isabel brought him back to his senses by saying sharply, "What is wrong with you? Why are you staring at me so?"

Marcus's eyes dropped to his half-lifted hand and he stared at it in horror. Good God! A moment more and she would have been in his arms and he would have been kissing her. Kissing her in a manner that would have shocked her right down to her pretty little gold slippers. Struggling with the sensation that his world had tilted on its axis, he shook his head. Taking a deep, steadying breath, he said testily, "Nothing is wrong with me." His gaze fell on the riot of roses behind her and, seeking a distraction, he muttered, "I wasn't staring at you, I was, uh, admiring the roses."

Her eyes narrowed. Hands on her hips, she demanded, "Are you foxed?"

Marcus shook his head, not blaming her in the least for thinking him drunk. He *felt* drunk, but not from any spirits concocted by man. Regaining some control over his brain, he said quickly, "I hope you haven't been waiting long."

She studied him a moment longer then shrugged. "No, I haven't been here long."

He forced a smile and asked, "What did you want to discuss? We knew there was the possibility that Whitley would mention the engagement to someone and we discussed our options thoroughly this morning." He frowned. "It was unfortunate that it had to be Edmund who heard the news first, but now that the news is public—perhaps sooner than we liked—we won't have to skulk around waiting for the ax to fall. We shall accept the congratulations of our friends with a pleasant smile . . . and in a few weeks or a month or so, we can stage a very loud, very public argument and you can cry off." More certain of his ground, he grinned at her. "I shall act a perfect beast; everyone will feel sorry for you and congratulate you on your near escape." When Isabel remained silent, he added, "You can even throw your betrothal ring in my face—*that* should resolve our problem."

"I don't have a ring," she said dryly.

"That is easily rectified," he replied with a smile.

Marcus fumbled in his vest pocket and brought out a dazzling sapphire and diamond ring. Almost shyly for such a usually confident man, he murmured, "I know it's not a new ring, but it is a family heirloom: my grandfather gave it to my grandmother upon the occasion of the birth of my father. She wore it until the day she died. Mother never wore it, she never cared for it overmuch." When Isabel remained silent and just stared at the ring, he added hastily, "You don't have to wear it if you don't want to and if you positively loathe it,

I can buy something different that you *will* like." Her frozen stance and deafening silence was unnerving and awkwardly, he explained, "After I, uh, received your message this afternoon, I realized that, er, we would probably need a ring. Before riding over here this evening, I looked at the family jewels hoping to find something suitable. This ring caught my attention. It, uh, made me think of you."

Wondering why she suddenly felt like bursting into tears, Isabel stared mutely at the glowing sapphire ring. The ring was just the sort of jewelry that appealed to her, and the knowledge that Marcus's grandmother had treasured the ring that Marcus was offering to her made the tears even harder to blink back. A lump lodged in her throat.

Avoiding precisely this kind of situation had been one of the reasons she had been against a sham engagement in the first place. How could she accept his grandmother's ring knowing it was only pretend? How could she accept all the congratulations of friends and family knowing that it was a lie?

Her heart aching, Isabel bit her lip and looked away. The falsehoods were only beginning, she thought painfully. The announcement had been only the first of many to come and the expressions of wild delight on the faces on her son and father-in-law flashed through her mind and her misery deepened.

For the past several hours, Edmund had gamboled at her heels like a puppy, prattling on and on about how happy he was that she was going to marry Mr. Sherbrook. "I *like* Mr. Sherbrook," Edmund had said numerous times, a sunny smile creasing his face. "I'll miss living at Manning Court to be sure, but Sherbrook Hall is very nice and I can come and stay with Grandfather whenever I want. It isn't like we'll be living miles and miles away." He'd hugged her tightly and exclaimed, "Oh, Mother! This is grand! I know that Mr. Sherbrook will not be my real father, but if I had to have a stepfather, I'd lief it be him more than anyone else in the whole world."

Every word her son spoke had been a dagger in her heart. Unable to listen to his delighted prattle any longer, she had fled to her rooms. Feeling more in command of herself, she had bathed and dressed for dinner, lingering at her dressing table as long as she dared, hoping to avoid further discussion about the engagement. But hurrying through the house this evening on her way to the east garden, she had been waylaid by her father-in-law. Clasping her hand in his, he looked her up and down, a twinkle in his eye. "You look very grand tonight," Lord Manning complimented her. "I think being engaged is good for you; I've never seen you in such looks." Pinching her cheek affectionately, he scolded, "Naughty puss, keeping such an important event a secret from me." His face softened and he said, "I cannot tell you how happy this makes me—and not just because of Mrs. Appleton. You are too young and too lovely to spend the rest of your days a widow. Sherbrook is a fine man and I cannot think of anyone I'd rather see you marry." For a moment a shadow crossed his features, then he shook himself and added huskily, "Hugh would have wanted for you to marry again. It would have made him unhappy to know that you have buried yourself away from the world and I'm certain that he would have approved of Sherbrook. Edmund needs a younger man's hand to guide him and it is past time for you to have a husband. Sherbrook will do very well for you."

Feeling the worst kind of fraud, Isabel blinked back tears and scurried to the garden. Her thoughts, as she had waited for Marcus's arrival, had been unpleasant and painful, but they had only confirmed her earlier decision. She could not deceive Edmund and Lord Manning in such a craven manner. Imagining the devastated expressions on their faces if the betrothal were to end in anything but marriage, she shuddered. How could she face them? Having raised their hopes and expectations, how could she disappoint them in such a manner? No. She could not—even if it meant a marriage she did not want. Looking at the ring he held in his fingers, she reminded herself acidly that this situation was all his fault and that it wasn't *her* fault if there were unforeseen consequences . . . consequences he might not like. The ring put the seal on her earlier decision and she took a deep breath, her way clear. Marcus didn't know it yet, but there would be no broken engagement. She would marry him. And God help them all.

Staring at the proffered ring, she knew the last time it had been given to a woman it had been done with love and delight, and that only made the ache in her heart deepen. This should have been a joyous occasion, but the sight of that ring held in Marcus's fingers only made her want to cry. Confronted with her decision that there would be no pretend engagement, she knew that Marcus would honor his word and marry her. So, why, she wondered bleakly, did that notion fill her with despair?

Ignoring the lump in her throat, she gingerly stuck out her hand and allowed him to slip the ring on her finger. As the ring slid onto her finger, something clenched inside of her. Why did this feel so right, when it was all so very wrong? To her surprise, the ring fit as if made for her, and she glanced up at Marcus.

As if guessing her thoughts, he said, "Grandmother was delicately made. My grandfather used to tease that he had to shake the sheets to find her." Softly, he added, "He adored her all of his life and she him. They had a long, happy marriage."

Her eyes on the ring, Isabel said thickly, "Thank you. I shall treasure it for the time that it is mine."

Too full of emotion to say more, Isabel motioned for him to follow her into the bower. When they were both seated on the stone bench, her hands in her lap, her eyes on the gleaming sapphire and diamond ring that lay warm and heavy on her finger, she sought to gather her thoughts.

Marcus watched her for several seconds, aware that she was troubled. "What is it?" he finally asked when he could bear no longer to see her look so unhappy. "Did you mistake Lord Manning's reaction? Is he upset with the news?" He smiled faintly. "Or is it Edmund? Perhaps he wasn't as fond of me as you thought?"

Isabel shook her head. "No," she said quietly. "They are both over the moon about it."

With one long finger beneath her chin, Marcus gently turned her face in his direction. "Then what, my dear? What makes you look as if you are facing the gallows?"

Her eyes met his. "I don't think," she said miserably, "that you've thought of all the ramifications of telling Whitley that we were engaged."

He frowned. "What do you mean? So far nothing has happened that we didn't anticipate."

Looking down again at the ring on her finger, she asked, "After you received my note this afternoon, did you write your mother with the news of our engagement? Or your cousins? Aunts?"

Still frowning, Marcus shook his head. "No. I thought I would wait until tomorrow to write Mother."

"But you are going to write her?" she pressed, still not looking at him.

"Of course! She has to know." He was silent a moment, then said slowly, "And if I don't write them, my cousins and aunts will learn of it from my mother." He sighed, the inkling of the problems facing them beginning to trickle into his brain. "I suppose I'd assumed we could keep the news of the betrothal fairly local, I didn't realize until just now precisely how far the ripples would spread."

"Do you think your mother will be happy to hear of our engagement?" Isabel asked neutrally.

Marcus laughed. "Oh, I expect that Mother will be like Lord Manning—delighted with the news. She's mentioned, upon rare occasion, that she'd like to see me marry. She's always had a fondness for you and I expect that she will be thrilled to learn that we are engaged." He smiled faintly. "And don't forget; Edmund is a favorite of hers."

Isabel looked at him then. "And will she be equally happy when we break our engagement in a few weeks?"

He stiffened and he stared at her, the image of his mother's face crumpling and tears shimmering in her eyes flashing before him. Just as his mother would be overjoyed at the news of his engagement to Isabel, she would be utterly desolated at its ending. And his other relatives that would have been drawn into the net, what of them? What of his cousins, Julian and Charles, how would they feel? They would, he was positive, be pleased that he was on the brink of marriage, but how would they feel when they learned that his engagement was over? What about Nell, Julian's wife? Daphne, Charles's bride? And his aunts, the other members of the far-flung Weston family and all his friends? They would be, he knew, full of congratulations at the news that he was finally marrying, but how would they react when they learned the betrothal had been ended?

Marcus didn't doubt that some would take it in stride and dismiss it with a shrug, but others . . . Others, he thought horrified, like his mother, would be crushed or, like Nell, deeply saddened when they learned the news. Nell, especially, would mourn the ending of the engagement and try to console him, and he knew that Charles and Julian would give him manly, silent support but would be very disappointed that the betrothal had ended and they would suffer for him. And his mother . . . his mother would suffer most. He swallowed with difficulty. His face felt hot, his chest tight. Good God! How could he do that to them? Raise their expectations, knowing it was all a lie and that there was never any question of marriage taking place? In that moment, the trap, the trap of his own making snapped shut.

He stared at Isabel, the realization that there would be no escape, no ending of their engagement apparent in the expression that crossed his face. In a voice devoid of emotion, he said, "It would make my mother very, *very* unhappy if the engagement were to end. She would be devastated. . . ." His gaze dropped to the ring on her finger. "Many people," he admitted reluctantly, "especially those dearest to us, will be hurt and disappointed if we do not marry." A shudder went through him. In a low voice he added, "Call me a coward if you like, but given the choice, I believe I would rather face a fire-breathing dragon empty-handed than tell my mother that we do not suit and have changed our minds."

Isabel smiled bitterly. "Exactly."

Marcus's gray eyes met hers. "I suppose this is what you wanted to talk about?"

Isabel nodded. "I thought," she said quietly, "that we might be able to brush through this entire . . . situation, without incident." Her voice thickened. "You were not there and did not see how ecstatic both my father-in-law and son were with the news of our engagement. It would be cruel to play out this farce knowing . . ." She fought for composure. Her eyes dark with emotion, she said, "I cannot mislead them in such a heartless fashion."

Marcus agreed. It would indeed be cruel to lead everyone to believe there would be a marriage between them knowing full well that they planned nothing of the sort. The engagement would have to stand . . . and eventually they would marry. The sensation of a noose tightening around his neck assailed him for just a second, but then he shrugged it off. Marriage to Isabel would not be so very bad. And if he *had* to marry . . . A crooked smile curved his long mouth. "It would seem, my dear," he said wryly, "that we are well and truly engaged and that instead of planning the ending of our engagement, we will be planning our wedding."

She hadn't been aware of how important his reaction to the knowledge that they could not just blithely call off the engagement had been to her, but at his words, a great sense of relief rushed through her. She'd known that he was an hon-

orable man and she'd been certain that he would not cut up
rough. He'd already indicated he would marry her if events
warranted it, she'd reminded herself, but it was one thing to
speak hypothetically and another to actually carry through
and there had been a tiny nagging doubt at the back of her
mind. It cheered her to know that she had not been mistaken
in his character and that he understood precisely the reasons
why they could not end their engagement.

But this was only the first hurdle they faced, she thought
tiredly, her relief vanishing as if it had never been. Thinking
of her marriage to Hugh and the promise she had made as he
lay dying, panic flooded her. The other hurdle might not be
so easily cleared. . . .

Unwilling to dwell on the future and what it held, she
forced herself to meet Marcus's smile, and say lightly, "And I
hope that you have learned the wisdom of thinking before
you speak."

A genuine laugh escaped from him. "Of that I think you
can be safely assured." Lifting her hand, he bent his head and
pressed a soft, warm kiss to the back of it. Holding her fingers in his, his eyes searched hers. "This isn't what either of
us planned, but I think we shall do well together, you and I."

She wanted to believe him, wanted to believe that they
would have a good marriage together, but inwardly she
quaked. No, marriage wasn't what either of them had
planned and their marriage, she thought miserably, would be
a great deal less than he could conceive.

Dinner was a pleasant, if not entirely comfortable, affair.
In addition to Mrs. Appleton, resplendent in a shot silk gown
in pleasing shades of soft blues, Isabel's uncle and aunt, Sir
James and Lady Agatha, had also been invited. Edmund,
looking very adult in a dark blue jacket and a neatly tied cravat, had been allowed on this special occasion to join the
adults for dinner. Isabel's only admonishment had been that
he would have to content himself with lemonade instead of

the champagne everyone else would be drinking. He made a face, but then he grinned at her. "I'll wager Mr. Sherbrook would let me drink champagne."

She'd smiled back at him, her heart aching just a little at how much he looked like his father in that moment. "Perhaps," she said lightly, caressing his cheek. "But he isn't your stepfather yet. Until he is, I make the rules."

With his usual sunny nature, Edmund accepted her decree and was on his best behavior throughout the evening.

Naturally, everyone was astonished by the news of the engagement, and during much of the meal, in between the various toasts that were drunk to Marcus and Isabel's health and their future together, there were exclamations of surprise from the other diners.

"Oh, but aren't you just the sly one," said Lady Agatha, her dark eyes full of speculation, and perhaps just a touch of malice, as they rested on Isabel's face. "Keeping secrets and hiding behind the fiction that you couldn't abide each other. It was very clever of you; no one had any idea that an engagement was in the offing."

Even in her youth, Agatha Paley had been a handsome woman rather than a pretty one. Tall and thin, with black hair, her features were almost mannish, her nose long, her chin pronounced and her eyes deep set under heavy dark brows and as she approached her fiftieth year not even age had softened her looks. In Isabel's opinion, Agatha had always been a cold, unfeeling woman and her marriage to Sir James had changed nothing. There was a long history of discord between the two women: before marriage to Sir James, Agatha had been Isabel's governess, and the longing to escape from Agatha's rigid rules had been partially responsible for Isabel's rash marriage to Hugh Manning.

Returning to England as Hugh's widow and taking her place with her son in Lord Manning's household had saved Isabel from finding herself once more under Lady Agatha's thumb. It had also prevented the inevitable open conflict between the two women. In the intervening time, Isabel had worked hard at making some sort of peace with the other woman and making certain Edmund knew his great-uncle and the house his mother had grown up in. Agatha and Isabel would never be fond of each other, but they had managed to form a polite relationship; but every now and then, Agatha's claws still showed. Isabel could not help showing some of her own.

Forcing a smile, Isabel glanced at her aunt and murmured, "Yes, we were very careful; one does so hate to be the object of gossip and innuendo. I'm certain you of all people understand."

Isabel's reason for keeping the courtship quiet was remarkably similar to the one Agatha had given out when her sudden marriage to Sir James fifteen years ago had caused a nine days' wonder in the neighborhood. Beyond a tightening of her lips, Agatha gave no other sign that the barb had found its mark.

Aware of the strained relationship between the two women, Clara Appleton rushed in, saying brightly, "Oh, I just think it is so romantic!" She sent a warm glance toward Marcus. "Your mother, I know, will be delirious with delight once she learns of the engagement. If she's said it once, she's said a hundred times how happy she will be when you marry and set up your own nursery."

Marcus smiled at her. "And of course, we all know that I live to please my mother."

"Oh, la, don't you take that tone with me," Clara replied, shaking a teasing finger at him. "Your mother has told me often enough what a wonderful son you are."

"It's a fine match, no doubt about it," remarked Sir James, his pleasure obvious. Well into his seventies, with his merry blue eyes and chubby pink cheeks and only a few tufts of white hair circling his bald pate he had always reminded Isabel of an adorable little cherub. They made an odd couple: Sir James rotund, Agatha thin, and because of his short stature, his nearly bald head barely bobbed above his wife's shoulders. In fact to Isabel's mind, Agatha towered over him like a black, thin-legged stork next to a round little partridge.

Raising his glass high, Sir James said, "Another toast! May the pair of you have a long and happy life together." He smiled warmly at Isabel. "Ah, my dear, your father would have been delighted at this happy turn of events. So everyone drink up: to Isabel and Marcus—long life and happiness."

"I'll drink to that," said Lord Manning, a broad grin on his face. In fact, Isabel didn't think he, or Edmund for that matter, had stopped smiling since they'd learned of the engagement. She'd had no intention of ever marrying again, but now that fate had conspired against her, she was glad that her coming nuptials had given the people she loved joy.

The toast having been duly drunk, Lord Manning set down his glass and asked, "When is the wedding to be? I presume sometime this summer?"

"Yes," agreed Marcus.

"No," blurted out Isabel.

Suddenly the cynosure of every eye in the room, Isabel flushed and muttered, "We, uh, haven't decided yet." Throwing Marcus a warning look, she said, "We intend to discuss it tomorrow, don't we?"

Marcus grinned. "Indeed we do."

The rest of the evening passed smoothly, but Marcus and Isabel had no time alone until he prepared to ride home. The other guests had departed several minutes ago; Edmund had retired hours ago and, with a wave of his hand, Lord Manning had bid them good night and discreetly disappeared upstairs.

Since Marcus's horse was still tied to the lime tree at the edge of the garden and he had dismissed Isabel's offer of a servant to fetch the animal, she accompanied him into the garden. As they walked through the quiet night, the black sky above them dotted with winking diamonds, Marcus said, "It went rather well, didn't it? The only awkward moment was when your father-in-law wanted to know when we are to be married." He stopped and looked down at her. "So when are we to marry?"

"Perhaps sometime next summer?" she offered.

Marcus stared at her incredulously. "Next summer?" he said in tones of disbelief. "Absolutely not!"

Having awakened this morning with no idea of marriage to anyone, he was astonished to find that the idea of a long engagement to Isabel found no favor with him. "No," he said decisively. When Isabel looked ready to argue, he said, "Please remember that putting off the date of our wedding does Manning and Mrs. Appleton no good." Thoughtfully he added, "And if we delay the wedding too long, it will certainly cause speculation and gossip."

Feeling as if she was standing on a crumbling cliff with only an unending expanse of wave-tossed seas below her, Isabel asked tightly, "Then when do you suggest?"

"Late July, early August," he replied promptly.

"Are you mad? That's only a few months away," she said, aghast, her comforting little plan of postponing the wedding for as long as she could shot down in an instant.

He nodded. "I realize that, but the timing is perfect. We shall be engaged a decent enough time—what two, three months before the wedding? Everyone will have departed London by then and returned to their estates for the summer. The Little Season isn't until September, so the wedding shouldn't interfere with anyone's plans."

Her expression troubled, Isabel gazed up at him. "Marcus, I don't think you understand . . ."

He stopped her from speaking by placing a finger against her lips. "Hush. You think I don't know what you are about? You are trying to please your father-in-law and Edmund and yet avoid the one thing that would make them happiest: our wedding." His gaze bore steadily into hers. "We will be married late July or early August, you may choose, but Isabel, it *will* be this summer."

Her eyes glittered with temper. "I just remembered what an autocratic beast you can be at times," she snapped. "I would remind you that I am not your ward any longer."

"I have not," he murmured, a note in his voice that she'd never heard, "thought of you as my ward for years." His hands caught her upper arms and he propelled her gently against him. "Since this morning," he said with his lips only inches from hers, "I find that I can only think of you as a most desirable woman. *Most* desirable."

Isabel's heart leaped at his words, but it was the touch of his lips on hers that sent her pulse rocketing through her body. His mouth was warm and knowing on hers, the sensation of his lips pressing against hers so seductive and beguiling that against her will she surrendered to his kiss; her arms crept around his neck and her lips parted.

Marcus groaned when her mouth opened for him, lust and delight mingling into one powerful emotion. He kissed her deeply, his tongue sliding into her mouth and rubbing suggestively against hers. She tasted wonderful, warm and intoxicating, and his grip on her arms tightened and he pulled her small frame closer to him. He'd meant only to bestow a friendly kiss upon her lips—at least that's what he told himself—but Isabel was too yielding, her response too irresistible for him to abandon the drugging seductiveness of her mouth.

A man's driving passion for one particular woman, and only one woman, rose up within him and he was blind to anything but how desperately he wanted her. His mouth fused with hers, his hands dropped to her bottom, lifting and guiding her lower body against his swollen member. It was unbearably arousing to feel her softness sliding against him and he was consumed with the sudden anticipation of the hot pleasure that would be his when he joined them together. Intent upon his goal, he bunched up her gown, his heart nearly exploding when his seeking fingers touched her naked flesh.

Drowning in his embrace, beset by emotions that had long lain dormant, Isabel was brought rudely back to reality by the feel of his big warm hand caressing her naked buttock. Shocked by the spear of desire that went through her as he kneaded her flesh, and the stunning intimacy of the moment, she gasped and broke their embrace.

Catching him by surprise, she twisted her head away and shoved with all her might. He made no attempt to stop her escape; his hands immediately fell to his sides and half-sobbing she scrambled away from him. Her cheeks burning, with shaking fingers she frantically tugged and pulled at her gown, chagrin and embarrassment flooding through her. She would not look at him and her voice thick with tears, she said, "That should not have happened. I swore to Hugh that I would always. . . . I never should have—Forgive me!" And then she was gone, snatching up her skirts and running away from him as if her very life depended upon it.

Marcus stared befuddled into the darkness where she had disappeared. Now what, he wondered, was that all about? And what in the hell had she sworn to Hugh?

Chapter 5

Marcus was frowning when he arrived home several minutes later and entered the house. He'd spent the intervening time as he'd ridden his horse through the darkness toward Sherbrook Hall considering Isabel's reaction. She'd not been repulsed by his actions and she'd been a willing participant in their embrace, he knew that much. So why had she run away? He had no quarrel with her wishing to stop things before they went much farther, and he was secretly appalled at how close he'd come to completely losing his head, but surely she hadn't needed to disappear like that. And what the devil did she mean by those cryptic words? Especially the part about Hugh?

Having told Thompson not to wait up for him, Marcus threw his riding gloves on the marble table in the elegant foyer, picked up the candle his butler had left burning for him, and wandered into his office. After lighting several candles, he spent a few minutes coaxing a fire into being in the fireplace that dominated the far wall. A thoughtful expression on his face, he poured himself a brandy from the tray of liquors and glassware Thompson kept filled and ready on a tall mahogany chest and walked over to his desk.

He set down his brandy on the corner of the desk and then stood staring blankly at the snifter, his thoughts on Isabel. Part of him was enormously satisfied by the way she had reacted to his kiss, but the ending . . . He scowled. Hugh Manning was not, he decided grimly, going to be a part of what went on in their bedroom. Marcus would allow no ghosts in his marriage bed.

Hugh Manning had been dead for ten years or more and Marcus found it impossible to believe that Isabel was still in love with her husband. She hadn't responded, he reminded himself, like a woman whose heart belonged to a dead man. She'd been warm and willing; the memory of her arms clasped around his neck and the way her lips had parted beneath his confirmed his opinion. So what had gone wrong?

That passionate interlude had startled Marcus. Since they were to be married, naturally he'd hoped that they'd find pleasure in each other's arms. He just hadn't expected to be so completely overwhelmed by the most basic, intense desire to possess a woman that he'd ever experienced. It occurred to him, and with no little unease, that for the first time in his life, he'd been controlled by his emotions. If Isabel had not brought things to an end he might very well have crossed the line, and that knowledge annoyed him. He should have handled the situation with far more finesse. Instead, he thought irritably, he acted like a randy youth with his first woman.

Marcus hadn't reached the age of nine and thirty without having become adept at the art of dalliance. He might have been discreet about his conquests, but he'd never been a monk and there had been more than one little opera dancer who had enjoyed his protection over the years. But while he appreciated the charms and the sensual gratification to be found in the arms of the various women he kept, his emotions, beyond lust and perhaps amusement at their antics as they coaxed another expensive bauble out of him, had never been touched. His mistresses had satisfied a physical need and, while he took pleasure in their company and bed, he likened it to the same pleasure and enjoyment he took in an exceptionally delicious meal or a particularly fine bottle of liquor: something relished for the moment and then forgotten. He doubted that, if he lived to be a hundred, he'd ever forget that blaze of passion that had ignited within him the instant his mouth had touched Isabel's. What had happened tonight with Isabel made him realize that until he'd kissed her, held her in his arms, he had never experienced *true* desire—and it unnerved him.

With Isabel ardent and willing in his embrace, the world had receded and he'd been oblivious to anything but how wonderful she felt in his arms; been aware of nothing but of the potent sweetness of her kiss and the arousing softness of her body crushed against his. Marcus made a face, not liking that he'd been fully at the mercy of his most basic instincts. He'd been immune to everything but a pounding desire to push aside those concealing skirts and mate; and mate, he admitted uncomfortably, was the only way to describe the primitive emotions that had reigned over him. If Isabel hadn't brought their embrace to an end, he conceded with a little bit of shock, well, he wouldn't have been responsible for what would have happened next. He frowned, knowing full well what would have taken place: he'd have possessed her fully there in the garden and damn the devil!

He shook his head. Something must be very wrong with him, he decided. He'd gone from placidly expecting each day to follow the rhythm and routine of the day before to rashly announcing to an utter stranger that he was engaged to a woman he'd avoided like the plague for the past decade. What's more, he'd discovered that the idea of marriage to *her* wasn't at all distasteful. No, he thought, not distasteful at all, remembering her sweet mouth beneath his and the feel of her bare little buttocks in his hands. His body reacted instantly to images that flashed across his mind, his blood running hot and thick through his veins, the organ between his legs suddenly swollen and heavy, and he wondered wildly if he was turning into a satyr and or libertine like his grandfather, the Old Earl. . . .

Horrified at the idea of following in the Old Earl's footsteps, Marcus resolutely kept his mind off of anything remotely connected to matters of the flesh. His face set in grim concentration, he shrugged out of his form-fitting dark blue jacket and tugged loose the starched white cravat, tossing both items over the oxblood leather settee that faced the fire. Seating himself behind the desk, after taking a sip of brandy, he pulled out several pieces of paper and began to write.

His mother should hear of the news first, he decided after a moment's thought. He took a deep breath and then quickly and decisively wrote, giving her little more information than the fact that he was engaged to marry Isabel Manning and that the wedding would be held sometime in late July or early August. That first, most difficult message completed, he settled down to write the remainder. Eventually there was a pile of notes on the edge of his desk, all essentially repeating the same information he'd written his mother. He paused in his efforts, reviewing the names of the people who should hear of the engagement directly from him.

The Weston clan was large and far flung, and, although Marcus was closest to his cousins Julian, the Earl of Wyndham, and Charles, and to a lesser extent his young cousin the Honorable Stacey Bannister and Stacey's mother, his mother's youngest sister, there were other relatives. Many other relatives, he admitted, wincing, some he probably didn't even know about. He sighed. The Old Earl had been known for his prodigious number of by-blows scattered from one end of the British Isles to the other and Marcus was grateful he could safely ignore all those relatives born on the wrong side of the blanket. But that still left three other aunts and who knew how many cousins?

Deciding that he needed only to notify his other aunts, leaving it up to them to spread the news to their children, he once again began to write. The last three letters written, he stared with satisfaction at the pile. His mother's he would have hand delivered by a servant to London; the others could be sent by post.

He eyed the pile of notes for a long time. His fate was sealed. Not only had the engagement been announced tonight at Lord Manning's, but once these notes were received, the news would spread like wildfire through the *ton*.

Pushing back his chair, he sipped his brandy and contemplated the future. Within a matter of months he'd be a married man and his life would never again be the same. But, he reminded himself, Isabel would be in his bed every night. A distinctly carnal expression crossed his face. Marriage, he decided, would have its benefits.

Roaming the confines of her rooms at Manning Court, Isabel couldn't think of one good thing that could come of her marriage to Marcus Sherbrook. In fact, she saw only disaster ahead.

Wearing a nightgown of the finest cambric, she paced in front of a pair of long windows that overlooked the gardens, her gaze kept firmly away from the direction of the rose arbor. One thing she did *not* want to think about was what had occurred when she had lost her head in Marcus's arms. With the same steely effort she had exercised over her life since Hugh's death, she forced her thoughts away from that passionate interlude and considered her future.

How could her life have changed so dramatically, so disastrously, within twenty-four hours? There'd already been trouble enough on her horizon, but nothing that she couldn't handle—and nothing approaching the magnitude of her marriage to Marcus! She'd awoken this morning knowing she'd have to deal with Whitley, but she'd never expected to end the day engaged to Marcus! A half-hysterical laugh bubbled up inside of her. Whitley she could handle, but Marcus . . . Pain twisted in her heart. Unable to think of Marcus without feeling like bursting into tears, she considered the situation with Whitley.

Whitley was a problem, no denying it. She already knew

that it had been a ghastly mistake to pay him any money in the first place and that she dared not pay him one penny more—no matter what he threatened.

Rubbing her head, Isabel sank down on her bed. *And I wouldn't have paid the bastard even two days ago if he hadn't caught me by surprise,* she thought bitterly. A chill blew through her when she remembered looking up from the roses she'd been cutting in the garden to find Whitley standing in front of her, that well-remembered, annoying little smirk on his face. While living in India, she had often itched to smack that same smirk right off his face, and she discovered that the itch had not gone away. She'd never understood Hugh's friendliness for Whitley and she had always been wary of him and his poking and prying.

An expression of distaste flitted across her face. How often, all those years before, she wondered, had she caught him snooping around the house, even one time pawing through the papers on Hugh's desk? How many boring afternoons had she sat through the sweltering heat of India listening to the wives of Hugh's colleagues gossip about Whitley's ceaseless nosing about. Her lip curled. The wives might gossip about him, but all of them invited him to their homes and acted as if they considered him quite charming. *Even I did,* Isabel admitted with disgust. But she'd never liked him, not even when Hugh had first introduced her to him, and she'd never fallen for Whitley's facile charm.

The English society in Bombay had been small and insular and, like all such societies, much of their entertainment had come from speculating on the doings of each other. Most of it had been innocent and not unnatural considering the situation, but there had always been, in Isabel's opinion, something decidedly nasty about Whitley's interest in the happenings amongst his friends and neighbors. Even before Hugh had died and she had returned to England, she'd come to believe that Whitley was dangerous and no friend to Hugh or herself.

A quiver of fear went through her. And dear God, I was right! Her hands suddenly felt clammy thinking of that original meeting with Whitley in the garden. She'd not been happy to see him, but she hadn't been frightened, at least not at first.

It had taken her a second to realize that Whitley was alone; no servant had escorted him to her and he had bypassed the normal route, avoiding being seen by any of the inhabitants of the house. He'd been sneaking and creeping around again, she thought disgustedly.

Her dislike boiling to the surface, in a sharp voice she had asked, "Did no one answer the door?"

Whitley's smirk had grown and he'd said, "I thought it best if we had a moment or two of private conversation before you introduced me to your father-in-law. We have much to discuss, you and I: old events in India, events I doubt Lord Manning would find interesting." His cold eyes locked on her face, he had drawled, "There's no need for him to know everything that happened in Bombay, now is there?"

Dread had filled her. Face white, she had stammered, "W-w-what are you talking about?"

"I think you know very well what I'm talking about." He looked sly. "Of course, I don't really have to speak with Lord Manning and tell him about those days of old, now do I? There's no reason to upset an old man by letting him learn that his son was not the paragon he thought or that you are not quite as you appear. I suppose," he said carefully, "if someone made it worth my while, I could just leave the way I came and ride away with no one the wiser that I had even been here."

Her thoughts scrambling like squirrels around a tree, Isabel had latched onto the most important part of his statement. He would go away. For money. "Wait here," she said breathlessly. "Don't let anyone see you." Throwing down her tools and the woven straw basket half-filled with roses, she'd dashed to the house.

It had taken her a few moments to gather up what ready money she could lay her hands on. She thanked God that she still had a large portion of the generous pin money that Lord Manning gave her every quarter, and to that, in her desperation, she'd even added in a diamond necklace and earrings. In those first frantic minutes, she'd have given Whitley anything he'd wanted simply to make him go away.

And that, she decided angrily, had been her first mistake. If she'd faced him down, she'd have ended the situation then and there, but had she done that? No. Like a scared little ninny-hammer, she'd panicked and thrown the money at him. He'd kept his word—gone away, all right—but like a tiger having tasted blood, he'd come back for more. And he'd keep coming back, she realized soon enough . . . unless she did something to prevent it.

She stared down at her clenched hands in her lap. I made a mistake, but I didn't repeat it. I stood up to him the next time, she reminded herself. I told him he'd not get one penny more.

Her mouth thinned. She'd been frightened but determined when she'd ridden out to meet Whitley this morning. Whitley had, she reminded herself, no proof of anything. He *had* to have been fishing, bluffing, she told herself repeatedly. He had to have been hoping to either startle the truth out of her or scare her into giving him money.

A mirthless laugh came from her. Well, the bastard had succeeded on one level: she'd given him money. But never again, and she cursed her foolishness for letting Whitley panic her in that manner. She should have stood firm and laughed in his face, or offered to introduce him to Lord Manning. Taking him to meet her father-in-law would have been a calculated risk, but it would have been worth the gamble. Whitley could know nothing for certain; she and Hugh had been so very careful, knowing that the stakes were enormous and that one slip, one mistake, would be tragic. There *was* no proof, she told herself again, but even knowing that no proof existed, it did not, *could* not, dispel the anxiety that clawed in her breast or lessen her terror.

Whitley's reaction to her refusal to give him more money hadn't surprised Isabel. She'd known that he could be violent. She'd seen him lose his temper once with one of his native servants and take a whip to the poor fellow. Isabel felt certain that only Hugh's quick intervention had saved the man's life.

Thinking back on the confrontation with Whitley this morning, she realized that she should have been better prepared. It was unlikely that Whitley would be fool enough to strike her or harm her in any measurable way, but she could see that the situation had been dangerous. Isabel grimaced. I should have brought one of Hugh's pistols with me and shot the bloody blackguard. For a moment, she dwelled on the satisfying image of Whitley lying dead on the ground, a bullet hole between his eyes.

She smiled grimly. She could have done it. Hugh had been uneasy with leaving her and Edmund alone in a foreign country for weeks, sometimes months at a time, while he traveled on the company's business. They'd had no near neighbors and, with only unreliable native servants around for her to turn to in unsettled times and a countryside rife with deadly predators and poisonous vipers, Hugh had made certain she knew her way around a firearm. When he was home, on countless sultry mornings before the heat of the day became unbearable, he'd taken her into the relative coolness of the jungle to practice with a variety of pistols. A bittersweet ache bloomed within her. Those had been some of the most pleasurable times she'd spent in India. Hugh had been proud of her, and after a difficult start, and Lord knew it had been difficult, the possibility of a happy marriage had loomed on the horizon. Her lips drooped. And then a king cobra had ended everything.

Shaking off the depressing thoughts, she stood up and began to pace again. She hoped that the situation with Whitley had been defused, but she suspected not. He wouldn't give up easily and she knew that, while he may have gone to ground at the moment, he'd circle around and come back again and try to frighten her into running like a terrified sambar doe in front of a stalking tiger. She snorted. *That* wasn't going to happen. She was prepared now and wouldn't let her guard down.

Isabel rubbed her forehead, the headache she'd been fighting all evening becoming more insistent. How she'd managed to keep that insipidly happy smile on her face all through dinner mystified her. *I must be a better actress than I realize,* she mused, *because heaven knows I never felt less like smiling in my life.* And tonight, she thought wearily, was only the beginning. . . .

During the coming weeks and months there were going to be many occasions like tonight. She and Marcus would be constantly in each other's company, constantly under the eyes of interested friends and relatives. The whole neighborhood would be excited about their wedding and, through it all, she would have to smile and nod and pretend that she wasn't terrified of the future, terrified of forgetting and losing herself in Marcus Sherbrook's embrace.

A tremor of half fright, half pleasure coursed through her at the memory of his warm mouth on hers. His kiss had been everything she'd ever foolishly dreamed that it would be, and for those brief treasured moments she'd been able to forget why it was madness and simply revel in his embrace, revel in the power of his kiss, in the hot, sweet sensations that raced through her, but then . . . then she'd come to her senses and remembered. . . .

Bleakly, she stared out into the darkness. *Oh, Hugh,* she thought miserably. *How could you die and leave me alone this way? What am I to do?*

The news of the engagement of Mrs. Hugh Manning and Marcus Sherbrook swept through the neighborhood with all the speed and wonder associated with a shooting star blazing across the night sky. Marcus had known that it would cause talk; he just hadn't expected it to cause *that* much talk, nor that everyone from the lowliest scullery maid to the loftiest member of the aristocracy in the area would find the news so very interesting. By the time his engagement was five days old, he was heartily sick of it. Glaring out the window of his office on a sunny Tuesday afternoon, he swore that if one more of his male friends or neighbors expressed their astonishment that he was going to marry *Isabel Manning* of all people, they'd discover just how handy he was with his fives. As for the female portion of the neighborhood, they were all clamoring to know the date of the wedding. He scowled. And that was the one question he couldn't answer.

His scowl deepened. And Isabel! The little wretch! Just what game was she playing? Every time he brought up the subject of setting the date of their wedding, she'd vanished like a puff of smoke. One minute they were talking and the next—poof!—she was gone and he was left talking to air. In fact, he thought grimly, since their betrothal had been announced, she had proven irritatingly elusive. It wasn't, he argued, that he intended for them to live in each other's pocket, but he'd certainly assumed they'd see each other more than they had these past days. They had things to discuss, a wedding to plan. There were decisions to be made, living arrangements to be decided upon, and blast her! She was always in a hurry to be somewhere else and simply did not have a moment to give him—or so she said. Why, he'd wager that since their engagement he hadn't spent more than twenty minutes at a time in her presence, and always, he reminded himself, his scowl deepening, with someone nearby. If he didn't know better he'd think she was afraid to be alone with him.

The sound of several vehicles and horses pulling up to the front of the house caught his attention and, still scowling, hoping it wasn't more curious friends or neighbors coming to call, he strode from the library. Like the well-trained servant he was, Thompson was already in the foyer ahead of him preparing to open the heavy oak doors.

"It is your mother, sir," Thompson said, smiling. "One of the gatekeeper's boys took a shortcut through the park and just came rushing into the kitchen with the news."

Marcus knew very well why his mother had come home, but he was still startled that news of his engagement had compelled her to leave London at the height of the Season. Touched by this sign of maternal devotion, he strolled out of the house to greet her.

His bad mood lifted as he caught sight of the entourage that awaited him. In addition to the large and lumbering family barouche drawn by four elegant grays, there was a coach that held several servants and behind that there were two heavily laden vehicles. His mother was notorious for the number of items she felt were absolutely necessary for her comfort when away from Sherbrook Hall and, looking at the assemblage before him, he smiled. His cousin Julian was of the mind that an invading army could probably get by with less than Aunt Barbara took for a few months' stay in London. Marcus tended to agree with him.

Even though he knew why she had left behind the delights of London and had returned home, he was still a trifle surprised at her unexpected arrival. His mother never traveled anywhere without an armed male escort, convinced that bandits and highwaymen lurked behind every tree, and Marcus had been half prepared for a summons to London for the express purpose of accompanying her on the journey home. That she had foregone such precautions was astounding and made him wonder if she had finally accepted his oft-repeated assurances that no self-respecting bandit or highwayman would dare hold up such a large party.

The mystery of his mother's sudden boldness was solved when he noticed a tall, fashionably attired gentleman in the act of dismounting from a restive black horse. She'd found an escort. Studying the man, Marcus frowned. Except for the black hair curling from beneath a rolled-brim beaver hat, Marcus could tell little about the man. He appeared to be a stranger, and yet there was something familiar about him, something about the lean-hipped, broad-shouldered build . . .

Puzzling over the stranger's identity, Marcus strolled toward the barouche. He and the stranger reached it at the same time and when the man grinned at him, Marcus stopped as if he'd been poleaxed. He still didn't know the man, but he'd have recognized those features anywhere: except for the difference in eye color, the man bore a striking resemblance to the face Marcus saw every morning in his shaving mirror. The man was clearly a Weston. He had the same black hair, the same rugged features, right down to the swooping black eyebrows, deep-set eyes, strong jaw, and wide-lipped mouth. Only the nose was a bit more aquiline, but the olive, almost swarthy, complexion was all definitely Weston. His heart sank. Had his mother befriended one of the Old Earl's by-blows?

Grinning at him, the stranger said, "You don't recognize me, do you? I'm not surprised, I doubt we've met a half-dozen times and then only briefly. I'm Jack Landrey."

"Aunt Maria's oldest son?" Marcus asked cautiously. "The one who was in the Army?" Jack nodded and as they shook hands, Marcus said, "Heard you got shot up in Egypt. A leg, wasn't it? Battle of Alexandria back in '01?"

"Not one of my more gratifying moments, I can tell you," Jack answered with a smile.

Smiling back, Marcus said, "I can imagine. But wait, that's not the only time you were wounded, was it? Didn't I hear from someone that a couple years later you nearly lost an arm fighting in the West Indies?"

Jack shrugged. "Yes, but one of those dashed island fevers was the worst of it."

Morbid curiosity prompted Marcus to say, "Seems to me I remember that you were also wounded last year at Copenhagen with Sir Arthur, weren't you?"

Jack shook his head and admitted sheepishly, "It was a horse that caused me grief that time. Rank beast unseated me in the midst of fighting and I broke my leg when I fell." He made a face. "After that, I decided perhaps fate was trying to tell me something. I sold out my commission and came home. Arrived back in England in January."

"What your cousin is completely failing to mention," said Barbara in exasperated tones as Marcus opened the door of the barouche and prepared to help her down, "is that he is no longer plain Mr. Jack Landrey. He is now Lord Thorne, Viscount Thorne."

Jack laughed. "Forgot."

"Newly inherited?" Marcus asked, liking a man who could forget being elevated to the ranks of the Peerage.

"Very. Not two months ago," Jack admitted. "Distant cousin, second or third, died without issue, and I woke up one morning to find myself a viscount. Gave me a queer start, I can tell you. Mother is in the boughs over it and, of course, my brothers and sisters are thrilled." Jack made a face. "I'm still not certain how I feel about it. Old fellow left plenty of blunt to go with the title, but the estate and farms have been allowed to fall into rack and ruin. First day at Thornewood, I put my foot through the dining room floor." He shook his head. "I foresee a great deal of money and work being expended on the place to bring it up to snuff."

Putting her hand on Marcus's arm as they walked toward the house, Barbara gave Jack a fond look and said, "Yes, and you shall enjoy every moment of it. Your mother wrote me that you have been like a caged beast since you've come home to England. She thinks overseeing the rebuilding of the estate will give you something to do—and keep you out of mischief." Turning her gaze to her son, Barbara's brow lifted and she said, "Speaking of mischief: you have been very busy while I've been in London, haven't you?"

Marcus grinned at his mother's understatement but there was no time to reply; they had reached the house and

Thompson was greeting his mother. Leaving Barbara happily issuing a multitude of orders to Thompson—rooms for Jack and his valet, the disbursement of trunks, bandboxes, and valises from the wagons—Marcus bore Jack off to his office.

Offering Jack a glass of hock, Marcus said, "Thank you for escorting my mother home. I appreciate it. I hope it didn't disrupt your plans too much."

"Good God, no!" exclaimed Jack, taking a seat on the oxblood leather settee. "I'd rather face a horde of savages intent upon my demise than the hallowed halls of Almack's."

Marcus laughed. "I don't blame you. London has its amusements but Almack's is not one I find to my liking."

Jack took a swallow of his hock. "From what Aunt Barbara said, it appears that you managed to get yourself engaged with no help from the matchmaking mamas that haunt London this time of year." He grinned and added, "She's ecstatic, by the way."

Though cousins, they were virtually strangers to each other and there were a few awkward moments, but these were soon left behind. Jack's mother, the sister next to Barbara in age, the Honorable Maria Weston, as she had been known then, had outraged her family when at seventeen she had run away and married an impecunious lieutenant in the Navy. The Old Earl had not been happy with the match and Maria and her lieutenant had received a chilly welcome the few times they'd returned to Wyndham Manor. Proud and very much in love, Maria had turned her back on her family, and contact with the main branch of the Westons for the past thirty years or so had been scanty at best. Even though the Old Earl had died decades ago, and the young lieutenant had gained the rank of Vice-Admiral before her husband's death three years previously, the estrangement that began during the Old Earl's lifetime created a breach that remained somewhat to this day. Marcus thought it interesting that his mother appeared to have taken Jack under her wing.

Deciding that if Jack had his mother's approval, and liking

his first impressions of him, Marcus set himself out to put his cousin at ease and soon the two men were conversing as if they had known each other for years. Though Maria and her brood had remained at a distance, she had maintained some contact with her siblings, mostly through letters, and Jack and Marcus were able to find some common ground. By the time Barbara stuck her head around the door to his office, Marcus and Jack were quite at ease with one another.

At Barbara's entrance, Jack set down his empty glass and rose to his feet. Smiling from mother to son, he said, "I'm sure that the pair of you have much to discuss. If you will direct me to my room, I shall give you some privacy."

Once Jack had been borne away by Thompson and Barbara had settled herself comfortably in an overstuffed leather chair, she looked up at her son and said simply, "Tell me. All."

Lying was not Marcus's forte, but he'd known this moment was coming and he'd prepared himself. Not quite meeting his mother's gaze, he said, "Before you left for London, you made it clear that I should make some changes in my life. Decided marriage would be one way. Knew you liked Isabel. Offered for her. Accepted me."

Barbara stared in dismay at her tall handsome son, her heart sinking. Instead of the love match she'd dreamed of, it was obvious that Marcus, in his usual unemotional way, she thought irritably, had chosen a marriage of convenience. She frowned. She could understand Marcus's motives, but what of Isabel's?

Thoughtfully, Barbara studied her son. Marcus's actions, while vexing, she could understand, but Isabel's had her puzzled. It had not escaped her attention that Marcus and Isabel's marked avoidance of each other was a little *too* obvious. She'd long suspected that the pair of them were attracted to each other, but both were too stubborn and proud to act on that attraction—or acknowledge it. Perhaps Isabel had realized that she didn't really dislike Marcus after all? In fact, quite the opposite?

Barbara sighed. Whatever Isabel's reasons, it was her son's that concerned her most. She'd so longed for Marcus to fall wildly, madly in love that she hadn't cared who the woman was; if Marcus loved her, Barbara would have welcomed a milkmaid into the family. But if she'd had to choose a wife for her son, Isabel would have topped the list. She'd had never simply wanted her son to marry, she'd wanted him to be helplessly, *passionately* in love with the woman he eventually married—which, it was apparent, he was not.

Well, it might not be a love match, she admitted resignedly, but she had hopes for the future. Married, they'd have to be in each other's company and propinquity was known to make miracles.

Forcing a smile, she looked at Marcus and asked, "So when is the wedding to take place?"

Chapter 6

Marcus nearly groaned aloud. Trust his mother to ask the one question he could not answer! Reluctantly he said, "We haven't set a precise date yet, but we've agreed that the wedding will take place in either late July or early August."

Barbara glanced down at her hands in her lap. Well, that sounded promising. At least there didn't seem to be a long engagement in the offing and she'd been half prepared for that. And, she thought pleased, Marcus seemed unhappy with the delay in setting a date for the wedding. Perhaps his emotions were more involved than she realized? Had she detected a note of impatience in his voice?

She glanced up to see him studying her, a quizzical expression on his face. "What?" she asked. "Why do you look at me so?"

"Unless you're a fortune teller," he said, smiling faintly, "when you left for London, you had no idea that I planned to marry, and I'll wager that Isabel Manning would have been the last woman you'd expect me to marry, yet you don't seem the least surprised."

Barbara shrugged and said, "You are my only child and I have tried very hard not to be an interfering mother. I raised you to be self-sufficient and you're old enough to make your own decisions and have been for years. I have long thought it is past time that you married and started your nursery but I assumed you would marry when it suited you. Obviously that time has come." She smiled. "As for Isabel being the woman you've chosen to marry . . . why not? She's an eligible, wealthy, attractive young woman from a respectable family. You've known each other all your lives, you come from similar backgrounds, and you've some interests in common—horses come to mind—and you even like her son, so why shouldn't you marry each other? Your marriage seems quite timely and practical to me."

His mother's words pricked him. There was nothing wrong in what she said but hearing her lay out all the logical reasons for his marriage annoyed him. When he thought of marriage to Isabel—and he'd thought of little else since the night of their betrothal—he didn't think in such prosaic terms as eligibility or common interests. No, there was nothing prosaic about his thoughts about Isabel. When he wasn't thinking of strangling her, he was aware of the emptiness that consumed him when he was away from her, or he was imagining her smile, her laugh; but mostly, he admitted, he was thinking of how very much he wanted her in his arms and in his bed.

A frown on his face, Marcus said, "So the marriage doesn't bother you?"

"Good heavens! Why should it? I am very fond of both Isabel and Edmund." She flashed him a wide smile, saying truthfully, "I am thrilled that you are going to marry Isabel; she will be good for you."

"You make her sound like a mustard foot bath," he said dryly.

Barbara laughed. "She will certainly be a spring tonic for you. Now, how do you feel about hosting a small dinner party on Friday evening to introduce Jack? With so many of our friends in London, we will be quite thin of company, but

I think we can put together a pleasant table. Naturally, we'll invite Isabel and Lord Manning, as well as several others, like Clara Appleton, who eschewed the Season this year." She smiled slyly. "And perhaps by then you and Isabel will have decided upon a date for the wedding and it can be announced."

Marcus doubted the latter, but he agreed with his mother's plans to introduce Jack to their circle of friends. They spoke on the matter for several moments before Marcus inquired about his mother's trip to London and Barbara in turn asked after local events.

A glimmer of a smile in his eyes, Marcus asked, "Did my news disrupt your plans in London terribly?"

She laughed. "No, truth be told, London was extremely tiring. I find that I like my familiar things around me and my normal routine."

"Hmmm, seems to me that you've scolded me often enough for saying the same thing."

"Hush!" she said, her eyes dancing. "As a respectful and dutiful son, you are to do as I say, not as I do." Leaning forward, Barbara demanded, "Now tell me: what do you think of Jack?"

Marcus shrugged. "On the basis of our short acquaintance, he seems a decent enough fellow. I think he will prove to be an enjoyable companion."

"My impression exactly! He was a delightful and entertaining escort during the trip from London. And if half of what I hear from his mother is true, he has led a most exciting life. The adventures he has had for a young man not yet five and thirty!"

Feeling a trifle ruffled by the wistful, almost envious note in his mother's voice, Marcus muttered, "Aunt Maria is probably well used to learning that he is lingering near death's door."

"Oh, I know," said Barbara, "she has often written to me

how she worries about him. My heart goes out to her and I am most thankful that you have never given me a moment's worry." Unaware that she had just added insult to injury, she added, "It was so fortunate that he came to call on the same day I received your exciting news. I was just about to write you and request your company for the journey home, when the butler informed me that Jack was in the foyer wishing to pay his respects."

"I'd wondered how he came to escort you from London. I didn't realize that you knew him well."

"I knew of his exploits from my sister, of course," Barbara admitted, "but until I saw him in my sitting room in London, I hadn't laid eyes on him for years." She smiled. "His mother wrote him that I was in London and urged him to come to call. I'm sure it was the last thing he wanted to do, but he did and it all worked out splendidly."

Idly, Marcus remarked, "Seems surprising that such a dashing buck would tear himself away from London to escort home an older female relative he hardly knows."

"Yes, I thought so, too, but he says that he has a friend staying in the area and that he'd take the opportunity to visit with him." She frowned slightly. "Now what was his name? Jack said the fellow retired from the Army just a short while ago. A major, I think. Now what was it? White? No. Whitlow? No, that isn't it either."

Marcus stiffened. "Would it by chance be Whitley?"

"That's it!" His mother beamed at him. "Do you know Major Whitley, too?"

"I've met him," Marcus said carefully. Jack was a friend of Whitley's? A coincidence?

"Oh, this is grand!" said Barbara happily. "Jack will be so pleased that you know his friend. If you let me know where he is staying, I shall invite him to dinner on Friday night."

"No," said Marcus in a voice she had never heard from him. His features grim, he added bluntly, "You are to have nothing to do with Whitley. Order Thompson to refuse him entrance should the man have the temerity to come to call. He is not an appropriate person for you to know."

Startled, she stared at her normally amiable son, wondering where this hard-eyed, stone-faced stranger had come from. "But *Jack* knows him," she said helplessly. "You must be mistaken. Surely Whitley cannot be so very bad?"

"I am sure," Marcus said harshly, "that *Jack* knows all sorts of people and some of them," he finished ominously, "are *not* the sort one would wish for a closer acquaintance."

It wasn't until after they had dined and Barbara had bid the two gentlemen good night that Marcus had a chance to bring up Whitley's name. The two cousins were comfortably seated once again in Marcus's office, partaking of snifters of brandy. A small fire burned on the hearth to chase away the faint chill of the May night, and candlelight cast a golden glow over the room.

Marcus was sprawled in the overstuffed leather chair near the fire, a snifter of brandy held in one hand. Jack sat on the oxblood settee, his long legs stretched toward the fire, his brandy resting on a nearby mahogany table.

Taking a sip of his brandy, Jack grinned at Marcus and said, "This is a far cry from some of the places I've bivouacked over the years. More nights than I care to think of I've gone to bed in a drafty tent, slept on the cold, wet ground with moldy cheese, stale bread, and sour wine my only sustenance—if I had that!" He leaned his head back against the settee and sighed blissfully. "A full stomach—my compliments to your cook, by the way—a warm fire, a snifter of fine brandy, and an entertaining companion; what more could a man ask for?"

"Little else," Marcus replied with a smile. Even with his suspicions aroused by Jack's relationship with Whitley, Marcus found it impossible not to respond to his cousin's easy charm. *Damn it, I like the bloody fellow*, Marcus thought ruefully. *And just because he knows Whitley doesn't mean anything.* But Marcus was surprised and a little disappointed, although he had no reason to be, that Jack associated with someone like the major.

Marcus knew the major's type. One met men like Whitley in the halls and gaming clubs along Pall Mall or in the high-priced brothels favored by the gentlemen of the *ton*. The major and his ilk were amusing companions for drinking and whoring, or any number of masculine pursuits, but they were generally *not* people someone introduced to the ladies of the family. Whitley's bold manner with Isabel bothered him more than he cared to admit and he wondered what Hugh Manning had been about calling someone like Whitley friend and letting him be on familiar terms with his wife. He certainly wouldn't let a bounder like Whitley within a mile of *his* wife, even if the polite world was full of men like the major. One didn't, Marcus thought protectively, subject the females of the family to fellows of Whitley's stripe.

The fact that Jack knew Whitley wouldn't have normally aroused Marcus's interest, but Jack's knowing him, coupled with Whitley's manner toward Isabel, raised alarms all through him. Of course, he reminded himself, Whitley and Jack had both been military men, and it was possible their paths had crossed more than once in the course of their careers. He frowned. Perhaps that's all it was: Jack simply knew Whitley in the most superficial way. But that didn't make sense. Why would Jack leave London at the height of the Season to travel to a small seaside village in the country to visit someone he only knew in passing?

Marcus took a sip of his brandy and decided to plunge right in. "Mother says that you have a friend staying in the area. A Major Whitley?"

A peculiar expression crossed Jack's face and Marcus was immediately aware that Whitley's name had provoked some emotion within Jack. And it wasn't friendly.

Jack hesitated, then said, "Ah, yes. I heard from, um, friends that Whitley was visiting around here, and since I would be in the area, I thought I'd look him up."

"A small world, isn't it?" Marcus said, watching him closely. "I happen to have met your friend Whitley just days ago."

"Did you now?" commented Jack. "Quite a coincidence."

Marcus nodded. "I thought so."

Jack tossed off some brandy. "When you met my friend, did he, perhaps, mention where he was staying?" He smiled, but Marcus noticed it didn't reach his eyes. "It'll save me having to look for him."

"The Stag Horn Inn near Salcombe, about a half hour's ride from here."

"How convenient," Jack said, staring at the amber liquid in his snifter.

"He a good friend of yours?"

"Not precisely," said Jack, a note in his voice that made Marcus wonder just what sort of "friendship" Jack had with Whitley.

"Still, you traveled all the way from London to visit him," Marcus prompted.

Jack grinned at him. "No, I traveled all the way from London to enjoy the company of your charming mother. Whitley being in the area is a, er, bonus." Tossing off another swallow of brandy, Jack looked at him and asked, "So how did you meet Whitley?"

Marcus hesitated, wondering how much to tell. Deciding that there was little to be gained in prevaricating, he said simply, "My fiancée, Isabel Manning, introduced us. She's been a widow for nearly a decade now and it appears that Whitley was good friends with Isabel and her husband, Hugh, when she was in India several years ago. Apparently, Whitley recently retired from the Army and, with time on his hands, he is looking up old friends and making their reacquaintance—at least that's what he said."

"Oh? And he just now decided to visit her? After ten years?"

"Again, that's what he said."

"You don't believe him," Jack observed, staring keenly at Marcus.

Marcus took a sip of his brandy. "Not a bit," he said cheerfully. Glancing at Jack, he said, "I think the man's a bounder and up to no good. I've already told my mother to have our butler refuse him entrance should he come to call." Thoughtfully he added, "And I must say that he's not the sort of fellow I'd expect you to call 'friend.' "

Jack made a face. "But then you don't know me that well, do you?"

"Can't deny that, but if I suspected for one second that you were of Whitley's ilk, you wouldn't be sitting here right now," Marcus said levelly. "Relative or not, I'd have sent you packing the moment Mother was inside the house."

Jack stood up and helped himself to another brandy. Walking to the fireplace, he set his snifter on the mantel and, resting one arm along its length, looked down at Marcus still lounging comfortably in the overstuffed chair.

After a moment, Jack asked, "Does the name Roxbury mean anything to you?"

"The Duke of Roxbury?"

Jack nodded.

Suddenly several things became clear to Marcus and a grin spread across his face. While he had only met Roxbury in a social setting, he knew from Julian that Roxbury was not the dilettante old aristocrat he played for the benefit of the *ton*. It was whispered in a select group of gentlemen that the old duke rubbed shoulders with unsavory members of the lower orders and wild young bloods of the *ton* as easily as he dined with society leaders, prime ministers, and members of their cabinets. Roxbury wasn't in politics, but according to Julian, the old duke dabbled quietly in the background at the behest of the government. It was because of Roxbury that Julian, in his younger days, had undertaken several dangerous missions for the duke in France. Julian seldom mentioned his days as a spy for Roxbury and through him the British government, but Marcus was aware of Roxbury's penchant for harnessing the talents of the bored, daring members of the aristocracy for his own uses.

Still grinning, Marcus sat up in his chair and exclaimed, "You're working for that old devil Roxbury."

Jack didn't bother to deny it. He merely shrugged and said, "He knew I was bored and he asked me if I would look into a little matter for him. He mentioned your name and intimated that it might be advantageous for me to reacquaint myself with you and informed me that your mother was currently visiting London." Jack flashed him a shamefaced smile. "I went to call on your mother for the express purpose of testing the wind. I'd hoped, at the worst, that she'd suggest that I visit you one of these days. I'd planned on arriving on your doorstep with a polite note from your mother and seeing where things went from there." He shook his head in amazement. "I couldn't believe my luck when she told me that she was leaving for Sherbrook Hall just as soon as she could arrange it and would I mind escorting her." Jack grinned. "I leaped at the chance, I can tell you."

"So what's the little matter Roxbury wants you to look into?"

Jack hesitated. "Roxbury didn't say I shouldn't tell you; in fact, now that I consider it," Jack said slowly, "I think he thought that you might be useful."

"Probably had already learned of my engagement to Isabel and her connection to Whitley," commented Marcus. "From what Julian says of Roxbury, *nothing* slips by the old man."

"I wouldn't be surprised," Jack agreed.

"I don't know how useful I will be," Marcus said with a grimace. "My meeting with Whitley was, er, not friendly. Caught him harassing Isabel."

"And he's still alive?" asked Jack, surprised.

Marcus smiled grimly. "The pair of them made light of the situation and, short of calling Isabel a liar, there was little I could do." An expression of disgust crossed his face. "I did try to provoke the fellow, but he wouldn't rise to the bait."

"That sounds like Whitley. From what Roxbury told me, his retirement was not entirely voluntary. There had been several incidents during his career in which Whitley's reputation was not enhanced and it was decided that his time in the Army should come to an end before he got more men under his command killed and wounded or did something that would embarrass the government."

"So why is Roxbury interested in him?"

Jack stared at his brandy for several minutes, putting his thoughts in order. Finally he looked at Marcus and said, "I suppose you've heard that there is an invasion planned for later this summer to help the Spaniards?"

Marcus nodded. "To be led by Lieutenant-General Sir Arthur Wellesley."

"Yes, Sir Arthur will lead the troops, but the government doesn't trust anyone in that nest of vipers Napoleon has made of the continent and—this is not common knowledge by the way—the present plan is to invade Portugal and then Spain."

"I may not have heard the specifics," Marcus said, frowning, "but rumors about the invasion have been circling for a while. How does Whitley fit into Wellesley's plans?" Marcus sat upright. Incredulously, he demanded, "Surely you don't suspect him of being a spy for the French?"

"If he is, the French don't know it yet, but Roxbury thinks that Whitley may be offering his services soon." Grim-faced, Jack went on, "Just before the major left London, he visited some old friends at the Horse Guards. As you know, the place is a hive of officers and officials and their friends, and none of them know what the next person is doing. Information leaks from Horse Guards like a sieve, but usually it is not of vital national interest. Embarrassing or irritating, yes, but nothing that can't be rectified. But shortly after Whitley's visit just a little over a week ago, a very important memorandum went missing."

"And this memorandum has to do with the Wellesley troop movements?"

Jack nodded. "Departure dates, landing sites, everything. There is time enough to change it, but we would have to find other places to land and that would delay the invasion . . . and put our allies in grave danger." Jack looked disgusted. "It's possible, and this has been discussed, that the memorandum will turn up on someone's desk or in a file where no one thought to look, but one of the people Whitley visited, a General Smithfield, is the last person known to have had the memorandum." Jack stared down into the fire. "Smithfield, for obvious reasons, didn't report its disappearance immediately. At first, he thought it was merely misfiled and wasted valuable time searching for it. By the time he admitted that he couldn't find the memorandum and the alarm was raised, he'd almost forgotten that Whitley had even been in his office."

"But he's remembered Whitley's visit now?" Marcus asked with a lifted brow.

"Yes, he has, but he doesn't know that his old friend Whitley has become our most likely suspect for the theft—if it has indeed been stolen," Jack replied. "All Smithfield, or anybody at the Horse Guards, knows is that a list was compiled of everyone who called at the offices during the crucial time the memorandum could have gone missing. When prompted, Smithfield did vaguely recall that Whitley, among others, had visited one morning within the time frame that we think it disappeared." Jack's lips thinned. "But since Smithfield practically holds court every day in his offices with all his old cronies, Whitley was just another name on the list."

"But not any longer?"

Jack shook his head. "Roxbury was able to eliminate everyone from the list except for Whitley and one or two others." He grinned. "I suspect those gentlemen are, even as we speak, being befriended by other individuals pressed into service like myself." His expression grew somber. "There is, however, a spy known as *Le Renard,* 'the Fox,' who has been at work in England for years, and Roxbury has long sought to capture him. Roxbury first considered the Fox the probable culprit, but to his mind none of the gentlemen known to have visited Smithfield seem likely to be *Le Renard*; they are in Roxbury's opinion too respectable, too timid, or too stupid. Of course, even he admits that being considered respectable, timid, or stupid could be a clever disguise." Jack sighed. "We can't rule out the Fox, but at the moment Whitley seems our most likely lead. His reputation is unsavory, he has a grudge against the government for forcing him to retire, and one of Roxbury's, er, cronies discovered that he left London the very next day after his visit to Smithfield for the Devon coast."

"And how did you find out that bit of information?"

Jack smiled. "Roxbury had his minions interview everyone Whitley had talked to and discovered a gentleman who remembered Whitley mentioning once that he thought he would look up the wife of an old friend who lived in Devonshire: a Mrs. Hugh Manning."

"Well, if that don't beat the Dutch!" growled Marcus, scowling at his cousin. "You were already aware that Whitley had come here to visit my fiancée?"

Jack had the grace to look guilty. "Roxbury told me that Whitley knew a Mrs. Hugh Manning from his days in India," he admitted. "Roxbury pointed out that Manning Court, where Mrs. Manning resided, was located conveniently near Sherbrook Hall—where my cousin lived." Not liking the look in Marcus's eyes, Jack said hastily, "I didn't know her name was Isabel or that she was your fiancée." When Marcus continued to scowl at him, he added, "You yourself admitted that Roxbury probably knew about the engagement and her connection to Whitley; don't blame me for what Roxbury knows."

Marcus snorted, half amused, half vexed. "Julian claims that a ferret can't fart in a henhouse that Roxbury doesn't know about it. After this, I'm inclined to believe him." He shot Jack a considering look. "You could have told me, you know."

"I really didn't know that the Mrs. Manning who knew Whitley in India was your betrothed until your mother mentioned it," Jack said. He sighed. "And I'll confess, once I knew of your relationship to Mrs. Manning, even though Roxbury implied I should, my mind wasn't made up about how much to tell you."

"I think," Marcus said to no one in particular, "that I have just been insulted."

Jack laughed. "As I said earlier, you don't know me very well, but conversely I don't know *you* very well either." Seriously, he added, "I had to base my decision as to whether to trust you or not on *something*. Your opinion of Whitley matches mine and that determined my telling you about Roxbury and the rest."

Not one to hold a grudge, and agreeing with Jack, Marcus nodded. "Very well, then," he said, "how do you propose to discover if Whitley has the memorandum or not?"

"Search his rooms would be the first step," Jack said. "If he has the memorandum, I'm convinced he has it with him."

Marcus agreed, saying, "The Devonshire coast is a known smuggler haunt and it is possible that he is here as much to see my fiancée as the possibility of finding a smuggler to sail him to the Channel Islands at least or mayhap even to France." He grinned at Jack and asked, "So when do we search his rooms?"

Jack grinned back. "Tomorrow night?"

"Excellent!" said Marcus. "What is your plan?"

Jack's idea was that Marcus would engage Whitley in conversation at the inn while he searched Whitley's rooms.

Marcus pulled on his ear and said, "That horse won't run;

you forget Whitley and I are a breath away from daggers drawing. He'd be highly suspicious of my sudden desire for his company."

Jack's face fell. "You're right. We'll have to think of something else."

"No, your plan will work," Marcus murmured, "if I am the one to search his rooms and you are the one to keep him safely occupied."

Jack didn't like it, but after several minutes of persuasive argument from Marcus he agreed.

They parted for the night and, after bidding Jack good night, as Marcus walked down the hall toward his bedroom, he marveled at himself. Had he just agreed to sneak about like a thief in the night and pilfer through another man's belongings? By Jove, he had! And he was looking forward to it.

Isabel could find little to look forward to these days. Edmund and Lord Manning could talk of nothing else but the wedding and, when she wasn't being bombarded by their questions, Marcus was demanding she name a date for the wedding. Feeling as if pursued by wolves, she thanked God that many of their neighbors and friends were still in London and she hadn't had to endure the inquiries from every lady of consequence in the neighborhood. Despite the lure of the Season there were still several local families that did not make the annual trek to town and she'd had to face the interested queries from several bright-eyed ladies about her sudden engagement to one of the most eligible bachelors in the area. Like a flock of twittering birds they milled around her asking question after question that she could not answer. And Marcus! He'd waylaid her more than once these past days pushing her to name a definite date.

Feeling hunted, she found herself escaping more and more often to her rooms, telling the butler to inform *any* callers that she was not at home. Her gaze fell to the scrap of paper she held in her hand that had been delivered by a footman just a few minutes ago. And now, she thought on the verge of hysteria, Whitley was demanding she meet him after dark two nights from now at the gazebo near the lake that divided the three estates.

Had it been such a short time ago, she wondered forlornly, that her world had been turned topsy-turvy? A wave of incredulity swept over her. She was engaged to Marcus Sherbrook! How in the world had she allowed that to happen? That damn Whitley!

She sighed, staring sightlessly at the note in her lap. It was unfair to blame Whitley; he couldn't help being a weasel and a scoundrel: this was all her fault. If she'd boxed his ears and sent him away that day in the garden none of this would have happened, but she'd allowed herself to panic and look where it had led: to the brink of disaster. Panic rose up in her throat nearly choking her, but she fought it back. She'd find a way. She had to.

Isabel stared hard at the note from Whitley, rage billowing up inside of her. She would not, she swore fiercely, let that wicked rascal beat her. Crumpling the note in her hand, imagining it was Whitley's neck, she jumped to her feet. She didn't know how she was going to handle her impending marriage to Marcus, but she could do something about Whitley and the threat he represented. In the note, Whitley implied he had proof to back up his threat, but she knew that was impossible. She and Hugh had been so careful. . . . But Whitley was a sly manipulator and, while he might not have proof, he could have some item, some *thing* that might cause speculation—and she dare not let him bring it forth.

Her mind made up to thwart Whitley and his plans, she started to throw the crumpled note into the fireplace to be burned the next time a fire was lit. Thinking better of it, she carefully, meticulously tore the note into tiny pieces before tossing them onto the hearth. Watching the pieces of paper flutter to the marble hearth, her jaw tightened. She'd beat Whitley at his own game. Some way.

Telling Barbara that he and Jack had plans, Marcus rode away from Sherbrook Hall with his cousin after dinner on Thursday evening. Along the ride to the Stag Horn they discussed their plan for Marcus to search Whitley's room. Jack still wasn't entirely comfortable with it, but he agreed that Whitley would certainly be suspicious of being approached by a suddenly affable Marcus. They were both aware that there were several problems with their current plan. Fortunately one major problem had been solved: they knew which room Whitley was renting at the inn and they had Jack's valet to thank for it. Marcus had first suggested that they send one of the stable boys to ask around about the major's lodgings, but neither man had liked that plan. Then Jack had hit upon using his valet. Fickett, a little gnome of a man, had been Jack's batman for years in the military and had loyally followed him out of the service. He suited Jack's needs, and as Jack had told Marcus, "I would trust him with my life, and more important, he can keep his bone box shut." That was good enough for Marcus, and Fickett had been sent to the Stag Horn the previous night to learn what he could. He came back with the news that the major was not a popular figure at the inn and that he was renting the best suite of rooms situated at the rear of the inn, specifically the northeast corner.

Knowing precisely which room Marcus had to break into was helpful, but they had no way of knowing where Whitley would be that night: he might be out carousing through the village, or worse, he might have retired early, either by himself or with a wench. But if they were lucky and Jack found Whitley at the inn, how was Jack to let Marcus know if he had engaged Whitley in conversation and could keep the major occupied while Marcus explored his room at the inn?

"It seems to me," Marcus said after a bit, "that the simplest solution is for me to wait hidden outside. If he's not there, you'll come out and tell me and we can decide what to do from there. I'll wait fifteen, twenty minutes after you go inside, and if you don't return, I'll assume you've engaged Whitley's attention and I'll set about getting into his rooms."

Their plan set they arrived at the inn. Jack went inside and, when he did not return after several minutes, Marcus took a deep breath and from his hiding place near the inn's stables crept around to the back of the inn. Fortunately, the back corner of the inn was covered in ivy and, using the heavy vines, Marcus quickly scaled the building and shortly found a partially opened window and silently slid inside.

Elated with his success and feeling rather dashing, Marcus immediately set about searching Whitley's rooms. Using only the light of one small candle he moved around the rooms, poking and prying. Beyond the normal places for Marcus to search, Jack had given him a few other places to look, but he found no false boot heels or bottom in Whitley's valises.

Aware that he had only a limited time, Marcus looked in those places first but found no hidden compartments anywhere. In fact, having made a thorough search of the major's belongings, careful to leave no signs of his actions, he found nothing out of the ordinary. The major was inclined toward the dandy set if the amount of starched cravats, fobs, seals, jewelry, and the three different quizzing glasses, each with a different styled handle, he found was any indication. There was also a pair of pale yellow pantaloons and a cherry-striped waistcoat that made Marcus wince when he spied them in the candlelight.

Dispirited but not willing to accept defeat, Marcus turned his attention to the major's bed. Despite a cautious inspection of the pillows and bedding, he found nothing of interest. On the point of leaving, he considered the bed one more time. He'd searched the bed itself, but what about *underneath* the bed?

Ignoring the sensation of foolishness, he knelt down and,

using his candle, looked beneath the bed. In the candlelight his astonished gaze spied a small boyish figure curled under the bed. Shadows danced over a face he would recognize anywhere.

"*Isabel?*" he croaked.

Chapter 7

"Marcus!" she exclaimed, her eyes widening in shock as she realized the grim-faced man staring at her in the flickering light was her fiancé. "What are you doing here?" she demanded, wiggling out from beneath the bed.

"I think," Marcus said dryly, having made way for her to crawl out from her hiding place, "that is my question."

Standing up, he helped her to her feet. If he had not known her so well, he would have thought he faced a boy. Hiding her red hair beneath a boy's cap and wearing a masculine jacket that had seen better days and a worn pair of breeches and scuffed boots, she could have easily passed for a youth of twenty.

Not meeting his gaze, head down, she swiped at the smears of dust that marred the front of her jacket and breeches, her thoughts jumbled. How, she wondered desperately, was she ever going to explain this? There simply was no explanation, at least no reasonable explanation, she decided glumly. She risked a glance at him and asked, "How did you find me?" Something occurred to her and her eyes narrowed and accusingly, she questioned, "Did you follow me?"

His expression hard and distant, Marcus said softly, "That horse won't run, my sweet. There are any number of reasons why I might be here, none of them, I'll admit, reflecting admirably on me, but your position is far more invidious. I've just found my betrothed hiding in the bedroom of a man she claims to not like very much." His gaze cool, he said, "I think I'm owed an explanation."

A burst of laughter from below reminded both of them where they were and, almost as one, they moved toward the open window.

"This isn't the place for the conversation we need to have," Marcus said as they stood side by side at the window, "but believe me, Isabel, we *will* have it."

Throwing one leg over the sill and blowing out the candle, Marcus said, "If you don't mind, I'll go first." Bluntly he added, "I don't trust you not to run away the moment your feet hit the ground."

Isabel flushed in the darkness since that very thought had crossed her mind. Accepting defeat, she gave a quick nod of her head. Frowning, she watched him slide lithely from the window and disappear into the darkness below. The dangerous-looking man she had confronted tonight was not the Marcus she had known all her life. From her position beneath the bed, hearing the sounds of movement, she'd known that whoever had entered Whitley's room through the window, the same one she had used only fifteen minutes previously, had made a thorough search of the room. She couldn't be certain, but she didn't think the person found whatever had prompted the search in the first place. Had he been after the same thing she had? But how could that be? Even she didn't know what it was she was looking for, so how could the as-yet-unknown person know what it was? Knowing now that the stranger was actually Marcus, she concluded that it would be too coincidental to believe that he had been searching for the same thing she had and she dismissed that thought. It was also clear that he hadn't been looking for her; he had been as shocked as she had been when they recognized each other. So why had that paragon of respectability, the darling of every parent with an eligible daughter, the highly regarded Mr. Marcus Sherbrook, been sneaking about in the dark, pilfering another man's belongings? The Marcus she knew would never have done anything so . . . so . . . impolite, she thought with a half-hysterical giggle as she followed him out the window.

Marcus was waiting for her, his hands closing around her waist before her feet hit the ground. Effortlessly lifting her away from the building, he set her down in front of him.

Keeping a firm hold on her, he jerked his head toward a small copse of woods that lay behind the inn's stables. "My horse is tied over there," he said quietly. "Where is yours?"

She looked over her shoulder in the opposite direction. "I left mine tethered behind old Mrs. Simpson's place just down the road."

With one powerful hand now manacling Isabel's wrist, Marcus headed toward the copse of woods where his horse waited, dragging her along behind him. "Fine. We'll go pick up your horse right now."

Isabel had learned a long time ago that there are some fights one can win and some one can't. This was one of those fights that she couldn't win, and so she meekly followed his lead, making no effort to escape. They reached his horse and, after untying the animal and mounting, he pulled her up in front of him.

They were silent as he guided the animal through the darkness, skirting the inn and riding to Mrs. Simpson's small cottage. The hour was late enough that the cottage was in darkness. There was no cause for alarm when Isabel's horse nickered softly as they approached and Marcus's horse replied: Mrs. Simpson was deaf as a post.

Once Isabel was mounted, Marcus prudently took the reins of her horse and, leading the animal, urged his horse back toward the inn.

"Where are you going?" Isabel hissed. "This is the wrong way."

"There's someone else with me," Marcus muttered over his shoulder. "I have to wait for him."

Marcus considered just leaving his cousin to his own devices and riding to Manning Court with Isabel, confident Jack could fend for himself. The fewer people who knew of tonight's debacle the better, but he balked at abandoning Jack without a word. His mouth twisted. He could hardly send Jack a note informing him of a sudden change in plans, nor could he risk Jack looking for him. Once Jack quitted the inn and didn't find him waiting, he would no doubt start looking for him in the last place he was known to be—Whitley's room. Marcus couldn't let that happen; it was too dangerous. He had no choice but to wait for Jack . . . which left him with Isabel. The last thing he wanted to do was to introduce Jack to Isabel under these circumstances, but postponing the frank conversation he had in mind by allowing her to blithely ride off to Manning Court—unescorted, he reminded himself—didn't seem like a good option either. And then there was Jack. . . . Jack would be eager for news of what he had discovered in Whitley's room, just as he was eager to find out if Jack had learned anything useful from Whitley. Neither topic was for the ears of Mrs. Manning. The exchange of information could be delayed until they reached Sherbrook Hall—which would be, he admitted, sighing, after he escorted his fiancée home and returned to the house a great deal later. Marcus made a face, not thinking much of *that* option.

He was, he conceded sourly, caught on the horns of a dilemma. The more he considered it, the more his mind boggled at the explanation he would have to give Jack to account for Isabel's presence—even if he bypassed finding her hidden under the bed in Whitley's room, not to mention the reason she was dressed as a youth! What possible reason could he give for any of it? He didn't even have an explanation for her actions himself yet, and he wouldn't get an explanation until he had the time to speak alone and at length with Mrs. Isabel

Manning, something that wouldn't happen in the short period before Jack joined them.

While the need to know *why* she had been in Whitley's room ate like acid in his belly, he realized that it might be simpler to postpone the confrontation with Isabel and send her on her way before Jack rejoined him. Which created another problem for him, and he struggled against the notion of her riding alone in the darkness to Manning Court. Even without the Whitley situation, every protective instinct he possessed was aghast at the idea of a gently reared woman riding unescorted through the night—and never mind that she had done just that to get here. Having her and Jack meet under these conditions was equally ghastly, and he couldn't decide which of his not very pleasant choices would be best.

Riding into the copse of trees at the rear of the stables, Marcus turned the problem over and over in his mind. He had come up with no solution when he halted their horses near where his horse had originally been tied. Marcus didn't like it, but it appeared that Isabel and Jack were going to meet tonight, unless he could think of some other way out of his dilemma. Turning to Isabel, he said, "We'll wait here. He shouldn't be much longer."

"Who are we waiting for?" she asked, curiosity evident.

"My cousin Jack."

She studied his big form barely visible in the darkness. It was devastating enough that Marcus had found her in Whitley's bedroom; the thought of someone else, a stranger, learning of it filled her with dismay. "Er, are you sure that's wise?" she mumbled. "I don't want anyone else to know about tonight, not even your cousin."

"No, it's probably not wise," he snapped, "but I don't have much choice. And I'm no more happy with having you meet Jack this way than you are." Thinking of all the complications before him, a strong sense of injustice overtook him. Finding Isabel hiding beneath Whitley's bed had been a direct hit between the eyes. Why had she been there? Why garbed as a boy? Was it because of some kind of perversion practiced by Whitley? His stomach lurched at the thought and bile rose in his throat. He took a deep breath, willing himself to think calmly. The hiding he could understand; if he'd been there and had heard someone else climb in through the window, he'd have hidden beneath the bed himself. There might be a reasonable explanation for all of it—none of which, he was convinced, he would like—but try as he might, he could only think of one reason that Isabel had been hiding in Whitley's room. Jealous rage clawed at his guts and he slewed around in his saddle and glared at her. "Are you and Whitley lovers?" he demanded.

Isabel stiffened. "How dare you!" she exclaimed, furious that he would even think such a thing. Her chin at a pugnacious angle, she added hotly, "You are insulting and presumptuous."

"You're my fiancée and I have just found you in another man's bedroom," Marcus said acidly. "I think I'm owed an explanation."

"What do you think I was doing there?" she taunted, too angry to watch her words. "Suppose I was there to meet Whitley? Suppose we are lovers? What are you going to do about it?" Hating herself for acting this way, she forced a nasty smile on her lips and murmured, "You realize, of course, that if you don't like the situation, you can call off the engagement."

"Oh, you'd like that, wouldn't you?"

"Indeed! I never wanted to marry you in the first place."

Riled beyond patience, he astonished both of them by grabbing Isabel and jerking her off her horse and onto his. Breathing heavily, holding her squirming body prisoner across the saddle in front of him, he snarled, "You listen to me, woman: you're mine! I'll not share you and, by God, we *shall* be married!" His mouth came down hard on hers and his lips crushed hers as he stamped his possession on her startled mouth.

This was no sweet kiss between gentle lovers; it was angry and desperate and full of a dark passion that overrode all thought. Marcus kissed her as he had never kissed another woman in his life, demanding that she respond, that she feel the same primitive emotions that lacerated his very being. And she did. After that first stunned second, Isabel no longer sought to escape; she strained against him, her lips as hungry and insistent as his, her hands clutching his shoulders as if she would never let him go. She wanted this. She wanted *him*.

Blind with need, Marcus lost himself in the wine-sweet intoxication of her mouth, kissing her again and again, heedless of anything but the woman in his arms and her wild response to him. His hand slipped to her breast and he cupped that small weight, urgent desire flaring through him at Isabel's soft moan of pleasure.

The snort and sudden upraised head of his horse ended the moment as if it had never been. Recalled to his senses, Marcus dragged his mouth from Isabel's and peered through the darkness. Someone was coming.

Cursing himself, wondering where his wits had gone, he swung Isabel back onto her horse. In the broken light of the moon through the trees, one swift glance revealed that her boy's hat was wildly askew, strands of her hair tumbling from beneath it to frame her features. She was as aroused as he, her eyes full of sultry promise and her mouth half parted as if waiting for his kiss. Breathing hard they stared at each other, desire swirling thick in the air between them, and it gave Marcus some comfort to know that it was not all on his part.

The recognizable clink of a bridle nearby jerked his attention away from Isabel and he looked in the direction of the sound, trying to focus his thoughts. A soft whistle carried on the night air and he recognized it as the one he and Jack had agreed upon before they had parted. The person slowly riding toward him through the trees was Jack. How in the devil, he wondered, was he going to explain Isabel to Jack? He smiled grimly. Devil take it! If Jack looked askance at Isabel or breathed a word of tonight, he'd probably just have to shoot him—and he'd really hate to do that.

Aware that Marcus's attention was elsewhere, Isabel glanced around, desperately hoping that a way out of this dilemma would present itself. She gasped when she spied the dangling reins of her horse. During their violent embrace the reins had fallen unheeded to the ground and, recovering her senses, her heart banging in her chest, she leaned forward and recaptured them. Her thoughts raced as she considered her next move. She wasn't a coward and generally didn't care about the finer nuances of the dictates of the *ton*, but even she saw no good coming from meeting Marcus's cousin while she was dressed as a boy and apparently out larking through the countryside alone after dark. There were too many questions that needed answering, questions she couldn't answer. Gathering her courage, gulping in a deep breath, she kicked her mount into motion. The animal gave a startled leap and, with Isabel's heels digging into its sides, the horse plunged through the trees. Breaking free of the woods, Isabel pushed her horse into a blazing pace and, by the time the road was reached, the animal was in a full gallop, mane and tail streaming in the air. In moments, the stables, the inn, and Marcus were left behind, and the only sounds she heard were the thudding of her horse's hooves on the road and the frantic beating of her heart.

Swearing under his breath, Marcus gave chase and his horse lunged forward, but almost immediately he realized that catching Isabel was only going to create more problems and, though it went badly against the grain, he jerked his horse and let her escape. Blast her! She'd won this time, he thought angrily, but by heaven the next round would be his.

Jack appeared out of the darkness. He hadn't missed the noise of the departing horse and, cautiously approaching Marcus, he glanced in the direction of the fading sound and murmured, "Trouble?"

Marcus's jaw clenched. "Nothing I can't handle," he muttered.

Jack's brow rose, but he said nothing as he brought his horse alongside. Together they guided their mounts to the road and Jack asked, "You find anything interesting?"

Marcus shook his head, disappointment leaking into his voice. "Not a damn thing. And before you ask, yes, I looked at his boot heels and for a false bottom in his valise, but I found nothing." Grimacing, he added, "The man owns a remarkable amount of jewelry; he has enough fobs and seals and quizzing glasses to open a shop on Bond Street. Sees himself as a bit of a dandy, but beyond that, there was nothing in his room that you wouldn't expect to find." Remembering that astounding moment when he'd discovered Isabel beneath the bed, he muttered, "And I looked everywhere—even under the bed—and believe me, I found nothing I was looking for!"

Jack stared between the ears of his horse, disheartened that Marcus hadn't found the memorandum or at least a clue of some sort. He'd known that his task wouldn't be easy and the odds were against them finding the memorandum so easily. But where, he wondered, had Whitley hidden it? His lips quirked. Assuming that Whitley had the dashed thing. It worried him that this might be a sleeveless errand and that Whitley was guilty of nothing more than being an unsavory society hanger-on.

"I assume that you found Whitley?" Marcus asked, interrupting Jack's ruminations.

Jack nodded. "Had a bit of scare, though; he wasn't present when I first arrived, and I was on the point of bolting to find you when he walked inside." Jack looked thoughtful. "Our friend the major was in a decidedly foul mood when he arrived. I gather he'd been gone to an assignation that did not go well. He made some ugly comments about the perfidy of women in general and especially the prime article that failed to keep the, er, appointment. I pity the absent ladylove when he eventually catches up with her—as he no doubt will."

Marcus had a very good idea of the lady's identity and, wishing to change the topic, he asked, "I take it, then, that you had no trouble making yourself agreeable to Whitley?"

Jack laughed. "Whitley wasn't quiet about his dashed hopes for the evening and I didn't have any difficulties in helping him drown his sorrows in several mugs of ale." Jack frowned. "Thing is, I don't think that Whitley's meeting tonight had anything to do with matters of the heart. He didn't give the impression of a man in the throes of thwarted passion. I could be wrong, but there was a note in his voice . . ." He shrugged. "Probably my imagination. At any rate, learning that I was your cousin, the major seemed quite interested in *you*, I might add."

Marcus growled, "Impudent busybody."

"He is that," Jack agreed. "Whether he stole the memorandum or not, I discovered that I don't care overmuch for Major Whitley. He is a blustering bully and a braggart, as well as an impudent busybody." He shot Marcus a look. "I'd take damn care to keep Mrs. Manning well away from him; old friendship or not, he's not a fellow I'd want any wife of mine to know." His lips thinned. "*Any* woman for that matter. Fellow's a damned libertine, the kind that seduces housemaids and boasts of his conquests. Don't like him."

Marcus frowned. "You and I share the same opinion of him, and I wonder what Hugh was at, allowing a bounder like Whitley to run tame through his house—which, from what Isabel had indicated, is precisely what happened."

"Your betrothed seems to be surrounded by unsavory characters," Jack observed idly.

Marcus sent him a narrow look. "And what precisely do you mean by that?"

"The major," Jack said, "wasn't the only new friend I made

tonight. Whitley and I were drinking at a table by ourselves when another gentleman came up and joined us. Just returned from London this afternoon. Fellow's name is Garrett Manning, lives at a place called Holcombe Manor, claims it is not far from Manning Court. Says he's Lord Manning's nephew. That true?"

"Unfortunately, yes." Marcus sighed. "Garrett is not a *bad* man but he is a profligate womanizer and a reckless gambler—and believe me, Lord Manning gives thanks daily that it is his own grandson who will inherit the title and not his rakehell nephew." Marcus half smiled. "Nearly everyone is of the opinion that, should Garrett inherit the estate and title, he would immediately turn Manning Court into a gaming den and brothel." Marcus's brow furrowed. "I am surprised that he left London at the height of the Season, though. I wonder why?"

"Your engagement," Jack said, "is apparently the reason for his return. I couldn't decide whether the engagement was agreeable to Manning or not, but the news certainly brought him hotfoot home from the city." He glanced at Marcus. "I wonder why your engagement to Mrs. Manning interests him so much? It should make no difference to him."

Marcus stared ahead into the darkness. "Hugh did well during his years in India, amassing a respectable fortune, and Isabel is an heiress in her own right—not counting the fact that her father-in-law dotes on her and would do anything for her. It is possible that Garrett had his eye on Isabel's fortune and planned one day, when it suited him, to court her. Since she rarely goes to London and is considered on the shelf, he probably assumed that she was his for the taking—when he got around to it."

Jack sent him a look. "He didn't, uh, consider you competition?"

Marcus grinned. "No, I'm sure he didn't. My fiancée and I have a rather tempestuous history and I am the *last* man Garrett would expect Isabel to marry."

Jack looked as if he'd like to ask more questions, but the subject was dropped and the two men turned to a discussion of tonight's activities. Arriving at Sherbrook Hall, they left their horses at the stables and walked to the house. Inside, they made their way to Marcus's office.

After poking the dying fire into life, Marcus threw on more wood and poured them each a brandy. They settled themselves before the fireplace, both contemplating the orange and scarlet flames in silence for several seconds.

"Perhaps Whitley does not have the memorandum," Marcus said eventually.

Jack shrugged. "That has already occurred to me, but it is telling that he departed London the very next day after his visit to the Horse Guards for a part of England where smugglers are known to be quite active."

Marcus snorted. "Which, I would remind you, includes nearly half the coast of England. But you are correct: we do have our share of smugglers, although I would have thought that Kent or Sussex would have been better for his purposes."

"I agree, but if he is trying to throw us off the scent, Devonshire, while known to be a smuggler haunt, isn't quite as obvious a location."

Marcus nodded. "And his professed longtime friendship with Mrs. Manning would make the destination seem logical." Silence fell for a few minutes before Marcus asked, "So what is our next step?"

Jack looked disgusted. "I don't know, but if he has the memorandum, he has to have it stashed away somewhere nearby. If he is planning on making a run for French-held territory, he'd want it close at hand. I can't imagine that he'd have left it in London." He cast a considering glance to Marcus. "Are you positive you searched everywhere in his room tonight?"

"Yes, I'm positive," Marcus said dryly. He'd heard the note of doubt in Jack's voice and didn't blame him; if their positions were reversed, he'd be doubtful, too. And would want to inspect Whitley's room himself. Marcus studied Jack and could almost see his brain turning over ways to get inside Whitley's room to make his own search. Wryly, he asked, "You're going to take a look yourself, aren't you?"

Jack had the grace to look guilty. "It isn't that I doubt you. . . ."

"You won't find anything," Marcus said. "And, in the interest of fair play, this time I'll run interference for you with Whitley and keep him at bay while you're busy in his room."

"Thank you," Jack said, grateful that Marcus hadn't cut up rough at having his thoroughness questioned or of having a second search done. Having Marcus keep Whitley distracted while he went through Whitley's things was another boon, but then he recalled the reason Marcus had been the one to search Whitley's room in the first place. "Won't he be suspicious of friendliness from you?" he asked. "You said your only meeting with him was not friendly."

"I said I would run interference," Marcus remarked dryly. "I didn't say I would be friendly."

Aware of Isabel's habits, Marcus was waiting for her just after seven o'clock the next morning on the narrow bridle path that ran between the two properties. As he waited for her, he realized that he knew far too much about her life and habits than the disinterested party he had believed himself to be should have known. It was, he admitted uneasily, as if a part of him, a part buried deep inside and unacknowledged until now, had always been keenly focused on her, always aware of her even as he kept his distance.

Riding a fractious black colt, Isabel came into sight and, thrusting his uncomfortable ruminations away, he urged his horse forward.

Isabel was so busy convincing the young horse she was riding that it would be impolite to unseat her that she wasn't aware of Marcus's approach until the colt stopped and half reared at the sight of another horse. She fought to bring the black under control and, once that was accomplished and the colt was content merely to dance and snort, she sent Marcus a wary glance.

"I'm surprised to see you out and about so early this morning," she said politely, ignoring the jolt of half pleasure, half panic his presence caused.

"You shouldn't be surprised," he said levelly. "I believe we have something to discuss."

She'd lain awake half the night trying to come up with a logical reason for being in Whitley's room but absolutely nothing occurred to her. Dreading the next meeting with Marcus, she had hoped to postpone the confrontation with him for as long as she could and intended to keep well away from him. He had, she thought miserably, just put paid to that frail plan.

She tried to rouse a healthy anger, tried to tell herself that it was none of his business and she didn't have to tell him anything at all, but even anger failed her this morning. The strain of dealing with the threat Whitley represented, the amount of dogged courage it had taken for her to climb into his room, and the terror she experienced when Marcus had found her had all taken their toll. Exhausted from a restless night, frightened of Whitley and what he might do, she felt as helpless as she ever had in her life. Not even in the horrible days after Hugh's death, alone in a foreign country with her very young son dependent upon her to bring them safely home, had she felt so alone and vulnerable. She was, she admitted, at her lowest ebb. And like an avenging god, Marcus was waiting for answers she could not give . . . dared not give.

She cast him a quick glance from beneath her lashes, her heart quaking just a little at the sight of those cool gray eyes and taut mouth. She knew that expression of old and she knew that he would not be dissuaded from his chosen path.

Her spirits sagged. Until she told him why he had found her in Whitley's rooms he would be relentless in his demand for an explanation. *And he deserves an explanation,* she admitted fairly . . . *but I have none to give him.*

Unaware that Isabel's expression reflected her inner turmoil, Marcus fought against the insidious urge to comfort her, to let matters rest. He knew in his very bones that, whatever her reasons for being in Whitley's room, they were of monumental importance to her and it had only been jealous rage that had prompted his accusation last night. His knowledge of her and some quiet reflection dictated that Isabel and Whitley were not lovers, but she was clearly, desperately unhappy . . . and frightened. The fright more than anything disturbed him. Isabel could be stubborn, infuriating, and utterly maddening, but she was no coward. He never questioned that unarmed and alone she'd face a pack of ravenous wolves defiant and unafraid, ready to fight to the death. Yet she was frightened now; something, someone had frightened her. Though he tried to hold onto it, the last remnants of his temper faded and a fierce desire to destroy whoever had caused that look in her eyes overrode every other emotion. *Except that of comfort,* he thought ruefully. At the moment his arms ached to hold her and he wanted to let her know that whatever lay in front of her, she was not alone.

Furious with himself that she could so easily distract him from his purpose, he growled, "I'm waiting, Isabel. Why were you in Whitley's room last night?"

His tone of voice brought her chin up and she said angrily, "May I remind you that I am no longer your ward? Do not speak to me as if I am an erring child."

"I have not," Marcus said, "thought of you as my ward— or a child—for a very long time." He brought his horse alongside the now-quiet colt and touched her lightly on the arm. Softly, he coaxed, "Isabel, sooner or later you're going to have to tell me." When she remained silent, he said, "Sweetheart, whatever it is, it can't be so very bad that together we can't fix it. Surely you have done nothing so shameful that you cannot tell me."

She stared stonily ahead, fighting the urge to burst into silly, feminine tears at the kindness in his voice. Damn him! Why couldn't he rage and rail at her like any other decent man would have when confronted with the situation he had found last night. But, oh, no, she thought dispiritedly, he had to be *understanding*, undercutting her defenses and making it so much harder to resist his persistence. She wanted to cast herself on that formidable chest of his and pour out everything, knowing that while he might be shocked and appalled, perhaps even disappointed, he would not abandon her. For a moment, she was comforted by that knowledge, but then she took a deep breath and pushed aside the treacherous emotions that threatened to swamp her. Her jaw firmed. For his own good, she could not involve him any more than he already was, but she also knew that he would not give up until he had at least some of the answers. She half smiled. Stubborn didn't even begin to describe Marcus Sherbrook. He would keep at her until she told him something. Could she tell him why she had been in Whitley's room without creating more problems? Did she dare?

She looked at him, her eyes meeting his. His gaze met hers steadily. It was all a matter of trust, she thought painfully, and there was no one she trusted more than Marcus—even if he was pig-headed stubborn.

Before she could change her mind, she leaned forward and said swiftly, "You must understand: Whitley is no friend of mine. He means me harm."

Something dark and dangerous moved at the back of Marcus's eyes, making Isabel glad that she was not the one who caused that expression. "I figured that part out myself," he said coolly.

"He has something of mine," she blurted out. "I went to his room last night to find it."

"Did you?"

She grimaced. "No, you came climbing in the window before I had been there much more than fifteen minutes and I had to scramble beneath the bed."

He nodded as if her words confirmed something he already knew. "What does he have? And how can it harm you?"

She raised troubled eyes to his. "I don't know," she said miserably. "I don't know what it is or how he intends to use it against me. I only know he has something and he claims that this something is a weapon that could destroy me."

Marcus studied her for a long moment. "Well, then," he said briskly, "we shall just have to take it away from him, won't we?"

Chapter 8

Isabel gaped at him. Torn between tears and laughter, she exclaimed, "And that's all you have to say? 'We'll get it from him?' Aren't you going to demand any answers from me?"

He glanced at her, a glimmer of a smile in the gray eyes. "Would you answer?"

She looked away. "I can't," she replied in a small voice. She glanced back at him, her expression woeful. "Oh, but Marcus, if I could . . . if there was anybody I could trust not to . . ." She swallowed and sent him a wobbly smile. "If I could tell anybody, it would be you."

"Thank you," he said gravely. He gave her a searching glance. "I trust someday that you will tell me."

Sighing, she nodded. "Yes, someday."

Though it went against the grain, with that he had to be content. Looking thoughtful, he asked, "Can you hazard a guess what it is that Whitley has? An indiscreet letter? A diary? What?"

"I've never kept a diary in my life." Ruefully, she asked, "Remember how my aunt used to nag me to do so? She said it would help change my writing from chicken scratchings into something a normal person could read. Believe me, it isn't a diary written by me." For a moment a pang of fear clenched her heart and she paled. But what of Hugh? she wondered frantically. Had he kept a diary? She cast her thoughts back to the days of her marriage. No, she would have known if he had. Hugh had not been the sort to keep a diary either, she reminded herself; he had been too busy keeping the accounts of the East India Company in order to waste any spare time on scribbling about the mundane events of his day. The notion of a letter held her attention for a second, but then she dismissed it. No, it could not be a letter.

She gathered herself together and confessed, "I cannot imagine what he has, or *thinks* he has; he has been very careful not to tell me anything that would help identify it." She bit her lip. "His note to me yesterday only stated that he had something of mine that, for a price, he would return. There was no hint what this item was, only that he had it and that"—she took a deep breath—"it would be in my best interests to have it back."

Frustrated by her unwillingness to trust him, he muttered, "Well, that's certainly helpful!" He glanced at her. "Perhaps he has nothing. Perhaps he is just bluffing."

"I've thought of that," she admitted. "But I dare not take the chance."

"And you're very certain you will not tell me what it is that allows him to make threats against you?" he demanded, his gaze intent upon her face.

Isabel shook her head. "Not until I have no other choice." Her expression imploring him to understand, she conceded, "I know I am being impossible, but . . ." She looked down at her hands holding the reins of her horse. "I cannot. I am sorry."

"Very well," he said disgustedly, "you won't tell me. So let us consider what I do know. You don't believe that it is a letter or anything in writing that he holds over your head. What do you think it is?"

"I don't know," she wailed. "I don't see how—" She stopped

short. Bitterly she said, "I simply cannot take the chance that he is bluffing."

"Then we shall assume that he is not bluffing." Marcus frowned, turning over things in his mind. "You were to meet him last night . . . where?"

Uneasily, she said, "He's obviously made himself familiar with the area because he wanted me to meet him at the gazebo by the lake." Wryly, she added, "I had no intention of meeting him and, knowing he would be away from the inn, I took the opportunity to search his room. I didn't know you would be doing the same thing." She paused as if struck by something for the first time and her eyes narrowed. "What were *you* doing there? You never said."

"And I don't intend to," he replied imperturbably. "My reasons have nothing to do with you or your problem." Grinning at her expression of outrage, he added smugly, "If you can keep secrets, so can I."

Blocked and not liking it, Isabel stared hard at the space between her horse's ears. She wanted to argue with Marcus, but she couldn't fault his words. But why, she wondered, had he been searching Whitley's room? Dismay smote her and she asked in a faltering tone, "He isn't blackmailing you, too, is he?"

Marcus laughed. "No, my sweet, he is not blackmailing me. I am too staid a fellow for someone like Whitley to know something about me that cannot stand the light of day. Now forget about my presence in his room last night and let us concentrate on your situation. I assume you have not yet heard from him again?" At her nod, he went on, "We can assume that he is not simply going to give up and go away. And we can be sure that he will contact you again." He looked at her. "You and Lord Manning are attending Mother's dinner party tonight?"

"To meet your cousin Jack," she said wryly. "The gentleman who was with you last night."

"You'll like Jack," he said, smiling. "And by then I shall have thought of some way to pull Whitley's fangs. In the meantime . . ." His smile faded and his face took on hard lines. "In the meantime, if you hear or see anything of our friend the major, you are to send a servant to fetch me immediately." He pinched her chin. "Without fail, Isabel. Without fail."

"Now why, I wonder, do I feel as if I am your ward again?" she asked of no one in particular.

He pulled her close, his mouth brushing tantalizingly across hers. "I'm very happy you are no longer my ward," he said huskily, "because if you were I could not do *this.*"

His lips caught hers and he kissed her deeply, tasting, savoring her increasingly addictive flavor as his mouth moved hungrily over hers. When he raised his head, they were both struggling for breath and her gaze was dazed and unfocused and his own was dark and full of desire.

The colt, which had behaved nicely until this moment, took exception to the nearness of Marcus's horse and suddenly cavorted off to the side of the bridle path. Recalled to her senses, Isabel automatically brought the youngster under control and the moment was lost. Ignoring the emotions still vibrating through her, she told herself that she was glad the embrace had ended. Glad that he was no longer kissing her, glad that his touch was no longer urging her to surrender. Very glad.

His eyes locked on her mouth, his body aching for more than a mere kiss, Marcus fought against his baser desires. He was not, he told himself doggedly, going to drag Isabel off her horse and indulge himself like a rutting boar. And, he thought suddenly with a grin, she'd most likely bloody my nose if I dared such a thing. Feeling more like himself and less like a lovesick moonling, he tipped his head in her direction and said, "Unless I hear differently, I shall see you tonight at Sherbrook Hall."

She nodded and, fearing and longing to be in his arms again, to feel those warm lips against hers again, she jerked the colt around and disappeared down the bridle path.

Since the Season was well under way, the dinner party to introduce Jack to the neighborhood was smaller than it would have been at any other time of the year, but that suited Marcus and Jack just fine. Having left the arrangements in his mother's capable hands—as if she would have let him have any say in the matter—returning home, Marcus bore Jack off to his office and they spent an agreeable time solidifying their growing friendship. Naturally, a large part of the time they spent together was taken up with speculation about Whitley and where he might have concealed the memorandum he'd presumably stolen from the Horse Guards. They also discussed how soon Jack could do a search of Whitley's rooms and convince himself that Marcus had not overlooked anything.

Having a fair idea how late his mother's dinner party would run, Marcus said, "I suggest we strike tonight, after the guests depart. Most of the people you will meet tonight are not the sort to remain late; the younger, livelier set is in London for now. I suspect we will have bid the last of our guests good night by midnight—if not before." He shot Jack a derisive glance. "Once you have allayed your suspicions that I did not overlook the memorandum last night, the sooner we can turn our minds to other things—such as where he might keep the memorandum."

"You're taking my lack of faith in you remarkably well," Jack commented.

Marcus shrugged. "Searching the room of a suspected spy is not something I can claim to be expert in and, while faint, the possibility does exist that I may have missed some vital clue. Considering the importance of what we are looking for, it would be foolhardy *not* to have other, more . . . experienced eyes take a second glance."

Jack nodded. "So how are you going to keep Whitley oc-cupied?"

Marcus smiled and something in that smile made Jack happy that he was not Major Whitley. "Oh, I have plans for Whitley," Marcus said. "Don't you worry about the major. I intend to keep him well away from the inn for quite a while; you will be able to search his room at your leisure."

The dinner party went smoothly and, though his mind was on other things, Marcus enjoyed himself—especially watching Isabel's expressive little face as toast after toast was offered to them and questions about their nuptials abounded. Isabel stammered and stuttered through most of the friendly interrogation and from time to time, Marcus took pity on her, deftly stepping in whenever she cast him a desperate glance. Everyone thought her manner charming and just as a bride-to-be should act, but Marcus wondered if he was the only one who saw that the coming marriage did not bring her great joy.

Several of the usual people were there: Lord Manning, Sir James and Lady Agatha, and Mrs. Appleton, along with a last-minute guest, her brother, Bishop Latimer—who had arrived unexpectedly that afternoon for a brief visit and had been hastily included in the invitation—to name a few. There was one person, however, whose attendance gave him pause. Having learned of his unexpected return to the neighborhood, Garrett Manning, Manning's nephew, was a last-minute addition to his mother's guest list and Marcus wasn't certain whether he was pleased or not to have the man sitting at his table.

Beyond his height and very blue eyes, Garrett bore scant resemblance to his uncle and the Manning family as a rule. Most of the Mannings were blond and fair skinned, but Garrett's coloring was dark, his complexion almost swarthy, and his hair as black as Marcus's own and, while charming, he did not exude the warmth and amiability that came so naturally to Lord Manning. There was a watchfulness about him and an air of dissipation that, oddly enough, enhanced his already handsome features. The wink of a small diamond stud in his right ear only added to the rakish air that hung around his elegant frame. As a gentleman with which to spend a pleasant evening gambling and drinking or to visit with at Tattersall's or other manly places of interest, Marcus could think of no one better. He smiled. Except, he admitted, his cousin Charles, the Charles of those reckless days before his marriage to Daphne. Garrett reminded him of that Charles in many ways and, like Charles, Marcus even liked him . . . a bit.

Occasionally, when he could tear himself from Isabel's taking features, Marcus discreetly studied Garrett, wondering at his unexpected return, wondering at his sudden friendship with Whitley. Garrett didn't look like a man whose hopes had been cut up by Isabel's engagement and Marcus didn't see any signs of a thwarted suitor in him. His manner toward Isabel was everything it should be: polite and courteous with no excessive familiarity. Which is as well, Marcus thought idly, because I'd dislike drawing his claret.

Jack was a great hit with everyone. The ladies fluttered around him exclaiming over his bravery and the gentlemen peppered him with questions on his service and his opinion of the war with Napoleon. Jack was an excellent raconteur and was clever enough not to dominate the conversation.

As Marcus had predicated, shortly after eleven o'clock the coaches and carriages were being sent for and there was a general, leisurely exodus from Sherbrook Hall. There had been no time for private conversation, but when Lord Manning stopped to exchange a few words with Garrett on the steps of the house, Marcus, who was escorting Isabel to the Manning coach, murmured, "I presume you've heard nothing from Whitley?"

Isabel shook her head. "No." She frowned. "After I didn't meet him last night, I feared the arrival of another note today, demanding another meeting. But there has been nothing." She bit her lip. "It worries me."

Marcus nodded, as if her words confirmed something he already knew. "Don't fret over it, my dear," he said. "Remember, you're not alone in this any longer; you have me at your side, and I don't intend for Whitley or anyone else to destroy your peace of mind." His eyes hardened. "If he contacts you in any way let me know immediately."

"He isn't likely to just give up," she warned.

A wolfish grin crossed his face. "And neither will I."

Less than an hour later, the guests gone and Barbara having bid the two gentlemen good night and retired for the night, Marcus and Jack slipped from the house and hurried to the stables. After saddling their horses, they rode away.

Pulling up their horses a half-mile down the road for one last exchange before they went their separate ways, Jack asked, "How do you know he'll meet you?"

Marcus smiled without humor. "Because, as I told you, I sent him a note requesting his presence: he believes it is from the lady who was absent from their rendezvous last night."

Frowning, Jack studied him. Jack liked the idea of Whitley being well away from the inn when he crawled through the window into his room, but he was wary about certain aspects of Marcus's plan. How did Marcus know that Whitley hadn't made other plans with the mysteriously absent lady? The ability to write was not common among the sort of woman Whitley was most likely to be meeting, so how did Marcus even know the lady could put pen to paper? His gaze narrowed. There was, he concluded, a great deal that his cousin was not telling him. Marcus was playing another game and dashed if he could figure out what it was. Jack believed that any game involving Whitley was a dangerous one and he was troubled about this easygoing cousin of his confronting the man alone.

"It's a good plan—if all goes as we hope." Reluctantly, Jack admitted, "I don't know that I like the idea of you tackling him by yourself."

Marcus sent him a look. "Now *that* is insulting. It isn't enough that you doubt my ability to search his room; now you doubt that I am capable of dealing with a cowardly braggart?"

"It's not that," Jack said unhappily. "Whitley may be a weasel, but weasels have teeth and you've never dealt with someone like him."

"Oh, good gad!" Marcus exclaimed disgustedly. "You sound just like Julian and Charles—or my mother." Patiently, Marcus said, "I may not have led the adventuresome life that you have, or done some of the dangerous, reckless things that Julian and Charles have done, but I assure you that I can take care of Whitley. You just do your part and get to the Stag Horn and into Whitley's room. Don't worry about me." Something dark and fierce moved in his gray eyes. "Worry about Whitley, if you want something to worry about."

They parted, Jack riding in the direction of the inn and Marcus, taking a shortcut cross-country, heading toward the gazebo near the lake. Jack had the longer journey and it was less than ten minutes later that Marcus halted his horse and, after dismounting and tying the animal to a tree, from the cover of the trees carefully reconnoitered the area. He had chosen this place as much as because Whitley had named it in his original note to Isabel as the fact that he was very familiar with it. Taking one long, assessing look around, he decided that his choice had been wise.

Gleaming like glass in the moonlight, the large lake that separated the Manning estate and his own from that of Isabel's uncle spread out endlessly before him, the far edges melting raggedly into the darkness of the night. In front of him and some fifty feet back from the lake a small gazebo shimmered ghostly white. The lattice-sided building was flanked and dwarfed by two enormous stone-rimmed goldfish ponds and had been built many years ago as a gift from Lord Manning to his wife. Tall, three-tiered stone fountains graced the center of each pond, the sound of the cascading water whispering through the quiet night. During Lady Manning's lifetime the area had been the scene of many happy gatherings of family and friends but in these latter years it was seldom visited.

Marcus had deliberately arrived early, well before the two o'clock time he had written to Whitley, but he was still cautious in his approach to the gazebo. As he had expected, the place was deserted and, having satisfied himself that Whitley had not arrived early, he approached one of the fishponds and stared down into the black depths. The occasional flash of gold in the faint light revealed that Lady Manning's goldfish still thrived amongst the reeds and water lilies that threatened in some places to engulf the pond. The ponds were enclosed by a short stone wall and finished off with a wide flat rim used by the ladies to sit and feed the fish. His booted foot resting on the smooth rim of the pond, Marcus smiled. He wondered if the major liked water. He hoped not.

The gazebo and fishponds were located in an open area, and he knew that if he wanted the element of surprise, he would have to catch Whitley before the other man left the concealment of the woodland that ringed most of the lake. Knowing which direction Whitley would be coming from made his task easier, and he walked into the trees and took up a position he decided would best fit his needs.

Well before the stated meeting hour of two o'clock Marcus heard the approach of a horse and smiled to himself. It seemed that he wasn't the only one who had wanted to be here early. Listening intently, Marcus moved silently through the night, tracking the horse and rider as they came nearer to the edge of the woodland.

When Whitley finally halted his horse and dismounted, Marcus was in position and he waited only until Whitley had tied the horse to a small larch sapling before striking. Spinning Whitley around, he hit him with a powerful right fist to the jaw. Whitley's head snapped back and Marcus followed the first blow with a sharp jab of his left fist to the stomach and another right to Whitley's jaw. Gasping and dazed, Whitley hit the ground. Marcus flipped Whitley onto his stomach and bound his hands behind his back as if he habitually did this sort of thing. The tasks completed in mere seconds, Marcus swiftly tied a black silk scarf over Whitley's eyes.

Marcus thought the scarf a nice touch. Whitley would most likely recognize his voice, but it was possible he wouldn't. Marcus didn't care one way or another if Whitley guessed his identity; his purpose in blindfolding Whitley was to keep him off guard and increase the sense of vulnerability the major was no doubt feeling at the moment.

Dragging Whitley upright, Marcus shoved him in the direction of the lake. Whitley stumbled and staggered and Marcus grabbed his arm and hustled him toward the gazebo.

With great calm, Whitley said, "I have money. Let me go unharmed and you can have it all."

Marcus laughed grimly. "I'm not a robber, my friend, and I don't want your bloody money."

Whitley started at the sound of Marcus's voice and his head turned in that direction. "Who are you?" he demanded. "Do I know you?"

"Now, why would I take the trouble to blindfold you, if I was going to tell you who I am?" Marcus retorted cheerfully.

"What do you want?"

"Just a little something you have that belongs to a lady."

Whitley stiffened and stumbled to a halt. "Never say that *Isabel* hired you?" he exclaimed.

"Ah, now that would be telling, wouldn't it?"

To his astonishment, Marcus was enjoying himself. It was

a fine night; he was doing a noble deed and teaching a piece of offal a lesson in the bargain. He smiled. And the best part was yet to come.

Reaching one of the goldfish ponds, Marcus shoved Whitley to his knees and dragged his upper body over the stone rim. With Whitley's head inches above the water of the pond, Marcus said, "If you want this to end now, you only have to give me what belongs to a certain lady."

Whitley laughed tightly. "You don't even know what it is, do you?"

"I'm afraid that doesn't matter to me. I want it, and if you're wise you'll hand it over."

"And if I refuse?"

Marcus didn't answer him. In a heartbeat, he plunged Whitley's head into the murky waters of the fishpond. Marcus waited a few seconds before pulling the major's head from the water. As Whitley sputtered and swore, Marcus said, "That was just to get your attention. The next time, I'll hold you under longer. Now, are you going to give it to me? Or do I have to continue?"

Whitley cursed viciously and Marcus said, "Ah, I take it that's a no?" And promptly submerged Whitley's head under the water once more. He left him there longer, and when he finally pulled him up, Whitley was choking and gasping for breath. "So," Marcus said softly, "do you want to give it to me?"

"Go to hell!" snarled Whitley.

"You'll beat me there," Marcus drawled and once again Whitley's head disappeared into the depths. Marcus couldn't deny that he'd taken a measure of pleasure from dunking Whitley but by now it was growing tiresome. Determined to end this as quickly as he could, despite Whitley's frantic thrashing, he held him under as long as he dared.

Finally yanking Whitley's head out of the water, his heart almost stopped and dismay filled him when Whitley lay unmoving. Fear as much as anything caused him to violently shake the man, and he was relieved when Whitley coughed, gagged, and gulped in a breath of air. He didn't want to kill the man . . . at least not this way.

Staring at Whitley's prostrate form, listening to his labored breathing, Marcus almost felt sorry for him until he remembered that this man threatened Isabel and, if Jack was right, England herself.

His voice full of silky menace, Marcus said, "Last time. Either give it to me, or the next time, I let you drown." When Whitley made no reply, he sighed and reached for him.

"Wait!" croaked Whitley.

"Don't waste my time. Either give it to me or . . ."

"I'll give it to you . . . but I don't have it with me."

Marcus knew a lie when he heard it and jerked him half upright. "Then I guess it's the pond for you, my unfortunate friend," he said cheerfully, certain that Whitley would cave.

He was right. As Marcus's hand tightened on the back of his neck, Whitley cried out in terror. "Wait! Wait! I lied to you. I have it. I swear I have it with me."

Marcus dragged him from his humiliating position bent over the rim of the pond and flipped him onto the ground. After making certain the black silk scarf remained in place over Whitley's eyes, he roughly pulled him up until Whitley was slumped against the short wall surrounding the pond.

"Make no mistake," Marcus growled, "if you play games with me, we'll start all over again—only I won't stop until I have what I want or you're dead. Your choice."

Whitley shuddered and muttered, "No games."

"Then give it to me."

"You'll have to untie me," Whitley whined. "I can't reach it with my hands tied this way."

Marcus slapped him. "Do you take me for a fool? Tell me where it is."

Whitley hesitated and then in a defeated voice, he said, "It's my watch fob. It's in my vest pocket."

Marcus's fingers found the heavy gold fob and pulled it

free. Examining it in the frail light of the moon, he realized that it was an unusually large object for a fob and closer inspection revealed that it wasn't a fob at all. It was a woman's gold locket. The urge to open the locket was unbearable but, reminding himself that he had no right to pry into something that Isabel had gone to great lengths to keep secret, he quelled the desire to discover what it was that seemed to have so much power over her. Besides, he admitted wryly, he wanted her to tell him herself. Unhooking the locket from the chain, Marcus slipped it into his own vest pocket.

Rubbing his chin he studied Whitley. He had been so focused on retrieving what belonged to Isabel that he hadn't considered fully what he would do once he possessed it. He couldn't just leave Whitley here bound and blindfolded, although that idea held appeal. Nor could he untie him and simply ride away. Whitley might be suspicious of his identity, but the moment the blindfold was removed, all doubt would be gone. And then there was Jack. Marcus had promised to keep Whitley occupied while Jack searched his rooms, but if he had figured the time right, Jack had accomplished his search and was even now riding back to Sherbrook Hall.

Marcus considered the matter for several seconds and then, whistling softly, he hoisted Whitley upright. Taking a knife from his boot, he performed a trick he'd learned from his cousin Julian. Against vehement protest from the major, Marcus proceeded to strip him naked by cutting away his clothing and slitting the sides of his boots down to the soles. He tossed the ruined boots and clothes into the pond; the major could go fish for them.

That chore done, Marcus turned his attention again to Whitley, who stood naked and shivering in the cool night air. Ignoring Whitley's startled yelp he carefully nicked the rope that tied Whitley's hands, making certain that several strands still held. Even with the weakened rope, he decided, it would still take Whitley a while to free himself—long enough for Jack to be well away from the inn before the major returned.

With his goal completed, Marcus said, "It's been a pleasure, my friend, but the hour is late and I'm afraid I must leave you now. You'll find your clothes, er, what's left of them, in the pond."

Shutting his ears to the virulent curses the major hurled at him, Marcus swiftly walked away and disappeared into the concealment of the forest. He thought about taking Whitley's horse, but decided that he had tortured the man enough for one night. Still, it wouldn't do to make things too easy for the major. He rode his mount to where Whitley's horse was tethered and, noticing the major's greatcoat neatly tied across the cantle of the saddle, he freed the garment and secured it to his own saddle. Whitley, he decided grimly, was going to have to make do with the clothing from the pond to hide his nakedness. But there was one more thing he needed to do and, leaning down, he nicked the girth of the saddle. He smiled. By his estimation, the cut girth would hold for a few miles before it gave way.

Satisfied with the night's work, he kicked his horse into a gallop and rode for home. He unsaddled and rubbed down his horse before putting him away in his stall. Giving the animal an affectionate rub on the forehead and a scoop of oats, and taking the pilfered greatcoat with him, he walked to his office at one end of the stables and tossed the garment onto a chair. Chores done, he strolled outside and seated himself on one of the stone benches that flanked the entrance of the building to wait for Jack.

Isabel's locket burned a hole in his pocket and he took it out and examined it in the moonlight. It looked old and was heavy and of good quality with attractive scrollwork decorating the front and back and he wondered if it was a family heirloom. The temptation to open it was overpowering and, though he told himself that as her husband-to-be he had every right, he could not bring himself to do so. Sighing, he put it back in his vest pocket. Secrets! How he hated them.

Ten minutes later, he heard the sound of an approaching

horse and stood up when Jack rode into view. Jack halted his horse and glanced down at Marcus. "You were right," he said disgustedly. "There was nothing in his room and, believe me, I searched everywhere." Marcus grinned and Jack laughed. "I'll not doubt you again." He dismounted and together they put away Jack's horse.

Walking side by side toward the house, Jack asked casually, "And your rendezvous with Whitley? I trust it went well?"

Marcus nodded. "Just as I planned it." Marcus smiled. "It was a most satisfying encounter."

Jack shrugged. "I'm glad one of us has something to be satisfied about. There was certainly nothing in his rooms that gave me any hope we shall find it."

"Perhaps he doesn't have it," Marcus offered as they climbed the steps to the house.

"There is that possibility, but he seems such a perfect culprit that I'm not ready to abandon the quest just yet." Looking thoughtful, Jack added, "After I'd searched Whitley's rooms, I had an enlightening chat with the innkeeper, Keating. Very talkative fellow, Keating. He mentioned that Whitley had made the acquaintance of one of the local smugglers, a Peter Collard by name. Do you know him?"

Marcus's mouth tightened. "Indeed. Collard's brazen actions are legendary in the smuggling community. Whitley's acquaintance with him gives credence to your assumption that he has the memorandum and is looking to sail to France—or places friendly to the French."

They had reached the heavy double doors of the house when the sounds of a horse galloping through the night broke the silence. Marcus turned, half expecting to see Whitley charging down the driveway. He frowned as he recognized the rider as one of the servants from Manning Court.

"Mr. Sherbrook! Mr. Sherbrook!" cried the young man as he pulled his lathered horse to a stop at the foot of the stairs. "I have a message from Mrs. Manning for you." Leaping from his mount, he waved a small envelope in his hand. "It's the baron, sir. He's taken mortal bad."

Isabel's note confirmed the servant's words.

Marcus, she wrote, *come quickly. The baron collapsed shortly after we returned home this evening. The physician has examined him and believes he is dying. Lord Manning insists that you be here. Isabel*

Chapter 9

After giving Jack a hurried explanation, Marcus rushed to the stables and within moments was once more riding through the night. This time, fear drove him and he pushed his mount dangerously as he cut across the countryside taking the shortest route to Manning Court.

When he jerked his sweating horse to a halt at the impressive entrance to Manning Court, he wasn't surprised to see the physician's black gig in the circular driveway or to find the house ablaze with lights. The Manning butler, Deering, rushed across the wide terrace to greet him.

"Oh, Mr. Sherbrook! I am so relieved that you are here," exclaimed Deering, his agitation plain to see. "It is just dreadful! We cannot believe that he is dying." Recalling himself somewhat, Deering said more formally, "If you will follow me, sir, I will take you to Lord Manning at once."

Quietly entering the bedroom of Lord Manning, Marcus slowly walked across the big room toward the dais dominated by a massive burgundy and gold silk-hung bed. In the flickering glow of several large candelabra placed strategically around the room, he saw the shape of the old baron beneath the heavy silk coverlet, his hands lying white and still on the fabric. Still garbed in the amber silk gown she had worn to dinner at Sherbrook Hall, Isabel half sat on the side of the bed, her head bent, her fingers gently brushing Lord Manning's. Beside her stood the physician, Mr. Seward, his long face grave.

Marcus cleared his throat and Isabel started. Looking over her shoulder and seeing him, she leaped to her feet and ran across the distance that separated them. Throwing herself into his arms, she gasped, "Oh, thank God, you came! He has been most insistent that you be here." She fought back tears. "It happened so suddenly. We came home and, after Edmund had gone to bed, we were enjoying a few moments together in the green salon before retiring ourselves, when he made an odd sound and crumpled to the floor." A shudder went through her as she relived that terrible moment. "I screamed for Deering and we managed to rouse him, but though he was conscious, his words were slurred and he didn't seem to know us. It took Deering and three footmen to get him up the stairs and into his bed. I sent immediately for Mr. Seward." Tears spilled unheeded down her cheeks. "Marcus, Mr. Seward says he is suffering from apoplexy and is *dying*."

"I wouldn't," Marcus said with more confidence than he felt, "give up all hope, my dear." Flashing her a comforting smile, he added, "The baron is pluck to the backbone and I do not believe that he is ready to stick his spoon in the wall just yet." Setting her aside, he walked to the dais.

Mr. Seward glanced at him, his expression grim, and said, "I do not know how much time he has." Disapproval in his voice, he said, "He demanded your presence. I did not think it wise but he was so greatly agitated I agreed that you should be here. Once he knew you had been sent for, he quieted and has been resting calmly. Do not, I pray you, allow him to become upset again: it may hasten the end."

Stepping up onto the dais, Marcus was stunned at the change only a few hours had wrought in his old friend. Lord Manning's features were gray and shrunken and he looked every one of his nearly seventy-five years.

Marcus carefully seated himself on the bed and took one of Lord Manning's hands in his. "Milord," he said softly, "it is Marcus."

The old man stirred and opened his eyes. "Marcus," he repeated with difficulty. A smile, more a grimace than a smile, crossed his worn features. "I fear," he managed, "that you find me not at my best."

Affection in his gaze, Marcus replied, "Indeed, milord, I have seen you look better—even after a night of deep drinking and wild wenching."

Lord Manning half laughed, half choked at Marcus's words. The blue eyes brighter, he said, "You were always good for me. Made me laugh even when I didn't want to." His gaze locked on Marcus's face, he said, "Seward says I've had my notice to quit, but before I go, there is one thing I want to see: you and Isabel married."

His features impassive, giving no clue to the grief churning through him at the thought of an old friend's death, Marcus stared at Lord Manning for a long minute. The baron's request didn't come as a surprise; he'd been half prepared for just such a request. Lord Manning was determined to see that Isabel was safely settled and his grandson in safe hands before his death. Before the pause became noticeable, Marcus nodded and murmured, "Since that is your wish, I shall do my best to see that it is accomplished." Forcing a smile, he said, "It is a good thing, is it not, that Mrs. Appleton's brother, Bishop Latimer, is staying with her. I shall leave you but a short while and obtain a special license." He glanced over his shoulder at Isabel's numbed expression and said, "While I am gone Isabel can send for the vicar and, when I return, we can be married."

Lord Manning nodded and dropped off into a deep sleep.

Leaving Seward to attend to Lord Manning, Marcus swept Isabel from the room. His gaze searching her face, he said gently, "It will not be the wedding we might have planned, but it will make an old man's last hours happy."

Tears flooding her eyes, she nodded. Tried to speak but could not. Visibly fighting for composure, she got out, "I would do anything for him. I love him as I would my own father. I cannot bear the thought of him dying." Anguish on her face, she cried, "What am I to tell Edmund when he wakes and find his grandfather has died?"

"Didn't I tell you not to give up hope? We must prepare ourselves for his passing, but we must not give way to despair either. Until this happened, he was a powerful, vital man. He is not dead yet and until he is, I refuse to countenance anything else. And if the worst happens, I will know that our marriage gave him peace of mind." He tilted her chin up and dropped a quick kiss on it. "Send word to the vicar and then go back in there and remind the old devil of everything he has to live for. Be strong for him." Concealing his own fears and anxieties, Marcus turned on his heels and strode away.

The faintest tinge of pink and gold was breaking across the horizon when they were all gathered once more in Lord Manning's bedroom. The number of people filing into the big chamber had grown considerably in the intervening hours. Before leaving Manning Court for Mrs. Appleton's residence, Marcus had placed a note to be delivered immediately to his mother in the hands of a sleepy-eyed servant. The note contained a brief explanation and warned her that if she wanted to be at his wedding, she best make haste. Consequently, she and Jack were two of the people standing silently near the silk-draped bed where Lord Manning lay so pale and quiet; Vicar Norris, who had arrived only minutes before them, stood talking to Mr. Seward in a low undertone nearby.

It wasn't to be expected that when Mrs. Appleton discovered the reason for Marcus's middle-of-the-night visit she would remain at home. Her soft face full of grief and blinking back tears, she insisted on returning with Marcus to

Manning Court to spend a few last precious minutes with the man she loved and had hoped to marry. Presently, she was standing at the side of the bed, Lord Manning's frail hand clasped in her warm, plump one. Bishop Latimer, when awakened and the situation explained to him, was not only willing to issue the license but was determined to be at his sister's side during her ordeal and had accompanied her to Manning Court.

While Marcus had been gone, Isabel had struggled with the question about whether to wake Edmund or not. Knowing how much he loved his grandfather, she reluctantly decided that he should be allowed to see him before the old man died. Edmund, his young face full of stunned misery, knelt on the other side of the bed, rubbing his grandfather's arm, his gaze painfully fixed on the lined features.

Deering, and the housekeeper, Mrs. Deering, his wife, having both grown up in the baron's household and their parents before them, stood side by side near the door, Mrs. Deering trying to muffle her sobs in a big white handkerchief. Marcus knew that several other longtime servants hovered anxiously just outside in the hallway, trying to brace themselves for the devastating news that the only master they had ever known was dead.

Despite the coming dawn and the many candles that had been lit and placed around the room, a gray gloom that had nothing to do with the lack of light seemed to smother the area. Mrs. Deering's quiet weeping by the door drifted in the air, adding to the depressing atmosphere. Not, Marcus thought, the best start to a wedding.

Hiding his own grief, keeping his features calm and placid, Marcus walked up to where Isabel stood near one corner of the bed watching her son and his grandfather. Touching her on the shoulder, he said, "Everyone is here. Shall we proceed?"

Her face white and strained, the golden-brown eyes huge

and filled with anguish, she nodded. Half dazed by grief, she was hardly aware of the other people in the room, hardly aware of what she was doing. She was numb and even the thought of marriage to Marcus couldn't break through the cloud of sorrow around her.

Once everyone was in place—Isabel and Marcus standing on the dais near the vicar at the foot of the bed, the others gathered nearby—Mr. Seward gently woke Lord Manning. Lord Manning stared blankly at the physician for a moment, then, as if remembering the circumstances, he glanced over and saw the others around the bed. After help from Marcus and the physician, he was half raised in his bed, and a pile of pillows placed behind his back. Sighing, he sank back against them.

Lord Manning's left eyelid drooped and when he attempted a smile it was clear that the left side of his face was partially paralyzed. Still, he managed a smile of sorts and said in a rallying tone, "You'd think from the expression on your faces that you were here for a wake instead of a wedding." Sitting up a little taller in the bed, the blue eyes sharper, he added, "I'm not ready to have dirt thrown in my face yet, so I'll thank you to get rid of those Friday-faces. Like to put a man off his feed."

His words lightened the atmosphere and, satisfied with the faint smiles that flickered here and there, Lord Manning looked at the vicar and, motioning weakly toward Isabel and Marcus, said, "I believe we are here to see these two married, so let us get on with it."

The ceremony was simple and brief and, within moments, Marcus and Isabel were pronounced man and wife. In a fog of misery, the ceremony passed Isabel by. She was aware of saying her vows, aware of Marcus standing so tall and imposing beside her, but the reality of what was happening didn't touch her. Her marriage was simply something to be endured before she could turn her attention back to her son and Lord Manning.

Marcus, too, suffered much the same depth of grief that consumed Isabel, and didn't pay a great deal of attention to the ceremony either. Like Isabel, most of his thoughts were on the old man watching them from the bed. Still, when it was time to kiss his bride, he did so and, for just a second, felt a flicker of satisfaction and delight. Isabel was his! His wife. He stared down into her upturned face and some deep, primitive emotion moved within him. Not desire, although that lurked beneath the surface, but something stronger, more lasting and more profound, and then the vicar offered congratulations and the moment passed and his focus again returned to Lord Manning.

There was not the open joy one usually finds at such an event, but the beaming expression on Lord Manning's face after Marcus had kissed his bride made up for it. The ceremony completed, at a nod from Seward Marcus ushered everyone from the room, until only he, Isabel, Edmund, Seward, and Lord Manning remained.

In the time before everyone had arrived, arrangements had been made for refreshments to be served in the morning room. It wouldn't be the gala breakfast normally associated with a wedding, Isabel admitted, but it would keep the servants occupied for the moment and give an air of normalcy to the situation for the others. She doubted that anyone would leave very soon. They would, she thought with an ache in her heart, remain until Lord Manning died.

Edmund sat down on the bed next to his grandfather, stroking the old man's arm again as if by his very touch he could stave off death itself. It seemed impossible to him that his grandfather was dying and he took comfort from the feel of his grandfather's warm, sinewy arm beneath his hand.

Isabel sat on the other side of the bed, forcing herself to smile. "We've all danced to the tune of your piping," she said teasingly, despite the lump in her throat. "Are you happy with the results?"

Lord Manning nodded. His words slightly slurred, he

murmured, "Indeed, I am quite pleased." He looked at her keenly. "And you, my dear? Are you happy?"

Isabel swallowed a lump in her throat. How could she be happy when he was dying? How could she ever be happy when she knew that her marriage, a marriage she had never wanted, might destroy everything she held dear? Willing a light note into her voice, she said, "Of course." She glanced at Marcus, who stood beside her. "I have a fine, handsome husband. What woman wouldn't be happy?"

"And I," said Marcus slowly, his gaze roaming slowly over Isabel's face, "have married the only woman that I ever wanted for a wife." It was true, Marcus realized with a small start. Marriage had never been in his plans for the future, but once he had become engaged to Isabel, his whole world had changed and a life without Isabel by his side as his wife had been unthinkable. A small part of him understood even before his stunning announcement of their engagement that buried deep inside of him had been the knowledge that there was only one woman in the world for him: Isabel. Yes, he thought slowly, he *had* wanted to marry her and had, perhaps, for a very long time. . . .

Lord Manning chuckled and Marcus's attention immediately switched to the old man. The baron was pale and obviously exhausted, but Marcus decided that his color looked better and that the frightening blank expression was gone from his eyes and face.

"How are you feeling?" Marcus asked softly.

Using only half his face, the old man quirked a smile. "Not as good as I would like." He closed his eyes. "I think I would like to rest now." His gnarled hand tightened on Edmund's. "But leave the boy."

Quietly, Marcus, Isabel, and Seward left the room. In the hallway, Marcus said to Seward, "Why don't you join the others downstairs for some refreshments? Mrs. Sherbrook and I will stay in the sitting room, and if there is any change, we will ring for you immediately. And if you wouldn't mind, please ask Deering to send up a tray for Mrs. Sherbrook and myself. We'll leave the selection to him." He glanced at Isabel's wan face. "But some hot tea would certainly be in order."

Seward hesitated and Marcus said, "Lord Manning is resting comfortably now and there is nothing that you can do but fret him. He will either recover or die. His fate is out of your hands."

The physician took a deep breath, nodded curtly, and disappeared down the stairs.

Marcus guided Isabel into the pleasant sitting room that adjoined Lord Manning's bedroom and, after seating her on a dark blue damask sofa and telling her what he planned to do, he walked back into the bedroom to speak to Edmund. Lord Manning had already fallen asleep, but Edmund looked up when Marcus approached.

Smiling at the boy, he said, "Your mother and I will be in the sitting room. I shall leave the door ajar and, should you have need of us, just call out."

Edmund smiled shyly and nodded.

Returning to the sitting room, Marcus took a seat in a high-backed chair covered in blue and gold striped velvet to the side of where Isabel sat like a little wraith. Her bright red hair glowed like a flame in the candlelight and the skirts of her amber gown spread out against the dark blue material of the sofa made a pleasing contrast. The strain of the evening was evident in the purple shadows under her eyes, the unnatural paleness of her skin, and the tightly held curve of her mouth—not to mention the unconscious twisting of her hands in her lap. Certainly, no one looking at her, he thought ruefully, would ever take her for a woman just married. At least, not happily married, he amended.

Reaching across, he laid his big warm hand over her cold smaller ones. Her fingers immediately clutched for him and her eyes lost that distant stare as they met his.

"It has been an eventful evening, has it not?" he said quietly.

She gave a small choke of laughter. "You could say that." Her gaze dropped to their entwined fingers. "How do we go on from here?" she asked unhappily. "Th-th-there hasn't been any time to discuss any plans before we m-m-married." She swallowed. "I know we are married, but I—" Her voice closed off and a flush stained her cheeks.

Having a good idea where she was going, he smiled and raised her chin until she was forced to meet his eyes. "Isabel, I am not about to demand my conjugal rights tonight," he said softly, "if that is what worries you. You may tell Deering to prepare a bedchamber for me, and for the next few days at least, you may pretend that I am merely a guest. When my mother returns home, I shall have her see to it that a trunk is packed for me and delivered here by one of the servants." He flashed her a whimsical look. "I will not deny that this is not the way I envisioned my wedding night, but there is more at stake here than our enjoyment of the marriage bed. I do not intend to disrupt Lord Manning's household any more than necessary, and that includes removing you and Edmund to Sherbrook Hall or forcing myself into your bedroom. We are married. God willing we will have a long life together. There will be time enough for us in the future."

Her face glowed and she leaned forward saying earnestly, "Oh, Marcus! Thank you! You are being most understanding." She turned to look at the opened doorway that led to Lord Manning's bedroom. "I-I-I am afraid that at present I can think of nothing but . . ." Her voice was suspended by tears.

"He's dear to me, too," he said somberly. His expression bleak, he added, "If he dies, the next few weeks will be painful and neither one of us needs to be worried about the changes our marriage brings." He took a deep breath. "Once this is behind us we can concentrate on our changed circumstances."

Relief almost made Isabel giddy and the cold iron claw that had been lodged in her belly since she realized what the baron was about vanished. Sinking back into the softness of the sofa, she looked at Marcus, thinking that he looked attractively roguish with his black hair tumbling across the broad forehead and his cravat slightly askew. The bottle-green jacket was not of the first stare nor were the breeches and boots in their usual pristine condition and they added to the roguish air. She smiled to herself. None of them probably looked their best. Her lashes lowered hiding her eyes and covertly she studied him, this man who was now her husband. He was dearly familiar and tonight with his tired, rumpled elegance he drew her as he had at no other time. She knew an urge to caress that wide brow, to soothe the lines of weariness and strain she saw on his dark face, to wipe away the unhappy cast to his fine mouth. The image of that mouth hard against her breast sent a stab of needy desire streaking through her and she gasped in dismay. How could she think of such a thing with Lord Manning dying in the next room?

"What is it, my dear?" Marcus asked, hearing that soft sound.

To her great relief, there was a tap at the door and, at Marcus's command, Deering walked into the room carrying a large silver tray. His face was composed, but the quick glance he sent toward the open doorway leading to Lord Manning's bedchamber revealed where his thoughts lay. Placing the tray on a mahogany table at one end of the sofa where Isabel sat, he bowed and said gruffly, "Cook has been busy since Lord Manning was first stricken. You will find warm cross buns, apple fritters, some ginger biscuits, as well as slices of rare sirloin, rashers of bacon, coddled eggs, and tea and coffee."

Marcus smiled at him. "Please send her my compliments. My wife"—and only Marcus knew what pleasure it gave him to say those words—"may enjoy the biscuits and tea, but the sirloin and eggs are precisely what I need right now."

A slight smile flitted across Deering's face. "Indeed, that is precisely what Cook said, when I protested." His eyes slid again to the open doorway and his voice lowered. "Is there any change?"

Marcus shook his head. "None for the worst, at least. He is resting peacefully with his grandson at his side."

Unable to think of a reason to remain, Deering bowed and reluctantly left the room.

While Isabel picked at her crisp, spicy biscuit and sipped tea, Marcus helped himself to a large plate of rare sirloin, coddled eggs, some warm buns, and two apple fritters. It had been a long time since he had last eaten. For several minutes there was a companionable silence as Isabel nibbled her biscuit and stared blindly into space and Marcus concentrated on the food on his plate.

His plate empty, and feeling somewhat revived, he rose to his feet and said to Isabel, "I'll be right back. I'm going to see how milord is doing and if Edmund would like one of the apple fritters while they are still warm."

Quietly entering the room, he discovered Edmund and Lord Manning sound asleep. Edmund lay curled next to his grandfather and Lord Manning's arm rested around the boy's shoulder. Marcus's heart ached as he stared at the pair of them. Losing the baron would be hard on all of them, but Edmund would suffer the most. Poor little bantling. So young to have lost first his father, now his grandfather. Remembering his anguish when his own father died, Marcus vowed that he would do his best for the boy and try his damnedest to fill the old baron's shoes.

As if aware of Marcus's presence, Lord Manning's eyelids fluttered and he awoke. His gaze met Marcus's and he gave another of those painfully crooked smiles. "Are you angry at the way I galloped you to the altar?"

Marcus shook his head, a faint gleam of laughter in his gray eyes. "Indeed, I thank you for it. Isabel was being coy about setting a date and you cleverly settled that matter for us." His gaze sharpened. "And that was your plan, was it not?"

The old man carefully removed his arm from Edmund and admitted, "She appeared to be happy about the engagement, but she is an independent little devil and I feared that once I died, she'd find a way to cry off. There are valuable lands and a large fortune at stake and they will be Edmund's when I am gone, but until he reaches his majority, Isabel and the boy need protecting and a man's hand on the reins."

"Don't let Isabel hear you say that," Marcus teased, even as he assessed the old man's state. Except for the obvious paralysis on the left side, he looked remarkably well. His color was good, his eyes clear, and he was speaking, if with difficulty, coherently—an encouraging sign.

Lord Manning chuckled. "I know. I have no doubt that she is more than capable of running the estate and overseeing the Manning fortune, but she would be fighting against convention and she and the boy would be vulnerable to those less scrupulous individuals who might think to prey upon them. As her husband, you will protect them."

"I would have in any case," Marcus said quietly.

Lord Manning closed his eyes, exhaustion once again sweeping over him. "I know," he said in a low, slurring tone. "I know, but this way is better and I can die knowing that they are safe."

Marcus touched the old man's hand where it lay limply on the side of the bed and Manning's eyes opened. Marcus flashed him a twisted smile. "Think about living, my lord, and less about dying."

The old man smiled faintly and fell asleep once more.

Leaving Edmund and Lord Manning, Marcus turned and walked toward the sitting room. He met Isabel at the doorway.

"Is he all right?" she asked anxiously. "You have been gone so long, that I feared . . ."

Taking her by the arm, he escorted her back into the sitting room. "Calm yourself. They are both fine. Lord Manning awoke and I spoke a few minutes with him. That is what delayed me."

"He spoke with you? What did he say?"

"Merely that he was happy to see us married."

She smiled uncertainly. "And you? Are you happy?"

Marcus pulled her into his arms. Staring down into her face, he said softly, "Our engagement may have come about by accident, but if you believe anything, believe that there is nothing that I wanted more than to marry you."

Her eyes searched his and something in his gaze, in his face, made her heart race. Was it possible, she thought wildly, that her most private, most cherished dream had come true? Did Marcus love her? Or was it mere affection for a one-time ward that she saw in his eyes? Despair swept through her. If he had married her still thinking of her as his irritating ward and out of a sense of duty, she might as well throw herself into the lake and drown. But if . . . if he had married her seeing her finally as the woman she was, seeing her as a woman who would love him with all her heart until the day she died . . . Hope flared in her. Oh, if that was what she saw in his eyes, then she was the happiest of women.

She knew that dark face and those cool gray eyes almost as well as her own; they had long haunted her dreams, but she could not determine if she was seeing reality or what she wanted to see. It seemed incredible that he could love her, and inwardly, she winced. She had certainly done nothing to make herself appealing to him and yet remembering those moments in his arms . . . Warmth suffused her and she felt a delicious tingle deep within. He had wanted her. Wanted her as a man does a woman, wanted her as she had longed for him to do since she had been seventeen years old.

A flush stained her cheeks and her gaze dropped. Playing with a button on the front of his jacket, she muttered, "Very prettily said."

He bent his head and nibbled at her ear. "Dear, sweet wife, I have many pretty things I will say to you soon."

She tilted her head and teased, "And no scolding?"

His eyes glittered and he pulled her closer. "No, no scolding. I have other methods of chastising an unrepentant little termagant like you." His lips caught hers, and desire for her never far from him, exploded into being. His mouth hardened and he kissed her thoroughly, making no effort to hide his sudden, rampant arousal. Feeling as if he would split his breeches, Marcus fought for control, but like a caged animal sensing freedom, his body had other ideas and he crushed her next to him, kissing her with an escalating urgency.

Isabel, as helpless as he, returned his kiss with fervor, delighting in the feel of that tall, hard body pressed so tightly against hers, delighting in the drugging sensation of his lips and tongue taking her mouth. Her nipples hard and aching, her lower body aflame, her arms closed around his neck and she pushed herself even closer to him.

They kissed passionately, the depth of their hunger for each other growing with every passing second. Rational thought clouded by the most basic needs pulsing through him, Marcus sought her skirts and lifted them, growling softly when his seeking fingers found the soft, naked flesh beneath. He cupped her buttocks, positioning her against the swollen rod between his legs and rocked against her, but it wasn't enough. Not nearly enough.

Tearing his mouth from hers, he glanced around for a place to lay her down and it was only when his gaze took in their surroundings that his thoughts became lucid. Christ! He was in Manning's sitting room and he was preparing to make love to Isabel on the baron's sofa!

Struggling to regain control, he determinedly set Isabel from him. It was difficult. Her face was sweetly flushed, the beautiful golden-brown eyes were drowsy with desire, and her soft mouth was far too appealing for his peace of mind.

But the knowledge that Manning lay possibly dying in the other room acted as a douse of cold water.

Isabel blinked and Marcus knew the exact moment that reality came crashing back to her. She gasped and spun around to look at the opened doorway. Her face horrified, she looked back at him. "Dear heaven! How could I forget, even for a moment . . ."

Marcus grimaced. "We are both not ourselves tonight."

She gave a half-hysterical laugh. "Indeed. That is an understatement." Fighting to regain her composure, she shook out her skirts, her face flaming as a thrill shot through her remembering Marcus's big, warm hands moving across her buttocks. Her spine ramrod straight, she forced herself to sit down again on the sofa and deliberately took a sip of her tea. It was cold, but drinking it gave her something to do.

Needing something stronger, Marcus spied several decanters and glassware atop an intricately carved lowboy on the other side of the room. Crossing to the lowboy, he splashed some brandy into a snifter, tossed the liquor down, and poured another.

After taking in a deep, steadying breath he returned to his chair. Seated again, he took a sip of his brandy and cast his mind about for a topic to take their minds off of each other and the old man in the other room. Recalling his adventure tonight—last night, actually—he grinned.

"I have something for you," he said and, putting down the snifter, reached into his vest pocket. The gold locket he had taken from Whitley in his hand, he offered it to Isabel. "I believe this is yours."

Isabel blanched and shrank away from the object in his hand as if it were a deadly cobra. She sprang to her feet and, looking terrified, she ripped her gaze away from the locket and stared at him. Her voice thick and rusty, she croaked, "Where did you get that?"

Marcus frowned. This wasn't the reaction he had expected. He glanced down at the locket, studying it for the first time. What was there about this piece of jewelry that caused her such alarm? What secret did this object hold? More important, what secret could it contain that Whitley felt she would pay anything to keep hidden?

Chapter 10

Marcus stared from her to the locket, frowning. His gaze settling on her face, he said, "I'll say it again—don't you think it's about time you tell me what is going on? Whitley obviously felt that this locket holds some power over you." His gaze narrowed. "Is this what you were looking for in his room?"

She hesitated, looked at the locket, then away. "Not exactly," she finally said. "I told you the truth when I said that I didn't know what he had, just that he meant me harm and that he had something that could, indeed, harm me."

"And this locket could harm you?" he asked incredulously.

"Yes. No. Oh, I don't know!" She took a deep breath. "But I couldn't take the chance that Whitley did possess something, some item that would . . ." She looked away again, biting her lip. "It is very complicated," she finally said.

Marcus snorted. "Apparently." His gaze traveled over her averted features. "I don't suppose you'd like to explain this complicated matter to me?"

She gave a bitter laugh. "No, I wouldn't." Her gaze hard and direct, she added, "I will not lie to you; if I can avoid telling you, I will. If I have my way, it will go to the grave with me." At the objection she saw on his face, she sighed and said wearily, "I know. And before you say it, I'll agree that it is unfair and obstinate of me, but believe me, Marcus, if our positions were reversed, you would do the same thing." She looked at the locket and asked softly, "May I have it?"

He regarded her thoughtfully for a moment and then wordlessly handed it to her. The locket was warm from his hands and Isabel stared down at it for a long time, her gaze tracing the intricate pattern engraved on it. Memories came flooding back and tears filled her eyes. Pressing the locket to her bosom, she smiled shakily at him. "Thank you," she managed in a thick voice. "It is very precious to me."

Marcus bowed. "You're welcome."

"How," she asked, the locket still clutched to her breasts, "did you get it from Whitley? He would not have easily given it up."

Marcus grinned. "You're quite right about that, but I can be, ah, very persuasive when the necessity arises." His grin faded and he crossed the room to stand in front of her. His expression grave, he said, "Isabel, you know that I will never allow Whitley or anyone else to ever harm you. Are you certain that you will not tell me what is going on?"

She hesitated, and then Edmund, having wandered into the room, said from behind them, "Mother, Grandfather is sleeping quietly right now. Do you think I could leave him long enough to wash my face and dress for the day?"

Isabel started, guilty relief flashing across her face. Rushing over to her son, she said, "I think that is an excellent idea. You run along and I'll go sit with him while you are gone."

The moment lost, Marcus made no move to stop her when she sent him an uncertain smile over her shoulder and disappeared into Lord Manning's bedroom.

By mid-morning, though the baron continued to sleep, it was apparent to everyone that he would not be dying within the next few minutes, and the vicar, Jack, Marcus's mother, Mrs. Appleton, and Bishop Latimer departed for their homes.

Mrs. Appleton would be back almost immediately. Her plump little chin quivering, she told Marcus, "I shall return within the hour. I need only to see my trunk packed and my brother settled before I return." Her eyes filled with tears and, in a choked voice, she said, "This was not how I envisioned my first time staying here."

Marcus patted her on the shoulder and murmured, "Do not despair, Madame. Lord Manning may confound the physician yet."

A less woebegone look on her face, she dabbed at her eyes with a dainty scrap of lace and exclaimed, "Oh, I do so hope that you are right!"

The house seemed quiet after their exodus, but shortly, the news having spread through the neighborhood, friends of the baron came to call, expressing their dismay and inquiring after his health. Marcus calmly dealt with all of them, having told Isabel that the best place for her was at the baron's side. Smiling faintly, he said, "Go to him, my dear. It is where you long to be." She'd hesitated and he'd said, "Naturally, if you wish to handle this yourself, I shall leave you to it and go see to Lord Manning's needs myself."

It was the right thing to say and Isabel fled up the stairs leaving him in command of the lower floor, which was, she thought with amused irritation, precisely what he planned.

Of course, the news of the unexpected wedding had also spread, and in between expressions of concern for the baron there were congratulations given to Marcus on his marriage. It was, he decided wryly, a most bizarre situation: accepting condolences and congratulations at the same time.

His own trunk arrived from Sherbrook Hall along with his valet, Bickford, who was currently upstairs busily unpacking in the large bedroom Isabel had selected for Marcus. "I've told Deering to put you in the bedroom adjacent to milord's," she said, "and Mrs. Appleton will be directly across the hall." She glanced at him. "It is all so very strange, is it not?"

"Indeed. I'm quite certain I did not envision the first nights of marriage sleeping alone in a bedroom next to my wife's ex-father-in-law," Marcus replied dryly.

Isabel suppressed a giggle that bordered on the hysterical and disappeared up the stairs once more.

In between the comings and goings of the various visitors, Mrs. Appleton, her maid, and several pieces of luggage had returned and a solicitous Deering had escorted her to her bedroom.

There was a slight lull and Marcus, feeling the effects of a long, anxious night, rang for Deering and requested a pot of very strong, very hot coffee and a decanter of cognac. As if by magic the pot and decanter had instantly appeared and, after taking a sip of the coffee liberally laced with the cognac, Marcus asked Deering, "Everything under control upstairs?"

Deering allowed a faint smile to cross his face. "Yes. Edmund and Mrs. Man—Sherbrook are both asleep on the sofas in Lord Manning's sitting room. Mrs. Appleton and the physician are with him."

"Any change?"

Deering's smile vanished. "No, but he appears to be resting comfortably; even Mr. Seward said so."

"Well, then, we shall have to hope that Mr. Seward knows what he is talking about."

Deering was not gone five minutes and Marcus had just settled himself in a large overstuffed chair when he heard the sound of an approaching vehicle. Sighing, he rose to his feet and glanced out the window at the spanking pair of black horses pulling an elegant Highflyer that swept up to the front door. He wasn't surprised to see Garrett Manning handling the reins.

A moment later, Deering showed Garrett into the green salon and departed. Observing the other man's elegant cutaway deep blue jacket, buff breeches, and gleaming Hessian boots, Marcus felt rather grubby in his old bottle-green coat and crumpled cravat and thought longingly of a hot bath, followed by several hours of sleep.

"My dear fellow! A wake and a wedding all on the same night," Garrett exclaimed as he crossed the room. Sticking out his hand, he asked, "Do we mourn the old man or celebrate your wedding? Or both."

The very real concern in the blue eyes robbed the question of any flippancy and, shaking Garrett's hand, Marcus said, "No mourning. The old man is holding his own."

There was no disguising the relief in Garrett's face. He gave a sharp laugh. "I know you will find it hard to believe but I do have affection for him."

Marcus nodded. "And he for you, although he wishes you just a bit less of a rake."

Garrett shrugged. "One seldom gets what one wishes for." He quirked a brow at Marcus. "So I am to wish you and the lovely Isabel happy?"

"Yes. Your uncle wanted to see us married before he . . . and we obliged him."

Garrett looked at him keenly. "Do you think he's dying?"

"It was a near thing, but as of now, no, I don't believe he is dying. The physician may disagree with me, but I think that if he was going to die, he would have done so by now." Reluctantly, he added, "But he has not escaped unscathed and I fear he will never be the man he once was."

Marcus relayed the events of the previous night and the extent of the effects of the stroke. "He may recover completely," Marcus said as the topic came to an end. "But only time will tell that."

"May I see him?" Garrett asked.

Marcus considered him. Lord Manning loved his nephew even if he disagreed with his lifestyle and Garrett appeared to have deep affection for his uncle. He shrugged. "I have no objection. Let me ring for Deering to show you upstairs."

"Ah, a moment, if you please?"

"Of course, what is it?"

Garrett made a face. "I'm not sure." Looking uncomfortable he muttered, "You may think me meddling in something that is none of my affair, but I feel compelled to speak." He half smiled. "After all, you could say that we are now related and I am only looking out for the best interests of the family."

Marcus nodded, wondering where this conversation was going.

Garrett cleared his throat, clearly ill at ease and not certain of his ground. "I don't usually go around sticking my nose in what doesn't concern me," he began reluctantly, "but I would be remiss if I didn't warn you to be careful of that fellow Whitley, who is staying at the Stag Horn in the village."

Marcus's gaze sharpened. "And why is that? What do you know of Major Whitley?"

Garrett pulled on his right ear where the diamond stud gleamed in the morning light filling the room. "Last night, after I left your mother's dinner party, I rode into the village looking for some amusement." He grinned at Marcus. "I'm afraid that I find country life somewhat dull and I was not inclined to drink alone. I stopped at the Stag Horn, thinking to nurse an ale or two before calling upon, ah, a lady that I visit from time to time when I am home." He smiled ruefully. "There was a convivial group gathered in the tap room and, with one thing and another, I never did get to her house." Looking reflective, he continued, "It must have been somewhere around four o'clock and I had just decided to leave when there was a great commotion and Whitley staggered into the inn. He was in a terrible state. He was disheveled, his clothing damp and hanging on him by mere strips; his face was bruised and he was screaming that he had been robbed and attacked by a madman who had tried to drown him."

Marcus's lips twitched, but his face the picture of concern, he murmured, "How shocking! The poor fellow."

"Hmm, yes, it was shocking, especially since we don't as a

rule have that sort of thing happening in the neighborhood," Garrett said slowly, not having missed that slight twitch of Marcus's lips. "Once Keating had ordered a warmed blanket for Whitley to wrap around himself and poured him a generous brandy, the major had quite a tale to tell. He claimed he was riding home from visiting a friend, a female friend he declined to identify, when he was attacked. The robber, not content with making him empty his purse and having slashed his clothing with a knife, leaving him perilously close to naked, had also tried to drown him. He was rather vague about the location where all this occurred, yet had no trouble recalling other less important details." Garrett made a face. "Perhaps I am too hard on the fellow. He certainly had a bad night and, once the robber made off, his troubles were still not behind him. Unbeknownst to him, this nefarious individual also cut the girth of his saddle. The girth gave way a few miles from the site of the attack and he had been dumped onto the road. His horse naturally galloped back to the stables, leaving him to walk in his ruined boots, also cut to pieces and soaking wet, I might add, to the inn."

"What a deplorable incident!" Marcus said with what he hoped was enough outrage to still any suspicion that he had anything to do with Whitley's misfortune, though why Garrett should think he had escaped him. "I'm sure that Whitley must be thinking of leaving for London at first light."

"No, he's not," Garrett said, his gaze fixed on Marcus. "After the first flurry of excitement had died down and the crowd had dispersed leaving him alone, I joined him by the fire hoping to find out more, if I could."

"And did you find out more?" Marcus asked in a bored tone.

Garrett's lips thinned. "No one else was around and so he spoke more freely than he would have otherwise. Whispering and constantly looking over his shoulder, he intimated to me that he believed that *you* were his robber and he swears to get his revenge on you."

Marcus's brows rose. "Now that's the silliest damn thing I've ever heard! The man must have lost his wits. Why would I attack a man I barely know? I only met him one time and, quite frankly, did not care for him. Allow me to assure you that the Sherbrook fortune is large enough and safe enough that I have not been forced to repair the family coffers by stealing from the likes of Whitley."

Garrett studied him for a moment. "Which is exactly what I told him, but I warn you, Sherbrook, you have an enemy there and he is determined to do you harm."

Marcus bowed. "And I thank you." He did not know Garrett well, but Marcus was beginning to think that given the chance, Lord Manning's nephew might make a very good ally. Garrett might be wild and reckless, but it appeared he had qualities that would make him a good man to have at your back in a fight and Marcus liked that. It was clear that Garrett didn't quite believe that Marcus had been Whitley's attacker, but he didn't *dis*believe it either.

Smiling at him, Marcus said, "Indulge me if you would. . . . Is Whitley a particular friend of yours?"

Garrett snorted. "Never laid eyes on the man until the other night."

"Yet he told you, a virtual stranger, that he suspected me? For all he knew, we are great friends. I wonder why he was so free with his suspicions with you?"

"He was half drunk by then and knew from our previous conversation that I was related by marriage to Mrs. Manning." Garrett grinned. "He was exhorting me to do all within my power to stop the wedding and save Mrs. Manning from a disastrous marriage. He had, he said, being an old friend, only her best interests at heart and he would be devastated if she married a man he labeled a blackguard and a robber in the bargain."

Marcus's gray eyes glinted. "Is that right? I may just have to go pay Whitley a visit and set him straight on a few points."

Garrett laughed. "Not necessary. I promised to show him

how handy I was with my fives and vowed to put a fist in his bone box if he spread such a rumor around the neighborhood."

"It seems I am in your debt," Marcus replied lightly.

"My pleasure." He cast Marcus a troubled glance. "Be careful, Marcus. He means you harm."

"Again, thank you for the warning." Reaching for the bell rope that hung nearby, Marcus added, "If there is nothing else, perhaps you would like to see your uncle now?"

Following Marcus's lead, Garrett nodded and said, "Yes, I would like that very much."

After Garrett, escorted by Deering, had departed, Marcus settled down in a comfortable chair, poured himself another cup of coffee, and sipped it, his mind busy with what he had just learned. He'd made no real attempt to hide his identity and so he wasn't surprised that Whitley had guessed who he was. That Whitley had voiced his suspicions aloud to Garrett did surprise him, though. Why? On such short acquaintance did he think Garrett was of his same ilk? Or had Whitley been too drunk to watch his words? Marcus decided that it was most likely the latter, but it was also obvious that Whitley had been casting about trying to cause trouble in any manner he could. He took a sip of his coffee. Yes, that sounded like Whitley. Thinking of the wedding ceremony performed some hours ago, he smiled. Whitley was going to be very, *very* unhappy when he heard the news.

The day that followed was without incident. Beyond the occasional caller that afternoon and messages of congratulations and concern, the household settled into a more normal routine. Lord Manning slept most of the time, but he roused enough to drink some barley broth and weak tea several times throughout the day. In the afternoon, his valet carefully bathed him and helped him into a fresh nightshirt. Lord Manning was weak and tired, but Marcus felt confident that the old baron was no longer at death's doorway.

As he had said to Isabel, Marcus had not expected to spend what was technically his wedding night sleeping alone in a bedroom adjacent to his wife's ex-father-in-law, but as he sank into the welcoming softness of the feather bed that night, he decided it was just as well. He'd been over twenty-four hours without sleep and he rather doubted that he'd have been up to the memorable wedding night he'd envisioned. As sleep caught him, he smiled. He might be exhausted at the moment, but he suspected if Isabel's snug little body had been pressed next to his that sleep would have been the last thing on his mind.

Marcus rose the next morning feeling much refreshed, and a bath and a change of clothes only helped his sense of well-being. Entering the morning room shortly thereafter, he learned from a beaming Deering that Lord Manning had passed a restful night and had even insisted upon leaving his bed to eat his breakfast at a table hastily set up in his bedroom. Heartened by the good news, after a breakfast of rare sirloin and ale, Marcus went to visit Lord Manning. While he found the baron much improved, it was apparent that the old man was facing a long recovery. Marcus chatted with Lord Manning and Mrs. Appleton, who sat by the bed with a lap full of knitting, for a few moments and, having satisfied himself that Lord Manning seemed to be improving, he took his leave and returned downstairs.

Learning that his bride was in her office in the stables, he was on the point of leaving to find her when Jack rode up astride a big gray gelding. As he slowly walked down the last few steps to greet Jack, from the taut expression on his cousin's face Marcus knew that this was no casual visit. Something serious was afoot. An icy dagger slid through his bowels. He couldn't help but think of the suddenness in which the baron had gone from a strong, vital man to an invalid; his mother was no longer a young woman. . . . "My mother?" he demanded. "Is she all right?"

"My visit has nothing to do with your mother," Jack said

hastily, swinging out of the saddle. "I left her in a fine mettle."

Marcus kept silent as a groom came up and took the reins from Jack's hand. The groom walked off with the horse and the two men entered the house. As soon as they were closeted in the green salon, Marcus demanded, "If Mother is all right, why the devil are you here—and looking, I might add, as if the end of the world is near?"

Jack gave a short bark of laughter. "Surely not that bad?"

Marcus permitted himself a slight smile. "Near enough. Now what is it?"

His expression once again grim, Jack said, "Sherbrook Hall was broken into last night."

Marcus stared at him. "Broken into? Housebreakers?" he asked, astonished.

Jack shrugged. "Could have been, but I rather doubt it. This housebreaker seemed to have very specific tastes and bypassed all the silver and plate and appeared to be most interested in what the library and your office might contain. Both rooms were thoroughly searched and left in a shambles." Carefully, he added, "Your mother and Thompson and the housekeeper assure me, from what they can see, that nothing was taken. An odd sort of housebreaker, don't you agree?"

Throttling back his anger at the invasion, Marcus snapped, "You think the housebreaking has something to do with Whitley, don't you?"

Again Jack shrugged. "This is a quiet neighborhood. Housebreaking is uncommon, *especially* housebreaking in occupied houses and, having gone to all the trouble to break in, to take nothing. . . ."

Marcus rubbed his chin. "He took nothing because he didn't find what he was looking for." He frowned. "Or . . . if he is convinced that I am the person who attacked him, and I have it on good authority that he may very well think that, then the whole object could have been simply to strike back at me."

"Garrett has talked to you, I take it?" At Marcus's curt

nod, Jack went on, "He talked to me, too, relating his conversation with Whitley, so that possibility also occurred to me. Whitley strikes me as a tit-for-tat sort of fellow," Jack admitted. "He might very well have broken in and left the rooms in a jumble simply for spite. There was an unnecessary degree of violence and destruction about the whole affair that arouses the suspicion that our housebreaker was venting his rage."

"It has to be that," Marcus said slowly. "Unless . . ." Unless, the unwelcome thought occurred to him, Whitley had been looking for the locket. What the devil, he wondered, was in the bloody thing?

"Unless?" Jack prompted.

Since it was not his secret to reveal, Marcus made a face and said, "Nothing, I am merely thinking aloud."

Jack looked at him closely. Marcus was not a very good liar, but he could hardly call him on it and he was willing to let the moment slide. "So what do you want to do?" Jack asked.

"For the moment my hands are tied. We don't know that it was Whitley who broke into the house and I can hardly walk smash up to the man and give him a leveler, now can I?"

"You could," Jack said with a grin.

Marcus grinned back. "And I may yet. I assume that you have taken steps to insure that if our housebreaker returns he will not find the house such an easy mark?"

"Yes, Thompson has ordered stout locks installed on the doors and for two of your strongest footmen to sleep on the ground floor of the house for the time being."

The two men discussed the situation, but when nothing new came to light, eventually Jack took his leave to return to Sherbrook Hall. Marcus was thoughtful after his cousin rode away, wondering about the break-in and the locket, but deciding not to waste time in useless speculation, he pushed the subject away . . . for the moment. Whitley was going to have to be dealt with sooner or later and a most un-Marcuslike look crossed his face and his hands curled into fists. Whitley was going to learn *painfully* that it was rude and impolite to break into another man's house. . . .

The next twenty-four hours neither dragged nor sped by, but passed at a steady pace. The baron appeared to improve by the minute and, by the next day no one, not even the dour Mr. Seward, considered him at death's door any longer. Tuesday morning Lord Manning had eyed the bowl of barley broth on his tray and insisted that if they didn't want him to die of starvation, someone dashed-well-better see to it that he was served some decent food and not this bloody tasteless pap. Edmund let out a whoop, Marcus and Isabel exchanged delighted looks, and Mrs. Appleton's plump little face was wreathed in smiles. Deering, grinning in a most unbutlerly way, was elated and returned shortly with a tray groaning with scrambled eggs, ham, rashers of bacon, spiced applesauce, and a plate piled high with toast. With Mrs. Appleton seldom far from his side, the baron continued to recover rapidly, and while there were still lingering effects from the stroke, notably a slight droop of his left eyelid and weakness on his left side, by Friday he was finally able to leave his bedroom.

The night Lord Manning joined the family for dinner in the dining room was a joyous one and the staff and family rose to the occasion. The crystal gleamed, the silverware glittered, and the linen tablecloth, tenderly washed and ironed by Mrs. Deering herself, was as white as new-fallen snow. Deering and the footmen moved effortlessly about the big room, seeing that nothing was lacking—and Cook? Well, Cook had outdone herself. Flemish soup; spring lamb, surrounded by early peas and tiny potatoes; fat, green asparagus; buttered lobster; creamed cauliflower; a fine veal roast; and jellies and creams of infinite variety graced the table. Dressed as if for a London soiree—Isabel in a charming confection of rose crepe, Mrs. Appleton wearing a gown of green striped silk, and the gentlemen, including Edmund, in dark coats and pale knee breeches—were all gathered around the table ready to enjoy the leisurely meal. Mrs. Appleton's brother, Bishop Latimer; Garrett; Jack; and Marcus's mother had been hastily invited to celebrate the baron's return to health.

Several toasts were offered and, at the end of the meal, somewhat slowly, the baron rose to his feet and offered a toast. Smiling at Marcus and Isabel, he said, "To the newlyweds: Marcus and Isabel, may you have a long and happy marriage." The toast was duly drunk and then, a twinkle in his blue eyes, Lord Manning said, "I think it is past time for the pair of you to begin your life together. There is no longer any reason for you to be underfoot here at Manning Court. I think within the next day or so that the new Mr. and Mrs. Sherbrook should take up residence in Sherbrook Hall."

Isabel's heart stuttered in her breast. "Oh, but, milord, you still need—"

"Hush, my child," admonished the baron. "These past days you and Marcus have placed my needs above your own." He smiled tenderly at her. "While I am most grateful, it is time for your sacrifice, willing though it is, to cease. You have your own lives to live and you don't need to be wasting any more precious days on a doddering old man."

"But—" Isabel began helplessly. It was happening too soon, she thought frantically. She'd assumed she had weeks, perhaps months before she'd have to face the reality of being Marcus's wife, and yet, if the baron had his way, tomorrow night she'd be installed in Sherbrook Hall and there would be no escape. She glanced at Marcus, almost as if seeking his aid.

Their eyes met and, after a long moment, Marcus looked at Lord Manning and said lightly, "As you well know, milord, it is no sacrifice. We do this gladly, for as long as need be. Isabel and I are planning on being married a long time. Another week or two will cost us nothing." It wasn't what he wanted to say but he could not ignore the appeal in those big tawny eyes of hers. The days since their wedding had been hell as far as he was concerned. Knowing his *wife* lay just down the hall from him had kept Marcus tossing and turning in his bed at Manning Court every bloody night for nearly a week. He didn't want to think of the evenings he had paced the dark halls of his lordship's house, aching and yearning to lie abed with his bride. That she felt entirely different had not escaped him and he wondered at her reluctance. Did she find him repulsive? Now *that* was a rather lowering thought.

His mother's words broke into his speculation. "I think it is an excellent idea!" Barbara Sherbrook said bracingly. "Now that the marriage has taken place and his lordship is returning to health, I have been thinking of going to Brighton. I don't wish to return to London and, besides, before long everyone will be coming to the seashore, anyway." Smiling at her son, she added, "Jack and I have discussed it and he has some business in town and is willing to escort me to Brighton before leaving for London." She beamed at Isabel. "I think a new bride should have her home all to herself for a few months before she has to put up with a meddling mother-in-law."

"And I'm sure that you would be wishing me to the very devil," Jack chimed in. He glanced at Garrett. "As soon as your mother is settled in Brighton and I see to a few things in town, I shall return." He grinned at Marcus. "You needn't worry I'll be underfoot; Garrett has begged me, in view of your marriage, to keep him company at Holcombe."

Marcus looked from Jack's guileless face to Garrett's impassive one. Now what the devil were those two up to? And when had they become such fast friends? It was true he had been preoccupied of late, but what about the memorandum and Whitley's possible involvement in its theft? Had Jack decided Whitley was innocent? Had the memorandum been found and was no longer a concern? But wouldn't Jack have told him?

Garrett murmured, "Jack and I thought you might enjoy some privacy."

"Did you now?" Marcus commented. "How very kind of you." He cast a look around the table, before his gaze came to rest on Isabel's face. Smiling ruefully, he said, "Well, my dear, it would seem that everybody has been very busy on our behalf and that we would be churlish not to accept the plans they have made for us."

Isabel slapped on as happy a smile as she could and said, "It is very kind of everyone and we thank you." Something occurred to her and she glanced at Mrs. Appleton, sitting across the table from her. "Will you be returning home soon, too?"

Mrs. Appleton blushed like a green girl and the baron cleared his throat. When Isabel looked at him, he said, "And that brings me to the most important toast of the evening." His gaze on Mrs. Appleton, he said softly, "A toast to my future bride! Clara has done me the honor of accepting my proposal."

Several more toasts were drunk and there was an excited chatter around the table. When the first flush of conversation had begun to die down, Marcus asked, "When is the wedding? In the fall?"

Lord Manning shook his head. Grinning at Marcus he said, "Clara and I liked your wedding so much, we've decided to do the same. Her brother will provide the special license and he will marry us in the morning!"

Chapter 11

From the expressions of those gathered around the table, it was apparent that Marcus and Isabel were the only ones who were taken by surprise by Lord Manning's announcement and the plans put forth by his mother. Even Jack and Garrett seemed to know what was afoot. Now that he considered it, Marcus realized that there had been an unusual amount of activity in and out of the house all day long, but he had thought nothing of it. Even his mother's early arrival, which had coincided with Bishop Latimer's arrival and their private visit with Lord Manning and Mrs. Appleton before dinner this evening, had not seemed out of the ordinary. It was obvious now that they had all put their heads together and plotted tonight's stunning announcement. But there was more to follow and, looking proud and thrilled at the same time, Edmund blurted out, "And I am to go with Mrs. Sherbrook to Brighton!" His face flushed with pleasure, he said, "She says that as my new grandmother, it is her duty to see that I gain some town bronze." Nearly vibrating with excitement, the brilliant blue eyes glittering, he added, "Oh, Mother! Is it not grand? Once Grandfather marries Mrs. Appleton, I shall have *two* grandmothers instead of none at all!"

The ground cut beneath her feet, Isabel could only smile and nod. While the other arrangements might fill her with trepidation, she could respond wholeheartedly to Edmund's open delight. "Wonderful, indeed!" she said, smiling warmly into her son's face. Only to herself would she admit that she was dreading the removal to Sherbrook Hall and what would come. . . .

On a lovely morning near the end of the first week in May, Lord Manning took Clara Appleton to be his bride. The wedding party had grown slightly; the vicar and his wife, as well as Sir James and Lady Agatha, had been apprised of the impending nuptials and were in attendance. After a charming exchange of vows in the gardens abloom with roses, a wedding breakfast was served that put to shame anything the finest London chef could have prepared. By end of the meal, though there was a broad grin on his face, the baron was looking tired and there was a flurry of good-byes as the house quickly emptied.

The intervening twenty-four hours had flashed past Isabel in a blur. She had overseen the packing of Edmund's things that would go to Brighton with him and the packing of her own most necessary items for removal to Sherbrook Hall. While Deering and the staff had eagerly thrown themselves into the preparation for the wedding, there was still much that called for Isabel's attention, and she had spent hours consulting with Deering, Mrs. Deering, and Cook to ensure that all went without incident. She had tried to confer with Clara on some points, but Clara had merely patted her cheek and murmured, "My dear, I shall be quite happy to leave everything in your capable hands. Tomorrow will be soon enough for me to take up the position of lady of the house." Beaming at her, Clara had added, "There is no use confusing the staff with the pair of us giving them orders, and I know that you shall do a splendid job."

Freed from any restrictions that might have been imposed upon her by the bride, Isabel had set to work seeing that the baron's wedding was without incident. From the erection of the blue silk canopy under which the bride and groom would stand and the bouquets of lilies and baby's breath that adorned the corners, to the tiny puff pastries filled with shrimp served at the breakfast that followed, all had passed by her for approval. She was glad of the distraction because it kept her from dwelling on what the night might hold for her.

Her trunks had been sent over to Sherbrook Hall hours ago; Lord Manning, his bride by his side, had retired upstairs; Jack, Mrs. Sherbrook, and Edmund had been the last to leave and after hugging Edmund she had waved them good-bye only a few moments ago. She had bid a tearful farewell to Deering and the other servants and now Marcus's carriage awaited her just outside the big doors of Manning Court. Standing alone in the entryway of the house that had been her home for a decade, she felt bereft and fearful of the future.

I should be happy, she told herself fiercely. *My son has two doting grandmothers where before he had none. Lord Manning, whom I love dearly, is on his way to recovery and has one of the kindest women I have ever known as his bride. I am not leaving him alone. He and Clara will be happy here together. There is so much in my life,* she thought wretchedly, *that should make me happy. I have a handsome husband. A good man. A man,* she admitted with a catch in her heart, *I have loved nearly all my life. So why am I so miserable?*

One of the doors opened and Marcus stood there, smiling at her. "Are you ready, my dear?" he asked quietly.

Suppressing all her fears and anxiety, her head came up, her spine stiffened, and, pulling on the lavender gloves that matched her muslin gown, she murmured, "Yes. I am." She glanced around the entry hall one more time. "It isn't," she said as much to reassure herself as anything, "as if I'm moving that far away."

Marcus had not been idle during the preceding twenty-four hours. With Isabel enmeshed in the plans for the wedding and the packing to remove to Sherbrook Hall, beyond giving Bickford his orders, there was little he could do at Manning Court. Deciding this would be an excellent time to talk to Jack before his cousin left to escort his mother and Edmund to Brighton, and from there to travel to London, he excused himself and rode home.

Looking slightly harassed, Thompson met him as he walked across the wide foyer. "Mr. Sherbrook! I didn't expect to see you until you brought home your bride. Is all well?"

"Yes. Everything is fine. I just wanted a word with Jack before he left for London."

"Oh. You'll find him and Mr. Garrett in your office." Thompson paused and, a frown creasing his forehead, he said, "I hesitate to bother with what may be nothing. . . ." At Marcus's questioning look he said in a rush, "There has been some suspicious activity around the house at night ever since the break-in. As you know, since then, we've taken to locking the house after dark and have had two of the footmen, young Daniel and George, sleeping on the main floor of the house. Both of them have said that more than once they thought they heard someone attempting to find a way into the house, but when they've investigated, they've found nothing out of the ordinary. It happened again last night." His expression troubled he said, "I do not understand it. Daniel and George are convinced that someone is still trying to get into the house. The whole affair has been most unsettling."

Marcus kept his features bland, but his brain was working furiously. What the devil was Whitley up to? Or was he mistaken in believing that Whitley had been the culprit in the first place? It made no sense for the intruder to be anyone other than Whitley, but if so, then why was the man still skulking about the house? Deciding he'd have a conversation with the two footmen later in the day, Marcus sought to allay some of Thompson's concerns. "This past week," Marcus said mildly, "has been one of great ups and downs. All of us have had our normal routines turned topsy-turvy and the break-in certainly only added to the extraordinary events taking place. As for George and Daniel, I will speak with them later this afternoon." He smiled at Thompson. "Knowing those two rascals, I suppose they imagined a horde of bloodthirsty robbers hiding in the shrubbery. Things are returning to normal and I suspect that the situation will resolve itself harmlessly before much time elapses." *Especially,* he thought savagely, *if I get my hands on Whitley.*

Putting away Thompson's disturbing revelations for the time being, Marcus strode through the house in search of his cousin. As Thompson had said, he found Jack closeted with Garrett in his office. Both men looked comfortable as they sprawled in the chairs by the empty fireplace and Marcus sensed that he had interrupted a private meeting. He noted the friendly ease between the two men, but wasn't surprised. They were of the same age and background and the pair of them, though they would vigorously deny it, were adventure mad. Smiling, he continued on into the room and half sat on the arm of the sofa that faced the fireplace and the two men.

Talk was general for several moments, with the baron's impending nuptials taking up the lion's share of the conversation.

"So," Marcus said to Jack after a while, "how long do you think you will be in London?"

Jack shrugged. "I don't know. Garrett and I were discussing that very thing when you came in."

"That and a mutual acquaintance of ours," Garrett said with a wry grin. "Roxbury."

Marcus looked astounded. "Never tell me," he said as he looked from one face to the other, before his gaze settled on Jack, "that his grace has enlisted someone *else* in our little problem."

"Indeed he has," Jack admitted. "I would remind you that

there is some urgency to the matter and Roxbury felt that you and I might have our hands full and that another pair might be useful."

Since there was no way to tiptoe around the subject, Marcus motioned to Garrett and said, "Am I to understand, then, that Garrett is fully in our confidence?"

Jack nodded. "I was bowled over when he gave me the note from Roxbury the day after you married Isabel."

A hint of embarrassment on his face, Garrett said to Marcus, "I apologize for not telling you at once, but Roxbury was vague about who was involved. I was told that I should see Jack and give him the letter of introduction that Roxbury provided. Jack and I had only spoken briefly before I came to call at Manning Court and he hadn't mentioned, at that time, your involvement. When Jack and I met later, he told me all, but there was never a moment to bring you current."

"Actually," Jack said, "it has been a good thing. With you tied up at Manning Court, Garrett's help has been much appreciated. Between the pair of us we have been able to keep a close eye on Whitley."

"For all the good it has done us," Garrett said disgustedly. Glancing at Marcus, he added, "I have spent far too many nights drinking with the man. I am noted for being a good tankard man myself, but I am appalled at the amount of liquor he can consume—and still be coherent." Thoughtfully, he continued, "The liquor *does* loosen his tongue, but so far he has said nothing that would help us."

Thinking of Thompson's concerns, Marcus inquired, "Were you with him last night?"

Garrett nodded, curiosity evident in his eyes. "As I am most nights. Why?"

"Thompson informed me that someone has been trying to get into the house. There was, if my two footmen are to be believed, another attempt last night. Whitley seems the most likely candidate."

Garrett made a face. "Well, I don't crawl into bed with

him, so I can tell you nothing of his activities once we part."
He looked thoughtful. "Now that I think of it, there have
been a few nights that Whitley has retired early, and by that,
I mean around midnight. It's possible that he's been sneaking
out later." Garrett frowned. "As I recall, he had an early
night last night."

Jack was frowning, too. "I wonder why Thompson didn't
mention any of this to me?"

Marcus grinned at him. "While you may have been running tame through my home with my blessing, my servants,
thank God, still remember that I am master here. It probably
never occurred to Thompson to say anything to you. He
most likely didn't want to trouble a guest with a minor irritation. Remember, he doesn't know what is in the wind."

Jack nodded slowly. "You're right." He glanced at Marcus. "What do you make of it?"

Marcus shrugged. "At best, it is merely Whitley's way of
further twisting my tail. At worst . . ." Marcus scowled. "At
worst, he's up to something dangerous and means to attack
me in some manner to pay me back for my supposed attack
on him."

"Think that's it," Garrett chimed in. "He doesn't say a lot,
but when he gets to drinking it's clear he holds a vicious
grudge against you. He'd do you damage if he could."

Marcus shrugged again. "Let him try," he said with a note
in his voice that made the other two men look at him sharply.
He merely smiled and said to Jack, "It appears for all our efforts and suspicions, we have still not discovered any sign
that Whitley has the memorandum."

"No, and that is one of the reasons why I am returning to
London," Jack admitted. "I must speak with Roxbury and
discover if anything else had turned up." Jack looked down-
cast. "I fear that we have been wasting our time and that the
document must either have been taken by someone else, or it
really is lost in the files at the Horse Guards." His expression
bleak, Jack added, "That bloody memorandum is some-

where and, until it is found, whether in Whitley's possession or not, none of us can rest easy." He sighed. "If only we could eliminate Whitley. . . ."

Marcus stared at the tip of his boot, wondering if another dip or two in the fishpond would loosen Whitley's tongue. He suspected not. Having possession of a locket and whatever secrets it held was not quite the same thing as having a document that could lead one to the gallows for treason.

"I've considered getting the man alone and beating the truth out of him," Jack said abruptly, echoing Marcus's thoughts. Wryly, Jack added, "Of course, he could be innocent."

"I know we haven't found any trace of the memorandum, but I don't think he's innocent. He's up to something," argued Garrett. "Don't forget Keating told me that he's seen Whitley being very cozy with Collard, and I know for a fact, when in his cups, Whitley alludes to Collard being in his confidence. Now, he could just be bragging to make himself seem more interesting by being acquainted with someone of Collard's stripe, but I think not. Our major holds himself in rather high esteem, and I can't imagine him rubbing shoulders with one of the local smugglers unless it benefited him in some way. And the only benefit I can see to that relationship is that Collard *is* a smuggler and has contacts with his French counterparts on the continent."

"But that brings up another question," Jack said. "If Whitley has the memorandum and has made contact with Collard, why the devil is he still here? Why hasn't he lit out for the Channel Islands or France and taken the bloody memorandum with him?"

"Because," Marcus said slowly, "he's waiting to hear from the French." At the skeptical looks of the other two men, he added impatiently, "He has something very valuable and he's not a stupid man. He might have previously met the person he's dealing with in France and trusts him. It's even possible that he has already made arrangements for the transference of the memorandum in exchange for gold, but I doubt it. If he stole the memorandum, it was probably a spur-of-the-moment act. From everything we know, his visit to the Horse Guards that day had nothing sinister about it; he was merely going to visit old acquaintances and listen to gossip. Spying the memorandum on Smithfield's desk and having the opportunity to whisk it out from under his very nose must have seemed like divine intervention." He smiled grimly at the other men. "But having the memorandum and making it profitable is another thing. I don't know about you but, if I were in his position, I wouldn't just hop on the first smuggler's ship to France and go traipsing into Paris waving the memorandum under the noses of Napoleon's generals. I'd want to make certain that, number one, I could get back to England with my head still attached to my neck and, number two, that I was well paid for the memorandum and not cheated."

"Of course!" Jack exclaimed, his deep blue eyes glittering with excitement. "He has no guarantee that whomever he meets to give the memorandum to won't just steal it from him and possibly kill him. They have nothing to lose."

"Don't forget: having gotten his price, and presumably in gold, he has to get it back to England," Marcus reminded him.

"So it's most likely that he's using Collard as a go-between to work out the exchange and to transport the money back to England," Garrett muttered. "Which, knowing Collard, would be damn risky. I wouldn't put it past Collard to murder him and keep the gold." Glancing at Marcus, he asked, "I wonder if Collard knows what Whitley is up to?"

Marcus shrugged. "Who knows? But while Collard is a smuggler, known to be dangerous and ruthless, and though he might thumb his nose at our Revenuers and trade with the French, in his own fashion, I'd like to think that he's a loyal Englishman." Staring at Garrett, he asked, "How well do you know Collard?"

Garrett smiled ruefully. "Probably better than you. In my, ah, wilder moments, I've been known to consort with, uh, some characters that would never grace the drawing room of even the least member of the *ton*. I know him and his reputation and I'm aware of a cask or two of truly exceptional French brandy that has found its way to my cellars at Holcombe. And while I've shared more than the occasional tankard with him and others at Keating's inn, we are not bosom friends."

"Bosom friend or not," Marcus said, "I think he would trust you, or rather *not* mistrust you. You could join him in a drink at Keating's place and discreetly direct the conversation toward his recent activities without raising suspicion." When Garrett nodded, Marcus continued, "What we really need to know is if he has made the crossing to the Channel Islands or France recently. It isn't something he'd tell just anybody, but he might drop a hint—especially if you plied him with enough liquor. And if he dropped a name or two, so much the better."

' "I might be able to get some information from Keating himself," Garrett said. He grinned. "Nothing happens in the area that the innkeeper at the Stag Horn doesn't know about. And if he doesn't know about it, his wife most certainly will!" Looking thoughtful, Garrett added, "Keating might also be a very good source to find out how Whitley spends his days." Ruefully, he said, "The various searches of Whitley's room have not gone unnoticed by the major. He's complained to Keating that the servants at the inn have been pilfering his belongings and, since most of the servants are related to Keating, the complaints did not sit well with our innkeeper. I think Keating would be quite happy to fill my ear with his own complaints about the major."

"Very well, then," Marcus said, rising to his feet. "You find out what you can from Keating and Collard, and you, Jack, will be off to London."

"What about you?" Jack asked. "Never say that you are bowing out?"

Marcus shook his head. "No. But there doesn't seem to be much that I can do at the moment that can't better be done by the pair of you." He smiled. "I am a newly married man and, for the next few days, at least, I would very much like to concentrate on my bride."

Returning later that afternoon with Isabel at his side, Marcus considered his next step in the wooing of his recalcitrant bride. Isabel continued to prove damned elusive, and there had been few moments for private conversation—or anything else—since their sudden marriage. Despite the demands Lord Manning's illness placed on her, he was well aware that she could have found more time for them to be together if she had wished and that she had used the baron's ill health as a barrier to keep them apart. Marcus didn't begrudge her the time she had spent with the old man; he'd spent many hours with him also, but that was now at an end. There would be, he thought with anticipation as the curricle swung into the wide, circular driveway in front of Sherbrook Hall, no reason why tonight his bride would not sleep in his bed.

Pulling the horses to a gentle stop, he smiled down at Isabel, who sat beside him in the vehicle. "Your new home awaits you, madame."

She smiled shyly up at him. "It is not so very new, you know. Have you forgotten? I practically grew up in your house."

Her breath caught at the intent look in his eyes. "I've forgotten nothing," he murmured in a thickened tone. Then he grinned and said, "Including what a troublesome little hoyden you were."

Ignoring the stab of disappointment she felt, she forced a light note into her voice and challenged, "Aren't you afraid that I shall prove an equally troublesome wife?"

Throwing the reins to the waiting groom and alighting from the curricle, he walked around to the other side to help her down. His hands on her waist, he lifted her effortlessly from the vehicle. Holding her next to him for a moment longer than necessary, he bent his head and gently bit her ear. "I'm sure I shall think of enjoyable ways to deal with a vexing wife, ways that would have been totally reprehensible if used on my ward." Not, he admitted wryly, that from time to time, certain disgraceful thoughts hadn't crossed his mind—especially in those last few months before she had run away and married Hugh. As he slowly set her down, for a moment he wondered what would have happened if he had given into just one of those thoughts and taken her in his arms and kissed her. . . .

The sensation of that soft bite and his warm breath against her ear sent a tremor through her body and Isabel was embarrassed and astonished to feel her nipples harden beneath her lavender gown. Heat bloomed low in her belly and she stared mesmerized up into that darkly handsome face. The normally cool gray eyes were locked on her mouth and something in their expression both frightened and elated her.

A polite cough behind the couple ended the moment and Marcus turned casually and murmured, "Ah, Thompson, eager to meet your new mistress?"

Thompson bowed, his bald pate gleaming in the afternoon sunlight. "Indeed, I and the entire staff have been waiting eagerly for this moment." Straightening, he said simply, "It is my very great pleasure to welcome you to Sherbrook Hall, madame."

"Thank you," Isabel said, smiling at him. Even as a child she'd liked Thompson, learning that behind his austere features lay a soft heart.

Since her return from India a decade ago, she had stayed away from Sherbrook Hall as much as possible, but the friendship between the Sherbrook family and her father-in-law had made that impossible. To please Lord Manning and to keep her avoidance of Marcus from becoming too marked, she had attended a few dinners and the occasional soiree hosted by Marcus's mother, but had been an infrequent visitor. And yet, knowing that this would be her home, when she entered the spacious vestibule with its gold-flecked marble floor and elegant crystal chandelier this time, she was aware of a powerful sense of homecoming. There had been changes over the years to the house, yet it all seemed dearly familiar and all the memories of those days when she had been Marcus's ward and had treated Sherbrook Hall much as she had her own home came flooding back.

Isabel had always loved Sherbrook Hall, with its ivy- and rose-covered gray stone walls and gleaming bay windows. It was a grand place, grander than Denham Manor, but Barbara Sherbrook had decorated Sherbrook Hall with soft, warm fabric and colors, imparting an elegant yet welcoming décor to even the most formal of rooms.

The staff was waiting to be introduced to the master's bride and, again, Isabel was struck by how familiar so many of them were. She remembered Cook well, recalling the numerous warm buns and biscuits she'd eaten as a grubby child at the scrubbed oak table in the large, airy kitchens at the rear of the house. The housekeeper, Mrs. Brown, was no stranger either, and Isabel recalled Mrs. Brown's kind touch as, more than once, scolding all the while, she had cleaned and doctored her numerous small scrapes and cuts. There were new faces, of course, but many of the staff had known her as a child and for someone else what might have an unnerving introduction to a sea of strangers only increased Isabel's feeling, after a long, turbulent journey, of having finally reached home.

The crowd of servants dispersed to go about their duties and Isabel and Marcus were left standing alone in the vestibule. He grinned down at her and said, "A bit overwhelming, wasn't it?"

She smiled. "Not too bad. At least I knew half of them.

And since I am familiar with the house," she said, her eyes not meeting his, "I think we can forgo the formal tour, don't you?"

"Good God, yes!" He studied her for a moment, noting the slight stiffness of her body and the wariness creeping into her expression. Did she think he was going to pounce on her the moment she stepped foot in the house? He sighed. The thought had crossed his mind, but he wasn't a rutting boar. He paused. At least he hoped he wasn't. Reluctantly pushing aside the idea of a lazy afternoon spent making love, he said, "Shall I leave you to settle in? Thompson can show you to your rooms." It wasn't what he wanted to say, but the look of relief that crossed her face told him it was exactly what Isabel needed to hear at the moment.

Suddenly tired of being the thoughtful, considerate gentleman instead of the passionate bridegroom he burned to be, Marcus muttered something under his breath and dragged Isabel into his arms and kissed her soundly. He'd meant to kiss her once and leave, but the sweet allure of her mouth destroyed his resolve. He crushed her to him, his lips hard and hungry on hers, his tongue delving deep into her mouth. Consumed with desire, oblivious to anything but the soft, tantalizing body in his arms, Marcus kissed her again and again, each kiss longer and more intimate, more demanding than the last.

Isabel had no defenses against him. She was tired of fighting him, weary of fighting the dictates of her own body. She was his *wife*. Their mating was inevitable and, with a little shudder, she surrendered, forgetting the past, forgetting the secrets. . . .

Dizzy with longing and desire, she kissed him back, her fingers digging into his upper arms as she strained closer, needing, wanting his big, hard body pressed solidly against hers. He was aroused—she could feel the rigid length of him sliding between them as they kissed—and a flood of warmth and dampness surged through her as he cupped her bottom and held her hard against him. But it wasn't enough, and he lifted her, fitting her to him so that the swollen rod of flesh was tightly lodged at the junction of her thighs. She trembled as he moved against her, shockingly intimate sensations rocketing through her.

It was the insistent chiming of a small ormolu clock that sat on a nearby marble table that brought Marcus back to his senses. He lifted his head, realized where he was, and thrust Isabel away from him as if she had scalded him.

Breathing hard, he glanced around, his expression wild. Christ! He was in his own vestibule in the middle of the afternoon! A moment or two more and he'd have thrown her down on the floor and taken her there.

Running a shaking hand through his hair, he said thickly, "Ring for Thompson, he will take care of everything." He brushed past her, spun on his heels, and turned back to jerk her into his arms once more. He pressed one, hot, searing kiss on her lips and then pushed her from him. A febrile glitter in those gray eyes, he said thickly, "I'll see you later." There was both a promise and a threat in his voice. Moving as if the hounds of hell were on his heels, he disappeared out the front door, leaving Isabel standing alone in the vestibule.

Dazed, she stood there for several moments, her thoughts and emotions in a jumble. Gradually, her breathing calmed and some semblance of normalcy returned to her. She touched a finger to her lips, astonished it didn't come away singed.

She might have still been standing there if Thompson, carrying a fresh bouquet of white lilies and pink rosebuds, hadn't come into the vestibule. He stopped, startled to see her standing there by herself. His expression concerned, he asked, "Madame? Is there something wrong? May I be of service to you?"

Isabel shook herself and smiled blankly. "No. No. Everything is just fine. Marcus, um, just left." Still half dazed, she groped for words and managed, "He said that you would, um, show me to my rooms."

"It will be my pleasure," Thompson said. Setting down the crystal vase of flowers on the marble table and turning back to her, he said, "If you will follow me, madame?"

Marcus learned nothing new from George and Daniel when he interviewed them later that afternoon in his office in the stables. After the two boys darted away, he stared out of the window for several moments, turning the conversation over in his mind. He was inclined to go along with the explanation he had given Thompson earlier: George and Daniel had allowed their imaginations to run wild. The boys were young, both not more than fifteen and, while tall of stature and broad of shoulder, they were still children. He didn't doubt that they had heard *something,* but it could have been anything—from the wind rattling around a door to the brush of tree limbs against the windows. Relieved to have settled that matter, he considered the matter of Whitley's original break-in. The sensation of violation rippled through him again and his hand formed into a fist. Whatever the outcome of Whitley and the memorandum, before Whitley was much older Marcus intended to have a private moment with the major. Not only had Whitley invaded his home, he had dared to threaten Isabel, and Marcus discovered that he could not tolerate either act. A fierce smile crossed his handsome face. Yes. He would have a moment or two alone with Whitley before this ended. A moment the major would remember for the rest of his life. . . .

Whether by design or coincidence, it was evening before Marcus and Isabel met again. Both excruciatingly polite to the other, they dined alfresco in the sprawling beautiful gardens that surrounded the house. After dinner, a quiet meal in which neither did full justice to the expertly prepared dishes, they strolled in the direction of the lake, a gibbous moon casting a silver glow over the water. The scent of lilacs and roses drifted on the air and a faint breeze stirred the leaves and branches of the various shrubs and trees as they wandered down one of several meandering paths. Clouds scudded across the star-sprinkled skies, heralding the possibility of a spring shower.

Outwardly serene, Isabel was a mass of chaotic emotions. Tonight she would become Marcus's wife in more than just name, and she was eager and terrified of what would come. Risking a swift glance at his lean face, she wondered what he was thinking. Was he looking forward to making love to her? Bored by the idea? A little ball of warmth bounced down low in her belly. No, he wouldn't be bored; that torrid embrace in the foyer this afternoon told her that much. But when he finally made love to her, would she be just another woman to him? Would he feel nothing more for her than he did for any of the other women he had undoubtedly made love to in his life? He was no libertine, but he was certainly no monk.

Isabel knew a great deal about Marcus Sherbrook; she'd known him as a guardian, as a neighbor, and even, in an odd way, a friend. He had always been so self-contained, unruffled, presenting to the world a calm, measured face, but of late, she'd learned that behind that calm, measured surface, a different man existed. Behind his cool manner lurked a man who could kiss her senseless and make her knees melt, and it was that man—that passionate, demanding male he kept well hidden—that had her heart racing and her pulse pounding in anticipation of what would come.

The first light drops of rain fell and Marcus halted abruptly. As the drops increased, he murmured, "Well, this certainly puts paid to the romantic seduction under the moonlight that I had planned for tonight." He glanced down at her, a light comment hovering on his lips, but rational thought fled as his gaze locked on her half-parted lips.

Knowing how it would end if he touched her, he fought the primitive desire that he had kept carefully banked all evening. Struggling against the overwhelming urge to take her into his arms and allow passion to rule him, he finally managed to force himself away from her. He had barely taken a quick step back when the sound of a shot shattered the night air and his left cheek was struck by flying splinters as the bullet buried itself in the tall beech tree only inches from his head.

Chapter 12

Marcus's first thought was of Isabel and he dove for her, knocking her to the ground and shielding her with his body. For a frozen second, they lay there, both of them breathing hard, listening intently. Then they both heard it: the unmistakable noise of a large body crashing through the underbrush. Neither had any doubt that it was the person who had fired the shot . . . the shot that had come perilously near to ending Marcus's life.

Isabel struggled to push Marcus aside. "Get off of me, you big oaf," she hissed impatiently. "Whoever shot at you is getting away."

Marcus rolled aside and rose to his feet, but before he could help Isabel, she jumped up and plunged into the woods in furious pursuit of the shooter. In two long steps he caught her, jerking her to a stop. "What the hell are you doing?" he demanded angrily. "Trying to get yourself killed?"

Ignoring the rain and the blustery wind that accompanied the sudden storm, Isabel wiped away a dripping lock of hair and glared at him. "I'm trying," she enunciated carefully from between clenched teeth, "to discover who fired that shot. You, on the other hand, are being obstructive."

"And you," he said with equal care, his teeth as clenched as hers, "are too hot at hand for your own good." He took a deep, calming breath, tamping down the temper, engendered as much by fear for Isabel as fury at the boldness of the attack. Only when he was certain that he had command of himself did he ask with more than a little curiosity, "What did you intend to do if you caught him—bite him?"

So enraged she thought seriously of biting *him*, she spun away and, arms crossed over her bosom, stared into the darkness. The noise from the assailant's rush through the forest had stopped, but in the distance, above the rain and wind, they heard the faint sound of hoofbeats as a horse galloped away. "You let him get away," she ground out and, turning on her heel, she marched to the house.

Marcus followed her more slowly, frowning. The attacker could have only been Whitley, but what the devil was the man thinking? Whitley could have so easily missed and wounded or killed Isabel. Something cold and hard lodged in his chest. Attacking him was one thing; doing so in a manner that endangered Isabel was something else again. His mouth set in harsh lines he caught up with her as she mounted the steps and prepared to enter the house.

An anxious expression on his face, holding a lantern, Thompson met them at the door. George and Daniel, just behind him, wearing much the same looks, were also holding lanterns. At the sight of Marcus and Isabel looming up out of the rain, relief spread across his features, Thompson stepped back and cried, "Master! We heard the sound of a gun and feared the worst."

Marcus smiled and said calmly, "There was nothing to fear; your mistress and I are unhurt. A poacher must have strayed too near the house."

Thompson looked offended. "As if your gamekeeper would allow such a thing!"

Brown eyes bright and eager, George, the smaller of the two footmen, blurted out, "I'll wager it was that housebreaker, come to murder us in our beds!"

Marcus ruffled George's hair and laughed. "I doubt it." George appeared to be more excited than frightened about the prospect of his imminent demise. "Whoever was out there is gone," Marcus explained. "Before we returned to the house, we heard the horse galloping away and, with this rain, no one, poacher or murderous housebreaker, is likely to be skulking about. I suggest that you all return to your duties. Mrs. Sherbrook and I are retiring for the night."

Her maid, Peggy, was nowhere in sight when Isabel entered her rooms, but signs of Peggy's industry were evident in the neatly turned-down bed and the fine lawn nightgown and matching robe that lay across the cream and green silk coverlet. Wasting little time, Isabel stripped out of her damp clothes and slipped into the nightgown. Chilled from the rain, she bypassed the lightweight robe on the bed and, crossing to the dressing room, opened one of the big mahogany wardrobes that lined the wall. Her fingers quickly found the yellow woolen robe she had been searching for. Wrapped in the warmth of the wool, she took a brief moment to take down her hair from the topknot of curls she had worn for the evening. She spent another moment swiftly brushing the thick auburn locks. With her hair waving gently about her shoulders, she stepped back into her bedroom and was pleased to find that Peggy had once more anticipated her needs and was busy placing a tray on one of the satinwood tables scattered about the large room.

An expression of fondness in her blue eyes, Peggy glanced up from her task and said, "I thought that you might like a spot of hot tea on a night like this. There's some warm milk if you prefer that. And some biscuits."

Nearly twenty years Isabel's senior, Peggy had been her personal maid ever since Isabel had taken up residence in Manning Court. They had begun as strangers, and in the beginning Isabel had been a little intimidated by Peggy's brisk manner and blunt ways, but over the years a warm relationship had developed between them, a relationship that went well beyond that of maid and mistress.

Satisfied that all was in order with the tea tray, Peggy picked up the other robe from the bed and disappeared into the dressing room. Returning, she ran a critical eye over Isabel and, seeing her shiver, ordered, "Now into bed with you! You're chilled and the last thing you need to do is catch cold."

Isabel didn't argue. Tossing aside her robe, she slipped under the covers, sighing with bliss to find that despite it being the month of May, Peggy had warmed the sheets. With a bank of pillows at her back, Isabel sat up in the bed, the covers folded across her lap, and gratefully accepted the cup of hot, steaming tea Peggy brought her.

After taking a sip, Isabel said with a smile, "What would I do without you, dear Peggy? You think of everything. A toasty bed and hot tea—wonderful!"

Peggy snorted. "As if it takes any brains to realize that, on a rainy night, warmed sheets and a hot drink wouldn't be appreciated."

Her eyes dancing, Isabel said meekly enough, "It is indeed appreciated. Thank you."

"You're welcome." Reaching for the discarded woolen robe, Peggy laid it carefully over the arm of a nearby chair and then cast an eye around the room, as if daring anything to be out of place. Finding all to her satisfaction, she patted the tight bun of light brown hair at her neck and said, "Well then, if that will be all, I shall retire for the night. Unless, of course, you need me for something else?"

Isabel shook her head. "No. No. I'm fine. I'll see you in the morning."

The big room was very quiet after Peggy left, and Isabel sipped her tea thinking about the incident in the garden. A thrill of fear knifed through her when she remembered that terrible moment when Marcus was nearly killed. But knowing he was safe and nearby, she experienced again the unutterable relief she'd felt when she'd realized that he was unharmed. She bit her lip. It was wonderful that he had escaped unscathed, but there was no denying that someone had tried to murder him! And despite his claim that it was probably a poacher, she wasn't having any of it. There was no pretending, she thought stubbornly, that if he hadn't moved when he did he might very well be lying dead in the garden.

Pushing aside the terror at the very thought of him being dead or even gravely injured, she considered the attack itself. Whoever the attacker had been must have been both foolish and desperate. Foolish because Marcus was respected and well liked, beloved almost, amongst his many, far-flung friends and relatives. His death or injury by a cowardly assailant would have caused an outcry heard all the way to London. And risking a shot at him in the rain, with woodland obscuring the target and under fitful moonlight had been the act of a desperate man. Her gaze narrowed. There was only one person she could think of who was both foolish and desperate and would have had a reason to harm Marcus. Whitley!

So intent was she on the path of her thoughts, not even Marcus's appearance in her room distracted her. Frowning, still considering the implications of her conclusions, she watched him enter from the pair of double oak doors that divided their two bedrooms.

Wearing a black and crimson silk robe, he strolled across the room as if he did it every night. A faint smile on his lips, he approached the side of her bed. She looked, he thought besottedly, utterly adorable. Staring at her sitting there in the bed scowling up at him, her mane of flame-red hair flowing wildly about her shoulders, those incredible golden-brown eyes fixed on him, Marcus acknowledged something he had known for a long time: he was helplessly in love with her.

Dazed by the admission, he simply stood there staring, mesmerized. Completely under her spell, he took a second to realize that her lips were moving and that she was talking to him.

"What?" he asked stupidly. "What did you say?"

"I said," she replied impatiently, "that your attacker had to have been Whitley. There is no one else who has any reason to try to kill you."

There wasn't much point in trying to dissuade her, and so he met her eyes and nodded. "Yes, I'm fairly certain that it was your friend, the major, who shot at us tonight."

"He's no friend of mine!"

"I agree. I suspect that Whitley's only friend is himself."

"Most likely, but what are we going to do about him? He can't be allowed to creep about the neighborhood taking shots at you whenever the mood strikes him." Her eyes full of fear, she said, "Marcus, you might have been killed tonight. . . . If anything were to happen to you . . ." She stopped, her voice suspended by tears. Looking away, she finally managed miserably, "This is all my fault! I put your life in danger. I should never have asked you to intercede for me." Her gaze fierce, she glanced up at him. "I should have killed him the moment I laid eyes on him, shot him like the venomous reptile he is!"

"I don't disagree that Whitley appears to want killing, but I would appreciate it if you would allow me that task," Marcus said quietly.

It was the very quietness of his tone that made her look closely at him, her eyes widening when she saw the resolve in those calm gray depths. Her breath caught. "You really mean to kill him, don't you?" she asked, half horrified, half approving.

He sighed. "Probably. It's not something I will take pleasure in, but you called it correctly: he is a venomous reptile and I can no more allow him to live than I could a viper in the stable."

"Oh, Marcus," she cried, "you will take care? He is dangerous."

"And so am I, my dear, so am I."

The words were said softly, but it was that very softness that sent a shiver down Isabel's spine, and she looked at him with new, wondering eyes. Until this moment, if anyone had told her that Marcus Sherbrook could coolly consider the possibility of killing another man, she would not have believed them. Nor would she have believed him capable of actually doing it; but hearing that note in his voice, seeing the icy resolve in his eyes, she realized that there was much behind the calm, polite façade he showed the world. Her heart banged in her chest, memories of his ardent kisses and bold caresses sweeping through her mind. Oh, yes, she thought warmly, there was so much more. So *very* much more!

Their eyes met and suddenly Whitley and the events of the evening evaporated. Desire swirled in the air between them. There was only the two of them, alone in her candlelit bedroom on a windswept, rainy night. . . .

Marcus's gaze dropped to her nightgown, the peaks of her nipples visible through the delicate lawn fabric. She was naked beneath that frail garment and tonight there would be no more delays, no more reasons why he could not make love to his wife. No more reasons why he could not claim his love. His loins tightened and the passion he'd kept so carefully caged sprang free.

Isabel saw the change in him, saw his eyes darken, recognized the frankly carnal curve to his mouth and, half fearful, half eager, she closed her mind to anything but the knowledge that tonight she would well and truly become Marcus's wife. Her body tingling in anticipation, when he reached for her she fairly launched herself into his arms, her mouth eager for the touch of his and what would come.

His lips came down hard and hungry on hers, his hands on her upper arms, pulling her against him. There was no thought of denial in her response, her mouth opening beneath the onslaught of his, heat rising through her as his tongue delved deep. When he lifted his mouth from hers, she moaned in protest, unabashedly seeking his lips.

He laughed huskily and muttered, "A moment, sweet; we are both wearing far too many clothes."

In a second, her gown was whipped over her head and tossed onto the floor; his robe joined it almost immediately and then she was jerked back into his embrace.

Warm flesh met warm flesh and Isabel trembled at the sensation of her naked breasts flattened against the muscled, hair-roughened wall of his chest. His mouth was insatiable, his kisses more and more urgent as he laid her down on the bed. She jumped when his hand closed over her breast, the gentle kneading, the caressing thumb at her nipples sending spirals of hot longing through her.

Marcus had meant to take his time, but he'd been bedeviled by dreams of holding her, making love to her for far too many nights to go as slow as he wished. Telling himself he'd be more tender, gentler the next time, he ravaged her slender body with his mouth and hands. Those tempting little breasts called to him and his lips dropped lower and, with a groan, his hot, searching mouth fastened onto a nipple.

Isabel arched under his touch, the sensation of his warm tongue curling around her nipple unbearably exciting. Her fingers clenched in his thick, black hair, pulling his head closer, reveling in the intimacy of the moment. She was full of longing, aching, yearning, *burning* to become one with him. His mouth worked magic against her breasts and honied heat cascaded through her as his teeth lightly scraped across her sensitized skin. When his big, heavy hand drifted to the thatch of curls at the junction of her thighs and she felt his fingers exploring the soft flesh he found there, she moaned, surging up against him, inviting, begging for deeper penetration.

A fierce smile of satisfaction crossed Marcus's face when his finger sank slowly into her and he found her wet and ready. He wanted to play, to explore, but he dared not. He was so hard, so aching and full, that he feared if he did not take her, he would shame himself.

He shifted, sliding between her legs. His hands holding her hips to his liking, his lips fastened on hers and, as his tongue took her mouth, his swollen member slowly entered her. She was tight, her inner flesh slick and warm against him and he was so lost in the scarlet haze of pleasure that he plunged through the frail barrier before he realized what had happened . . . or the significance of it. But the second after he breached her, he *knew*. His eyes snapped open and he stared down into her face.

In a welter of pain, shock, and pleasure, Isabel lay still beneath him. It took all the courage she possessed to meet his gaze. She tried to speak but words failed her. He looked very dark and dangerous as he loomed over her with black hair falling across his forehead and his gray eyes smoldering with desire, but accusation and suspicion were also there in the hard gaze that pinned her to the bed.

Passion riding him hard, Marcus couldn't think. Questions flew through his mind, but they were clouded, drowned out by the feel of her soft body beneath him and the primitive desire to seek release from the mating hunger that clawed and screamed through him. He shook his head, trying to concentrate, but he couldn't; her body singing its siren song, desire drumming so wildly in his veins that it drove all else out of his mind. His eyes closed and his mouth closed demandingly over hers as he withdrew slightly and thrust himself back fully into her. Pleasure jolted through him and he was lost. Again and again, he plunged into her, each stroke coming faster, deeper than the one before, his hips moving in an ancient, urgent rhythm, frantically seeking to prolong the pleasure, yet demanding the sweet release, the scarlet oblivion.

The first shock of his taking filtered away and, with every stroke of his body, a fire, a desperate ache, grew deep in her loins. Her body no longer her own, she was swept up in the moment, her hands sliding to his driving buttocks, and she caressed him, urging him on, wanting, wanting, oh wanting she knew not what. A spiral of pleasure, pleasure so sweet she cried aloud at its intensity, exploded through her and the world spun away.

Her cry was his undoing and Marcus gripped her hips tighter to him and with a low groan, he thrust in once more, allowing ecstasy to take him where it willed.

Except for their labored breathing, the room was very quiet as slowly, reluctantly, Marcus slid from her body. He lay beside her a moment, then, saying nothing, rose from the bed. Heedless of his nakedness, he walked into her dressing room and found the pitcher of water he knew would be there. He poured a small amount of water into the china bowl and, taking up the washcloth neatly laid next to it, walked back into the bedroom.

Half dazed by her body's ardent response to Marcus's lovemaking, small aftershocks of pleasure still radiating through her, Isabel watched him disappear into the dressing room, her gaze mesmerized by his tall, lithe form. She shivered with delight as she remembered the feel of his lips on her breasts, the sensation of his big body moving over hers. But all too soon, reality came crashing back and she jerked upright, looking about for her robe, thinking she'd rather *not* face him stark naked. The sudden movement caused her to wince just a bit and, at that reminder of her changed state, a small, almost proud smile flittered across her face. She was a woman now. The smile fled as soon as she remembered the look in Marcus's eyes when he realized that she had been a virgin, and she decided that she definitely needed her robe before he came back. He was going to have questions, a lot of them, and he wasn't going to necessarily like or approve of her answers, and she'd just as soon have on her robe. Being naked left one feeling vulnerable and this was one time she couldn't afford to be vulnerable.

Though she knew he was right in her dressing room, Marcus's reappearance startled her as he walked back into the bedroom and, before she could stop herself, she shrank back against the pillows of her bed. He halted and stared at her for a long minute before he continued toward the bed. Putting down the bowl of water and washcloth on the table next to the bed, he said bitingly, "Stop that! I don't believe that I've ever beaten a woman in my life—even when given great provocation. I don't intend to start now."

"I d-d-didn't think you meant to strike m-m-me," she stammered. "You startled me."

Ignoring her comment, he reached over and moved one of her legs, his mouth tightening at the degree of blood he saw on her thigh. His jaw set, he picked up the washcloth and, after dipping it in the water, began to clean away the signs of what had happened between them.

The silence was so loud in the room Isabel thought her head would burst from the very lack of sound as Marcus quickly washed the stains from her thighs. Embarrassment crawled through her at the intimacy of the moment and she moved, trying to avoid his touch. The tightening of his hand on her thigh warned her to cease and she let him have his way. He said nothing and, staring at his bent head as he worked on her, Isabel wished desperately that he would say something. Say anything. Rail at her. Hurl accusations at her. Demand answers, an explanation.

Just when she thought she would scream to break the oppressive silence, he asked carefully, "So whose child is Edmund?"

She stiffened and her eyes burning gold, she said fiercely, "*Mine!* He is my son and has been since the moment of his birth."

He looked at her then, the gray eyes cool and assessing. "Don't lie to me," he snapped. Tossing the cloth in the china bowl of water, he said, "Proof of your lie is right here before us."

She glanced away. "In every way that counts, Edmund is my son."

"I hate to point this out to you," Marcus said, "but the last time there was a virgin birth, there was a star over Bethlehem." His voice hardened. "Tell me the truth. Tell me why you've allowed everyone to believe that Edmund is *your* son, the child of your marriage to Hugh." His eyes flashed. "From the moment you arrived from India, you deliberately foisted an imposter on the baron and allowed an old man to believe the child he adores is his rightful heir. Explain, if you can, how it comes about that the next Baron Manning will be illegitimate—with no lawful claim to the title or estates. And tell me, if you please, why I should help you continue with the charade." He leaned forward, his dark face inches from hers and demanded harshly, "Did you even marry Hugh? Or was that a lie, too?"

Frightened and angry at the same time, Isabel took refuge in temper. Her head snapped up and she glared at him. "Hugh and I were married in London by special license. You can check that out for yourself if you don't believe me!" she retorted furiously. Shoving him aside, she slid from the bed and snatched up her warm, yellow robe. Yanking it on, she roughly tied the belt around her waist. Feeling better with something to cover her nakedness, and her first burst of anger dissipating, she looked up at him and said helplessly, "It was what Hugh wanted. Even before Edmund was born he insisted that the boy's true heritage could never be revealed." Her throat thickened with memories of those first tense, miserable days in India flooding through her. She'd known from the beginning that some decision would have to be made about the coming child, but all during the long, uncomfortable sea journey to Bombay, she'd pushed that knowledge away. She—they all—were trapped in a terrible tangle, one in which an innocent child's life hung in the balance and it was all her fault. Her damnable, *damnable* fault! If only she had not been so impetuous and convinced Hugh to marry her. . . . Guilt smote her and her eyes filled with tears. "It's all my fault," she muttered, staring down at her feet.

"I doubt that," Marcus said acidly. "You could hardly have conjured Edmund up out of thin air all by yourself."

Despite the gravity of the moment, Isabel almost smiled at his comment. Trust Marcus to be so prosaic.

Standing up, he grabbed his robe and shrugged it on. He was shaken more deeply than he had thought possible. The knowledge that Isabel had been a virgin had filled him with exultation . . . and remorse that he had not taken greater care with her. But except for that one second of sanity, his whole being had been focused on easing the carnal demons that rode him. Merged with her soft body, coherent thought had been beyond him. It was only afterward, in those few moments he lay beside her on the bed, that he considered all the implications.

Feeling as if he had stepped off into a chasm, Marcus struggled to make sense of what he knew—or thought he knew. Isabel had been a virgin. That was a fact that he knew. His eyes dropped to the pink-stained water in the bowl. She had never borne a child and Edmund could not be her son.

He frowned. The boy was clearly a Manning, and he didn't doubt that Edmund was Hugh's son, but *not* Isabel's. So why had she returned to India claiming that Edmund was her son? To give himself time to think, and to destroy evidence of her loss of innocence, Marcus gathered up the bowl and cloth.

Isabel watched him as he efficiently cleaned up all signs of blood, carefully rinsing the cloth he had used on her and then, taking the bowl with the stained water with him, he walked over to one of the windows and, opening it, threw out the evidence. Setting down the bowl on the table next to the bed, he finally turned and looked at her.

His gaze locked on hers, he said bitterly, "I'm now part of your lie. No one but the two of us know that you and Hugh never consummated your marriage and that Edmund is not your son."

She nodded, too full of emotion to speak. She had always known that Marcus would never betray her secret and Edmund's, but it wasn't until this very moment that she understood what she had thrown away by not telling him. Never once had she given him any chance to decide for himself whether he wanted to be part of the lie that she had lived since the moment she had first learned of Edmund. Intent upon insuring her son's position—and she could never think of Edmund as anything but *her* son—determined to keep the vow she and Hugh had made on that long ago, hot, tragic day, she had never considered Marcus's role in the lie. Never realized the choices she had made for him.

There was no one in the area, she admitted miserably, who was held in higher esteem than Marcus Sherbrook. Everyone, from the most titled aristocrat right down to the lowliest scullion, knew that Marcus Sherbrook was a man to be trusted, an honest, fair man. And now she had made him part of the lie she lived every day.

Her hand rose, as if to reach out to him, then fell to her side. "I'm sorry," she said baldly. "I never meant to involve you."

"And how did you think to keep me out of it?" he demanded, not certain which infuriated him most: that she had not trusted him with the truth, or that she had insured that it would be impossible for him to do anything but continue the conspiracy. "You had to know that once I discovered that you were a virgin, I would know the truth."

Her ready temper spiked and, eyes bright with anger, she said, "If you will remember, I tried everything I could to end our engagement." She pointed a finger at him. "This is your fault! I never wanted to marry you. You forced this marriage upon me, and if you had not married me, you'd have been none the wiser. So don't blame me!"

Marcus grimaced. She had him there. "Very well," he agreed. "It is my fault that we are married and because of that I'm now privy to some unexpected truths—or lies if you will." His gaze narrowed. "Is this what Whitley was blackmailing you about? Edmund?"

Isabel ran a hand through her tumbled locks. "Yes," she said tiredly.

"How much does he know?"

"He can't prove anything and, if I hadn't lost my head that first day and given him money and had brazened it out instead, he would have gone away. I think." She sighed. "But once I had given him money, he was like a jackal scenting a tiger's kill: he knew there was something in the wind; all he had to do was keep circling around until he found it."

"But he has no proof of anything?"

She sighed again. "Not that I know of. The locket is the closest thing to proof, but in and of itself, it proves nothing." Her eyes met his. "But I didn't know what he had and I couldn't take any chances." Her eyes pleading for understanding she added, "But even without the locket, even if he couldn't prove anything, all he would have had to do was to plant suspicion and speculation in other people's minds about Edmund's legitimacy and Edmund's life would have been blighted and the baron's peace destroyed. The circumstances of my unexpected marriage to Hugh caused, I'm sure, a great deal of gossip here at home. And when the announcement of Edmund's birth arrived at Manning Court, I don't doubt there were some raised eyebrows when certain people counted on their fingers and realized he was an eighth-month child." She laughed bitterly. "Of course, it was probably no more than anyone expected of me, but if anyone had been paying attention, they'd have realized that Hugh wasn't even in the neighborhood when Edmund had to have been conceived." Wearily, she added, "While Hugh was alive we always worried about that, but there was no reason for anyone to look farther or to actually try to prove that Edmund wasn't anything beyond what we claimed: Hugh's and my son." Her hand closed into a fist and she threw Marcus an appealing look. "But if Whitley were to start asking questions, poking about, offering idle speculation, it's possible, though unlikely after all this time, that someone might uncover the truth. I could not take that chance."

Marcus cast his mind back to those painful months after Isabel had run away and married Hugh. Too well did he remember the gossip and speculation; even more did he remember the sly looks and smug smiles exchanged between several old tabby cats when the baron, delighted and proud, talked of his grandson, Edmund. He should have realized the reason behind the looks at the time, but he had still been reeling from the knowledge that Isabel was lost to him forever . . . and that she had borne a son to her husband. Even now, he felt the knife-edge of black despair he'd suffered then. He shook himself. That was over. Isabel was his wife now. A fierce, satisfied smile crossed his face. And she had never been Hugh's. . . .

He studied her wan little figure, aware that it didn't matter too much to him what lies or half-truths she and Hugh may have concocted around Edmund. All that mattered to him was that she was here and she was his wife. His wife. Not Hugh's. Never Hugh's.

Marcus tried to feel remorse over the intense pleasure that knowledge gave him, but it was beyond him. He wasn't, he thought wryly, *that* noble. Reminding himself that there were greater things at stake here than his personal gratification, he forced himself to concentrate on the lies surrounding Edmund's birth. Putting aside the right and wrong of it, she'd borne this burden alone for over a decade and, while he might have been furious that she had never given him the chance to share that burden, he was keen to hear the truth.

He glanced around the feminine room and grimaced at the two dainty chairs. It was going to be a long night and he sure as the devil wasn't spending it sitting in one of those fairy-sized chairs.

Abruptly, he said, "Come to my room. There's a fire." He looked at the teapot, shuddered, and muttered under his breath, "And something considerably stronger to drink than scandal broth."

Isabel was grateful for the interruption and she said nothing when he took her hand and fairly dragged her from her bedroom to his. Only after he was ensconced in a burgundy mohair-covered chair near the small, cheery fire and had shoved a snifter of brandy into her hand did he say, "Now tell me. All of it."

Chapter 13

Isabel looked around the comfortable room lit only by a pair of tall, silver candlesticks on the wide, carved oak mantel, gathering her courage and trying to think how to start. For too many years, she had lived with the fear that someday the events surrounding Edmund's birth would be made public and everything she and Hugh and Edmund's mother had tried to do would be destroyed. Not so many lives would be ruined now—Edmund's mother and Hugh were dead—but Edmund and Lord Manning were very much alive and it was for them that she had lived the lie. She glanced over at Marcus's hard face. A lie that was no longer hers alone . . . Stalling for time, she sipped the brandy. The liquor warmed a path from her throat to her belly and, knowing the moment could not be postponed, she took a deep breath and said, "Her name was Roseanne Halford."

Marcus started. "Not Ham-Handed Halford's only child?" he asked incredulously.

Isabel shrugged. "I don't know, but probably. Roseanne came from a very well-connected family." Leaning forward, she said fiercely, "She wasn't just a little nobody. Her birth and family was as good as yours and mine. Her father had even arranged her marriage to the heir to a barony, although it was never publicly announced."

Marcus frowned, recalling some old gossip about Halford

and Lord Brownleigh, known to be great friends, and the possibility of a match between Halford's daughter and Brownleigh's heir. The unexpected death of Halford's daughter while touring in Italy had cut up both families and ended any hopes of the two families uniting. If Roseanne Halford had died in India, the direction Isabel's tale was going, then it appeared that Halford had done some altering of the facts surrounding his daughter's death.

When Marcus made no reply, keeping her eyes on the fire, Isabel said softly, "Hugh met her when he was traveling in the north of England and when . . ." A knife-blade of pain sliced through her as she remembered that awful day. She took a deep breath and pushed on, saying, "And when she died, I wrote to a Mr. Halford at Vyne House in Bellingham to tell him that his daughter had died." Her face hardened. "I didn't tell him how she died, only that she had been visiting some friends in Bombay and had taken ill and died suddenly."

"Vyne House is Halford's country estate," Marcus said quietly. "So his daughter and Edmund's mother are one and the same." He hesitated, waiting for Isabel to take up the story; when she did not, he prodded, "She and Hugh met and . . . ?"

Tiredly, Isabel said, "They fell in love. Hugh offered for her, but her father turned him away." She flicked a glance at him. "At that time, Hugh was not in line to inherit the title and Mr. Halford informed him that he had a better match in mind for his only child."

Marcus nodded. "Halford was ambitious."

"And his ambition killed his daughter," Isabel said harshly. "If he had allowed her to marry Hugh, she might still be alive." Sadness overcame her and she muttered, "Even Hugh might still be alive. He . . . he was so unhappy after she died that he stayed away from home as often as he could. If it hadn't been for Edmund . . . and me, I don't doubt he'd have lost himself in the jungles." Her hand closed into a fist. "If it had been Roseanne waiting for him at home, he wouldn't have been sleeping in that wretched hut in the middle of the jungle where he was bitten by a cobra."

Attempting to distract her, Marcus asked, "Hugh and Roseanne, uh, anticipated their vows?"

"They were in love," she said dully. "They didn't mean to, but . . ." Her eyes daring him to say otherwise, she declared passionately, "Hugh was an honorable man. He intended to marry her. He would never have deserted her. When her father crushed their hopes he begged her to run away with him, but at the time she was too timid to defy her father. Hugh left Bellingham with neither one of them having any idea that she was already carrying his child."

Isabel rubbed her forehead and said painfully, "And then I met him by the lake and ruined everything by convincing him to marry me." She raised tragic eyes to Marcus. "It is all my fault! If I had not badgered him into marrying me out of hand none of this would have happened."

"You didn't get Roseanne pregnant," Marcus said dryly.

Isabel bit back an unhappy spurt of laughter. "No, but I created an insurmountable impediment to their happiness."

Discovering a streak of selfish single-mindedness, and not too interested in Hugh and Roseanne, Marcus asked with suspicious idleness, "Since you and Hugh were married, how is it that the marriage was never consummated?"

"I know the match was my doing," she admitted, "but if I could have undone it, I would have. It all happened so fast, there was no time to think, to reflect . . . to come to my senses. One moment I was sitting beside the lake begging Hugh to marry me and take me to India with him and the next we were at the Manning townhouse in London and married." She bit her lip. "Almost immediately, though we said nothing to each other at the time, we both realized that we had made a horrible, horrible mistake." Her expression miserable, she added, "We spent a horrid afternoon together, trying to pretend that we were thrilled with the marriage.

And that evening . . ." She swallowed. "And that evening when he came to my bedroom, I locked him out. He was my husband, but he was a stranger and I was frightened. I spent the night huddled in bed terrified. Hugh went downstairs and got roaring drunk."

Marcus tried to feel sympathy for Hugh and failed, but he had no trouble applauding Isabel's actions. "And the next morning? What happened then?"

"Hugh was very kind. He said that we were both under a great deal of strain and that we had all of our lives together; there was no need to rush. He was sailing for Bombay within two days and we had much to do before he left. He said that we could put off any intimacies until I had arrived in India. He swore that he would court me as I should have been courted before we married, and only when I was comfortable would we consummate our marriage."

Marcus couldn't fault Hugh's reasoning. "But I take it Roseanne appeared before this admirable plan could be put in motion?"

"Yes. Hugh made all the arrangements for my sailing to India on a ship that was leaving two weeks after his. He hired a companion for me, Mrs. Wesson, and had spoken with a young colleague of his, Mr. Akridge, who was sailing on the same ship that I was, to act as my escort. Before he left, he set up accounts for me to draw on and made a list of purchases I was to make—or rather, his man of business in London, Mr. Babb, would make." She smiled faintly at Marcus. "Hugh was very capable and he made certain that I had nothing to worry about."

"Until Roseanne showed up on your doorstep. Which is what I presume happened?"

Isabel nodded. "Yes. Precisely one day after Hugh sailed. She was terrified her father would find her and exhausted from the desperate journey to reach Hugh before he sailed. Meeting me devastated her." Isabel shuddered. "I'll never forget the look on her face and the horror in her voice when she cried, 'His *wife?*' and fainted dead away at my feet."

"Couldn't have been very pleasant for you."

"No, it wasn't! By the time she roused, I had ordered William, the butler, to take her upstairs to one of the bedrooms and had summoned a physician. He had just begun to examine her when she came to." She shook her head. "Poor Roseanne! She was so confused, so startled and frightened when she woke in a strange bedroom with a strange man bending over her. It took us several moments to calm her down and assure her that she was safe and that we meant no harm."

Isabel took a sip of brandy, her gaze on the fire, her thoughts far away. Finally she shook herself and looked over at Marcus. "She was a very sheltered, sweet girl and she would have been perfect for Hugh." She smiled faintly, memories rushing through her mind. "Roseanne was biddable and agreeable and so very willing to please that one couldn't help liking her."

"You apparently did."

She nodded. "By the time she died I loved her dearly and I would have done anything for her. I know you'll find it hard to believe—she and I only knew each other little more than six months—but in that short time, she became the sister I never had. There was no jealousy between us; I didn't love Hugh, had never been in love with Hugh, and more than anything in the world, I wanted them to be together—as they should have been. I blamed myself for the situation we were all in, but Roseanne"—her eyes filled with tears—"Roseanne blamed herself and tried to comfort *me*!"

"I would remind you that it wasn't your fault. Hugh had no business running away with a chit just out of the schoolroom! If anyone is to blame," Marcus said grimly, "it is Hugh. Not you. Not even Roseanne."

Isabel smiled sadly. "I think you are forgetting how determined I can be when I want something. I gave Hugh no chance to think about what we were doing. I pushed him into the marriage."

"You were seventeen!" Marcus said furiously. "He was a man of thirty or more. He should have known better."

Isabel waved a dismissing hand. "It doesn't matter now. What matters now and what has mattered all along is Edmund and his fate."

Marcus took a grip of his unexpected show of temper and muttered, "Yes, yes, of course. Tell me the rest of it."

"Once the physician and everyone had left us alone, in her fear and despair, Roseanne blurted out that she was pregnant with Hugh's child. I was horrified because it changed the whole situation. It was no longer just a case of not being able to marry the man she loved, but there was a child at stake now. She would have been ruined, but worse, the child would be branded a bastard, just another by-blow of a well-born gentleman. From the beginning, Roseanne and I were united to prevent that from happening, and fortunately, so was Hugh."

Marcus's grandfather, the Old Earl, was noted for cluttering the English countryside with his bastards, so Marcus was well able to understand and sympathize. He'd always been appalled by his grandfather's numerous illegitimate children, even if the Old Earl had carelessly acknowledged and provided for them, but even the Old Earl's blessing never took away the stigma of illegitimacy. The ranks of the *ton* were closed to them and their position in life was not always easy. Hugh had tried to act honorably and Marcus would not fault him on that even if he blamed him for the situation. Finding Isabel staring expectantly at him, he said, "So you and Roseanne sailed to India together to lay the problem at Hugh's feet—where I might add, it belonged."

"Yes. I dismissed Mrs. Wesson and substituted Roseanne in her place. I ordered Mr. Babb to make the necessary arrangements and to buy the extra items we would need." She looked down at her robe, unconsciously pleating and un-pleating a section of it. "The trip to Bombay was ghastly. Our quarters were cramped, the food toward the end nearly uneatable. It took over four months and Roseanne was sick through most of it. Her constitution was not robust and I feared she might die or lose the baby. I was terrified the whole time."

"I assume you kept Mr. Akridge in the dark?"

"Oh, definitely. We hardly ever left our cabin." Isabel looked guilty. "I suppose even then I was thinking of a way to protect Roseanne and her child, and the idea of passing the child off as mine with Roseanne acting as his nursemaid had already crossed my mind. There were several difficulties but none that I didn't think we could overcome. I was certain that Hugh would agree to it. The main problem would be the timing of the baby's birth." She glanced at Marcus. "Edmund is actually six weeks older than everybody believes."

"I'd already worked that out." He took a long swallow of his brandy. Seeing his snifter was empty, he poured himself another and, standing by the fire, his arm resting on the mantel, he looked across at Isabel and asked, "So how did Hugh react when the pair of you showed up on his doorstep?"

"Oh, Marcus!" she breathed, her eyes sparkling. "You should have seen his face when he saw Roseanne. It was as if the brightest light in the universe had illuminated it. And the love . . ." She choked back a sob. "His whole face, his entire being radiated his love for her. He was overjoyed to see her." Her voice thickened. "And then his gaze fell upon me. . . . It was dreadful. The worst moment of my life."

"Good God! The bastard surely didn't blame you?" Marcus exclaimed, outraged at the notion.

Isabel shook her head. "No. Never! It was just that one moment his dearest dream appeared to have come true and the next he realized what a nightmare we were all in."

"One of his making," Marcus snapped.

"Perhaps," Isabel agreed, not wanting to argue with him. "And despite the difficulties that lay before us, he was beside himself with joy at the news that Roseanne was carrying his child."

"I suppose none of you considered an annulment?" he demanded sarcastically.

"Yes, Hugh did. But time was not our friend. Obtaining an annulment in India was out of the question. By the time I could return to England and the annulment could be secured, the child would have been born." She stared off into space. "If Roseanne had lived, I'm certain that we would have faced the scandal and found a way to end the marriage—provided the child could have been protected." She looked up at him, pleading for understanding. "All three of us were determined to save the child—and Roseanne, too—from a life of disgrace and shame. We hadn't thought out all of the ramifications, but we all agreed that as far as the world was concerned I was the one who was pregnant. Within days of our arrival in Bombay, I wrote the letter to the baron telling him that I was with child."

"Yes, I know," Marcus said tightly, remembering too well the fury and pain he had felt at the news. The baron had been so happy, laughing and constantly talking about his coming grandchild, and Marcus had walked around wanting to smash his fist through a stone wall. He took a deep breath. "He even chided Robert for being a laggard in producing an heir."

"You do understand," Isabel said earnestly, "that at the time we had no idea that Edmund would end up being the heir? We all assumed that Robert and his wife, Georgine, would have children. Even after Hugh died and Edmund and I returned to England, though they had been married for several years, everyone, myself included, still expected Robert and Georgine to have children." She smiled in memory. "I remember how excited we all were when Georgine announced that she was pregnant. Edmund was looking forward to having a cousin to play with and, of course, the baron was delighted at the prospect of another grandchild and hoped for a boy, Robert's son and one day, his heir." She sighed and shook her head. "No one ever expected that Robert and Georgine, along with their unborn child, would die in that yachting accident, leaving Edmund next in line for the title."

Considering everything, Marcus suspected that—God forbid!—if he had ever found himself in Hugh's position he would probably have done the same; done everything within his power to see that his son didn't suffer for his father's mistake. Or that the woman he loved was not shamed before the world. He didn't blame Hugh for wanting to protect Roseanne and to insure his son's position in the world. As for Edmund becoming the next Lord Manning? Isabel was right: none of them had been prepared for the deaths of Robert and Georgine. Scowling, he stared down at his bare feet showing beneath the hem of his robe. He wanted to rage against someone; wanted to vilify Hugh, for all the lost years, but he could not. Isabel might have lived a lie, might have passed off another woman's son as her own, but had any real wrong been done? Roseanne Halford would have been an eminently acceptable bride for Hugh, and if they had been married, Edmund would have been Lord Manning's legitimate grandson, the legitimate heir to the barony. Was anyone going to be harmed by allowing the lie to continue?

For a moment, he considered the implications for Garrett Manning, then shrugged. Garrett was wealthy enough on his own; he didn't need Lord Manning's estate or money. And while Garrett might have enjoyed a title, from what he knew of the man, Marcus imagined that it didn't matter much one way or another to him.

He took a swallow of brandy. There wasn't much of a decision for him to make, he realized. He'd already made his choice the moment he had destroyed all evidence of Isabel's virginity. He smiled wryly. Besides, he was hardly going to *complain* that his wife had been a virgin.

Her gaze fixed painfully on his face, Isabel asked, "What are you going to do?"

He smiled gently at her. "Nothing. Absolutely nothing. As far as the world—and myself included—is concerned, Edmund is your son."

Isabel burst into tears. "Oh, Marcus! Thank you! You cannot know how I have feared . . ." Her voice suspended by tears, she could only stare at him, relief from the terror of discovery that she had lived with all these years suddenly overwhelming.

Marcus bit back a curse and setting down his snifter, jerked her into his arms. "Hush," he murmured. "Hush." He shook her gently. "You little goose! How could you believe that I would ever do anything that would harm you or Edmund?" He caught a tear on one fingertip. "I love him, too. I would never want him to suffer the stigma of being labeled Hugh's bastard, or watch the joy die in the old man's eyes."

Gulping back sobs, Isabel buried her head against his chest. In a muffled voice, she sniffed, "I did trust you, you know. It was just that it had been my secret for so long that I d-d-didn't know what to do. Everyone else was dead and there was no one I could talk to about it." With tear-drenched eyes she looked up at him. "I promised Hugh and Roseanne," she said thickly. "On the day Roseanne died, we swore together that no one would ever know the truth. And Hugh and I vowed that as far as the world knew, Edmund was *our* child."

Marcus kissed her on the forehead and, settling down with her in his arms in one of the chairs by the fire, he asked quietly, "Roseanne died in childbirth?"

He felt rather than saw the nod of her head. "It was a difficult, difficult birth." She trembled and his arms tightened around her. "There was so much blood and she was in such pain and so frightened. There was a physician, Mr. Evans, but he could do nothing. It was a long, hard labor and she was exhausted by the time Edmund was born. We laid him in her arms and she kissed him, begged me to swear that I would never reveal the truth, and then just slipped away from us."

"How did you manage to hide what was going on? Surely

you met Hugh's friends and colleagues, such as our friend Major Whitley?"

Isabel shook her head. "No, not until after Edmund was born. Once we all agreed that Edmund was to be my son, within days of our arrival in Bombay, Hugh removed us to the high country where we would have more privacy and not have to worry about the British residents in the city. During those first months, Hugh discouraged visitors, giving out that I was sickly and unable to receive visitors, but that as soon as the baby arrived, I'd be back in Bombay and eager to meet everyone." The worst of her tears over, she nestled her head on his shoulder and said, "Roseanne's death devastated Hugh. We buried her very quietly near the house where we lived; Hugh owned several hundred acres there. After she died Hugh informed everyone in Bombay that my companion that had accompanied me from England had died from one of the fevers. It was horrible for him. He had lost the love of his life, yet he had to pretend that everything was wonderful and that he was joyfully anticipating the birth of his first child." Her gaze far away, she murmured, "When we buried her, his grief was so new and raw, I was terrified that he would throw himself into the grave with her. I know that only the fact that Edmund was alive kept him from doing so." She sat up a little straighter and brushed the tears from her eyes. In a stronger voice she went on, "Evans's knowledge that the baby's mother had died terrified us, but we could do nothing about it. He was a taciturn man and kept to himself and seldom left the area where we were. Even if he spoke out, it would be our word against his and why would I claim as my son another woman's child?" She sighed. "His knowledge gnawed at us, but we didn't want to make the situation worse by offering him money to keep his mouth shut. We just had to trust that fate would help us."

"Rather risky, wasn't it?"

"Terribly. But at the time we could think of no way to lessen the risk."

"You don't think that Whitley talked to him? And what he learned from Evans isn't what set him on your trail?"

She shook her head. "No, I'm almost positive it could not be. Evans drowned the following year during the rainy season trying to cross a river, and to my knowledge Whitley and Evans never met each other."

Evans's knowledge of the truth bothered Marcus, but he suspected that if Whitley had actually talked to the man and knew that it was the companion who had given birth and not Hugh's wife, he would have been bolder in his attempts to blackmail Isabel. His actions smacked of a man without a very strong hand.

Breaking into his thoughts, Isabel said, "We kept Edmund's birth a secret for nearly six weeks and then Hugh had to pretend that his son had just been born, all the while mourning Roseanne's loss. And because Edmund was supposedly born six weeks later than he really had been, I had to remain in seclusion for several more weeks before I could return to Bombay with my one-month-old child." She smiled reminiscently. "For the first year of his life everyone marveled at how *big* he was for his age."

"You didn't resent the position you were put in?" Marcus asked with a lifted brow.

Isabel shook her head. "I loved Edmund from the moment he was born and I loved his mother. I made a promise to her to always protect him, but it was an easy promise to keep."

"I notice you said that you loved Edmund and Roseanne, but you didn't mention that you loved Hugh. Didn't you?" As he waited for her answer, jealousy clawed in his chest and he was ashamed of his emotions.

"I did love Hugh," Isabel admitted, "but more as a big brother. He was always kind and considerate of me." She looked at the fire, her thoughts far away. "I can't say what might have happened if he had lived. I would never have been the love of his life and he would never have been mine, but we might have managed to make a pleasant life together and make our marriage real eventually."

Marcus didn't like the empty hole in his gut that her words caused. He might have studiously avoided her this past decade but there had always been a part of him that had been glad that she had been living at Manning Court, a part of him that had been tantalizingly aware that she had no husband. . . .

"What about the locket?" he asked abruptly.

"It was Roseanne's. If you study the face of it, you can see in the midst of all the filigree work, her initials, RH." She frowned. "I have no idea how Whitley came across it. I can only assume that Hugh had kept it, unable to destroy it as we did everything else of hers, and that Whitley, with his constant snooping around, found it."

Marcus nodded. "That would make sense." He glanced down at her. "Are you ever going to let me see what is in the locket?"

She flushed. "Of course! Would you like me to get it for you?"

"Yes."

Isabel scrambled from his lap and, trailed by Marcus, walked quickly into her bedroom. She walked up to a dainty desk that had come with her from Manning Court. Opening one of the drawers, she removed it and, reaching into the back of the desk, found the spring that opened the secret compartment. Reaching into the compartment, her fingers found the locket and she brought it forth.

Looking at Marcus, she said, "I thought of just putting it in my jewelry box and having Lord Manning keep it in his safe, but I feared . . ." She shrugged helplessly. "This was the safest place I could think of to hide it."

She handed him the locket and, for a moment, Marcus just held it, staring at the filigree work. Isabel was right. If one looked hard enough and, he thought wryly, knew what to look for, one could make out the entwined initials of RH. With a flick of his finger, he opened the locket. On each side of the locket was a beautifully painted miniature; one of a man, the other a woman. He recognized Hugh Manning immediately. The woman, he assumed, was Roseanne Halford.

He glanced at Isabel. "Hugh and Roseanne?"

"Yes. Hugh had the portraits commissioned and bought the locket just before her father denied his suit. He had meant the locket to be a betrothal gift—one of many. When Roseanne's father rejected him, Hugh gave her the locket anyway, hoping that . . ." She sighed. "I don't know what he hoped, but he gave it to her just before he returned to Manning Court and prepared to sail to India."

Marcus studied the portrait, thinking that Roseanne had been a pretty girl and he understood now how strangers could mistake Isabel and Roseanne for each other. Like Isabel, Roseanne had red hair; it was not the vivid red of Isabel's glossy locks, but a lighter shade of auburn. Someone who knew the two women would be unlikely to mistake one of them for the other, but they shared enough similarities to fool the unfamiliar. Roseanne's eyes were blue and her features lacked the vitality and verve that characterized Isabel's, but again, a passing acquaintance could be forgiven for mistaking the two. Marcus smiled to himself. Of course, he was probably prejudiced—never in a million years could he have mistaken Roseanne for Isabel.

He looked at Isabel and asked, "Was she similarly built?"

Isabel nodded. "She was perhaps an inch or two taller than I am, but you wouldn't notice it unless we were standing side by side." Reluctantly, she admitted, "Roseanne was also more, er, rounded than I am."

Marcus walked across to her. Tipping her chin up, he said huskily, "My sweet, you are round enough to please any man." He brushed his lips across hers. "Your, er, roundness certainly pleases me."

Isabel blushed, but it was one of delight. "Th-th-thank you," she stammered.

Marcus laughed and pulled her into his arms. "No, don't thank me. You have an enticing little body and visions of you naked in my bed have bedeviled me for days."

Isabel would have preferred to continue this very gratifying conversation, but the locket and what Marcus intended to do with it preyed on her mind. Stepping away from him, she asked, "Now that you have seen the locket and what it holds, what do you propose to do with it?"

He, too, would have preferred to dwell on her charms and their effect on him—this was, after all, their wedding night—but the existence of the locket and what it represented pushed ideas of further dalliance with his bride away for the time being.

Frowning, Marcus stared down at the locket still clasped in his fingers. "The locket proves nothing but that Hugh had been enamored of Roseanne prior to his marriage to you, but its very existence in the wrong hands could raise all sorts of doubts about Edmund's parentage."

"Especially if someone like Whitley started gossiping," Isabel said unhappily, "about how I and my companion disappeared almost immediately upon our arrival in Bombay to Hugh's estate in the high lands." An expression of fright crossed her face. "The whole tale hangs together as long as no one looks closely at the facts. Several of the servants that were at the Manning townhouse in London are still alive. Roseanne and I were very careful to hide her pregnancy and she was in the early days then, so I don't think any of them even suspected," she admitted. "But they did know of her unexpected arrival and the fact that I dismissed Mrs. Wesson and substituted Roseanne in her place." She sighed. "As for Mrs. Wesson or the physician who first examined Roseanne or any others who might be able to remember those days before we sailed for Bombay, I know nothing of them or their whereabouts. And the servants in India . . . we tried to keep them at a distance, but I'm sure some knew or guessed the truth. If Whitley talked to one of them—or more horrifying still, actually brought that person to England—the consequences would be horrible."

"I don't think we have to fear anyone from India appearing on our doorstep. If Whitley had someone who was actually there at the event, it would have given him a powerful hand, but from what you've told me, he never did more than imply he knew more and threatened you." He glanced down at the locket. "I think this was all he had—besides the fact that you went into seclusion from the moment you landed in Bombay until you appeared with your son, which on the face of it is not unusual. Women of your station are always retiring to await the birth of their child."

Isabel took an agitated step away from him. "I know what you say is true and I never believed"—she flashed him a faint smile—"in my darkest moment that Whitley had anything substantial. My fear was that he could, and would, create a whirlwind of gossip and speculation, and that for the rest of his life Edmund would have to endure the whispers about his birth. Most of the *ton*, after the first flurry of gossip, would ignore it, but questions would always linger and he would always have the stigma hanging over his head. I couldn't let that happen."

Speculation in his gaze, he asked, "Assuming the worst and that Whitley spread his lies, if Lord Manning had asked you outright, what would you have said?"

Her eyes met his steadily. "I would tell him," she said calmly, "that Whitley was a liar and blackguard and that Edmund was Hugh's and my son. With no doubt."

He nodded as if he agreed with her. His eyes fell to the locket once more. "I think this bit of jewelry needs to disappear," he said quietly.

Distressed, she asked, "Must we destroy it? They are his

parents. I thought that . . ." She sighed. "No, you're right. I could never tell Edmund the truth."

"Christ! I should hope not," Marcus exclaimed. "What would be the point?"

"You're right, I know." She looked at him, her eyes full of misery. "I just feel so guilty."

He shook his head. "Don't. The time for any guilt is long past."

She nodded reluctantly and, fingering the locket in his hand, she asked, "What are we going to do?"

"Come with me," he said and walked back to his bedroom. Once there, he pried out the two pictures and, walking to the fireplace, tossed them into the small fire that burned there.

Isabel stood beside him, relief and pain mixing together as she watched the small portraits disappear in the flames. When there was nothing more to see, her eyes still on the flames, she asked, "And the locket?"

Marcus stared down at it a long time and then he tossed it onto the grate. From the wood box nearby he added several more logs to the fire. "The heat of the flames won't completely destroy it, but the fire will obliterate the initials."

She raised her gaze to his dark somber face. "Thank you," she said softly. "I knew it had to be done, but I could not bring myself to do it."

He pulled her against him and smiled down at her. "Edmund's entire life depended upon its destruction; eventually you would have brought yourself to do it."

Leaning against his hard length, she asked, "He's safe now, isn't he?"

"Yes, he's safe," Marcus answered. And will be even safer, he thought, once Whitley is no longer alive.

Chapter 14

When Isabel awoke the next morning, she was surprised to find herself alone in her own bed. Staring at the silken canopy overhead and remembering what had happened after the locket and portraits had been destroyed, she flushed over her whole body.

With vivid clarity, she remembered Marcus scooping her up in his arms and carrying her to his bed. A smile on his lips that made her heart thud and her lower body turn to liquid honey, as he lay her down, he murmured, "And this time, my sweet, I shall make love to you the way I should have the first time." And he did just that.

The flush along her entire body deepened as memories of the previous night flooded through her. His touch, his kisses, had been maddeningly soft and seductive, and when he finally merged his big body with hers, she had been frantic, aching to feel that first long slide of his swollen member sink deep within her. If the first time he had made love to her had been wonderful, she thought with a wide, satisfied smile, the second time had been, oh, utterly splendid!

Marriage to Marcus was everything she had ever dreamed it would be. She had been terrified of his reaction to her virginity and all the lies it would reveal, but she should have known that Marcus would never fail her. She sat up, her eyes widening. Why hadn't she realized that before? He had never failed her and, even when she had been at her most furious with him, she had known deep within herself that his actions had all been simply to protect her, whether as a wayward ward or an outrageous neighbor. Her pulse leaping, she wondered . . . could he *love* her? Did he love her as a man loves a woman? Were his emotions stronger and more powerful than she had ever suspected? Was what he felt for her something more than mere obligation and fondness?

She sat up in bed, her gaze blind and her thoughts chaotic. She never doubted that he had a fondness for her, but had she in her inexperience been oblivious to the fact that there might have been some other feeling behind his concern for her and his care of her? When Whitley had been badgering her that morning on the path, he had charged in with his stunning announcement of their engagement. And when she had desperately needed to discover what it was that Whitley had held over her head, he had obtained the locket for her. Even more important and telling, last night when he had discovered the truth about her marriage to Hugh and Edmund's true parentage, he had not hesitated a moment, but had immediately joined her in covering up the truth. She had lived in fear and dread of her wedding night, terrified that once Marcus learned the facts surrounding those fateful days in India that Edmund's life, Lord Manning's joy and her own reputation would be shattered. She frowned. Now why had that ridiculous thought ever crossed her mind? Why had she even for one moment considered that Marcus would betray her? Had he ever? Of course, she argued, he could be just protecting his own reputation, but couldn't his behavior be explained as that of a man with more than just a fondness for a woman? Didn't his actions smack more of a man that cared deeply, perhaps was even *in love* with that same woman? Oh, she certainly hoped so!

Joy bubbling up through her, she slid down from the big bed and, after grabbing her robe, danced around the room. Oh, could it be? Could Marcus love her? As passionately, as greatly and intensely as she had loved him for what seemed her whole life?

"Well, someone is very happy this morning," remarked Peggy, walking into the room with a large silver tray covered with various pots, plates, cups, and saucers. Putting down the tray on the small table near one of the chairs in the room, she beamed at Isabel. "Marriage seems to agree with you."

Too happy to be embarrassed, Isabel flung her arms around Peggy's waist and said, "Oh, Peggy! It does! I am very happy indeed."

Her face full of fondness, Peggy pinched her cheek. "And you deserve it, poppet. I've long thought that you and Mr. Sherbrook would make a grand match."

"Did you?" Isabel asked, reaching for a piece of toast. "Why?"

"Why, it's plain as the nose on your face that the pair of you were in love with each other."

Isabel frowned. "Oh, I hardly think that's true. We avoided each other for years."

Peggy snorted. "That may be, but I know the look you got in your eyes whenever he came to call on the baron, and the way you would mope around the house for hours after he had left."

"I may have," Isabel admitted reluctantly, chagrined that she had not hidden her feelings better, "but that doesn't mean that he cared one whit for me."

"You silly little goose! I suppose you think his kindness to Edmund all these years was simply because he enjoyed being climbed all over by a little boy not out of leading strings? I can't tell you the times I've seen Marcus in his fine London clothes wrestle on the ground with Edmund. Or the times I've noticed his eyes following you around the room when he came to dine or attend some gathering at Manning Court."

"Did they?" Isabel breathed, her face glowing.

"They did, indeed!" Peggy replied, grinning. "And you were just too blind too notice it."

* * *

Isabel rushed through her bath and resented the time it took to dress and for Peggy to arrange her bright hair in a topknot of curls. While Isabel fidgeted, Peggy calmly wound a length of gold and green plaid silk ribbon through the top-knot and pulled a few tendrils of hair down and left them to dangle near her cheeks. Only when her hair was arranged to Peggy's satisfaction was Isabel finally able to escape. Picking up the skirts of her green sprigged muslin gown, it was with a light step that Isabel flew down the stairs of Sherbrook Hall in search of her husband. *My husband,* she thought giddily. *Marcus Sherbrook is my husband.*

The object of her thoughts stepped out of the morning room just as she paused on the bottom step, and her heart felt as if it would jump right out of her chest and into his hands. At the sight of him, so tall and handsome and beloved, standing before her, a joyful smile lit up her face.

Rocked back on his heels by that dazzling smile, Marcus stared at her, thinking, when he could think, that she had never looked so beautiful to him, or so dear. His thoughts somewhat fuzzy, after a second he croaked, "Good morning. I thought that you would still be abed."

Though a rosy blush stained her cheeks, she walked up to him and, standing on her tiptoes, brushed a kiss across his chin. "My bed was lonely," she said shyly, "without you in it."

Marcus groaned and instinctively his arms tightened around her slender form. Leaving her warm and naked alone in bed this morning had been one of the hardest things he had ever done. Even after he had carried her back into her own room and pulled up the covers over all that delectable, silky skin, the urge to sink down beside her and waken her with a kiss had been almost overpowering. He had denied himself then, but he could not now. His mouth found hers. They kissed for a long time, and when Marcus finally raised his head and put her from him, they were both breathless and aroused.

Amazed to feel her nipples hardening and that sweet ache of anticipation flaring into being between her thighs with just one kiss, she stared dazed at him.

Marcus was not much better. The urge to pick her up and carry her back up to bed and soothe the raging hunger just the sight and taste of her had caused, he struggled to gain command of himself. They were in the bloody entry hall, for heaven's sake!

Snatching her hand, he dragged her into the morning room. Shutting the door behind him and leaning his broad shoulders back against it, he pulled her into his arms once again.

She flowed into his embrace, her arms clasped around his neck and her face upturned for his kiss. Beneath his buckskin breeches, his body was hard and responsive against her and, feeling the thick, rigid bulk nudging her softness, she gasped with pleasure.

Marcus kissed her again, this time letting his hands roam at will, cupping her buttocks, positioning her where he liked. Kissing her, having her feminine curves pressed so tantalizingly against him was a blissful agony, especially since his every nerve screamed for him to take her.

Marcus lifted his head and gazed wildly around the room, and then slowly, reluctantly but firmly, set her aside. Smiling wryly, he said, "I can hardly make love to you amongst the breakfast dishes."

Isabel forced herself to glance around the room. It was a handsome room. A woolen rug in subtle tones of cream, rose, and pale blue lay on the gleaming oak floor; ivory drapes flecked with rose hung on either side of a bank of windows, and comfortable chairs were placed here and there. The cherrywood sideboard was laden with various covered dishes and the oval table with its pristine white linen tablecloth and centerpiece of hothouse lilies and ferns graced the center of the room. Tall crystal salt and pepper shakers, cream and sugar pitchers, and dishes full of jam were scattered across the table; signs of Marcus's meal were evident in the empty plate, cup, saucer, and glass at the head of the table.

Marcus was right, and she giggled at the picture of trying to make love in the midst of all the various items on the table. Her eyes dancing, she said, "Indeed not. Besides, what would Thompson say?"

Almost on cue, there was a tap on the door.

Marcus obligingly moved away from the door and Thompson, carrying a steaming plate of coddled eggs, walked into the room. He bowed slightly and, smiling at Isabel, said, "Your maid said that you were awake and that you were very fond of coddled eggs."

"Thank you," she said and, though breakfast had been the last thing on her mind, she obediently found a plate and helped herself to some of the coddled eggs. Thompson fussed over her, pouring her a cup of coffee and offering her a rasher or two of bacon and some fresh strawberries and cream.

Marcus watched, amused at the antics of his butler. It would appear that his wife had stolen another heart.

After Thompson departed with the admonition that she ring should she need anything else, anything at all, Marcus strolled up to the sideboard and, taking another cup, helped himself to another cup of coffee. Seated himself, he looked across at Isabel as she made short work of her eggs.

"Hungry?" he asked, smiling.

She grinned. "Always. Don't you remember when I was a child the prodigious amount of food I ate?"

He nodded. He had many pleasant, delightful memories of her, many of them here in this very room as well as countless others all throughout the house and grounds. Idly, he wondered if their lives would have been different if he had not been placed in the position of being her guardian while still a youth himself. If their lives had not been so intertwined and they had not been placed in the position of adversaries, would he have recognized the affection he'd always felt for her was something deeper, more powerful?

His gaze blind, he stared down at the crisp white table-cloth. To this day he could remember as clearly as if it had happened yesterday, the first time he had laid eyes on her. She had been an infant, perhaps less than six months old, but already she sported a head of flaming hair and was snatching at life, at what she wanted, with tiny hands. He smiled. Too well did he remember the moment those big eyes, still with the cloudy blue of babyhood, had fallen on his uneasy nine-year-old self. He had been visiting at Denham Manor with his parents, and Sir George had been proudly showing off his infant daughter. Ignoring the cooing adults, her gaze fastened unerringly on him, Isabel had gurgled with laughter and reached out with both hands for his. Tentatively, and at the urging of his mother, he had put forth one finger. With another happy gurgle, Isabel's fingers had closed tightly around his, and for a long moment they had simply stared at each other.

Marcus shook his head at the memory. Could the bond between them have occurred then? It seemed incredible to consider it; he had been a grubby schoolboy at the time with scant interest in squalling infants, but *something* had happened between them in that moment.

"You are very quiet. What are you thinking?" Isabel asked.

"I was thinking of the first time I saw you," he said with a grin. "You were a squealing infant and determined to have your own way even then."

She grinned back at him. "Some things never change, do they?"

He laughed. "Indeed not! Now, how would you like to spend the day?"

A mischievous gleam in her eyes, she said, "Touring your

stables. I must see for myself that you have the proper quarters for my horses, especially, if Tempest is to be housed here."

They did precisely that and, as they wandered through the stables and Isabel took stock of the situation, Marcus smiled as he watched her, thinking that few brides would wish to spend the first days of marriage tramping up and down the aisles of one barn after another. With indefatigable energy, she dragged Marcus willy-nilly behind her as she inspected the stalls, the tack rooms, the sleek, blooded horses; spoke knowledgeably with the grooms and stable boys; viewed the nearby paddocks; and ended with a lengthy conversation with Worley, his head stableman.

Marcus said little during this, content simply to watch his wife, content simply to be in her company, but he suspected that his pocketbook was going to sustain a considerable drain on it before Isabel's notions of how her and their horses should be stabled. He was right.

It was late afternoon as they walked slowly back toward the house. Her hand was resting on his arm and they strolled in silence for a moment, enjoying the gentle May afternoon the scent of apple blossoms and roses borne in the air.

"Well?" Marcus finally asked.

She peeped up at him. "It's going to cost a great deal of money."

He nodded, a smile lurking in his gray eyes. "From the bits and pieces I overheard between you and Worley, I had already come to that conclusion."

"I do have my own fortune, you know," she said briskly. "The entire cost doesn't have to come out of your purse."

"Isabel," he said, a warning note in his voice.

"Very well. Worley and I both feel that we need at least one additional barn." When Marcus remained unmoved, she added, "Two would be better. After all, I have several horses of my own. And we think that a series of covered walkways between the various barns would make movement of horses and humans much more convenient during inclement weather."

"Convenient," Marcus said neutrally, thinking of the looming construction projects and the disruption they would cause for months—to him as well as the horses and stable crews. For a moment, he thought of his calm, quiet, well-ordered life before that fateful morning he had met Isabel and Whitley on the path leading to Manning Court. Sherbrook Hall would soon house an energetic twelve-year-old boy, a boy whose mother was already beginning the changes that would forever alter the serenity that had once been his. But was serenity the correct word, Marcus wondered? Odd, but when he considered life before recent events, the word *boring* came to mind.

He glanced down at Isabel, who was regarding him uncertainly. Married to Isabel, he suspected that "boring" was never a word that would cross his mind or lips for the rest of his life.

Some devilish imp made him ask, "Suppose I refuse to countenance any of it?"

To his delight and no great surprise, her eyes narrowed, her chin took on that stubborn slant he knew too well and, snatching her hand from his arm, she said hotly, "You would not dare!"

He laughed and, pulling her into his arms, he swung her around. "Of course not. I intend to be a very meek and doting husband."

She snorted. "What a rapper!" Her pugnacity faded and, just a flicker of concern in her eyes, she said, "I know it will be a huge undertaking and that the cost will not be light, but Marcus, it really *is* necessary if Sherbrook is to become a leading stud farm."

"Is that what we intend to do?" he asked innocently.

Realizing that he was teasing her, she grinned at him and, flinging her arms around his neck, said happily, "Absolutely!"

They enjoyed a light luncheon eaten alfresco in the courtyard at one side of the sprawling house and, afterward, ambled companionably through the extensive grounds that
spread out in all directions, their conversation skipping effortlessly from one topic to another. Having lived in the same
area and having known each other all of their lives there wasn't
the unfamiliarity that plagued most newlyweds; there was an
easiness between them not given to many. That wasn't to say
that sexual awareness didn't simmer in the air between them,
or that their hands and eyes didn't often meet, or that they
didn't linger a while in the shadows of shielding trees where
passionate kisses and soft murmurs were exchanged.

Dinner passed in a dreamy haze and, by the time Isabel
climbed into her bed, her body was one long ache of anticipation. Apparently Marcus was in the same state, because
she had barely pulled the sheets up when the connecting door
between their rooms opened and he strode into her bedroom.

At her bedside, he stripped off his black silk dressing robe
and slipped naked under the covers with her. Half propped
up on his elbow, he stared down at her, his gaze drifting to
the delicate lace that trimmed the modest neckline of her
nightgown.

"I think," he said huskily, "that you are wearing far too
many clothes." And promptly removed her nightgown. Sliding down beside her now nude body, he sighed. "Ah, this is
much better." He turned his head to look at her. "Do you
know this was all I could think of all through the day?"

Her body tingling from the nearness of his, she murmured,
"What? Bed?"

He smiled and caught her to him. His mouth brushed hers,
his big, warm hands beginning an intimate exploration.
"No," he muttered against her mouth. "I was thinking more
of this. . . ." And his lips slid like fire down her breast, where
they tasted and teased her nipple. "And this," he added, his
hand moving lower, across her flat belly, down to the curly
hair at the junction of her thighs. He parted the tender flesh,

stroking and exploring before slowly sinking a finger deep within her. Her hips rose to meet his caress, inviting more, and he complied; adding a second finger, he played with her, coaxing her into wild abandon.

Isabel moaned as he worked her, excitement and pleasure spiraling up through her body. She could not think, she could only feel and marvel at the sensations he aroused. Demandingly, she sought his mouth and, surprising and delighting both of them, kissed him as thoroughly and deeply as he did her.

With her hot little tongue thrusting into his mouth, her hips pumping against his hand, Marcus gave into the urgent hunger he had fought all day. His tongue found and mated with hers as he pushed apart her thighs and slid between them. With one heavy thrust he was buried tightly within her. Her fingers dug into his arms and she writhed wantonly beneath him, urging him on, driving him mad with her soft cries and seductive body. He was lost in ecstasy and the world blurred. . . .

Afterward, they lay locked in each other's arms, their breathing gradually returning to normal. Reluctantly, Marcus slid from her body and lay beside her. With her head resting on his shoulder, her silky skin brushing against his, he savored the moment. The knowledge that she was his, that this was just one night in the many they would spend together, filling him with a joy, a happiness he had never thought would be his.

But as he lay there darkness crept into his vision of their future together and he tensed. Whitley.

Even though half asleep, Isabel felt his body tense. "What is it?" she asked, alarmed.

"I was merely thinking of our friend Whitley," he admitted reluctantly.

"He's no friend of ours," she said sharply. "If you will remember, he shot at you just last night and it was only luck that he didn't kill you." She sat up, the sheet partially falling from her body, allowing Marcus an enticing glimpse of one rosy nipple. Shoving back her disheveled hair, she said, "In fact, I think it would be a good idea if we killed him."

His hand behind his head, Marcus regarded her thoughtfully. Though neither one of them had mentioned Whitley's name all day, he suspected that the major and the danger he represented had never been far from either of their minds. It was interesting that Isabel had just voiced the conclusion he had come to last night.

"Just murder him?" he asked carefully. "In cold blood?"

She looked taken aback, the reality of what she had just proposed sinking in. Biting her lip, she looked at him, troubled. "It would be in cold blood, wouldn't it?" she asked in a small voice.

He nodded. "One could even say with malice aforethought."

"I could kill him with my bare hands if he attacked someone I loved," Isabel began then stopped. After a second she shook her head and said wearily, "But I don't think I can sit here and calmly calculate a way to murder him."

"My sentiments exactly," Marcus confessed regretfully. "He wants killing, and in the right circumstances I could kill him without hesitation." He sighed. "I have a problem murdering him based on what he *might* do."

She cocked her head to the side, thinking hard. "He doesn't have the locket. To our knowledge he has no one to collaborate his suspicions. How dangerous do you think he really is?"

"I don't know. If he started telling anyone who would listen about the companion who accompanied you to India— even if he just breathed one word that there was something havy cavy about Edmund's birth; that he'd heard the servants talking or whatever. . . . He could claim he'd talked to the physician who attended Roseanne—how could you disprove it? He doesn't need proof. All he needs is to breathe one word about there being something smoky about Edmund's birth and it will spread through the *ton* like wildfire. After the first titillating rounds, most of the *ton* will dismiss it for the scandal broth it is. But there will always be those who . . ." He flashed her a somber look. "Gossip could be as devastating as proof, and once it begins, the rumors will follow Edmund for the rest of his days. The question is can we risk the gossip—if Whitley chooses that path?"

Her expression miserable, she said, "And if we wait until he starts the rumor, it will be too late to kill him."

Marcus nodded. "Killing him then would only add fuel to the speculation. So the question is this: do we plan cold-blooded murder to try to stop something that might never happen, or do we take the chance that he will simply fade away and we will never hear from him again?"

"Oh, God! Such a terrible choice!" Her eyes flashed. "He's a terrible man and I'd like to wring his neck for putting us in this position."

"Don't blame you there," Marcus said. "But it doesn't answer the question."

"I know that," she snapped. "I would do anything for Edmund and Lord Manning, but I can't, tonight at least, bring myself to contemplate deliberate murder."

"I suppose," Marcus offered slowly, thinking back to Julian's killing of Lord Tynedale a few years ago, "I could force a duel upon him and kill him." The idea appealed. One could argue that the challenge was cold-blooded, but the actual duel would give Whitley a fighting chance. Thinking of his own prowess with the sword and the pistol, Marcus gave an icy smile. But not much of one.

"You will do no such thing!" Isabel shouted, furious with him for even considering putting his own life at peril. She hurled herself across his chest and, staring deep into his eyes, she demanded, "Promise me! Promise me right now that you will not fight him in a duel."

"I can't do that," Marcus answered levelly. "He may offer me provocation that I cannot ignore."

For a tense moment they stared at each other. Isabel knew

from the implacable expression on his face that there was no swaying him and, miserably settling for what she could, she said thickly, "Then promise me you will not deliberately provoke him."

Marcus hesitated. Then reluctantly, he agreed. "I will not deliberately provoke him."

It was the best she could hope for and she fell into an uneasy sleep bedeviled by nightmares of Whitley, pistol in hand, standing over Marcus's dead body.

Whitley would have been delighted to know that he was disturbing Isabel's sleep and, perhaps to a lesser extent, pleased that he had placed both Marcus and Isabel on the horns of a dilemma. Of course, *he* would have had no such compunction. If he'd had his way, Marcus would be dead at this very moment.

It had been a stroke of luck that the opportunity to kill Marcus had come his way. He had been skulking about Sherbrook Hall considering another assault on the big, sprawling house when he had heard the sounds of people approaching. He'd barely crouched down behind some bushes when Marcus and Isabel strolled by. He had already assumed that it was Marcus and Isabel walking in the garden and the moonlight allowed him to confirm their identity. Stealthily, he had followed the oblivious pair and, thinking of all that he had suffered at their hands, the ugly taste of revenge rose up so strongly in his throat that, consumed by rage, he had dragged his pistol free and fired.

He regretted taking that risky shot at Marcus last night. But not for the reasons one might suppose. His only regret was that he had *missed* Marcus and by doing so had put him on his guard.

While Marcus and Isabel had spent an enjoyable day together, Whitley had spent the day sitting in a corner of the inn, imbibing tankard after tankard of ale, brooding over the unfairness of fate. When darkness fell, he changed from ale to brandy and, as the hour grew late, his thoughts grew blacker.

Things were not going well for him. Even that bloody Collard, back from a run to Cherbourg two days ago, had not brought him the news that he wanted. Which was probably as well, he thought bitterly, because at the moment, he was in a rather awkward position. He scowled. Blast it all! If it weren't for Isabel and Sherbrook . . .

They were going to pay, he promised himself viciously. Isabel had upset his plans, beyond that first paltry amount, by refusing to be cowed into giving him money to keep his mouth shut about what he suspected. Then that damn Sherbrook had nearly drowned him and taken from him the only thing he had to give his threats any credence. Sherbrook had humiliated him. Had not only stripped him of his clothes, but his pride and something far more valuable than a piece of trumpery jewelry. It was Sherbrook who stood between him and all his dreams of a tidy future.

In the time since the engagement of Sherbrook and the widow Manning, Whitley had convinced himself that he really had wanted to marry Isabel. Never mind that she wasn't to his liking; for her fortune, he would have made himself endure her scrawny body and hot temper. But not for long, he mused, no, not for long. Wives died all the time. His marriage to Isabel would have been of short duration and he would have played the grieving widower for all it was worth and taken great solace in her fortune. He smirked. Not hers any longer, but *his*.

He cast a bleary eye around the taproom of the Stag Horn and his lips thinned. Instead of having to put up with these country bumpkins he could be comfortably ensconced at Manning Court—he glared at his snifter of brandy—and enjoying excellent brandy, instead of this swill that he suspected the innkeeper watered down. His money worries would be over. He would live in a fine home, servants at his beck and call, and it would be his wife's fortune that kept him in a style that had always eluded him.

While the thought of killing Sherbrook brought him pleasure, Whitley did not want to hang for it, and he knew, unless fate presented him with a foolproof opportunity, that killing Sherbrook was unlikely. It was probably just as well, he admitted morosely, that his shot had missed last night. For the moment, killing Sherbrook wasn't possible, but there must be a way that he could cause trouble. . . .

A way presented itself, and a cruel smile crossed his face. He no longer had the locket, and approaching Isabel was out of the question, but what if . . . what if he called on Lord Manning? He liked that idea. The old man was just as vulnerable as Isabel had been and would, now that he considered it, probably be an easier mark. Yes, he should have thought of that approach first. Manning had the most to lose. Yes, he would call at Manning Court tomorrow. It would be just a polite visit wherein he mentioned that he was an old friend of Hugh's passing through the neighborhood and had thought to call upon his old friend's widow . . .

He chuckled to himself, imagining Isabel's consternation when she learned of his visit. She'd pay. She'd pay him anything to keep him away from the old man. Happy with his plans for the morning, and thinking he would enjoy some female companionship, he stood up unsteadily and staggered outside, calling for the stable boy to bring him his horse. An accommodating widow who enjoyed his patronage during his stay lived just a mile out of the village.

Whitley had been too engrossed in his drunken misery and vengeful thoughts to note any strangers in the taproom or the pair of intelligent eyes that idly watched his every move. If he had not been quite so drunk, he might have noticed the gentleman who had sat half-hidden at a table in the shadows by the stairs and have realized instantly that Collard had not told quite the truth about his trip to Cherbourg. . . .

The stranger paid his bill and slowly wandered out of the inn, timing his progress so that Whitley had already mounted his horse and was riding down the road. He quickly reached his own horse tied out of sight at the side of the inn and, swinging into the saddle, discreetly followed Whitley.

He waited until they had left the village behind before he struck. Kicking his horse into a gallop, he bore down on his prey.

His brain befuddled by drink and lost in his thoughts, Whitley had no warning of danger until it was too late. He heard the approach of a horseman behind him, had only a moment to realize that the racing horse behind him was coming too fast and was likely going to collide with his own on the narrow track before his head exploded in a blaze of pain and blinding light.

Chapter 15

Whitley woke with a ferociously aching head and the scent of the sea in his nostrils. Groaning from pain, he glanced around, astonished to discover that he was in one of the many caves carved out along the shoreline by the powerful Channel waves. What the devil? He struggled to rise from the pebble-strewn floor of the cave and the first faint quiver of fear shot through him when he realized that he was bound hand and foot. And, as his gaze fell upon the gentleman leaning casually against the wall of the cave, that he was not alone.

"*Bon!*" said the stranger. "You are awake at last."

"Where am I?" croaked Whitley.

"It does not matter, *mon amie*," replied the other man. "What matters are the answers you shall give me to the questions I shall ask, *oui*?"

Thinking feverishly, Whitley tried to get his bearings, tried to make sense of what had happened. He remembered drinking at the Stag Horn last night, vaguely remembered riding on his horse . . .

Whitley twisted around, squinting at the faint light that filled the front half of the cave. It was daylight, so some period of time had passed. God! He wished he could think clearly. If only the incessant pounding in his head would cease!

He glanced over at the stranger, taking his measure. The stranger, who regarded him with a cool smile, was tall, his build lean and muscular, and his clothes—from the nankeen breeches to the superbly fitted dark blue coat—were those of a gentleman. His features were even and not unattractive and his hair was dark, as was his complexion. From his speech, Whitley assumed he was French.

Excitement coursed through him. Dragging himself up into a sitting position, Whitley rested his back against the wall of the cave and muttered, "Collard *did* deliver my message, after all."

The stranger nodded. *"Oui."*

Uneasy with his position, but feeling a little braver moment by the moment, Whitley demanded, "But why did he lie to me? And who are you? Why am I being treated like this? Charbonneau shall certainly hear of your high-handed actions, I can tell you that—and he won't be pleased. We are good friends."

"Monsieur Whitley," said the stranger, "we will deal much better with each other if you allow *moi* to ask the questions."

"I'm not answering any of your damn questions until you tell me what this is about," Whitley blustered. "You've had the audacity to tie me up like a common criminal, and I don't appreciate it one bit." Frowning, Whitley demanded again, "Who the bloody hell are you?" The stranger's brow quirked at Whitley's tone, but he did not answer. More confident and angry, Whitley declared angrily, "This is an outrage! I am a British subject and this is British soil and you have no right to treat me this way. I insist that you untie me this instant!"

The stranger straightened from his languid position against the wall and walked to Whitley and calmly kicked him in the face. Whitley screamed from the pain, blood gushing from his nose and lips.

"First of all, I'm afraid that you are in no position to *insist* upon anything, and I did tell you, did I not," said the gentleman in perfect King's English, "that I ask the questions."

Blinking from the pain, Whitley stared up at him in horror. "You're *English*!"

The man smiled. "I am," said the stranger, "whatever I wish to be. English. French. Spanish." He shrugged. "Whatever the situation calls for."

Confused and uneasy, Whitley sought to make sense of the situation. This man could not have come from Charbonneau. Which meant that his cleverly worded message to his long-time acquaintance on Napoleon's staff had fallen into the wrong hands and that could only happen if . . . Fright bloomed throughout his body. "Collard betrayed me," he said dully.

The gentleman nodded. "Collard and I have served each other's needs well over the years," said the stranger. "And when we met on his latest trip to Cherbourg, he mentioned you and said he thought you were up to something that might interest me. For a generous price he gave me your letter to Charbonneau."

Whitley had been very careful in what he had written to Charbonneau, fearful of what would happen should his letter fall into the wrong hands. On the surface his letter had simply been that of one old friend to another. Thankfully, he had written no specifics, but he had alluded to previous mutually beneficial meetings, meetings that could be construed as only references to former pleasant times and leaving the door open to another, hopefully delightful, meeting with Charbonneau.

A surge of confidence went through him. This fellow may have read his message to Charbonneau and, while he might think that there was something in it for him, he couldn't *know* anything.

"I'm afraid that I don't quite understand," Whitley said. "What could my letter have to do with you? I have known Charbonneau for years. We often correspond with each other."

"Via a smuggler?"

Whitley flushed. "France and Britain are at war. The normal avenues of communication are not open to me."

The words had hardly left Whitley's mouth before his captor kicked him again in the face. Harder.

As Whitley writhed and howled on the floor in pain, the man bent lower and said softly in his ear, "Do not waste my time. Tell me what is so important that you sent a seemingly innocuous letter to a member of Napoleon's inner circle. And do not tell me again that it was merely a note to an old friend."

"Go to hell!" Whitley spat, scooting as fast and as far away from the other man as possible.

"I shall no doubt do just that," the man said, pacing beside Whitley. He kicked him again, this time in the ribs, and added, "And if you do not answer my questions, I assure you that you shall be there before me."

Whitley felt a rib snap and pain splintered through his chest. Breathless from pain, fear gnawed in his gut. He risked a glance at the other man and the cold glitter in those dark blue, almost black eyes terrified him, but greed overrode his fear. "I don't know what you're talking about," he cried. "I swear to you, I merely wrote to an old friend."

"Have it your way," said the stranger and spent the next several minutes viciously applying his boot to any part of Whitley's thrashing body he could reach. When he finally stopped, Whitley lay unmoving with his back to him, only a shuddering whimper now and then giving sign that he was still alive.

"Tell me what I want to know," said the man in the same calm tone he'd used earlier. Whitley only mewled and struggled to wiggle away. The stranger sighed.

Removing his coat and lying it on a large boulder, he extracted a knife from his boot. He flipped Whitley over to face him. Squatting on his haunches, and with his face only inches from Whitley's, he asked quietly, "Do you truly wish to die? Is what you have worth your life? Wouldn't it be better to simply tell me . . . and live?"

Through his battered lips, Whitley managed, "Why should I? You're going to kill me anyway."

"Not if I like what you have to tell me."

The man showed Whitley the slender-bladed knife he held in his hand. "I am very adept with this little instrument. I can keep you alive for hours, but before you die you *will* tell me, *mon amie*, what I want to know." He smiled. "Of course, you could tell me now and save both of us time and pain."

"If I tell you, you won't kill me?" Whitley asked eagerly.

"I already told you I would not."

His body one long shriek of agony, Whitley eyed the knife. How much more of this torture could he bear? Was it worth dying for? Sickly, he realized that there was no safe way out for him. If he didn't tell, he would die. If he told, he *might* live. And so he told.

When he finished speaking, he held his breath. Would he live? Or die?

His thoughts turned inward, the stranger remained silent for a long moment. Then rising gracefully to his feet, he said, "You are a fool. Too foolish, almost, to live."

When Whitley whined and shrank away from him, the man said disgustedly, "Oh, stop that. I have no intention of killing you."

Leaving Whitley where he lay, he turned away and, after slipping the knife into his boot, he shrugged into his coat. He looked at Whitley and said, "I suggest that you consider another continent for your retirement. I understand that there are parts of America that remind one of England." His gaze icy, he added, "Be aware that should you cross my path again or should I hear of any further meddling in things that don't concern you, I shall make it my business to hunt you down and slit your throat—as I should do now. Understand me?"

Hardly daring to believe his luck, Whitley nodded vigorously.

The stranger swung on his heel and began to walk away.

"Wait!" called Whitley frantically, struggling against his bonds. "What about me?"

"I'll send Collard," the stranger said without slowing his stride or looking back. "He'll set you free. And Whitley: I suggest you leave this area within the hour of being set free." He glanced back at him. "If I hear that you have not . . ."

Whitley gulped and nodded and breathed a sigh of relief when the man disappeared. Alone in the cool, dim cave, despite the agony knifing through his body, Whitley fought to escape the ropes on his hands and feet. Had the man lied? Had he left him here to die?

The bonds held tight and, when the pain racking his body grew too great, Whitley simply lay there panting and exhausted, hoping the stranger had told the truth. He waited what seemed like hours, testing the ropes from time to time, but always ending up flopping back down flat on the rough surface of the cave, defeated. When he finally heard the sound of someone scrambling over the rocks near the entrance of the cave, he could hardly believe it.

"Collard! Collard! Is that you? I'm in here!" he shouted.

It was Collard and, seeing the man's stocky form in the faint light filtering in from outside, Whitley had never been so happy to see anyone in his life. "Thank God you came," he cried happily, forgetting that Collard had betrayed him.

Collard said nothing. He walked up to where Whitley lay and, taking out his knife, knelt down on one knee behind him.

Eagerly Whitley thrust his bound hands out for Collard to cut. Collard snorted, grabbed Whitley's hair, jerked his head back, and sliced his throat as neatly as a butcher dispatches a goat.

Whitley bleated once, twitched and lay still. When he was certain Whitley was dead, Collard stood up, carelessly wiping his blade on his pants. "I don't care what the man said," he muttered to himself, staring down at Whitley's corpse. "It never pays to leave behind a witness."

*   *   *

The newlyweds heard nothing about Whitley's disappearance until Saturday afternoon when Garrett came to call. Marcus and Isabel spent a pleasurable morning wandering through the stables and barns, Isabel pointing out the changes she wanted to make and, since he thought her ideas were excellent, Marcus nodding in agreement. They smiled and laughed often, their hands touching and their bodies brushing against the other's as they walked. Anyone observing them could tell in an instant that they were lovers and deeply in love. When Thompson announced Garrett, Marcus was in his office trying to catch up with various estate matters and Isabel was closeted with the housekeeper, familiarizing herself with the routine of the household and discussing the few changes that having a boisterous twelve-year-old boy in residence would require. At Garrett's entrance, Marcus threw down the sheaf of papers duly presented to him that morning by his bailiff with relief and rose eagerly to his feet, hand outstretched.

After the two men shook hands and exchanged warm greetings, they seated themselves in a pair of overstuffed chairs on the far side of the room.

"I do apologize for barging in on you this way," Garrett said ruefully, "but I felt it was important that you know that Whitley has apparently disappeared."

Marcus looked shocked. "Disappeared? What do you mean? He left the Stag Horn?"

"I mean precisely what I said, 'disappeared.' Whitley rode away from the inn on his horse very late on Wednesday night and no one has seen him since. Keating admits that Whitley was foxed when he left, but not too drunk to mount his horse and ride away. Most disturbing of all, his horse was in the stall when the stable boy woke Thursday morning, but there has been no sign of Whitley since then."

Frowning, Marcus said, "I assume that no one has found him lying with a broken neck in a ditch somewhere?"

Garrett shook his head. "That was the first thing Keating did Thursday afternoon when he discovered that Whitley was not in his rooms. He was certain that was exactly what they would find, but a search found nothing. No body. No signs of anything amiss all along the road for a few miles in either direction. Of course, it's possible that whatever happened occurred some distance further, but that doesn't seem likely. Keating was fairly certain that Whitley had been going to visit Mrs. Halley when he left and, when they did not find his body, Keating then thought to see if perhaps Whitley had remained at Mrs. Halley's longer than expected."

At the mention of Mrs. Halley, both men smiled slightly.

Mrs. Halley was an accommodating widow of an uncertain age who lived in a tidy cottage a few miles from the village. When she had moved in five years ago, there was some speculation that "widow" was an honorary title, but since she was an amiable soul with genteel manners and plied her business very discreetly, she was accepted into the village by all but the most puritanical. While Marcus had never visited the widow, it didn't surprise him that Whitley had been a client.

"I take it he was not there?"

"No. Mrs. Halley said that she had not seen him since last Sunday . . . when he had come to call."

Marcus rubbed his chin. "The horse in the stables is troublesome. Someone returned the animal."

"I agree." Garrett leaned forward. "I don't like it, Marcus. When I was at the inn last night and inquired after Whitley and learned what I did, I insisted that Keating let me see Whitley's room. He did. The room looked like just what you would expect. His clothes, everything was still there. It looked like he had just stepped out and had every intention of returning. Keating has the wind up and I don't blame him. Whitley had no reason to disappear and, if he was going to leave the area, why didn't he pay his bill, pack his things, mount his horse, and ride away? His disappearance makes no sense."

"Unless he managed to make contact with someone who was interested in buying the memorandum," Marcus said grimly. "It's entirely possible that the French are now in possession of the memorandum and that Whitley is feeding the fish at the bottom of the Channel somewhere."

Garrett nodded. "I'd already thought of that." He frowned. "Except the return of the horse, that bothers me. Why would someone do that? Why not just turn the animal loose? Or steal it, for that matter. I seem to recall it is a good-looking horse; any horse thief would be happy to take it."

"Probably because we're not dealing with a horse thief and I can think of one good reason not to simply turn the animal loose: whoever is behind this wouldn't want it found in the area where Whitley may have been dispatched."

"You think Whitley's dead, don't you?"

"I feel that is his most likely fate. I can't think of any other reason for him to disappear so mysteriously, leaving all his belongings behind. And since the horse was returned, we know that someone else was involved, because I'll wager that it wasn't Whitley who put the animal in the stall."

"You think he went to meet the buyer on Wednesday night and that they took the memorandum and killed him?"

Marcus nodded. "That's exactly what I think happened."

Glumly the two men stared at each other. "So the memorandum is probably in the hands of the French by now," Garrett said bitterly.

Marcus shrugged. "Probably. But until we find out what happened to Whitley we won't know for certain." Marcus stood up and took a turn around the room. Looking over at Garrett, he said finally, "We have to let Jack and Roxbury know."

"I've already done that. I sent off a message to Jack at first light."

"So until we hear from Jack or Roxbury we are at a stand-still," Marcus said. Stopping before one of the tall windows that graced the room, he stared out sightlessly at the beautiful, rolling expanse of garden that met his gaze. "It is possible that Whitley's disappearance has nothing to do with the memorandum," he said slowly, a moment later.

Surprise on his face, Garrett asked, "What do you mean?"

Marcus came back and sat down again. "One of the reasons why we never tackled Whitley directly was because we had no sure proof that he even had the memorandum. It is more than likely that a real spy, someone like that *Le Renard* Jack mentioned, has the memorandum. We had suspicion aplenty, and circumstances certainly put Whitley in a position to have snatched the memorandum, but all we really had were suspicion and circumstance."

"And," chimed in Garrett, frowning now, "his belongings were searched by both you and Jack and neither one of you ever found anything incriminating."

"Which didn't mean Whitley didn't have the memorandum, only that we didn't find it." Marcus sighed. "I wish I'd followed my first instinct and beaten the truth out of the man."

Garrett laughed without humor. "You, too? That thought crossed my mind more than once."

They shared a wry smile.

"I repeat: we still don't know that Whitley has the memorandum and if his disappearance is connected to it." A silence fell as they turned this thought over in their minds.

"Do you think we've been chasing shadows?" Garrett asked eventually.

Marcus grimaced. "It's possible. Considering the sort of fellow he is, or was, there are no doubt any number of people who would not shed a tear if he died or disappeared." *Myself among them,* Marcus admitted. Without question Isabel was not the only person that Whitley had attempted to extort money from over the years, nor would she have been last;

was it possible someone from Whitley's past had murdered him? Marcus liked that idea, but he was not entirely at ease with that explanation. The likelihood of Whitley having possession of the memorandum surrounding Wellesley's planned invasion of Portugal was too important to dismiss out of hand.

His expression troubled, Marcus stared at his gleaming boots. "If Whitley had the memorandum, where would he have kept it? As you mentioned, we've been through all his things and didn't find it. And if he were going to meet a buyer for the memorandum on the night he vanished, wouldn't he have brought it with him? And if he did, where had he hidden it so that none of us ever found it?"

"You don't think he left it in London, do you?"

Marcus shook his head decisively. "No. If he had it, he brought it with him. Besides, if he had left it in London and was preparing to meet a buyer, he would have had to go get it—and we know he never left the vicinity."

"Maybe he just buried it in the ground somewhere," Garrett offered dejectedly. "Or was wearing it."

An arrested expression on his face, Marcus considered that idea. Whitley *had* been wearing the locket. But thinking back to the night he'd stripped Whitley naked and tossed his clothes and boots into the fishpond, Marcus shook his head again. "That I doubt."

Rising to his feet, Garrett said, "I won't keep you any longer. It appears that we shall have to await Jack and whatever events transpire."

Long after Garrett left, Marcus sat in his chair, looking blindly into space. Considering only his own desires, it would be a good thing if Whitley were indeed dead. Edmund would be safe and he and Isabel could put the past firmly behind them. But if Whitley's death was connected to that damned elusive memorandum . . .

There was still enough time, he admitted, to change the date and place for Wellesley's invasion of the continent, but with Portugal eliminated it narrowed down for the French the most probable areas of a British landing. And that knowledge alone could cost Britain the element of surprise and the lives of countless good Englishmen.

Isabel found him there some time later and, seeing the worried expression on his face, she shut the door behind her and walked quickly to him. "What is it?" she asked, sinking down onto the floor beside his chair, her hand resting on his knee.

He looked at her, his heart lightened by the mere sight of her, and for just an instant, Whitley and the problems he presented vanished from his mind. He sat there simply taking pleasure in her nearness, smiling at her.

Impatiently, Isabel shook his knee. "What is it? And stop staring at me in that idiotic fashion."

He laughed and pulled her up into his lap. His laughter fled, though, as he considered what to tell her. About the memorandum? No. Whitley's disappearance? Yes. She'd hear it soon enough.

"Garrett came to call," he said slowly. "And apparently, our friend Whitley has disappeared."

Frowning, she twisted around in his lap and looked up at him. "What do you mean, 'disappeared'?"

Marcus quickly told her all that Garrett had related to him. The news that her nemesis had vanished didn't seem to please her any.

Sitting up, she said firmly, "I don't believe it. Whitley is a snake, and while I've wished a million times that he'd just slither away and go back to whichever rock he crawled out from under, I can't imagine him doing so."

"You don't think someone from his past might have caught up with him and murdered him?" Marcus asked with a raised brow. "If you will remember, we haven't ruled out murdering him ourselves."

She started to shake her head, then paused. Thoughtfully, she admitted, "That's possible, but if someone killed him, why isn't there a body? Why was his horse returned?" When Marcus shrugged, she said, "Exactly! If *I* was going to murder him, once I'd disposed of the body, I would have had a note delivered to Keating stating that I, Whitley, had been called back unexpectedly to London and for Keating to pack my belongings and send them by the first stage back to London. And I'd have sent along enough money to cover the bill and the stage—with a generous tip included. You wouldn't even have to have an address to send his things to, just instructions that his valise was to be left at the posting house and that someone would pick it up there. With all the comings and goings at the posting house, it would be days or weeks before someone noticed the valise, and by then no one would remember when it arrived or whose it was. As for the horse, it would have disappeared at the same time Whitley did, leaving everyone to assume he rode it back to London."

Marcus nodded. "It could work. But about Whitley's note: wouldn't someone realize it wasn't in his handwriting? And the horse? Would you dispose of it in the same manner you did Whitley?"

She shot him a disgusted look. "Do you think Keating has ever seen Whitley's handwriting? Or is that familiar with it? Or that he's going to keep the note? Of course not! What does Keating care that Whitley returned to London? As for the horse," she finished triumphantly, "I'd have sold it at the nearest horse market. Whitley certainly wouldn't be around to object."

Considering Isabel's scenario, Marcus decided that Whitley's disappearance had not been planned. Or, at least, not very well planned—because her plan would have worked. Whitley would have disappeared with no one the wiser. And the lack of a body and the return of the horse made it more likely that there was something else afoot. If a robber or thief had killed Whitley, why not leave the body where it fell? And the horse . . . What highwayman worth his weight would simply return a valuable animal? Still, Marcus could not dismiss the idea that someone from Whitley's past had a hand in the major's disappearance. Or an agent of France . . .

Isabel and Marcus had just arisen from dinner the next evening when Thompson appeared and said that Marcus had visitors awaiting him in his office. Having a fair idea who his visitors were, Marcus pressed a kiss on the back of Isabel's hand and, ignoring her questioning look, hastened from the room.

He found a worn-looking Jack and a grim-faced Garrett waiting for him in his office. Both men accepted the brandy Marcus offered and, after they were served, Marcus remarked to Jack, "I didn't expect to see you back so soon."

"You could have knocked me over with a feather when he strolled into the house a couple of hours ago," Garrett said. "He and the servant I sent with the note about Whitley must have passed each other on the road."

Jack smiled mirthlessly. "No doubt. And Whitley's disappearance is the worst news I could have received when I returned to Garrett's." Jack tipped back his snifter of brandy and took a long swallow. "Time is fleeting and within the week Wellesley's plans must either move ahead or be changed completely," he said frankly. "Portugal was our best bet for surprising the French, but now that Whitley has disappeared, we must assume that the memorandum is in the hands of the French." His gaze moving from one to the other, he added, "Roxbury and I discussed the situation and we concluded that we have wasted enough time—far too much time, truth be told." His jaw clenched and he ended with, "And that we would have to act quickly to get the truth out of Whitley by any means necessary."

"Beat it out of him," Marcus said levelly.

Jack's eyes met his. "Yes. The time for finessing is past. We've wasted what? A week? Ten days? More?" His fine mouth thinned. "Blast it! Why the devil did he have to disappear right now?"

"It doesn't matter any longer why he disappeared," Marcus said. "What matters is what we are going to do about it."

"I agree," Jack replied. "And since he has disappeared, we must assume that the memorandum is in the hands of the French and act accordingly. I shall leave for London within the hour and give Roxbury the unsettling news that Whitley has disappeared under mysterious circumstances."

"No, you won't," said Garrett decisively. "You're half dead on your feet. You'd fall off your horse before you rode five miles. I shall go to London. As long as Roxbury is apprised of the situation here, I don't think it matters which one of us brings him the message."

Jack looked like he'd argue, but Marcus said quietly, "Jack, he's right and you know it. Let him go."

Jack sighed. "Very well."

There was a smattering of conversation and then the three men rose to their feet, shook hands, and Jack and Garrett departed. Frowning, Marcus went in search of his wife. He found her upstairs in the sitting room adjacent to her bedroom.

Isabel looked up from the lady's magazine she had been leafing through, questions in her eyes.

Marcus smiled wryly. Now, how was he to handle this? She was going to demand to know what was going on and he had no easy answers for her.

Isabel watched him and her gaze narrowed. "You're not going to tell me what you spoke about, are you?"

He sat down on the arm of the sofa next to her and admitted, "Not all of it. I shall tell you, though, that Jack and Garrett are greatly mystified by Whitley's disappearance."

"Why should they care?" she asked reasonably.

Marcus knew that tone of old, and unless he gave her something that satisfied her, she would badger him to death, demanding answers to questions he could not answer. He thought a moment and then asked, "Do you remember when

I would ask about what hold Whitley had over you and you would not tell me?"

She nodded.

"Well, I find myself in a similar position. If I could tell you I would, but for the time being, at least, I can say nothing."

Isabel wanted to argue, and while she was eaten up with curiosity, she admitted that fair was fair. He had not pushed her when she refused to tell him her secret; she could hardly become angry with him for having one of his own. She was tempted to probe just a little, but the expression on his face told her that she would gain nothing. She sighed and, not happy about the situation, she asked in a small voice, "Will you tell me eventually?"

He smiled, his gray eyes warm and caressing on her face. "The moment I can, I shall."

With that she had to be content.

While Isabel might have been content, the stranger, who had spent the day hidden in the trees well away from the house and immediate grounds, was not. He had taken his perch high up in one of the big oak trees well before dawn, and at first light had begun scanning the outbuildings and the impressive home. Through his long spyglass, he had watched the servants come and go and had closely studied Isabel and Marcus as they had strolled about enjoying a fine Sunday morning. He'd also noted Garrett's call that afternoon and had watched him ride away, staring thoughtfully after him. Garrett might prove troublesome.

When darkness fell, he descended the tree and walked to where his horse had been staked out with food and water within easy reach. His expression was abstracted as he mounted and rode away.

His observations today only confirmed what he already suspected: the Sherbrook estate was too large to make his task simple and, as he reminded himself, time was running out. He had to strike and strike swiftly if anything was to be salvaged and, unfortunately, there appeared only one sure way that he could accomplish his task as quickly as possible.

If Whitley was to be believed, the key to solving his current problem lay somewhere within the vast Sherbrook estate. All he had to do, he thought with a grimace, was find it. And he could see only one sure way that would accomplish that task, swiftly and with as little violence as possible. He sighed. It wouldn't be pretty, but unless something else occurred to him in the next few hours, he wouldn't have much choice.

He shook his head in disgust. Christ! Sometimes there was little question, indeed, that he really was a bastard.

Chapter 16

Isabel woke Monday morning in Marcus's bed. She stretched luxuriously, delighting in the feel of a healthy body well used by an inventive lover. Smiling, she stared overhead at the silk canopy, thinking of the night just passed and all the marvelous things she had learned about her own body and her husband's as well. Marriage, she decided, was wonderful!

Though the hour was early, daylight just filtering in from behind the heavy drapes, before he left several minutes ago she vaguely remembered Marcus pressing a warm kiss on her shoulder and mentioning something about meeting his steward to tour several of the farms on the estate. He would be gone until late afternoon.

Yawning, she sat up in the bed and glanced around for her clothing. Spying her robe slung across one of the chairs and her gown tossed on the floor near the bed, she smiled again. Thinking of the way Marcus had made impatient work of her garments last night and the things he did to her with his mouth and hands, a delicious shiver went down her spine.

She left the bed and, shortly, bathed and gowned and having eaten the toast and tea that Peggy had brought up to her, she hurried across the foyer and out the massive front doors of the house. A smile lit her face as she stepped into the May sunshine and, happier than she had ever thought possible, after telling Thompson her destination, she fairly skipped to the barn.

Since Marcus was away and construction had not started on any of the improvements, she decided that a call on her former father-in-law and his bride was in order. During the few days she'd been in residence at Sherbrook Hall, though her attention had been taken up with other things, such as Marcus's lovemaking, Lord Manning's health had never been far from her mind. Today was the perfect time to pay a visit to Manning Court and see for herself how the old baron was faring.

As she walked down the wide aisles of the barn, in spite of all the good things in her life right now, there was, however, one tiny cloud on her horizon. It was so small and, she told herself firmly, not of the *utmost* importance, that she tried not to dwell on it or allow it to dampen her cheerful mood. Even as she tried to pretend it wasn't vital to her happiness, she knew she was lying to herself and, despite her best intentions, she couldn't help wondering how Marcus really felt about her. She knew her own heart, had known for years that she was madly, helplessly in love with Marcus Sherbrook, but what did he feel for her? Was it only mere affection he had for her? Or did he love her as a woman deserves, *needs*, to be loved by the man who holds her heart?

Even as she led her horse from its stall and absently refused the help of the stable boy who rushed forward to aid her, her mind was on Marcus and whether or not he was in love with her. Quickly and efficiently, she saddled and bridled her horse, a spirited little chestnut mare, and within moments was riding in the direction of Manning Court.

The mare knew the way and Isabel's thoughts were free to roam as the mare daintily picked her way through the dappled sunlight of the forestland that separated the Manning and Sherbrook estates. It was a lovely morning, but Isabel was only peripherally aware of her surroundings.

She didn't question for a moment that Marcus had a deep

fondness for her. Nor did she question that he took enormous pleasure in her body, in the marriage bed, but she couldn't pretend that theirs had been a normal courtship and marriage.

Their marriage, she admitted glumly, had not come about because Marcus had really wanted to marry her, but because of a series of complicated circumstances. She smiled faintly. His innate desire to protect her had prompted his brazen announcement to Whitley that they were betrothed, and she'd wager her best horse that it had never occurred to him that he might actually have to marry her. Recalling the expression on his face that night at Manning Court when he had realized that there was no way out of the engagement, her lips drooped. While he had shown no great distress, he certainly hadn't danced a jig of joy. Forlornly, she reminded herself that the wedding itself had been none of their making: the baron's fragile health had been as effective as a sword held over their heads. Again, Marcus had had no choice, but, she thought a bit more cheerfully, he had married her without the least reluctance.

She frowned. Had it been only his strong sense of honor and affection for Lord Manning that had prompted his actions? Or simply something more prosaic: the need for a son to carry on the Sherbrook name? She grinned at that thought. Marcus had never struck her as someone who worried about his legacy or what would become of his fortune and estates in the future, and she dismissed the notion that the need for an heir had been behind the ease with which he had accepted their betrothal and marriage.

Isabel had been so lost in her own musings that she had not realized how far she had traveled and, when the mare suddenly stopped, she looked up surprised to find herself in the courtyard in the front of Manning Court. A stable boy came running to hold her horse, the front doors of the mansion opened, and Deering, a broad smile on his face, hurried across the terrace to meet her.

"Oh, madame! It is so good to see you," he said in greeting. "And I know his lordship and Lady Manning will be very happy that you have come to call."

Jumping down lightly from the mare, Isabel handed the reins to the stable boy and ran up the steps to join Deering. As they walked toward the house, she asked, "I know it has only been a few days, but how is he doing?"

"Splendidly!" Deering cast her a sly glance. "And forgive me for being so bold, but I must say that marriage appears to agree with you also."

Isabel laughed. "Oh, it does, Deering, it does indeed."

She found Lord and Lady Manning sitting in a small stone courtyard at the rear of the house. Roses and peonies, with the occasional tall, graceful willow casting patches of shade here and there, surrounded the area. Shaded by one of the willows, Lord and Lady Manning were taking their ease in a pair of wrought-iron chairs, the hard lines softened by cushions in shades of green and gold. Several other chairs were scattered about and, off to one side, a round iron table held the remains of what had been a light repast.

A huge smile broke across Lord Manning's face at the sight of Isabel and, rising to his feet, he met her halfway. Holding her shoulders, he stared down into her face and said, "Now this is a pleasant surprise. Clara and I were just talking about you and Marcus and wondering how you were doing in your new home."

On tiptoe she pressed a kiss to his cheek and replied, "As you can see, I am doing well." She ran an assessing gaze over him, pleased to see that his gaze was bright and alert and that his color looked good. Most important, the ease with which he had arisen and walked to greet her banished the faint, lingering worry that his illness had left him completely crippled or incapacitated. He had not escaped unscathed, though, and as they rejoined Clara, she was conscious of the slight hesitation to his step and she noticed when he had gripped her shoulders that his left arm was weaker than she would like, but overall, he appeared to be making an excellent recovery.

After a brief hug and a kiss on Clara's sweetly rose-scented cheek, Isabel took a chair beside the pair of them.

"Would you like some tea, my dear?" Clara asked. "I can ring for Deering. I'm afraid what is on the table is cold by now."

Isabel shook her head. "No. I'm fine." She looked from one smiling face to the other and said, "And it would appear that the pair of you are doing just fine, too."

Lord Manning laid his hand over Clara's soft, plump one and said, "Indeed we are. We have decided that my illness was actually fortunate. Without it, you'd still be dithering on a wedding date and Clara and I would still be pining for each other." He beetled his brows at her. "Forgiven me yet for rushing you to the altar?"

"There was never anything to forgive," Isabel said truthfully. "But next time you wish me to do something, could you choose a less dramatic way to accomplish it?"

Lord Manning guffawed. "I've missed that tart tongue of yours, and Edmund's spirited presence." He flashed Clara an apologetic look and added hastily, "Not that Clara and I aren't content in each other's company."

"That's very true," Clara said, with a fond smile at him, "but it will be most enjoyable when Edmund is back and stirring things up a bit for the two of us." She looked at Isabel, an impish gleam in her eyes. "Too much peace and quiet will turn us into a pair of doddering old crotchets. Edmund will keep our step lively . . . and then, of course, I'm sure that you and Marcus will present us with some honorary grandchildren, won't you, my dear?"

For a moment, Isabel's mind went blank. With everything that had gone on recently, she'd not yet given any thought to a child. Why, this time next year, she realized excitedly, she could be holding her own child, her and Marcus's baby in her arms. Joy blossomed through her and she exclaimed, "Oh, I do, indeed, hope so!"

It was mid afternoon when Isabel eventually rode away from Manning Court and toward Sherbrook Hall, taking the path by which she had come. She had not meant to stay so long, but the older couple had pressed her to join them for an alfresco luncheon and she could not deny them. Relaxed and smiling, she was in no hurry to reach home, content simply to enjoy the warm afternoon and dwell on the miraculous path her life had taken.

The secret surrounding Edmund's birth was safe, and if she had not loved Marcus before, she would have adored him for the way he immediately became her ally in securing Edmund's future. The burden she had carried for so long had been lifted from her shoulders and, she thought with a faint smile, her pesky virginity had been taken care of, too. Marcus was . . . oh, *very* good at solving problems.

Clara's mention of possible children flitted through her mind and, dreaming of the children she might someday bear, she was oblivious to the world around her. Her mare gave her the first hint, stopping and snorting in the middle of the narrow path.

Jerked from her daydreams of gray-eyed, black-haired little boys and girls, her reaction was slow, and before she knew it, the horsemen were upon her. She barely glimpsed the pair of them, the lower halves of their faces hidden by handkerchiefs as they rushed out of the woods on either side of her, before a heavy dark blanket was thrown over her and she was lifted easily off her horse by one of them.

More outraged than frightened, she struggled to escape. "Unhand me, you blackguard!" she ordered. Her position, slung over the horse in front of the rider, made escape nearly impossible. Her arms were tangled in the blanket, and with her head dangling over one side of the horse and her feet the other, she could gain no purchase.

Her captor gave her buttocks a sharp slap and said, "Be still! You keep wiggling like that and you're going to end up falling on your head."

Enraged that he had taken such liberties, Isabel turned her head and bit him on the thigh.

"Jesus Christ!" the man gasped. "You bit me!"

"And I'll do more, if you don't release me at once!"

To her astonishment a soft chuckle met her ear. "Unfortunately, madame, that is beyond my power. Now, be a good little wench and this will soon be over with nothing hurt but your pride."

Isabel frowned. Her captor's voice was that of an educated man, his tone and words not that of a common footpad. What the devil was happening? Her breath caught, and she demanded, "Is Whitley behind this? Did he hire you to abduct me?"

"I think," said the stranger, "that I should be the one asking questions. Now hang on, we have some ground to travel." And he kicked his horse into a fast gallop that made talk impossible.

As the horse swiftly bore her away from the place of her abduction, the possibility that she might be in real danger occurred to Isabel. She wasn't frightened, exactly, but as her first burst of anger dissipated, neither was she sanguine about her position. The fact that both men had worn handkerchiefs over their faces made it impossible to identify them, and instinct told her that they were strangers to her. Or rather, she amended, she couldn't imagine someone she knew abducting her in this bold, insolent fashion. Which raised the question, why had she been taken in the first place?

The ride, considering her uncomfortable position, was not overly long, but they traveled at speed and had crossed, by her count, three streams. Crisscrossing? Covering their tracks? When the horses stopped a short while later, she breathed a sigh of relief. She had no idea where she was, but she knew that they couldn't be too far away from either Manning Court or Sherbrook Hall.

Her captor swung out of the saddle. A second later, he lifted her down and, like a sack of potatoes, threw her over his shoulder.

A hint of laughter in his voice, he said, "I apologize for the rough treatment, madame, but this is the easiest way to transport you to your, er, abode."

With her firmly anchored across his shoulder, he scrambled across the ground, climbing slightly, and as they climbed, Isabel heard the heavy breathing and the occasional vicious curse made by the other man as he followed. Her captor may have some polish, but his companion, if his speech was anything to go by, was as common as dirt.

Upon reaching their destination, the man carrying her pushed open a door—one not used often, she thought, if the creak and the scrape it made across the floor was anything to go by. Inside, she was set on her feet, her captor's hands on her shoulders holding her steady until she could stand by herself.

The instant his hands left her shoulders, Isabel grabbed the blanket and tugged at it, suddenly needing to be free of the smothering folds.

The companion saw what she was doing and yelled, "Damn her eyes! Grab her! She'll be free of that blanket in a moment."

Two hard hands caught her, stifling her movements and, in frustration, Isabel kicked out wildly. By luck, her foot connected with someone's shin and she was pleased by the sound of his painful yelp.

"Dash it all! Will you be still? I don't want to hurt you, but if you keep this up, you'll force me to do something you won't like."

"Well, I don't have no trouble at all putting her glimms out," snarled the companion.

Isabel sensed a movement behind her the second before something hard connected to the back of her head. Pain exploded through her brain and all went dark as she slumped senseless to the floor.

Cursing under his breath, the stranger leaped across her fallen body to grab both lapels of Collard's jacket. Shaking him savagely, he said, "By God, if you've harmed her . . ."

"You'll what, kill me?" Collard taunted. He tried to push the other man away, but was unable to break the iron grip. His face red, Collard demanded, "Who found this place for you? Who told you about Whitley in the first place? If I hadn't looked you up, you'd have no notion of what was in the wind."

"You're wrong," the stranger snapped. "I already knew about the memorandum, you fool, and the reason you found me in Cherbourg was because it was the logical place for it to surface."

"But I told you where to find him, didn't I?" Collard whined. "I've been useful to you, you can't deny that."

The stranger's hands fell to his sides and he said grimly, "I would remind you that even the best tool sometimes outlives its usefulness. Disregard my wishes one more time and we'll have an unpleasant parting of the ways."

Collard grimaced. "You're still angry about Whitley, ain't you?" When the stranger said nothing, just stared at him coldly, Collard muttered, "All right, maybe I made a mistake. But I didn't think it was smart to leave him around to wag his tongue."

"He wouldn't have. Besides, what could he have said that wouldn't have been self-incriminating? Whitley was a coward, but not a fool, and he'd have put as much distance between us as he could."

"Maybe that's so, but I still think . . ."

Ignoring him, the other man turned away and knelt beside Isabel's still form. Gently he removed the blanket from around her and carefully explored the back of her head. His mouth thinned when his fingers came away sticky with blood, but the steady rise and fall of her bosom told him that she was alive.

She was small enough for him to handle easily and he picked her up and set her on the one piece of furniture in the old wooden hut, a rickety chair probably as old as the ramshackle building. He glanced over his shoulder at Collard. "The rope. And the blindfold and gag, if you please."

Collard quickly retrieved the items, and a few minutes later, Isabel was tied to the chair. A black blindfold had been placed around her eyes and a gag had been put in her mouth. Sitting back on his heels, the stranger surveyed his handiwork.

Rising to his feet, he said, "That should keep her still and quiet long enough for us to accomplish what needs to be done."

"We're just going to leave her here?" Collard asked, frowning.

"Yes. As you said when you suggested this place, it's unlikely anyone would stumble across it, and with her tied, gagged, and blindfolded . . ."

Collard hesitated and, moving like lightning, the next instant the stranger had him pushed up against the wall of the hut, his hands around his throat. "Touch her," the stranger threatened softly, "harm her in any way, and it will be the last thing you ever do. I will not have an innocent's death on my conscience. Understand me?"

Eyes bulging from the pressure of those hands, his fingers clawing at the steel grip around his throat, Collard nodded.

The stranger let him go and said coolly, "Since we now understand each other, let us now conclude our business with Mr. Sherbrook."

Marcus returned home hours later than he had planned. Even though he had rushed his steward and he was quite certain that several of his tenants thought him somewhat brusque in his manner during his visit to their farms, it had still taken much longer than he had assumed it would. At every place they stopped, there seemed to be some matter of utmost importance to the farmer that ate away the hours, but finally it was over and he was riding home.

His thoughts were on Isabel and he was smiling as he turned his horse down the long driveway that led to Sherbrook Hall. Approaching the stables, his smile faded as he noted the crowd of servants milling around the small chestnut mare he knew Isabel favored. An ugly knot clamped in his belly and his face was set in hard lines as he approached the group.

At the sound of his horse's approach, the crowd turned as one and rushed toward him. The knot in his belly clamped even tighter when he saw that Thompson and the housekeeper, Mrs. Brown, were amongst them.

Dismounting, he looked at Thompson and demanded, "What is it?"

Thompson took a deep breath and said, "It is madame, sir. Her horse returned without her a while ago. Immediately, the alarm was raised and searchers were sent out to look for her, but so far no one has found any sign of her anywhere."

"Do you know where she was going when she left on her ride?" Marcus asked, astonished at how calm his voice sounded when inside he was a gibbering idiot.

Thompson nodded. "Yes, sir. As she left the house this morning she mentioned that she intended to ride over to visit Lord and Lady Manning." He cleared his throat. "I took the liberty, sir, of sending George to Manning Court with a note to Deering. I know that you would not want to alarm the old lord and his lady, and Deering knows how to keep his mouth shut. George brought back a reply from Deering: Mrs. Sherbrook rode away from Manning Court sometime around two o'clock this afternoon."

Marcus glanced at his pocket watch. It was coming on six o'clock. "When was her horse discovered?"

"Just a little over an hour ago, sir. Everyone has been searching for her since then. Several of the stable boys have combed every trail between here and Manning Court. The lake was even checked, but there is no sign of her. Only her horse."

Which told him bloody little, Marcus thought savagely. Whatever happened to Isabel could have happened as little as an hour ago or within minutes of her leaving sight of Manning Court this afternoon. Tamping down the sheer terror that raked up through his chest, he said, "Where are they? I wish to speak to them."

Within minutes Marcus was surrounded by about a dozen men, half of them barely into their teens. Whatever the age, however, every face wore the same anxious look. Keeping his own expression calm wasn't easy but Marcus managed it. The last thing his people needed was for him to panic.

His questioning of the stable staff gained him little and, hiding his own fears, he eventually sent them on their way. One young man lingered and Marcus glanced at him. "Ellard, isn't it?" he asked. When the boy nodded shyly, he questioned, "You have something you want to add?"

The boy, for he was little more than that, bobbed his head and mumbled, "Begging your pardon, sir, but there's a spot on the main trail where it looked to me like the missus was waylaid. The tracks are fresh, not more than a few hours old."

"Show me."

A moment later, Marcus and Ellard, the stable boy, were astride their horses and galloping away from the stables. Several minutes later, Ellard pulled his horse to a stop and, motioning for Marcus to follow him, urged his mount off to the side of the trail. They traveled in silence except for the soft thud of their horses' hooves on the dirt for another few minutes before Ellard said excitedly, "There, sir. See! The one track leads off toward home, which is most likely that of madame's mare, but the other two cut through the forest."

Marcus didn't claim to be a great tracker, but he'd hunted his share of game and it only took him a second to find the tracks, amongst the others on the trail that Ellard was point-ing to. He dismounted and carefully studied the ground. Widening the area, further search revealed signs where two horses had waited, each one hidden on either side of the trail. The tracks weren't more than a few hours old and it did look as if Ellard was right. A pair of riders had waited for Isabel's return and had captured her.

That blasted Whitley, Marcus thought as he stared at the hoofprints in front of him. He didn't know what was going on, but he was convinced that it was somehow connected to Whitley.

His face implacable, wordlessly, Marcus remounted and he and Ellard began to track the path taken by the other two horses. It was agonizingly slow work, the forest floor hiding the passage of the two animals, but here and there, a hoof-print was spied and they traveled deeper into the woods. After the second stream crossing they lost all sign of their quarry. They wasted another hour trying to pick it up again, but they found nothing.

By the time they returned to Sherbrook Hall, dusk was falling and, weary and more frightened than he had ever been in his life, Marcus dismounted and gave the reins of his equally weary horse to his stable master, Worley.

Worry in his eyes, Worley asked, "Anything?"

Marcus shook his head. "Nothing. But young Ellard proved to have a good eye. Reward him." Marcus hesitated, then added, "Calm your staff as best you can. Keep the spec-ulation down. Tell them that, oh, that Mrs. Sherbrook forgot to tell me that she was visiting friends and that her horse ac-cidentally wandered away."

Worley looked like he wanted to object, but something in Marcus's eyes made him shut his mouth with a snap.

The sound of an approaching vehicle jerked Marcus's head around, but the wild hope that had flared in his chest died when he saw that it was only one of his tenant farmers, Bartlett. The heavy farm wagon creaked and groaned as it rolled up. Bartlett pulled his horse to a stop and said, "Good evening to you, Master Sherbrook! I have something for you." He reached into the front of his jacket and pulled out an envelope. Handing it to Marcus, he said, "Fellow gave me a queer start when he stopped me on the road. Gave me a whole guinea, though, to deliver it. Said I was to put it in no one's hands but yours."

Hoping no one had seen the way his fingers had shaken when he had taken the envelope from Bartlett's hand, Marcus nodded and murmured, "Thank you." He glanced down at the envelope, already having a fair idea what was in it, and asked, "Could you describe the man who gave this to you?"

Puzzled, Bartlett replied, "Fellow acted as if he was a friend of yours. Wasn't he?"

Marcus shook his head. "No. Not a friend. What can you tell me about him?"

Bartlett pulled on his ear. "I'll be truthful, sir, I didn't pay him no mind, but as I recall he had the look of a gentleman, spoke like one, too. He was a well set-up fellow, rode a blood horse, but now that I think of it, he kept his hat pulled down over his face, so I'm not likely to recognize him again." Worried, Bartlett added, "I didn't do wrong, did I, sir?"

"No. You didn't do wrong. Thank you for your troubles," Marcus said, forcing a smile.

Bartlett grinned at him. "Wasn't no trouble, sir. Not for a whole guinea!"

Marcus waved him off and headed for the house. Entering the wide foyer, he was greeted by an anxious Thompson. "Any word, sir?"

"I suspect that what is in this envelope will tell me what I want to know," Marcus answered, waving it in front of Thompson. He sent Thompson an unflinching look and said, "As far as anyone is concerned, my wife neglected to tell me that she decided unexpectedly to visit with friends and will be gone for a few days. See that you inform the staff."

Thompson swallowed. "And her horse, sir? Is there a reason why it came home without her?"

"Probably because it became untied from the carriage in which she was riding." Giving Thompson another look, he held the envelope up and said, "It's all in here. Even her apology for upsetting everyone. Make sure that you spread the word around that it was all a mistake and that everything is fine." His voice hard, he repeated, "Everything is fine. Just fine."

Thompson bowed. "Very well, sir. I shall see to it."

Alone in his office, Marcus shrugged out of his jacket and tore off his cravat, his eyes on the envelope lying in the middle of his big desk. He didn't have to read the contents to know what was inside. From the moment he'd learned of the return of Isabel's riderless mare he'd been half braced for some sort of ransom note. Accidents did happen, but his wife was an exemplary rider, the mare not known for being particularly fractious. From the beginning he'd been aware that it was unlikely that Isabel had been thrown from her horse and, when a search turned up no trace of her, he'd fought to contain the panic that threatened to consume him. Finding the tracks with young Ellard had only confirmed his suspicions that there had been *nothing* accidental about Isabel's disappearance and the arrival of the note.

He splashed some brandy in a snifter and, with the snifter in his hand, sat down behind his desk. He studied the envelope in front of him like it was a deadly viper. All I have to do, he told himself, is open it and have my worst fears confirmed.

For a second longer, he sipped his brandy, staring at the slim envelope on the desk before him, trying to get his thoughts in order, considering all the angles. The temptation, however, to put an end to all his wild speculations was too overpowering, and with a curse he set down his snifter and snatched up the envelope. In one violent motion he tore it open.

There was only one sheet of paper inside and as he read the scant words written there, a chill blew through him. Dear God, no!

His face set and rigid, he crumpled the note in his hand and, starting to his feet, charged from the room. Heedless of anything in his path, he raced to the stables, nearly knocking down Worley as he sped by.

Reaching the door to his office in the stable, he flung open the door and gazed around wildly. There, on a hook against one wall, hanging neatly where one of the stable boys had put it, was the object of his search. In four swift strides, he was across the room and yanked down Whitley's greatcoat from the hook.

I should have known, he raged, as he laid the garment on his desk. *We knew the bastard had to have brought the memorandum with him. I* knew *he had to have it nearby but I never gave his bloody greatcoat a second's thought. I was a fool,* he thought furiously, *not to have paid more attention when I learned of the break-in and the other events.*

Darkness was falling and, needing light, Marcus lit a pair of candles and set them on the desk on either side of the garment. Forcing himself to act calmly, in the dancing light he slowly examined the fine woolen garment. It took him several minutes, but eventually his fingers touched a section of the coat that didn't feel right. There was no way that Whitley's hiding place would have been accidentally discovered and Marcus gave him credit for being clever. If he hadn't *known* the coat had to hide the memorandum, he'd never have found it. Only by carefully running his fingers over the welting in the lapels and noticing that one side was a trifle thicker and a bit more rigid than the other did he find the memorandum.

With a knife, he carefully slit the expertly sewn seam and his breathing quickened when his fingers touched a narrow cylinder of oilcloth. Getting it free of the coat, he brought it closer to one of the candles and almost reverently unrolled it. Inside were several tightly rolled sheets of paper, and as he read them, he realized how damaging to the British troops it would be if this information fell into the hands of the French.

His expression bleak, his jaw rigid, he stared at the memorandum in his hands. The ransom note had made no mention of the missing memorandum, but the moment his eyes had fallen upon the demand for Whitley's greatcoat in exchange for Isabel, Marcus had known precisely what Isabel's captors had been after. He cursed himself roundly for not realizing days ago that the very thing they searched for had been hanging in his barn office all the time.

His gaze fixed on the papers he held in his hand, he slumped down in a chair behind his desk, terror and despair tearing through him like cannon fire. *How can I,* he wondered dully, *not save the woman I love more than life? But how many lives may be lost if I hand this over to them? Am I not a traitor if I give them what they demand?* His heart twisted in searing anguish. He could not imagine a life without Isabel at his side, could not imagine allowing her to die when he had the ability to save her, yet how could he live knowing he may have gained her safety at the cost of how many lives of good, loyal Englishmen?

He took a deep breath. The possibility of changing Wellesley's plans had already been mentioned; didn't that make the memorandum before him useless to the French? Couldn't he with a clear conscience hand the memorandum over to Isabel's abductors and get his wife safely back in his arms? For a brief moment he considered it, but he knew it wasn't that simple.

Marcus wasn't a military tactician, but he understood how vital the landing in Portugal would be for Britain and her allies. Yes, other ports, other sites could be used, but Portugal might be the key to unlocking Napoleon's throttle hold on the continent and he held in his hands the document that could allow those plans—plans that had been in the works for weeks, months—to go forward. If those plans were changed, there was no telling how much more difficult, how many more lives would be lost because of it.

Marcus groaned and buried his head in his hands. His choice was simple. Save his wife. Or betray his country.

Chapter 17

For several minutes Marcus let black scalding despair wash over him at the terrible choice before him, but then he straightened suddenly and his gaze narrowed as he looked at the memorandum before him. He studied the document intently for several minutes, his fingers rubbing the edges of the paper. A desperate idea occurred to him and, swiftly rerolling the memorandum and placing it once more in its waterproofing oilskin, he stuffed it back into Whitley's greatcoat.

Blowing out the candles, with Whitley's greatcoat slung carelessly over his shoulder, he strode from his office in the stable toward the house. He didn't have a lot of time. The meeting was set for midnight and he had a great deal of tedious work to do before then.

I'm going to beat the bastards at their own game, he thought fiercely, *and I* am *going to get my wife back!*

Intent upon his own thoughts, Marcus was oblivious to his surroundings, and the notion that he might be watched never crossed his mind. Even if it had, it is unlikely he'd have spotted the watcher hidden amongst the shrubs and trees that were scattered charmingly throughout the area, but the watcher had him firmly in his sights. As Marcus walked swiftly down the broad avenue that led to the main house, the watcher kept pace with him, gliding invisibly through the glorious gardens and parklands tended so assiduously by the head gardener and his staff. Once Marcus entered the big double doors at the front of the house, the watcher slipped around the side of the house, determined not to lose track of Whitley's greatcoat. He'd considered attacking Marcus and taking the greatcoat from him right then, but after eyeing the strong build of the man walking toward the house, decided in favor of prudence.

Inside the house, Marcus went directly to his office, locking the door behind him. Thompson had already seen to it that the brass candelabra on either side of the fireplace had been lit and a small fire glowed on the hearth so the room was not in darkness, but Marcus lit a few more candles on his desk. Putting down the greatcoat and taking the memorandum from its hiding place once more, he carefully unrolled and considered it again at length. He was pleased to see that his first impression had been right. The paper the memorandum had been written on was nothing out of the ordinary and he'd wager a sack full of gold guineas that he had paper of a similar nature right in his desk drawer.

The paper had been his main obstacle and, convinced his rash plan would work, he sat down behind his desk and, after rummaging around his desk drawers, found precisely what he was looking for: several pages of paper. Paper that was *nearly* identical to those that the plans for Wellesley's invasion of Portugal had been written on. Checking his quill and ink bottle, he began the laborious task of copying the memorandum word for word, except for the locations and dates and the number of ships and troops—those he changed to whatever whim took him.

There was one fatal flaw in his plan and he was chillingly aware of it. If the ransom had come from Whitley and it was Whitley he was meeting to exchange the memorandum for Isabel, Whitley had to know the contents of the memorandum and would know the one Marcus handed him was a fake. But Marcus was taking the desperate gamble that Whitley had nothing to do with Isabel's abduction and that her captor had no idea what was in the real document.

The ransom note had given him no clue as to its author. Again, he didn't believe that it was Whitley. Whitley was a coward—look at his fumbling attempts to regain his great-coat—and while abducting an unarmed woman wasn't the act of a brave man, it did entail a certain amount of verve and boldness, traits that Whitley had never displayed. And then there was Whitley's disappearance. It was possible the disappearance was all smoke to hide Whitley's real actions, but Marcus rather thought not. The most likely reason for Whitley's sudden and inexplicable disappearance was because he was dead. Whether by accident, and the body not yet discovered, or murdered by an as-yet-unknown party, remained to be seen. Instinct told Marcus that whoever had engineered Isabel's abduction was new on the scene and was behind Whitley's disappearance. He was, he admitted brutally, gambling on a new set of players. Players that would never realize that they had been duped until it was too late.

The simplest explanation for this latest development was that this newcomer, or newcomers, had captured Whitley and, by ways he didn't care to think about, compelled him to tell them about the memorandum. Whitley was certainly dead; Marcus could not imagine him giving up the information about the memorandum easily. He paused for a moment, remembering that Whitley had given up the gold locket. . . . He shook his head. But the locket had not been the sure thing the memorandum was. Whitley's threats to Isabel had been nearly all bluff and he had little to lose by giving it up. But the memorandum . . .

His gaze dropped to the papers in front of him. The French would pay a king's ransom to get their hands on this information and Whitley knew it: he would not have given it up. Marcus was convinced that Whitley had to be dead and that he had died at the hands of whoever now held Isabel.

That Isabel was in the hands of someone ruthless enough to torture and murder filled him with dread and rage. Unconsciously, his hand clenched into a fist and he was aware that where his wife and her safety was concerned, he was quite capable of murder himself.

Reminding himself harshly that before he could take vengeance there was work to be done, he returned once more to copying the memorandum. Some time later, the chiming of the clock on the mantel jerked him from his task and he stared down, surprised at the duplicate document he had created. To the untrained eye it looked real enough; thank God he hadn't had to deal with seals or engravings. It had been the fact that the paper itself was of a common type and had not been altered in any way that had allowed him to take this desperate gamble. As for the contents themselves, some nameless clerk in the offices of the Horse Guards had written the original and, beyond a set of initials at the bottom of the last page, there weren't even signatures to worry over. Which was just as well, Marcus thought, since until this moment he'd never had reason to try his hand at forgery. But critically comparing the two sets of papers, he decided that his first attempt at forgery, and pray God his last, would do—provided Whitley hadn't given Isabel's abductors some idea what was in the document and that Whitley wasn't still alive and able to denounce the false memorandum. There were many things that could go wrong, but Marcus had his mind firmly closed against anything but success. He had to get Isabel back. Anything else was unthinkable.

Cloaked by the darkness outside, the watcher shifted slightly in his position behind an impressive clump of lilacs. He had a clear view of the interior of Marcus's office and, as night had deepened, the illumination from the candles had lit up the room like a stage. With great interest he had watched Marcus's actions and had smiled to himself when he realized what Marcus was about.

Inside the house, the document complete, Marcus carefully

creased and folded it into the shape and size of the original.
He undid it and refolded it several times so that the creases
lost their sharp, crisp look and more resembled that of the
true memorandum. When he was satisfied with his work, he
fitted the forged document with all its false information back
into the oilcloth and then the oilcloth into the seam in Whitley's greatcoat.

Rising from his chair, the original memorandum in his
hand, he walked across the room to the far wall and moved a
large gilt framed picture of Tempest that he'd commissioned
from George Stubbs more than a decade ago when he had
first bought the horse. Behind the portrait of the stallion was
a safe and, after opening it, Marcus placed the real memorandum in it.

Unaware that his every movement had been observed,
Marcus wearily sat back down behind his desk. Even though
he had created a passable forgery, the slashing claws of the
demon in his chest had not abated and he could not even find
solace in the knowledge that at least he had a plan to save his
wife and foil the enemies who sought to harm England. His
iron control cracked and he buried his head in his hands,
doubt strangling him. There was so much that could go
wrong and he had no reason to believe that he could actually
trust the person who had sent him the ransom demand.

Isabel, he realized bleakly, could already be dead. A low,
primitive moan of anguish rose up from deep inside him. He
could not bear to even think such thoughts. *I never even told
her I love her. . . .* She had to be alive. She had to be.

Isabel was very much alive and she had spent the intervening hours swinging between pure fury and frank terror. She
fought stubbornly against the despair and fear that battered
her, but it was no easy battle and occasionally her defenses
were breached and wretched despair won—but only for a
while. Anger kept some of the fear at bay, but she couldn't
entirely squelch the occasional flash of panic at the thought

of what would happen to her when her captors came back. Equally terrifying was the possibility that her captors would *never* return to free her and that, for some unknown reason, she had been left here to die.

Despite her fears and terror, she was not idle and, once she was convinced that she was well and truly alone, she struggled to free herself. She wasted time and energy fighting against the bonds that held her before admitting bitterly that she was unlikely to escape from the ropes that held her fast; her captors had tied her well. Undaunted, she tried another tack and, sliding off the chair onto the floor, she tried rubbing the gag and the blindfold against the rough, wooden surface of the chair, hoping to loosen or remove one of them, but to no avail. Forcing back tears of frustration and anger, panting from her efforts, she finally lay on the floor and considered her next move. Her hands were tied behind her back with a length of rope running from them down to her ankles where her feet had been tied together. She couldn't walk and she couldn't get her hands in front of her where she could remove the gag and the blindfold. For a moment despair claimed her.

Exhausted from struggling, she lay there on the floor and fought the bleak emotions that crowded through her. She could not escape, at least not at the moment, and having swallowed that unpalatable fact, she cast about for a reason for her predicament. Understanding *why* she had been captured might give her something to fight with—if her captors returned.

Abductions, highwaymen, and footpads were uncommon, almost unheard of in this area, yet in broad daylight two men had brazenly abducted her in the middle of Lord Manning's lands. There had been nothing about either man that gave her a clue to their identity, although from his speech she had concluded that one of them spoke like a gentleman. The other man had clearly been of a rougher sort, but beyond that she could not describe either man.

But why, she wondered, *why did they abduct me?* Her abduction was like something one would read in a novel from the Minerva Press: things like this didn't happen to women like her. She was a respectable woman, a member of the gentry, her life mundane and predictable . . . until Whitley had appeared. Behind the blindfold her eyes narrowed. That bastard!

Impatiently, she struggled into a sitting position and half leaned against the wall of the hut. It wasn't comfortable, but she felt less helpless than simply lying like a trussed hen on the ground.

Frowning, she reasoned that Whitley had to be behind her abduction. Could this all be tied somehow to her days in India? Was it connected to Edmund? Panic flooded through her. She took a deep breath, fighting back a flood of fright. No. It could have nothing to do with India or Edmund. Marcus had seen to that. All evidence had been destroyed. And Whitley, she reminded herself uneasily, had disappeared, and while she could not identify her captors, she knew that neither one of them had been Whitley. She bit her lip. He might not have been one of the men who abducted her, but Whitley was involved somehow—of that she was convinced.

She wasted several minutes in wild speculation, before coming back to the one thing she was convinced was true: this went back to Whitley. And if it was not connected to India and Edmund, then what? It had to have been something that occurred here in England. Something recent . . .

Her brow furrowed, she considered the problem. Whitley had retired from the military. That was recent, but she could make no connection with his retirement and her situation. Something occurred to her and she sat up a little straighter. Whitley wasn't the only newcomer to the neighborhood who had recently retired from the military. Jack Landrey, Lord Thorne, Marcus's cousin, had also retired from the military not too long ago. . . . Her breath caught. And then there was the mysterious meeting the other night between Marcus,

Jack, and Garrett—a meeting whose purpose Marcus would not tell her. Could that meeting have had something to do with Whitley? Was that the common denominator? She nodded slowly. It had to be. Nothing else made any sense. There was *something* that tied Whitley to her abduction . . . and whatever Marcus would not tell her about his meeting with Jack and Garrett.

It was thin, she admitted wryly, but she didn't dismiss it as she had several of her other more outrageous ideas. But even if she was right in her deductions, and she wasn't entirely convinced that she was, it didn't change her circumstances: she was still bound, gagged, blindfolded, and held captive and she knew not why.

Like a viper unwinding from behind a rock, it occurred to her that she could be in grave danger and that her life could be at stake. If she was being held simply for ransom, what if something went wrong? What if her captors had never had any intention of exchanging her for whatever it was they wanted so desperately? Again the ugly question crossed her mind: what if she had been left here to die? Stonily, she considered the knowledge that she might not survive this ordeal, that she might never see her husband or her son again.

Isabel flinched, recoiling from the very notion of never seeing Marcus or Edmund again. Choking terror reigned for a moment, but once again she fought it back and forced herself to believe that all would end well. She would *not* allow fear and hopelessness to beat her. She *would* survive this. She must! She had too much to live for, and she thought of those gray-eyed, black-haired little boys and girls she'd been dreaming of before her abduction, and Edmund, and most of all Marcus. . . . Yes. She had every reason to live.

Stiffening her resolve, she tried to calculate how many hours had passed since she had first been taken captive. It seemed like an eternity since she had been dumped here and her captors had left, and while an eternity might not have passed, she knew it had been a very long time. Blindfolded, she had no sense of the passing time, but she'd been aware for some time that the air felt cooler and she was certain that darkness had fallen. Someone would have realized hours ago that something had happened to her. If her captors had turned her horse loose, and she suspected that they had, eventually the mare would have ambled home. The alarm would have been raised. People, Marcus, would be looking for her.

A warm glow spread through her body at the thought of her husband and his rage at her abduction, his determination to find her. Yes, Marcus would be looking for her and she knew he would not easily give up. The image of his beloved face floated before her and, despite her best efforts to hold gloomy thoughts at bay, she wondered bleakly if she would ever see him again. Or her son? What of Edmund? If she were to die, he would well and truly be orphaned and her heart ached for him and what might be. Edmund would mourn her loss, but he would survive. He had a loving grandfather and she knew that Marcus would care for him and see to his future.

And what of Marcus? How would he react to her death? Oh, she knew he would suffer; he could not have made love to her the way he had without having some depth of feeling for her. A soft smile curved her mouth. Few men would have reacted as he had when he had discovered the truth about Edmund. If she had not already loved him, that moment alone would have won her heart. She never doubted that he held her in high affection and she had enough sense to realize that it was more than just honor, more than just a shared history or propinquity that bound them together.

There was no question about her feelings. She loved him. It seemed she always had. A small sob rose up within her. *But I never told him,* she thought miserably. *I never once let him see what was in my heart. I was too busy hiding my secrets, too busy pretending that he meant nothing to me . . . when he means everything to me!*

She sat there sunk in bitter remorse, cursing herself for all the opportunities she had squandered to tell her husband how much she loved him and swearing that if she lived, she'd not be so foolish in the future.

Her stomach emitted a very ungenteel growl, telling her better than anything else that the hour was very late. How much longer would she be held captive?

That thought had hardly crossed her mind when she heard the sounds of hoofbeats. In a mixture of relief and terror, she listened intently. One horse or two? One, she decided quickly. The gentleman or the other? Or someone else entirely? Whitley? She shivered. Please not Whitley.

The new arrival approached the hut and the door opened. "I see that you have been busy trying to escape," said the one she had dubbed the gentleman and she sighed with relief. She had hoped it would be him. She had no reason to trust either one of her captors, but intuition led her to believe that the gentleman was the lesser of two evils.

"And if you are uncomfortable," he said without a hint of compassion, "you have only yourself to blame."

Isabel muttered furiously from behind her gag.

He laughed. "Yes, yes, I know you would like to put a dagger in my liver, but since I am rather fond of it, I'm sure you'll understand if I don't oblige you."

She hurled another garbled insult at him, but he only laughed again and easily plucked her upright. "Come along," he said in a kinder tone. "Your ordeal is almost over."

With that he tossed her over his shoulder and carried her away from her place of captivity. Reaching his horse, he laid her carefully across the pommel of his saddle and mounted behind her. Making certain he had her securely in front of him, he kicked the horse into a brisk trot.

Isabel shifted, trying to find a more comfortable position, and again received a sharp smack on her bottom for her efforts. "If you want to fall off, just keep that up," said her captor. "So far nothing has gone as I'd planned and the last thing I need is for you to get your neck broken falling off my horse. Behave yourself and I promise this will all end happily." He chuckled. "Well, not for everybody, but in the main."

Despite his outward confidence, the gentleman was worried. It had been a number of years since he and Collard had worked together, and Collard's killing of Whitley disturbed him. When he'd had to leave to fetch Mrs. Sherbrook, he'd been uneasy about leaving Collard behind tonight. He no longer trusted him to follow orders and he'd had to choose between having Collard watch Sherbrook or having him go get Mrs. Sherbrook. He grimaced. He didn't like either choice, but in the end, he had not been willing to risk Isabel Sherbrook's life to Collard's less-than-tender mercies. If Collard would stick to the plan, all would be well, but he suspected that Collard had a different scenario than the one they'd discussed. He sighed. Christ. He supposed he would have to kill Collard, after all.

Uneasy about what Collard might or might not do, he urged his horse into a gallop. The horse surged forward and Isabel gasped. "Yes, yes, I know it's uncomfortable, poppet," he murmured, bending low against the horse's neck, "and I apologize, but it's necessary, so hang on."

The ride was very rough and she lost all sense of direction. Fortunately, it was not a long journey and, just when Isabel thought her head would become disconnected from her neck from the constant jarring motion of the horse's gait, the gentleman slowed his mount. The horse walked quietly for several minutes before the gentleman halted the animal. After sliding from the animal and tying it, he unloaded Isabel and once again slung her over his shoulder.

He was moving very carefully and silently and Isabel had the impression that he was sneaking up on someone or something. He stopped for a second and then she heard the opening of a door and he stepped inside a building. Walking swiftly, he hurried toward some destination. As she was carried along she heard the restive movement of animals, the smell of grain and hay, the distinctive scent of horses. Was she in a stable? He paused, opening another door. The next instant she was laid on the ground—ground that was heavily bedded in straw.

A stall? she wondered. It was obvious she was in a stable somewhere; even if she hadn't recognized the common smells, the blowing and snorting of the nearby horses would have alerted her, but where was she?

"This wasn't part of the plan," her captor said softly, "but I think you'll be safe here."

He moved and the next instant, she felt the rope that had linked her hands to her feet fall free. He patted her slightly on the cheek and whispered, "You're a smart little baggage. I'm sure that you'll manage to free yourself." He laughed low. "Eventually."

And then he was gone.

When she was certain he really was gone, Isabel wiggled around in the straw, struggling to get her hands from behind her back. She was agile, but it was not easy, the skirts of her riding habit thwarting her efforts to get her hands over her feet. After several fruitless attempts, she paused in her efforts. Breathless, she lay there listening, wondering where she was and what was happening with Marcus.

Isabel and her fate were foremost in Marcus's thoughts as he prepared to meet her abductor. The place for the exchange was not far, less than two miles away. The site was a well-known landmark: a huge, lightning-blasted oak tree in a small clearing adjacent to the trail that led to Manning Court.

Even though he had the forged memorandum, Marcus had still considered many different plans to free his wife in the intervening hours. Isabel's safe return was his main goal, but it galled him to just tamely hand over Whitley's greatcoat. He had no way of knowing if Isabel's abductors would keep their word, no way of knowing whether she was alive or not, no way of knowing whether he was riding into a trap. . . .

The idea of setting his own trap had crossed his mind, and

more than once he'd reached for paper to write Jack and ask his help. But each time, fear for Isabel's safety stopped him. What if, through his actions, he caused the very thing he feared: Isabel's death?

Through the long hours, he'd desperately tried to conceive of a way to thwart the enemy and regain his wife—alive. In the end, concern for Isabel's safety defeated him. He *dare* not risk her life in pursuit of revenge. The forgery was risky enough and he would take no further chances with Isabel's life.

His spirit in turmoil, Marcus stared blindly into space. His cousins Julian or Charles would have known precisely how to handle something like this, and they would have, he was convinced, come up with some daring plan. He cursed himself for having preferred the quiet, the mundane life. *If I had been more adventuresome,* he berated himself, *I would have been able to free Isabel in one clever move and confound her captors.* His gaze dropped to Whitley's greatcoat and disgust roiled through him. And what do I do? Instead of riding with sword drawn to save the woman I love, I forge a bloody memorandum!

Another glance at the clock on the mantel told him that he had run out of time, that within the next several minutes he would either have his wife back or . . . He furiously shook his head, unable to complete the thought. Hopeful, angry, eager, and anxious, Marcus rose to his feet and picked up Whitley's greatcoat. With the greatcoat hung over his arm, his jaw set, he walked from his office toward the front of the house, where his saddled horse awaited him.

Having safely deposited Isabel in the stables, the gentleman swiftly exited the building. If all was going as planned, Collard should already be waiting for Sherbrook near the lightning-blasted oak and Sherbrook was either on his way or would be leaving the house within the next few minutes to meet him. He stopped and rubbed his jaw. Collard wouldn't be happy when he didn't arrive with Isabel, but he wasn't particularly worried about it. Collard could think on his feet and he would, most likely, fob Sherbrook off with some excuse for her absence. He sighed. There was no avoiding it: Sherbrook was going to have several nasty moments before he arrived home and discovered that all was not lost. The gentleman smiled. Once Sherbrook arrived home, he would find his wife safe and sound waiting for him.

The sudden jabbing of a pistol in the middle of his back wiped the smile from his face and he stiffened. In a low voice from behind him, Collard said, "Now, fancy meeting you here. Lucky I spied you sneaking around the stable and waited for you to come back out. Since she ain't with you anymore, you must have dumped her inside. I don't remember this being part of yer plan."

"It wasn't," the gentleman said levelly. "But leaving her here doesn't change anything. Sherbrook still gets her back, just not when and where he thought he would." A feeling of helpless rage swept over him. Collard was going to ruin everything. "And you?" he asked coldly. "What are you doing here? Shouldn't you be waiting for Sherbrook?"

Collard laughed nastily. "Why should I have to follow the plan? You haven't."

"Very well, I didn't follow the original plan, but shouldn't *one* of us be meeting Sherbrook?" he asked sarcastically.

Jabbing the pistol deeper into the gentleman's back, Collard said, "Oh, I'll meet with Sherbrook, all right, but I did some thinking while you was gone and I was left to watch Sherbrook, and I've made my own plan." Greed and excitement coloring his words, Collard added, "Everybody knows that Sherbrook's a warm 'un; he'll pay her weight in gold to get her back. Dealing with the frogs don't suit me. I'm taking the woman from you and getting good English gold for her return. What you do is your business."

"You fool!" the gentleman burst out angrily and started to turn and face Collard, but the pistol stopped him.

"Don't move," hissed Collard, poking him harder. "I ain't made up my mind about whether to kill you or not, but you give me trouble and I'll shoot you where you stand."

"Yes, that would be smart," the gentleman drawled. "By all means shoot me and rouse the entire household. The moment you fire that pistol, how long do you think it would be before this place is swarming with men? Enough time, do you think, for you to retrieve her from the stall where I put her? It's a big stable. Do you really think you'll find her and reach your horse and simply ride away before they catch you?" He laughed without humor. "Somehow I think not."

"Shut yer bone box!"

A woman's voice rang pure and clean through the still night air and the gentleman knew that Isabel had finally managed to get her hands in front of her and remove the gag. In moments, the stable yard would be filled with sleepy servants, with Sherbrook at the fore. If all was not to be lost, the gentleman knew he had to end this. Now.

Startled by the sound, Collard half turned to glance in the direction of the voice and the gentleman used the distraction to pivot on his heel and attack him. They grappled together, both fighting to gain control of the pistol. It was a deadly battle, their bodies locked against each other as the pistol wavered between them, their breathing labored, their muscles straining to overpower the other, each aware of the passing seconds—seconds that could not be spared if they were to escape.

The pistol exploded between them and a form slumped to the ground. With a curse, the survivor threw the pistol to the ground and fled into the night.

In the act of mounting his horse, as the sound of the shot shattered the air, Marcus jerked around to stare in the direction of the stables. Fear such as he had never known bloomed in his chest and he kicked his horse into a mad gallop, swiftly covering the scant quarter mile between the house and stables.

Jerking the horse to a sliding stop, he leaped from the saddle, his heart jumping like a wild thing when he heard Isabel's raised, frantic voice coming from the stable. Lanterns were already lit in the sleeping quarters of the stables and sleepy-eyed stable boys were tumbling outside. Heedless of the body lying inches from his snorting horse's hooves, heedless of anything but Isabel, he raced past the first of the servants and charged down the aisle, following the siren song of his wife's voice.

Finding the stall where she lay still bound, he flung open the door and in one long stride was by her side. Kneeling beside her, he pulled her into his arms and rained kisses across her face.

"Oh, my little love," he cried brokenly. "I feared never to hold you again."

It took him but a moment to cut her bonds and, with strands of rope dangling from her wrists and ankles, Isabel looped her arms around his neck and melted into his big, warm body. She was safe at last. Marcus had her. Her cheek resting against his shoulder, the fear and terrors of the day vanished. She was home. And Marcus *loved* her!

Cradling her next to him, Marcus rose to his feet, and oblivious to the gasps and startled glances of the curious servants he passed in the aisle, like a conquering hero he strode from the barn, his most precious treasure held securely in his arms.

Chapter 18

Walking outside into the cool night air, Marcus and Isabel were met with a barrage of astonished gasps. Worley, with young Ellard at his heels, came rushing up.

"Sir! What is going on?" Worley demanded anxiously. In the light of the lantern he held, his anxious gaze took in Isabel's smudged, exhausted features, her creased and dirty riding habit, the pieces of rope dangling from her ankles and wrists, and the bits of straw clinging to the fine material and her hair, and he exclaimed, "Madame! Are you all right? What has happened to you?"

Nestled in her husband's arms, Isabel smiled wanly and said, "I am fine, Worley. It has been an exciting day, but it ended well. Do not worry."

Not convinced but knowing he would get no more than that, Worley turned his eyes to Marcus. "Sir," he said with commendable aplomb, "there is a dead man lying over there."

Unable to keep quiet a moment longer, forgetting both his place and his manners, Ellard said excitedly, "It's the smuggler Collard, sir! He's been shot dead."

Marcus said nothing for a moment, then glancing down at Isabel he asked softly, "Could you identify him as one of your abductors?"

She shook her head. "No. I know that there were two men, but they attacked so swiftly, enveloping me in a blanket or something, that I never saw either one of them. Before they removed the covering, one of them knocked me out, and when I awoke, I was blindfolded." She sighed. "I could recognize their voices, but other than their voices and my impressions of them, I can tell you nothing."

Every word hit Marcus like a blow and he fought to contain his rage against the two men that had laid rough hands on his wife, had dared to touch her at all. Dying had been too easy for Collard, he thought savagely. He hugged Isabel tighter to him. She was safe, he reminded himself. She was safe and that was all that mattered.

Pushing aside thoughts of vengeance, Marcus said to Worley, "Wrap the body in a blanket and get it out of sight. At first light send someone to notify the constable and the squire." Looking at Ellard, he added, "I have a horse somewhere around here. Will you fetch it?"

"Yes, sir!"

A second later, Ellard returned with Marcus's horse from where it had been contentedly cropping grass near one of the paddocks. Reluctantly, Marcus set Isabel down, just long enough to mount his horse. She came up easily into his arms and with her sitting in front of him, her arms once more looped around his neck, her cheek against his shoulder, they rode slowly home.

By now Sherbrook Hall was brilliantly lit and Thompson and a half dozen servants were anxiously milling around the front of the house, peering intently in the direction of the stables. As Marcus and Isabel appeared out of the darkness, almost as one they surged toward them.

"Master!" cried Thompson. "What has happened? We heard the sound of gunfire. Is everything all right?"

Similar sounds and questions came from the others around him. Peggy, her blue eyes worried, pushed herself to the front of the crowd. "Oh, my sweet mistress! What has been done to you?" she demanded, taking in Isabel's bedraggled state.

Isabel forced a smile. "I have had a most exciting day,

Peggy, an adventure, but it ended well and now I simply long for a bath, and perhaps Cook or someone else could find me a few morsels to eat?"

It was precisely the right thing to say: Peggy drew herself up like a general preparing for battle and said briskly, "I shall see to it immediately." Turning away, she pointed a finger at a couple of the younger maids. "Come with me, madame's bath water must be heated."

Thompson looked at George, the footman, and said, "Go this instant and wake Cook. Tell her that madame has come home unexpectedly and has not eaten. She is to prepare a tray for her immediately."

The servants vanished into the house as if by magic, leaving only Thompson, Isabel, and Marcus standing in front of the house. His features kind and concerned, Thompson said, "Madame, may I help you down?"

Isabel was gently lifted down, Thompson discreetly making no comment about the pieces of rope clinging to her wrists and feet. Marcus dismounted and, remembering Whitley's greatcoat for the first time, untied it and threw it across his arm. The last of the crushing weight he had borne since the moment he had read the ransom note lifted. Isabel was safe and so was the memorandum. Right now, it didn't even matter to him that one of the scoundrels had escaped. He smiled. He had beaten them. His gaze wandered to his wife. No, he thought jubilantly, *they* had beaten them.

But the greatcoat reminded him of pressing matters and, looking at Thompson, he said, "Tell George to prepare to leave for Holcombe within the next few minutes. He can ride my horse. Just as soon as Mrs. Sherbrook is settled, I'll have a note for him to deliver to Lord Thorne."

Thompson rushed away, leaving Marcus to escort his wife across the courtyard and into the house. Once inside, Marcus reluctantly handed Isabel over to Peggy's eager hands and excused himself.

"I'll be only a few minutes," he murmured, his gaze caressing Isabel's features. "I must write that note for Jack and then I shall find you."

"Madame needs to bathe and eat first," said Peggy with the impunity of a longtime servant. "A half-hour would be better for her."

Marcus bowed and said meekly, "Of course. Whatever is best for your mistress."

Triumphantly, Peggy bore Isabel away.

Tiredness washed over Marcus, but his step was light as he headed for his office. Entering the room, he tossed Whitley's greatcoat onto the nearest chair and sat down and scrawled a brief note to Jack, demanding his presence as soon as possible. Folding the note, he decided that it was going to be a very long night.

He rang for Thompson and, handing him the note, said, "This is for George. Tell him he does not have to wait for an answer. Oh, and tell Mrs. Brown to have a room prepared for Lord Thorne. I doubt Jack will be riding back to Holcombe tonight. I'll be upstairs with my wife. When Jack arrives show him here and notify me."

Despite the questions burning on his lips, Thompson bowed and departed. A moment later, the note was on its way to Holcombe and Jack.

Alone in the room again, Marcus poured himself a snifter of brandy and slowly leaned back in his chair and fully relaxed. It was over. Isabel was upstairs being fussed over by Peggy and soon enough he could turn the memorandum over to Jack and that would end his part in this whole affair. His mouth tightened. Collard's death bothered him not a bit, but he wondered about Collard's accomplice. Another smuggler? A Frenchman? Isabel might be able to answer those questions. And Whitley? Was he dead? Marcus strongly suspected so, but it didn't matter to him; what mattered to him was that his wife was home, unharmed, and the memorandum had been found and was residing in his safe. Soon enough it would be in Jack's hands and headed for Roxbury and London.

Glancing at the clock and deciding that he had tarried long enough he set down his snifter and left his office. Taking the stairs two at a time, he reached the upper floor and hurried down the wide hall toward his wife's rooms. He found her neatly tucked into bed, a bank of pillows at her back and a small tray across her lap. A larger tray, holding several covered dishes, sat on a nearby table. Of Peggy there was no sign.

Seeing him, Isabel set down her cup of tea and sent him a shy smile.

His heart fluttered in his chest at the sight of that smile and, heedless of anything but her, he sped across the distance that separated them. Knocking the tray askew, he jerked her into his arms and kissed her hard.

"I love you," he said in a shaken voice. "You mean everything to me. If something had happened to you . . ." His voice died away and he kissed her again. "I love you." With trembling fingers he brushed back a tendril of fiery hair. "I know ours was not a love match, but you must believe that I will do everything within my power to make you happy. I swear it."

Pressing sweet little kisses across his mouth and cheeks, she exclaimed, "Oh, Marcus, I love you, too—I always have!"

Astonished, he pushed her away slightly. "You love me? Truly?" he asked hopefully.

She smiled tenderly at him. "I was in love with you even when you were my pigheaded guardian."

He frowned. "If you loved me, why did you run away with Hugh?"

She sighed. "Because I was young and foolish and so miserable that I could think of nothing else to do. Things were so wretched at home, Aunt Agatha always pecking at me, and you . . . you only saw me as a troublesome ward and I so wanted you to see me as a woman." She toyed with a button on his jacket. "I was convinced you never would, that you'd always see me as a child and a brat at that! The afternoon after our fight over Tempest, I was sunk in the depths of despair and I just wanted to run away from everything. Hugh happened along at the wrong time."

Marcus settled himself on her bed: Isabel half sprawled across him. "Well, you're wrong about one thing: I was very much aware of what an enticing little chit you were growing into."

She sat upright, her eyes big. "You never gave any sign!" she accused.

He sighed. "Sweetheart, how could I? I was your guardian. It would have been dishonorable of me to have given you any idea of my feelings."

She scowled at him. "Well, I think you should have given me a hint. If I'd had the least—do you realize how much time we wasted? If only I'd known!"

"I was waiting for the guardianship to end," he explained patiently. "I had every intention of courting you once I no longer had any responsibility for you."

"Suppose someone else would have caught my eye while you waited?"

Marcus smiled like a tiger, thinking of Whitley's near drowning at his hands. "I'm sure I'd have thought of a way to discourage anyone fool enough to come courting the woman I had marked as my own."

"Oh, Marcus!" she breathed. "That's the most romantic thing you've ever said to me."

He pulled her up against him and kissed her until her eyes were starry and she was breathless. "For the rest of our lives together," he said huskily, "I have every intention of saying and doing the most romantic things imaginable."

"The time we've wasted," mourned Isabel, rubbing her head across his chest like a kitten.

"Well, you weren't exactly encouraging after you came back from India," he said dryly.

She looked up at him. "How could I be? You know why I couldn't marry anyone." Her eyes narrowed. "Besides, you never once gave any indication you felt anything for me but irritation and annoyance."

He grimaced. "What did you expect? You'd broken my heart. I was hardly going to lay it at your feet and take the chance you'd trample it again."

"What fools we've been," she said softly.

"That's in the past," he murmured, "we have the future to share and memories to make." He kissed her. "I love you, Isabel. Never doubt that. I think I fell in love with you the first time I saw you—a squalling infant in the arms of your nurse."

She looked delighted. "Oh, Marcus! Really?"

"Oh, Isabel!" he teased, the gray eyes warm and caressing. "Yes, really."

It was a joyous time in a day that had been so traumatic and fraught with danger and they reveled in the knowledge that they loved and were loved in return. Passion simmered between them and inevitably they made love, their coming together all the sweeter, all the more meaningful with love guiding every caress, every touch.

Mindful that Jack would be arriving soon, Marcus eventually rose from the bed and sought out his own room to prepare to meet him. When he was presentable again, lured by his wife's presence, he came back to her and, scooping her up in his arms, he settled in a comfortable chair near the bed. Nestled together, they talked of the things that lovers do until all too soon the knock on the door came and Thompson informed Marcus that Lord Thorne awaited him in his office.

Reluctantly, Marcus carried Isabel back to bed. "I have to talk to Jack. It's important."

Her eyes searched his. "Is it what you and Jack and Garrett were meeting about the other night and you couldn't tell me?"

He nodded curtly.

She caught his hand. "I'm involved, too. You can't tell me that my abduction today, yesterday, doesn't have some bearing on it. I want to be there."

He hesitated. "Are you up to it?" he asked. "There are questions I'd like to ask, but I didn't want to put you under any more strain tonight."

She grinned at him. "I'd be under more strain wondering what you and Jack were talking about than answering questions."

"Very well," he said with a faint smile. "Join us in my office when you are dressed."

Marcus found Jack pacing the floor when he arrived. Jack declined the offer of refreshments and demanded, "What the devil happened that is so important that I am dragged from my bed at this hour of the morning?"

Marcus said simply, "I have the memorandum."

"*What?*" Jack ejaculated, goggle-eyed.

Marcus nodded. "Yes, I know, astounding, isn't it? Whitley had the memorandum with him all the time—hidden in his greatcoat." He waved in the direction of the greatcoat, lying where he had flung it earlier. "If you'll examine it, you'll see where he hid it."

In one long stride, Jack crossed to the greatcoat and plucked it up and found the seam Marcus had opened. He pulled out the oilcloth-wrapped packet and, looking back at Marcus, exclaimed, "By Jove! This is wonderful! Wellesley's plans can stand as they are. I'll leave immediately for London. Roxbury will be happy to have this in his hand I can tell you!"

Marcus pulled on his ear. "Ah, not that memorandum. It is a long story, but what you hold in your hand is a fake that I concocted. The original is over here in my safe." Smiling, Marcus turned to indicate the location against the far wall and froze.

The safe and its concealing gilt-framed portrait had not been in his line of sight when he had entered the room and, focused on Jack and his reaction, Marcus had not even looked in that direction. But now, he was staring in frozen disbelief at the sight that met his horrified gaze.

The portrait was on the floor, leaning neatly against the book-lined wall, and the door to the safe gaped open. Smothering a curse, Marcus leaped across the room and frantically dug through the items in the safe. Everything was there . . . except the memorandum.

Jack was on his heels, having realized the significance of the opened safe at the same instant Marcus had. Marcus whirled to look at him with wild eyes. "It's gone!"

"But how? Who knew about the fake and where you put the original?"

"No one!" Marcus said. "No one." He glanced past Jack at the tall windows behind him. Blackness met his gaze, but he knew to anyone standing outside that inside of the room would have been lit up like a stage in a theater. Harshly, Marcus said, "Someone must have been watching me and realized what I was doing."

Pushing Jack aside, he snatched up a candelabrum and strode toward the door. "There's one way to find out. Grab that one," he said, indicating the twin to the candelabrum he held in his hand. "Follow me."

Flinging open the door, he nearly walked over Isabel, neatly dressed in a simple green muslin gown, who was just preparing to enter the room.

She took one look at Marcus's face and touched his arm. "What is it? What has happened?"

Marcus gave a shake of his head. "In a moment. I need to confirm what I believe happened. Wait in the office for us, we will be right back."

Hand on her hip she waited until the two men headed down the hallway and then followed them, picking up the candlestick that Thompson had left burning on a table in the entry. Stepping out of the house a moment after the two men, she walked along quickly, guided by the light of their candelabra. When Marcus spied her following him, he growled, "I thought I told you to stay inside."

She smiled sunnily at him. "Did you? I must have misunderstood you. But since I am here . . ."

Marcus snorted and continued on his way. Arriving at the side of the house and the area just outside his office, Marcus glanced at her and said, "We're looking for signs that someone hid out here and watched me in my office."

The flickering candles pierced the darkness and, though daylight would have made the task simpler, after a few minutes Isabel said, "Marcus, I've found something."

She had indeed. There in the soft dirt at the edge of one of the many flowerbeds that flowed around the house were several footprints. From the depth and overlapping of the prints it was obvious that someone had stood here for several minutes. Closer examination revealed that two different-sized boots had made the prints.

Once he and Jack confirmed what she had found, Marcus stepped into the footprints and looked inside the windows. His entire office could be clearly seen and anyone standing here would have had an excellent view of the inside—and everything he had done. Following the prints in the flowerbed, he moved to a position next to the window and easily lifted it. Sticking his head inside, he glimpsed the faint dirt smears on the rug. His expression grim, he shut the window and turned back to the others. "It's clear he entered this way. There are more signs inside the house."

Silently the three returned inside and to Marcus's office. Looking for them now, it was easy to find the occasional smudge of dirt that had clung to the bottom of the intruder's shoes as he had walked directly from the window to the safe. This time when he offered Jack a brandy, Jack did not refuse. Isabel accepted a small glass of ratafia, enjoying the scent of apricots that wafted up from it before taking a dainty sip.

Jack's brow rose at Isabel's presence and Marcus said

tersely, "I'll have no secrets from my wife. And after what happened today, she has every right to be here."

Jack took a drink of his brandy and said wearily, "Very well. Tell me what the devil is going on. And you can start with the reason you created a fake."

Marcus related the events of the day, starting with the discovery that Isabel had been abducted. He ended with finding her in the stables and the news that a well-known local smuggler, Collard, was presently lying dead somewhere in that same stable.

"Collard and his companion wanted you to betray England, risk the lives of those men for me?" Isabel demanded angrily, when he finished speaking. "Of all the dastardly deeds! Oh, I am so glad that Collard is dead!" Her face glowing she added, "And Marcus, it was so very clever of you to think of a fake!"

"I couldn't let you come to harm," he said thickly, his eyes locked on hers, "but neither could I turn over the memorandum to them."

"Of course, you couldn't," she exclaimed. "And I would not have wanted you to." She smiled lovingly at him. "But I am very glad that you came up with a way to thwart them."

"But it would appear that in the end he didn't," Jack reminded them sharply.

"No," Marcus admitted bitterly, "it would appear not." Staring down into the amber liquor, he muttered, "To think I had the bloody memorandum in my hand . . ."

"But you had no way of knowing that they were watching you," protested Isabel. "You couldn't have known. It is not your fault."

"She's right, you know," Jack said quietly. "I would have wished you'd have notified me the minute you found the memorandum. . . ."

"I couldn't," Marcus snapped. "It was my wife's life at stake. You would have only cared that Roxbury got his precious memorandum back!"

Jack flushed. "I would have helped you," he said tightly. "I can't deny that my first reaction would have been to get it to Roxbury, but I wouldn't have abandoned you and snatched it away from you and ridden hell-bent for London."

Marcus ran a hand through his hair and sent Jack an apologetic smile. "I've insulted you. I'm sorry. I wasn't thinking. Or rather all I could think of was Isabel's safety."

Jack nodded curtly. "Apology accepted." He took a quick drink of his brandy and, glancing at Isabel, he asked, "Can you tell us anything about the two that abducted you?"

Isabel made a face. "Not very much. As you know, I never saw their faces and their voices were not familiar. I do know that there were two of them. One of which we now suspect was Collard. The other one . . ." She hesitated and said slowly, "I had the impression that the other one was the leader and that he was of a higher social standing than Collard. He seemed to be the one making the decisions. His speech was that of a gentleman; in fact, I thought of him as the 'gentleman' and Collard as the 'other.' " She looked uncertainly from one man to the other and added, "It is hard to explain but the gentleman was almost kind to me."

"And that's all you can tell us?" Jack asked, disappointed.

Isabel frowned, trying to recall every word that had come from the gentleman's mouth. "He was worried," she said abruptly. "He said something about plans changing, that nothing had gone as planned. I don't think he trusted Collard."

"Was any mention made of Whitley?" Marcus asked.

Isabel shook her head. "No. They said very little in front of me and Whitley's name was never spoken."

It was a depressed little trio that occupied Marcus's office. There was joy that Isabel had been returned unharmed, but all of them were aware that the fateful memorandum was in the hands of the "gentleman" and no doubt on its way to the French even now. They had failed, and many men might die because of it.

Jack shook himself and, tossing off the last of his brandy, said, "I must leave for London now. The sooner Roxbury knows of this latest event, the sooner he can set things in motion to change Wellesley's plans."

Despite the lateness of the hour, Marcus didn't try to dissuade him. "You have everything you need?"

Jack smiled wryly. "Yes, even a full moon to light my way."

He took his leave and strode from the room.

Marcus had not forgotten that the squire and the constable would be arriving shortly after daylight and so, despite a strong inclination to stay delightfully wrapped around his wife's soft, warm body, he rose in the hour before dawn and dressed and prepared to meet the day. The squire and the constable were suitably shocked by Collard's death, but there was nothing they could do but shake their heads. The identity of his assailant remained unknown and they agreed that most likely it was a fellow smuggler. Marcus saw no point in suggesting otherwise. Neither mentioned the peculiar circumstances or the odd fact that the murder had taken place on the grounds of Sherbrook Hall.

"I never liked the man and I always knew that he would come to a bad end," remarked the squire as he mounted his horse and prepared to leave.

"Yes, indeed," said the constable, a bluff, hearty man known to frequently look the other way as far as the smuggling community was concerned. "No question about it, Collard was a bad 'un. Can't say as I'm surprised." He tipped his hat to Marcus and added, "I'll have someone pick up the body—don't you worry about anything. My best to you and your wife."

His official duties settled to his satisfaction, Marcus walked slowly back to the house. There would be no further investigation in the matter of Collard's death and, while the servants were aware that the mistress had been at the center of *something*, it had ended well and that was the end of it. Jack was well on his way to London and steps would be taken to keep Wellesley and his troops from harm. The escape of Isabel's gentleman gnawed at him, but Marcus decided he could afford to be magnanimous: Isabel was safe and in the end that was what mattered most to him.

Marcus and Isabel spent a delightful day together, wandering through the gardens, their hands entwined, stopping now and then to exchange dizzying kisses in the shadows and nooks that abounded. That evening, as dusk was falling, they had just finished an intimate meal in a courtyard at the side of the house, when the sounds of galloping hoofbeats and the creak and rattle of a fast-approaching vehicle caught their attention. With Isabel at his side Marcus strolled to the front of the house.

An elegant traveling coach pulled by four matched bays swung around the wide driveway. Lanterns winked in the deepening twilight on the corners of the coach and a pair of outriders flanked either side of the vehicle.

The coachman pulled the horses to a stop and the two outriders halted their steeds and dismounted. If he hadn't already spied the crest in the center of the door of the coach, he would have known the identity of his sudden guests.

A broad grin spread across his face and he said to Isabel, "It is Julian and Charles and their wives."

While the servants at the back of the coach leaped down to help the ladies alight, the two gentlemen approached Marcus and Isabel. Isabel had met Julian, Lord Wyndham, as a child, but she had never laid eyes on Charles Weston, another of Marcus's many cousins. No one had ever told her that Julian and Charles could have passed for twins and, when she first caught sight of them, she gasped at their similarity, right down to their keen green eyes. Like her husband, both of his cousins were tall, broad shouldered, and black haired, and though there was a lesser resemblance to Marcus, it was obvious that they were related.

Charles flashed a quick grin and said, "I see that your husband has not yet told you about his handsome cousins." He sent Marcus a look. "For shame!" Turning back to Isabel, he bowed and said, "I am Charles Weston and most happy to meet the woman who has finally brought him to heel."

Isabel giggled, charmed by his outrageous manner.

Julian smiled and said, "It is a pleasure to see you again, madame. And I congratulate you upon your marriage. I wish you happy." He flicked a glance at Charles and added, "You must forgive him. It is his nature to be incorrigible. Fortunately, he is also vastly amusing, so we put up with him."

Delighted though he was to see them, Marcus couldn't help saying, "You know that you are more than welcome, but what brings you so unexpectedly to my door?"

Wryly, Julian said, "Nell. She had a dream."

It was obvious Marcus and Charles understood the meaning behind that cryptic statement, but Isabel looked in puzzlement from one lean face to the other. Before she could demand an explanation, Nell herself came rushing up, followed by Daphne, Charles's bride of only a few months. The two women were very different in appearance. Nell's hair was a soft golden-brown, her eyes sea green in color and, though Nell was tall, Daphne towered over her by half a head. Daphne's hazel eyes were warm as she greeted Isabel and her thick black hair had been caught back in a neat chignon. Isabel, enfolded in scented embraces, could only marvel at fate. These beautiful women and handsome men were her relatives!

Several chaotic moments followed as the entire group wandered inside the house where a gaggle of servants was dispatched to help unload the coach and orders for bedrooms to be prepared were given. Eventually, they were all scattered about the library, Thompson happily overseeing the serving of refreshments. Once everyone had been served, Thompson waved the footmen from the room, bowed, and departed, shutting the big double doors behind him.

Conversation was general for several moments, the ladies sipping their tea, the gentlemen enjoying brandy, before Isabel asked Nell, "What did your husband mean when he said you had a dream?"

Her eyes somber, Nell murmured, "Marcus hasn't told you about . . . Charles's terrible half-brother, Raoul, and my nightmares about him?"

Scowling at her husband, Isabel said, "No. He hasn't."

Daphne leaned forward and asked softly, "Didn't he mention the ghosts we encountered at my brother's home in Cornwall either? It was only a few months ago."

Looking guilty, Marcus said quickly, "We're newly married, I didn't see the need to fill her head full of . . ."

He stopped and Charles finished dryly, "Nonsense?"

Isabel saved him by saying, "But what does any of that have to do with Nell having a dream?"

Deciding that now was not the time to drag up the past, Nell said simply, "I dreamed that you were in grave danger. I clearly saw you bound and gagged and blindfolded." She looked across at Marcus, her face compassionate. "I knew that Marcus was in anguish."

"She woke me," said Julian, "and insisted that we had to leave for Sherbrook Hall immediately, that we were needed here."

Charles took up the tale saying, "Daphne and I were visiting and when Julian woke me to tell me what was going on, we insisted upon coming with them."

"You knew I was in danger?" squeaked Isabel, incredulously. "But how?"

Nell made a face. "It is complicated to explain, but sometimes when I dream, I . . . see real events. I saw you and I knew we had to come."

Isabel's eyes got very big and round. "Oh, how very exciting!" she exclaimed. She looked eagerly at Daphne. "And ghosts? You actually saw ghosts?"

Daphne smiled. "Yes, we did. It was terrifying at the time, but the ghosts are at peace now."

Mournfully, Isabel said, "Such adventures you have had! I

wish I'd been there to see the ghosts; nothing so exciting has ever happened to me."

Forgetting himself, Marcus protested, "You were abducted only yesterday. You were held for ransom. You could have died! Wasn't that exciting enough for you? It certainly was for *me*!"

Charles gave a crack of laughter. "I told you that a wife would shake you from your humdrum existence!"

An incredibly tender smile crossed Marcus's face as he looked at Isabel and, uncaring of who saw or heard him, he said, "Indeed, you did. I just never imagined that she would make me the luckiest, happiest of men."

But Isabel was not to be distracted and it was Marcus's turn to laugh when she looked around the room and asked brightly, "And now could someone please tell me about the ghosts?"

Epilogue

The hour was going on three o'clock in the morning when Duke Roxbury arrived home to his magnificent townhouse in London. For appearance's sake he'd spent an hour or two gaming at White's but he did not enjoy himself, his thoughts more on a missing memorandum and its far-reaching implications than the cards in his hands. Lord Thorne's arrival just before midnight had been unexpected, but the news he carried had been devastating. *I was so sure we'd recover the memorandum,* Roxbury thought to himself as he absently handed his hat and gloves to his butler. *So sure. Yet, I was wrong. Right,* he reminded himself, *to suspect Whitley, but wrong to think that others, such as Le Renard, the notorious Fox, would not be following the scent.* He frowned. But the abduction and theft of the memorandum from Sherbrook's safe didn't have the feel of the Fox. No, there were other players, players he'd overlooked.

Within minutes of Lord Thorne arriving on his doorstep, despite the hour, Roxbury had instantly notified several of the top generals. They were probably at this very moment considering other landings; he knew that nothing of real consequence would be accomplished for several hours yet. Once a full staff at the Horse Guards was assembled for the day, the real work would begin.

His thoughts strayed for a moment to Lord Thorne, currently sleeping upstairs. Jack had been white with exhaustion after his frantic ride to London, almost swaying on his feet when he had been shown into Roxbury's library, and once he had relayed his message, Roxbury had insisted he stay the night. Jack had gratefully accepted, not liking the disturbance his unexpected arrival would cause at the Thorne townhouse this time of night. Roxbury sighed. The young man had done his best and he sympathized with Jack's feeling of crushing failure. Garrett had yet to be notified of the disaster and Roxbury no more looked forward to telling him about the theft of the memorandum from Sherbrook's safe than he had imparting the news to the generals.

With a heavy tread and heart, the duke walked down the wide hallway to his private study at the rear of the house. He felt very tired and old as he walked and he wondered if perhaps his days of usefulness in his own unique way weren't coming to an end. *I failed.* It was a bitter draught to swallow.

Entering his study, he shut the door behind him and stared blankly around the large, candlelit room. It was a handsome, masculine room befitting a man of his wealth and title. Amber figured bronze silk graced the portion of the walls not holding a series of floor-to-ceiling oak bookcases, their shelves crammed with leather volumes; drapes of amber velvet hung at the many windows. A pair of French doors opened onto a quiet terrace and a gold-veined marble fireplace dominated the opposite wall.

Roxbury fiddled with a few volumes of his vast collection of books, but nothing held his interest. Turning away, he strolled over to the French doors and, opening one, stepped out onto the terrace and stood looking up at the black sky as if he could find answers there. He sighed and, coming back inside, he walked over to his desk, where he sat for a few minutes, his fingers tapping aimlessly on the leather top as he stared blindly into space. Getting up a moment later, he approached the array of crystal decanters and gleaming glasses and snifters neatly arranged across a marble-topped table.

He stared for several seconds at the decanters before pouring himself a glass of rich, aromatic port. Glass in hand, he finally settled himself on a long leather sofa that faced the fireplace and gazed at the empty hearth.

The only comfort he could take from the entire debacle, he decided, was that he had been right to suspect Whitley of the theft in the first place. Not that he hadn't considered others and hadn't had those possibilities investigated. He had, and they had all come to naught. If there was anything good to come out of this, he reminded himself morosely, it was that at least they knew that the memorandum was in enemy hands— thank God, they were no longer dithering about *that!*

Intent upon his unpleasant musings, he had no indication that someone else was in the room with him until he felt the cold kiss of a pistol at the back of his neck and a man said, "If you value your life, your grace, do not cry out or turn around."

Roxbury sighed deeply. Just what he needed to end a perfectly foul evening: a brazen housebreaker!

"Take what you want," Roxbury said indifferently and took a sip of his port. "You'll not find much that is easily disposable in this room," he added helpfully. "Try the butler's pantry; there's bound to be a great deal of plate that would appeal to a common thief like yourself."

"Common?" mocked the man, a hint of laughter in his voice. "I like to think that there is nothing common about me at all and, while I appreciate the generous offer, your grace," said the man, "I'm not after silver candlesticks and utensils. I'm after gold . . . a great deal of gold."

His interest piqued, Roxbury asked, "And why should I give you a great deal of gold?"

The man chuckled. "Why, because I have something that you want very badly . . . a certain memorandum."

Roxbury stiffened and started to turn around, but the pistol pressed deeper into his neck and the intruder murmured, "No, don't turn around. I don't know for certain yet that we're going to do business and until I do we'll just keep things the way they are."

Irritated, yet undeniably excited by the man's words, Roxbury said, "I'm sure that we shall be able to come to an agreement, but I absolutely refuse to do business with a person I cannot see."

There was a hesitation, then the man sighed and said, "Somehow I expected you would say that."

Removing the pistol from Roxbury's neck, the intruder strolled around the end of the sofa where Roxbury sat and took a seat in a chair that was arranged at an angle to the sofa. There were only a few candles lit in the room and the intruder purposefully selected a chair that was half in shadows.

Roxbury watched him, noting the tall, broad-shouldered, loose-limbed body, the heavy black hair, and the cut and quality of the clothes his uninvited visitor wore. The dark blue coat looked to have come straight from the hands of Stultz, the man's linen was pristine, the starched cravat tied in a manner that would have won even Brummell's approval, and the black Hessian boots gleamed in the faint candlelight.

Roxbury smiled at the black silk mask the stranger wore. Lifting his glass, he indicated the mask and asked, "Do you think that fashion will catch on?"

The man smiled, his teeth a white flash in the shadows. "Perhaps, not, but it serves me well."

The light moment gone, Roxbury leaned forward and asked, "Do you have the memorandum with you?"

The man nodded and, reaching inside his jacket, extracted several folded sheets of paper and handed them to Roxbury.

Roxbury stood up and carried them to a candelabrum that sat on the far edge of the fireplace mantel. Quickly he scanned the material, his heart beating faster, his spirits lifting. It was the memorandum.

With a narrowed-eyed gaze, he looked at his intruder. "How did you come by these?"

The man stared down at the pistol he still held in his hand. "Not easily. Blood was spilt." Heavily, he added, "I doubt you'll find Whitley's corpse, but know that he is dead." Between the slits in the mask, his eyes met Roxbury's. "I did not kill him, but it is my fault that he is dead. As for those pages you hold, you know how I came by them. Lord Thorne is sure to have told you all when he arrived, just after midnight."

"You watched my house." It was a statement, not a question.

The man shrugged. "In my business one tends to be very careful."

Roxbury glanced down at the memorandum, already composing the note he would have delivered to the Horse Guards the moment he was done with his . . . guest. He considered the small pistol he always carried in his vest. Dare he risk it? He looked over at his visitor and discovered that the man's pistol was aimed at his heart.

"No tricks," the intruder said quietly. "If it will make it easier for you I suggest you think of this in the light of a mutually agreeable exchange. You get the memorandum and I get my gold."

For a long moment Roxbury studied him. As the man himself had stated, this was no common housebreaker. He had the manner and wore the clothes of a gentleman. There was arrogance in the set of his head, a cool confidence in the way he held himself. Even if his clothes and bearing did not bespeak the gentleman, his speech certainly did. And there was something familiar about him. . . .

"Who are you?" demanded Roxbury. "Do I know you?"

"I don't think you need to concern yourself about that," he replied coolly. "Our business has to do with those sheets of paper you hold in your hand."

"How much?"

The man grinned, showing his even white teeth again, and said, "I'll take that nice leather bag of gold you keep in your safe just for fellows like myself and you may keep the memorandum with my compliments."

Damn the man! Roxbury fumed. Was there anything he didn't know? It was true he did keep a large amount of gold on hand for . . . He half-smiled. The scamp was right. It was for fellows just like this impudent jackanapes.

When Roxbury remained silent, the intruder moved restlessly and said, "I know you have it, so don't try to fob me off with some excuse that it will take you time to fetch it."

"You seem to have studied me quite extensively."

"As I said, in my business one tends to be careful. Very careful."

Roxbury nodded and walked to the bank of books that hid his safe. There didn't seem to be any reason to hide the location of his safe; he suspected the fellow already knew *precisely* where it was. Opening the safe, he pulled out a large, leather bag filled with gold guineas.

After putting the memorandum into the safe and locking it, he carried the bag of gold back to the intruder. Tossing it to him, Roxbury said, "You may count it if you like, to see if it is enough."

The man caught the bag easily, the heft of the bag and the chink of the gold telling him that this night's work had been well worth the effort. Another grin was flashed Roxbury's way. "It will be enough, your grace." Rising to his feet, he bowed and said, "It has been a pleasure to do business with you."

He turned to leave and Roxbury commanded, "Wait!" When the man looked back at him, he asked, "You could have sold the memorandum to the French for far more than what is in that bag. Why didn't you?"

A bitter smile curved the handsome mouth. "There may be blood on my hands and I may be a thief and a robber and live by my wits, but I am no traitor to England."

Roxbury nodded. His gaze considering the man before him, he said slowly, "You're very clever and bold; I could use a man with your talents. Would you be interested in working for me?"

The intruder chuckled, shaking his head. "I work for no master, your grace. You'd find that I am not easily brought to the bridle."

"And do you think that men like Lord Thorne are easily brought to the bridle?" Roxbury asked curiously.

The intruder hesitated, then shook his head decisively. "I'm sorry to refuse you, your grace," he said with a hint of regret in his voice, "but Lord Thorne and the like have something I will never have. I would be of no use to you." And then he was gone.

Roxbury stared at the opened French door through which the man had disappeared. It never occurred to him to raise the alarm and, thinking of the precious memorandum resting in his safe, he decided that it had been a fair exchange, after all. Roxbury admired the boldness of the man, and oddly enough he wished his intruder well. There was, he mused, no reason for anyone to know that gold had been exchanged for the memorandum. It would be, he thought wryly, our little secret.

Seating himself behind his desk, he rang for his butler. There were messages to be written and delivered and he reached for his quill and ink bottle.

It was a few days before Jack and Garrett returned to Sherbrook Hall and related the amazing events in London. They came to call late one fine May afternoon and found Marcus and Isabel entertaining their guests, the Earl and Countess of Wyndham and Mr. and Mrs. Charles Weston, on the terrace. Garrett was vaguely familiar with both Lord Wyndham and his lady, and he had met Charles upon more than one occasion over the years. Daphne was new to him and he was instantly charmed by her friendly nature.

Jack had met both his cousins previously, but as with Marcus, they were almost virtual strangers and he had not yet met their wives. Introductions were made, congratulations were offered on his inheritance, refreshments served, and in no time everyone was at ease, chatting like old friends.

Isabel noticed immediately that both men seemed more relaxed and lighthearted and she puzzled over what had transpired in London to bring about this transformation. Once the niceties were dispensed with, unable to contain her curiosity any longer, she demanded, "Oh, Jack, tell us what happened! What did Roxbury say about the stolen memorandum?"

"Yes, do tell us," encouraged Charles. "Isabel and Marcus have brought us abreast of the situation, and we have all wondered how the loss of the memorandum will affect the war."

Jack hesitated, thinking of the stranger's admission to Roxbury that Whitley was dead. His gaze was uneasy as he took in the expectant faces of the women. "Uh, perhaps I could speak privately with the gentlemen," he finally muttered. "It, uh, isn't a topic for the ladies."

"Oh, pooh!" exclaimed Isabel. "We already know all about it, so there is no reason to think it is something only fit for the ears of gentlemen. I was abducted, Jack! I have just as much right to know what is going on as Marcus does." She gave his arm an impatient yank. "Now tell us. What happened?"

Marcus grinned at him. "You'll find that there is very little you can keep from intelligent women. You might as well tell them; they'll get it out of us eventually."

Jack capitulated. "By Jove! It is the most amazing thing," he said excitedly. "The very night I arrived, Roxbury had a visitor." He glanced at Isabel. "We're convinced it was your 'gentleman.' " His eyes gleamed. "Can you believe it? The fellow gave him the memorandum! He said he might be a thief, but he wasn't a traitor! So the French didn't get their hands on the memorandum after all." Looking around from one astounded face to the other, Jack laughed. "Yes, you may stare. I did when I woke in the morning and Roxbury told me that all was well. I didn't know whether I was on my heels or my head."

"The deuce you say!" burst out Marcus incredulously. "If he was going to turn it over to Roxbury, why the devil did he go to all the trouble of abducting Isabel and stealing it from us in the first place. We'd have turned it over to Roxbury."

Jack shook his head. "I don't know." He frowned slightly. "The man confessed to knowing that Whitley was dead. Knowing Roxbury, I'm positive that there is more to the matter than Roxbury is telling me, but the main thing, the most important thing, is that the memorandum is back at the Horse Guards where it belongs and Wellesley's plans are in full swing."

Alone in their private rooms later that night, Isabel said to Marcus, "I know it is unfeeling of me, but I cannot be very sorry that Whitley is dead. He was a bad man."

They were seated on a balcony just off Marcus's bedroom, enjoying the soft spring air, Isabel sipping a glass of warm milk, Marcus toying with a small glass of cognac.

Marcus nodded. "He probably didn't deserve to be murdered, though."

"How can you say that?" she demanded, outraged. "Marcus, he was trying to destroy Edmund's life and he was going to sell that memorandum to the French! Of course he deserved to be murdered!" She thought a moment, then added fiercely, "Or hanged."

Marcus couldn't argue with her logic and said, "You're right. Whitley got precisely what he deserved."

Satisfied that Marcus felt just as he ought, she asked, "What did you think of Jack's news?"

He shrugged. "It sounds like a Banbury tale to me. That fellow went to far too much trouble to simply hand the memorandum over so tamely. I think Jack is right. Roxbury isn't telling all he knows."

There was silence for a few minutes as they each mulled over what Roxbury might be hiding. Finally Isabel said, "It is very strange, isn't it?"

Marcus nodded and, tired of Jack, Whitley, and the whole affair, he said, "But enough of that . . . have I told you how very much I love you?"

She giggled. "Not for the past fifteen minutes."

"How remiss of me!" He rose and scooped her up into his arms. "I love you, Isabel," he said huskily.

"Oh, Marcus! I love you!"

Kissing her, he carried her to his bed. "And now," he said with a husky note in his voice, "I intend to show you exactly how very much I do love you." And did.

Marcus woke several hours later. Isabel was curled warmly next to him and for a moment he let himself revel in her nearness. He thought about waking her with a kiss and making love again, but despite his best efforts, his thoughts kept slipping away to Roxbury and the stranger who had returned the memorandum.

Deciding sleep would be impossible for now, Marcus slid from the bed and slipped on his dressing robe. Strolling to the balcony, he stared out at the darkness.

Where was Isabel's abductor? Marcus wondered. What sort of dangerous mischief might he be planning at this very moment? He stared for a long time into the night, his thoughts on the stranger, trying to understand what drove a man to do what he had done and why. A yawn took him. Enough of this useless speculation. Everything had ended well, he reminded himself, the gentleman had even, one might say, acted like a gentleman. . . . And that was the end of it. Like a shooting star the man had blazed into their lives and was now gone, never to be seen again. But as he turned away to rejoin his wife, Marcus had the unsettling notion that they'd not heard the last of Isabel's "gentleman". . . .